Blue Mou

Wayne H. Drumheller

Published by The Short Book Writer's Project
Wayne Drumheller, Editor and Founder
Publishing Platform: KDP.amazon.com
Distribution in USA by the author.

ISBN 13:978-1979995344
ISBN 10:1979995346
Blue Mountain Highway Home is published in the U.S.A.
Copyright © by Wayne H. Drumheller, 2018. All Rights Reserved.

Contents

Blue Mountain Highway Home
Light a flame in me
So others will see
What you've meant to me

Take me back to where I began
And can now live again
To sing my songs in loving jest
To be where I am blest

Let me travel back in time
Let me travel back in my mind
This song is not a good-bye
For we will meet again.

Remind me of heaven and its glory
While angels sing with me and hear my story
About my home where streams and stones
Let me know I am never alone

Take me to that river clear
And lay me down with a lover near
And make love in a Spruce Creek Stream
Where I can dance in forest and meadows green

Let my eyes see cotton white clouds
and blue skies gently go by
and I can feel the seasons and smile
If only for a little while

And let my heart, soul and spirit feel
What my body cannot heal
And dance with me with my lover by my side
To a feeling that I cannot hide

Blue Mountain Highway
Take me home to the place I know so well
and lay me down
So I can live again

A young Blue Ridge Mountain poet, country folk singer-song writer knows she has a year to live due to a chronic illness. A traumatic near death experience when she was nine, still causes pain and nightmares. She has been in counseling since the childhood experience happened. She prays for and dreams about a sign that will help her stop the nightmares and thoughts of suicide. She meets the person of her hopes and dreams in 1963, who could be the answer to her prayers.

They begin an ill-fated romance, a musical adventure and love affair that takes them to Columbia, SC, Washington, DC, San Francisco, Los Angeles, and the California Monterey Jazz Musical Festival before her sad return to her Rockfish River Valley home in 1964.

Cast of Characters

Jamie Marshall
A young singer song writer from Spruce Creek, Wintergreen, Va.
Wade Dhamner
Narrator and young soldier Nellysford/Wintergreen who meets Jamie
Ms. Wanda Thompson
Jamie's Grandmother
Sally and Hayward Dameron
Wade's Grandparents
Tom and Hanna
Lives and works on Ms. Thompson's farm
AB and Catherine Dhamner
Wade's Parents
Ned and Lillian in Columbia, SC
Lillian is Wanda's sister and Jamie's great aunt
Lilly and Thomas in Pacific Grove, California
Lilly owns Crusoe's, and is Wanda's sister and Jamie's great aunt
Lt. Colonel Lasiter
Wade's commanding office of CEDEC, Fort Ord, California
Stephanie
Registered nurse and fiancé to Lt. Colonel Lasiter
Sgt. Specialist, Dick Edlund
US Army buddy and soldier at CEDEC command
Sgt. 1st Class Harmon Faison, Drill Instructor at Fort Jackson, SC
Master Sgt. Kessler, NCO unit commander and instructors of CECOM
Marianne
Childhood friend and mentor to Jamie
Ms. Stevens
Clinical Social worker and counselor to Jamie
Connie & Ray Hershey
Wade's Friends and Mentors

217,231

That's the best estimated number documented by law enforcement, health, medical and educational officials in the United States of America of young people between the age of 12 and 20 who died annually of unintentional or intentional causes These include: auto accidents, physical assault, water accidents, agriculture and farm injuries, and other conditions such as heart, lung, kidney, liver and skin diseases. It also includes to a lesser extent, but no less significant, circumstances such as suicides, homicides and childhood conditions that may become fatal as other conditions are diagnosed in later teen years. And, for every young individual death, at least eighty family members, relatives or close friends were deeply impacted, by their loss, according to social, spiritual and mental health personnel by their loss. They all had hopes, dreams, fantasies, wishes and goals. This book is dedicated to them.

Leaving Home

My mother stirred the frying pan more slowly than usual. She turned the eggs two-three times before pushing them into the grits piled at the outer edge of the 20 rounder cast-iron-frying pan. She knew that the family really liked her cooking. Still, it seemed like she was taking a lot more time this morning.

With every turn of the eggs, she looked at me thumbing through the army induction papers we had signed together just two months before my high school graduation. I was seventeen and a half, and had received my formal orders to report this afternoon for my physical and deployment for basic training at Fort Jackson, South Carolina.

As the smell of grits, gravy, white ham and biscuits continued to drift from the wooden stove, she placed a copy of the Waynesboro New-Virginian by my plate. Carefully tucked within its folded pages were a brown leather writing notebook, a cigarette lighter, and a copy of *Profiles in Courage* by Senator John F. Kennedy.

We knew this Friday morning would come.

However, this morning was different. On any other early summer morning, and especially Friday mornings, my mother would be bustling about the kitchen barking out orders to wash our hands, stop fussing and sit down at the table. "Let's have breakfast while it's still hot." She would say.

This morning was different.

It was quiet. I was going to miss the sounds and smells of the farm, and the morning conversations that never seemed to cease on Fridays and Saturdays when my father was home from work at DuPont. But, on this morning there was no talk of chores or activities on the farm. We spoke in soft voices, reflecting on times past, and avoided talking about when I would come home again.

Now, she stood at the stove and said, "I don't want you

to forget where you're from, who you are and how to get home" as I opened the newspaper to a Rockfish Valley map and legend. This 21 miles long and 14 miles wide farm valley had been my home for seventeen years. It lay on the edge of the Blue Ridge Continental Divide. We lived on the eastern slope of what was once called the Appalachian Frontier.

It was a vast mountainous area formed not by ocean waters, but by a geological upheaval that created its rugged peaks and green pristine meadows and valleys. It was a reminder of the strength, independence, and love of country that had been given to me by five proud Scot-Irish-German generations of Marshalls, Colemans, Damerons, Rankins and Drumhellers.

We were descendants of back valley farmers and craftsmen of all sorts-spilling down into deep shadowed valleys suitable for mountain goats and wild pigs. Forced pastures pushed up against forest undergrowth, bordered by twisted briar and grape vines where plow shears had dumped them at the end of corn and tobacco rows over the years. Chickens of all breeds ranged wild on the high ridges above our house in the daylight. At night they hovered in slat barn rafters to avoid foxes and wild dogs on the prowl.

The flat iron frying pan my mother stirred eggs and bacon in had traveled hundreds of miles in the back of a Model 'T' Truck as part of a clothing and pantry order from the Sears-Roebuck catalog. The sound of a blue grass guitar and fiddle faded away on the brown and silver enamel Silvertone radio, as a voice barked out the farm market report--poultry, milk, eggs, wheat, corn prices were up, while side meat, corn starch and gabardine clothes were down--news of the world drowned away as the last of the dirty dishes piled on the side board of the porcelain sink to dry.

I was in the kitchen of the house my father had built in 1953 with a GI loan. The cinder block walls with roll out windows and floors covered with white linoleum would come back to me in memory many times over the next few years. The oily smell of the table cloth would drift into my thoughts, reminding me of the day it was purchased at Harris' Grocery Store in Wintergreen.

I was looking at the oak kitchen table with four buckets of drinking water from our recently dug well and momentarily wished that I wasn't leaving when my mother shouted, "You need to eat those biscuits before they get cold!"

Then she stirred the last of her black coffee into the gravy pan and removed it from the stove. She knew I would eat this plate, and probably the next one she would fill before I left for the bus station in Lovingston. She didn't say much more when she noticed me looking out the window toward the two-story chicken house and the roof of the barn, where my older brother had tried to fly when I was five, and he was eleven. She only stared at me as I caught myself laughing out loud.

This was home.

I didn't know how long it would be until I would see it again. I was going to miss it and the high Blue Ridge Mountains above our farm, with its parkway of endless scenic overlooks and picnic tables that attracted travelers to stop and take pictures of this idyllic valley.

I was still thinking about home and the farm when my mother tenderly brushed her warm fingers across my forehead to smooth my hair out of my eyes. She filled my coffee cup and placed the notebook in my lap, as she made me promise to keep writing when I could.

Then in his usual quiet manner my father appeared at the kitchen door. "Son, you have about an hour before we leave," he said, as I asked permission to walk around the farm before we left.

Going through the back kitchen door, I traced my fingers along the boards of the old pine-wood barn, and took a deep breath and inhaled the aroma of the barnyard floor, and the fresh smell of hay in the loft. I could hear our chickens clucking and pecking inside the barn as they had for years. I could also feel Guinea hens scratching and scraping the dirt path beneath my feet as I reached the corn shed, leaned inside and grabbed a hand-full of cracked corn. I stirred the freshly cracked corn in my cupped palm with my fingers and thumb.

I always enjoyed the feel of the sharp-edged grain just before the first toss to the chickens, as it sailed forward through the morning air. I could hear my father's voice in my head teaching and telling me what to do next, as the corn dust shimmered in a wide shaft of the sun's ray coming through the cracks in the barn wall.

The hens and pullets scrambled and fluttered from their nests to the dirt floor. As they pecked at the grain at my feet, I visualized the shadowy image of my grandfather tossing rye seeds and wheat corn while waving his hands and arms to the martial arts of Thai Chi, which he learned while serving in the Far East during World War I.

He moved westward as he lifted his body and arms high over his head. Then with an almost effortless motion, he turned his entire body in a pirouette, to face in an eastward direction, as he had done for years--always finishing with his face down and palms folding around his arms and then reaching outward.

Magically, this separated the hens and young pullets into a choreographic dance, as they pecked at the cracked corn and rye wheat husks sprinkled about the red clay floor.

On the far side of the barn, I spotted the old Victrola standing in the corner. My father had bought it and placed it there when we were little kids. He liked to serenade the chickens and pigs with Tommy Dorsey, Artie Shaw, Pete Fountain and other big band music. He believed it produced more eggs and softened the hams on the pigs and hogs-- that's what he told us when asked.

He liked talking to himself like that and telling us stuff that seemed to be true, but was hard to believe. I cranked the old handle while holding the turntable before letting it spin. The applause of the crowd and orchestra music blasted into the shadows of the shed and barn.

The hens seemed not to notice the scratches and wavering sounds as they retraced their steps and retreated to their perches and concentrated on laying eggs.

I had to laugh to myself about the times my brothers and I had placed nervous bantam hens on the turntable. We would let them spin around until they flew dumb-founded and half-dazed to the barn yard floor. They would keep turning in the dirt until their balance returned and their feet were firmly under them again.

I knew that both my grandfather and father would have a transformational effect on me, now and in the future, just as they had on the chickens at my feet. I was still smiling when I heard my father on the planks of the back porch. He had my suitcase and mother's bucket of jam and jelly biscuits for the trip to the induction center.

As we drove down the dirt driveway, my mother, brothers Eddie, Freddie, and little sister Sue, were leaning over the back porch railing waving.

I thought I heard my mother shout "You get on that Blue Mountain Highway and come home."

I'm sure it was only in my imagination, but it sure made me feel good.

Ride To Lovingston

Although I knew he had a lot to say, my father didn't talk much as we made our way down highway 151, and south on route 29 to Lovingston, Virginia. In fact, my father and I had seldom spoken until I turned twelve. And now, he said something that I knew I would never forget.

"You can learn a lot just riding down a road. One day it's just a foot path through the woods or a crossing in a meadow field. Indians, fur traders, frontiersmen, soldiers, travelers make their way west. Then it becomes a dirt path, maybe a single lane road for wagons and cars.

They gravel it--maybe it becomes a cadamine road. It's paved into one lane, two lanes of blue black asphalt highway like this one. Who are these people? Where are they going-- where've they been-who are they? What's their life about? We don't know. They're just faces in a windshield that we look at but don't see. I don't know. But this, I do know. People will come at you all your life. They'll push themselves into your mind. Most of them will quickly fade away, but some will become your best friends. You'll remember them all your life."

He started to stop and then said   "So as you leave home, I want to tell you a thing or two. I'm not going to tell you what to do, but I can tell you what I know. There will be sad times and good times. You will want more than life has given me. You'll want a bigger house, a better car, even more money, I'm sure. But what I know is that the days pass quickly. The nights can be lonely. Loved ones will misunderstand you. Lovers and wives will be your best friends. Keep the day to yourself and learn how to sleep well at night. Have nothing to be ashamed of and never, never forsake or be embarrassed by your family. We will be here as long as you live.

And when we're gone, we're gone. Remember me and don't forget who I am, and the words you say to your children someday will sound just like me." He finished in a somber voice that trailed off into a whisper as he peered more intently through the truck's windshield at the road ahead.

He went on to talk about making this same trip in 1942. He told me that I would think of home often, but I needed to keep my mind on my job.

"It will bring you home" he said, as we turned off business 29, and into the parking lot behind the bus depot. It wasn't much of a bus depot. It was an old Phillips 66 gas station, where they sold bus tickets at the front counter. I had bought my ticket a week ago.

We arrived just as the Trailway Bus was pulling into the side street. We parked behind it and I walked to the door with my ticket, notebook, and handbag. My father followed me.

As he gave me the lunch pail, I noticed that his hands were trembling, and his face had turned a little ashen gray. His lips moved, as words tried to skip across his tongue but nothing came out. I knew what he was trying to say.

We stood facing each other like two sentries on a faraway hill; one weary, the other looking to a fresh beginning. We never spoke, as he grasped my elbow in one hand, and shook my hand firm and long with the other. I turned away, not knowing what to say to this man I had always called 'father', and boarded the bus.

As I walked down the aisle to my seat, I looked out the window and imagined him turning around and waving good-bye to me, but he didn't.

Instead, I watched the back of his head, as he wiped his face and eyes with his big blue handkerchief before getting into the truck to head home.

Jamie

The bus ride down Route 29 to Charlottesville, would take about an hour, with stops in Rockfish and Schyler. The transfer to another bus in Charlottesville would make it about a two and a half hour trip to the Roanoke bus stop. We would stop at the top of Afton Mountain and the Blue Ridge Parkway on Highway 250 for road passengers. There would be stops in Waynesboro and Staunton before we finally arrived in Roanoke, one of the largest cities in Virginia outside of Richmond, the Capitol. I was tired and anxious from a sleepless night.

I leaned back into the seat, listening to the drone of the diesel engine and the whistle of the air streaming from the bottom of the passenger window.

The sounds had just whisked me away into anxious thoughts about home, and what my future in the army would be like, when a hand bumped my elbow and a voice chided, "Hi, my name is Jamie. I'm going back to the University in Charlottesville. Where are you going?"

Glancing away from the window, I noticed that the voice came from a shielded forehead under a wide orange brimmed cap. She made a striking figure with green eyes behind school boy steel-rimmed glasses. Her freckled face sparkled and the emerald eyes darted back and forth behind the rims. She seemed to vibrate while pushing a transistor radio hard against her right ear. Abruptly, she would jut out her chin and jam it forward against the invisible air, and hum as she moved her head to the rhythmical sounds, and her yellow pony tail danced back and forth through the back of her UVA baseball cap.

Turning her body in the seat to face me, she stretched the top of the white t-shirt with both hands. I could read the blazing red imprint, *Carpe Diem*.

She was smiling a half laugh, while popping Teaberry chewing gum between her teeth and lips. She was determined to get my attention. "Hey, come on, tell me where you're going. Everybody tells me my hair looks like a two-pound bag of spaghetti coming out of the back of my cap. You don't know me, but I know your grandmother. She's been a great friend to my family."

"Come on, talk to me. It will make the trip go faster. What's in the leather folder with the strap around it? I ride this bus all the time and it gets pretty boring," she continued as I interrupted.

"I'm going to join the Army," I said.

Without pause she continued "My older brother is in the Marines, stationed at Camp Lejeune. We don't see him much. He's supposed to get out next year. He may not come home. Not much work around here except farming and working at the Pie Company. I'm going to the University. Why are you joining the army?" she continued.

"What's at the University?" I asked as she continued talking in a rapid and nervous voice, as if this was all new to her.

"I'm supposed to be a sophomore, but failed freshman English. I have to make it up in summer school in four weeks" she returned, as she jerked her body hard and raised her knees in the seat to face me.

She kept talking, but I couldn't take my eyes off the delicate blue heart-shaped diamond tattoo on her neck, with a highlighted purple tear drop floating inside. Someone had delicately guided the needle along the fragile face and neckline scar, and surgically laid a thin layer of ink, that could and would fade with time.

The barely noticeable S curved scar on the back-side of her face appeared to have blended with the rest of her facial skin, as she had grown into an attractive, inquisitive young woman. The scar traced a thin, softened line down her face, starting just above the cheek bone, bending slightly forward, and then back again, and downward along the cleft of the jaw and the side of her neck. It ended just above her neck line where a heart shaped amber earring attached to a small gold chain, brushed back and forth.

"Everybody asks me about it" she blurted, as I tore my face and eyes away, embarrassed.

"It's OK. I was in an accident when I was nine. My mother and father were killed. I don't remember much. I just remember waking up in the hospital. I went to live with my grandparents a few days later.

They live in Wintergreen on Spruce Creek. I go visit some of my other relatives in South Carolina and Charlottesville on holidays and in the summer. What about you? Is your family going to miss you while you're gone? Do you have a girl friend? I got a million questions. What's in the leather notebook? Are you writing a book or something? What's in that leather binder under your seat? Some people say I never shut up!"

For some strange reason, I liked her. She had a wide eyed, inquisitive personality, and seemed to be a year older than me, but younger in spirit. I didn't know her, but apparently my grandmother did.

I was hoping to learn more about her when I blurted out stupidly "Did it hurt?"

"It hurt for a week or so until they took the bandages off. Oh, oh, you mean the tattoo. A little, but I had it done last summer. You want to touch it?"

"No, but tell me about your scar," I asked as I pulled my tin bucket from under the seat, opening the lid.

I was feeling really dumb for giving her a jelly and jam biscuit when she said   "This is really good!" She swallowed the biscuit in two bites and chased it down with her orange *Nehi Drink.*

"People don't ask! They stare. They treat me like I'm some kind of freak. I cuss a lot and sometimes call them names under my breath. A lot of people think I committed some kind of female sin for getting the tattoo. I don't care. Hell with them! Kind of pretty isn't it?" she said as she took my hand and cupped it against the side of her face.

Her skin was velvet soft and felt like smooth silk cream. She lightly guided my fingers cross her smiling face and down to the tattoo and stopped. I could feel a knot or slight bulge, but I wasn't sure.

"Now, that still hurts! Yeah, right there where they wired my jaws together from the impact of the ground. I even wrote a poem about it. I like to play it on my *Humming Bird Guitar* my grandfather gave me. Some people even say I sound like Joan Baez." She said.

Before I could say anything, she pressed my hand against her neck, pulled her guitar out of her backpack on the bus floor and started singing:

There will be a day when my pretty face will smile again. I'll forget the pain that took my mama and daddy away. Until then, I'll keep this tear drop in my heart, so that the harshness of life that tore us apart, Will make the flowers on their grave smile And I... Will be happy again.

As the last silent chord on her guitar dissipated into the sound of the diesel engine, she sank back into her seat while taking my hand from her face and gently placed it in her lap like a wounded bird.

I turned away and pushed my head back against the seat. We were both quiet. I had no words, only feelings, that I couldn't explain. It seemed like the right thing to do. She glanced at me from under the bill of her cap and I felt the grip of her hand tighten on mine. We knew we were approaching the bus station. The bus ride would soon be over for us. I'm sure she wondered if I would remember her, as a few tears drifted down her soft shadowy face. I could still feel the warm tears where she bent over and placed her forehead on the back of my hand and closed her eyes when we pulled into the bus station in Charlottesville.

Everyone got off. I took my suit case in the station for a tag, and bought my ticket to Roanoke. All the transfer lanes were posted on the lighted sign above the counter. My bus would leave in 40 minutes. I looked around for Jamie, but she had disappeared into the bus station or maybe was on her way to the university clinic she mentioned. I wanted to say good-bye. Maybe get her address. She was one of those people my father said would come at me.

I wanted to remember her, but apparently she was gone. I couldn't miss my bus. It would leave soon, so I walked around the station one last time, turned the corner, and headed for my bus.

Jamie was standing by the waiting bus door. She had strapped on her back pack and guitar over her right shoulder. The glare of a large incandescent light above the front bus window and door cast a lean female figure along the massive Greyhound bumper, dangling a partially smoked Lucky Strike from the thumb and forefinger of her left hand.

She handed me a folded note as she apologetically told me that she was very sorry for her behavior on the bus, and pleaded that I not forget her.

I think I heard her shout over the sound of the diesel engine and street traffic as I boarded the bus. "I know we'll meet again. I read, sing, and know a lot about a lot of things, and I think I'm going to be one those people you'll never forget. And, wait until you're on the bus to read my note!"

The Counseling Session

The group counseling session for children and young adults, led by neurologist, James Gamble, MD and Ph.D., and Shelby Stevens, MSW, Clinical Social Worker at the University Hospital, had been meeting for some three years.

It was started by Gamble, for children and young adults, who have received care for traumatic head injuries, especially those presenting long-term physical and mental anxieties, panic attacks, nightmares, and sometimes suicide attempts.

Jamie attended these monthly sessions every third Monday of the month. Attendance was strictly voluntary, but she felt compelled to be there. Attendees had to be under a doctor's care, either at the University Hospital, or any one of four regional medical clinics located at Jefferson-Albemarle rural support region.

She would have her 18th birthday in October and was under consideration for release, if her issues and concerns were deemed stable or improving. The attending physician and social workers who had worked with her, had seen some general improvement in her mood swings and conversations about wanting to die, but they could record no significant breakthrough to recommend her release.

This Monday would be different.

"Hello everyone, announced Gamble. Take your seats at the table, and we should be ready for lunch by 12:30.

For the record, Ms. Stevens will record your names and any comments you have for today's session."

"Charles, it's good to see you again, Ms. Steven began. Your new medication is working and you will be with our physical therapist after lunch."
"Anna, it's good to see your cast is off and the medication on your arm is working."
"Jamie, you are beaming today, and I'm sure you will have some good news once we get started."
"Alex, your mother called this week and told us about your job at Kroger. We want to hear about it."
"And, Sharon, let's move your wheelchair closer and we can start with you. OK?"
"Thank you, Ms. Stevens… Sharon can we start with you? Tell us about your last couple of weeks. We want all of you to talk freely and express your feelings and goals for the next two weeks."
The session started as it usually did with the attendees reluctant to talk, and Gamble and Ms. Stevens urging and probing them to talk. Sharon was quiet as usual, and Alex put his head on the table and pretended to sleep.
Jamie was typically quiet, and almost always talked about how she hated herself and those who made fun of her, except for today.
"I just met a soldier on the bus ride here. I talked to him almost the whole trip from Lovingston. He was kind and different than anyone I have ever met. He joined the Army, and I hope I meet him again. He did not stare at me, and listened to me. I even played my guitar and sang him a song. Was I silly? I wrote him a note, gave him my address, and asked him to write me. I feel so stupid, but I really liked him. He's the first boy I've talked to in three years….."
"Jamie, did you know him….?" Asked Ms. Stevens.

"No, but I think I know his grandmother who lives up on Spruce Creek. He just graduated from high school and his name is Wade....Wade Dhamner. He had never heard of me, but he liked my hat. His family grows apples in the valley, and this is his first time away from home....I...."

"Jamie, I want to hear more, but I would like to hear from the others, and maybe we can talk more at lunch." Gamble interrupted, as Jamie recoiled into her seat, pulled her guitar tight to her chest as she had on the bus earlier this morning, and promised herself she would only talk with her grandmother when she got home later today.

She had been through so much over the years, growing up in a home with an uneducated and abusive fundamentalist preacher father. Her mother tried to please everybody and spoiled the older bipolar brother who suffered from seizures and fits of rage, to savage threats to kill them all.

Jamie struggled to survive. Somehow, after her brother's rampage, her parents' death, and the house fire that left her body burned and jaw broken and disfigured, she struggled hard to remember.

The nightmares woke her in a panic sweat most nights, after her grandparents took her in following her stay at the university hospital burn and trauma unit. She could remember the hot fire, her older brother towering over her and striking her with a heavy pipe, and his face glared and he shouted 'I killed them. I killed them" as he pushed her out the window to the ground and the burning pine planks below.

Her grandparents protected her from young boys and girls who pointed and called her names. There were staring neighbors who looked at her only with sadness. Her adoring and loving grandparents nursed her, as best they could, back to some semblance of health, and provided the money for her monthly counseling and tutoring at the university hospital in Charlottesville.

Receiving no formal public education until she was 12, she read every book, magazine article, New Testament Bible, advertisement poster, and comic book that came into the house, or she could get her hands on.

Often described by her grandparents as shy, timid and quiet, but smart and musically talented, she built a world around herself that was filled with imaginary friends, a grandfather who religiously rubbed the lotions and salves on the scars, and helped bathe her fragile body in Spruce Creek. He washed away the peeling skin on her back; there only remained a thin jagged seven inch elongated scar and an even thinner S curved scar, on her left cheek and the side of her neck.

Her grandfather worried every day because of his own failing health and the 150 acre farm he could barely manage by himself. He even took her to South Carolina on her 12th birthday to see if younger relatives would take her in. He died of heart failure and a nagging cough that kept him awake most nights. Jamie remained with her grandmother on Spruce Creek near the Rockfish River, and now at almost 18, she had become a beautiful young girl, although remaining shy and introverted.

She liked to swear and cuss at passing cars, smoked a pack of cigarettes a day, played her guitar in her room to borrowed 45 rpm records. She dressed, as her grandmother lovingly said, "like a boy most of the time wearing baggy shirts and cut-off torn blue jeans."

She made lots of promises to herself. She wanted to change. She knew she wasn't a little girl anymore, and had thoughts and feelings that came to her that she couldn't always understand. She dreamed at night that things would be better for her. She prayed that her grandmother wouldn't die and leave her like her grandfather. She understood the books she read, and had a constant appetite for more, but she needed somebody or something strong in her life. She needed someone who she could love more than she hated her pitiful self.

And now, she sat quietly during lunch, although the doctor and social worker tried to get her to answer more questions. She wanted to talk and express her feelings, not answer a bunch of questions. She left the lunch room early and walked back to the bus station to wait for the 2:50 bus to Lovingston where her grandmother would be waiting to pick her up and take her home. While she waited, she wrote her first poem for Wade. She would mail it as soon as he sent her an address.

Trip to Roanoke

The bus ride to Roanoke was pretty uneventful.

I missed Jamie already. Meeting her was a pleasant distraction from the feelings I was having about leaving home and entering the service.

As she said, talking did make the trip go faster.

I wasn't sure why, but I knew I would never forget her long, wavy, strawberry yellow hair, blasting from the back of her baseball cap. I could see her deep green eyes and youthful smiling face that masked a life of loneliness and hardship. The smell of suntan lotion and coconut balm clung to my shirt sleeve, where she had tucked her head and shed a soft tear when I touched her face.

The heart-shaped diamond tattoo would haunt me until I knew the whole story. Maybe she would explain this in her note to me.

Even now with the wind blowing against the window, I could still hear her elongated vowels and sweet tea voice singing in my ears, as the miles passed by highway on 29 south and west 250 to Roanoke.

The passenger beside me smelled of summer heat and stale cigarette butts. I wanted to move, but all of the seats were taken.

As we headed down Afton Mountain, I kept looking back at the Blue Ridge Mountains disappeared from view. My family had made this trip many times on Saturdays.

This trip felt different.

Each passing mile marker pushed my past further away and pulled me into an unfamiliar future.

As we pulled into the Waynesboro bus station the passenger beside me jumped up and grabbed a brown paper bag from the overhead rack before the bus stopped. Cursing at the seated passengers, he rushed to the front, pushed past a few waiting passengers outside and disappeared down a dark side alley.

His body odor was still lingering on the seat beside me as a gray-haired middle-aged woman made her way down the aisle. She hurriedly placed her suitcase in the overhead compartment, dropped her heavy body down into the leather cushion and she settled her dark blue winter suit in the seat like a nesting hen, politely pushing me aside to the window.

Then reaching high over her head with both hands, she removed a long hat pin from her bun while holding onto her satin brimmed hat, and placed them both in her lap. She inserted the pin like a sword in the small ribbon band.

It was hot and humid. Tiny beads of sweat circled the waddle of her neck like small spring peas spilling from a clay bowl. The shaved stubble on her upper lip held the summer's moisture like dew on the bottom of a summer peach. She pulled a silk handkerchief from her purse and pressed it upward under her chin, and then across her upper lip, slightly smearing her freshly applied lipstick. Replacing the handkerchief, she removed a decorative gold compact from her purse and patted each cheek with talc powder. It had a cooling and calming effect on her.

It brought back memories of my grandmother sitting on the front porch in the summer, and patting her face with a powder puff. She smelled of lilacs and honeysuckle. It smelled sweet. We didn't talk. It was going to be a quiet trip.

She was still napping when we arrived in Staunton. She told me that she was going to Roanoke to see her granddaughter-- a student at Hollings Academy. They would be staying at the Roanoke Hotel. Her granddaughter liked it there. They could sit by the lobby fountain and eat in the restaurant. She described the veranda on top of the hotel, where one could see the whole town at night. She let me know that she had taught high school English, and written a book of poetry. She handed it to me to read. It was mostly about flowers and plants in her garden.

I glanced at a few poems and politely returned the book saying "Thank You." I had not read Jamie's note and took it from my pocket.

My name is Jamie Catherine Marshall.

That and my parents death is about the only thing I said that was true.

I live in Wintergreen on the Spruce Creek just below Wintergreen Mountain with my grandmother.

My mother and father are dead, but they did not die in a car wreck. They died in a horrible fire that raced through the pine clapboard house like a volcanic eruption pitching its heat ahead of the crimson exfoliates. My older brother is accused of starting the fire. He left that night and hasn't been seen since.

Anyway, during the fire my brother was shouting and yelling obscenities at our parents.

He then turned toward me and knocked me down with a metal pipe. I ran and he pushed me through a second story window to the ground below.

That's how I got the scar.

I cut my face on the glass and landed on an old pile of lumber. I have a scar on my upper back, but you would never recognize it. I almost died. I still have nightmares.

You must think I'm terrible for lying, but I hope you won't hate me once you finish this letter.

I'm a clinical outpatient at the University Hospital in Charlottesville. I go there every first and third Monday when I'm not attending school or staying with my cousin near Martha Jefferson Hospital.

Then I catch the bus back to grandmother's house. I've lived with them since I was nine. I've taken free college courses for the last two years. I've recovered physically from the injuries, but they say I still have some problems.

I was also burnt badly from the fire. I have nightmares. I worry constantly that my brother will return and do me harm. I take medicine for headaches, my mood swings, and some kidney problems. The doctors tell me that my kidneys may get better eventually. I write poetry, paint, sing and play a guitar with my initials 'JDM' carved into the popular wood that my dear, beloved grandfather made for me.

He died four years ago.

I am getting better, but the medicine and years of recovery have been hard on me and my grandmother.

One of my best friends in the world graduated three years ago from Nelson High School. She lives and works in Washington DC. She visits me occasionally when she's home. I would like to visit her sometime and see Washington DC. She knows so many famous people writers, artists, singers and business owners.

She was also the friend that drove me on my trip to the beach two years ago. That's when I got the tattoo. She paid for it. I also got a small butterfly tattoo to cover the scar on my upper back and shoulder. They say butterflies don't have a very long life-span. I'll show it to you someday.

My grandmother got pretty mad about it. Of course, she likes it now.

You were really nice to me. I feel bad about lying to you. I do that a lot. I know I'm never going to see most of the people I meet again. I hope we meet again.

You were the nicest thing to happen to me in a long time. I don't get that much.

People tell me they like my poems and songs. I love playing the guitar. It takes away a lot of the headaches and lonely times. I do a great impersonation of Patsy Cline and Janis Harris. I want to play and sing like Joan Baez on the radio someday, but that's just a dream.

I really liked the jelly and jam biscuit. I will tell my grandmother that I met you on the bus. You travel safe.

P.S. I hope you will write back and let me know where you are. Jamie Catherine Marshall, Rural Route 151, Box 4, Wintergreen, Virginia.

I folded the note and put it back in my pocket. I wasn't sure how I felt about her lying to me, but I promised myself that I would write the first chance I got.

Talk with Grandmother

"Grandma, don't get mad at me, but it happened just the way I dreamed it.

When I woke up this morning, I was feeling so bad about the diagnosis, the medicine, the counseling sessions, the way people pity me and how I am such a burden on you that I looked out the window this morning and asked God for a sign that my life would change.

And it happened on the bus to Charlottesville.

I met a boy, a soldier, on the bus. He was going to the induction in Roanoke, and I really like him. He liked my hat, my hair, my poetry, my tattoo and me. He was so

27

caring, not like most people I meet on the bus. Do you know the Dhamners' on Spruce Creek Mountain?"

"Yes, I know Sally and Hayward and some of the family down in Nellysford. They're good people. I've invited them to our family reunion but they have never come. He works all the time. He grows fine apples, peaches and makes his own *Appalachian Sunrise Brandy*. He raises cock fighting roosters. Your grandfather used to go over there and come home stinking drunk. I wish I hadn't gotten so mad at him about it, bless his soul. He had such a good time" she answers as tears came to her eyes.

"He was so good to me, grandma. Never met anybody like him. What am I going to do? I may never see him again. I wrote him a note. He promised to write, and I gave him my address. He probably won't. I feel really bad for telling him some lies about me. I just couldn't tell him the truth about the fire. Do you think he will write back to me?"

"If it's meant to be, he will. Now, let's get you home for dinner, and we can talk more then."

It had been a long day and Jamie was excited and energized, but she dozed off in the car. The gravel road to their farm house jarred her from her slumber and she looked at her grandmother with a smile. Supper would be fun and she couldn't wait to talk more about her day.

Roanoke

It was a bumpy ride around barricades and stops for flagmen to Roanoke; highway 11 south was under construction. Soon Interstate 81 would replace it, making a straight line of asphalt and concrete from Johnson City, Tennessee, through the Shenandoah Valley, to Winchester, Virginia. For now, the bus made its detours, switchbacks, and frequent stops along the two-lane highway.

We arrived at the bus station at two o'clock. I would have less than an hour to grab the last ham biscuit from my lunch bucket and make my way to the induction center. Once there, I could finish my written test and complete the physical exam. The four block walk took longer than I expected in the blazing summer heat. The sidewalk felt like a burning wood stove beneath my feet. My shirt was drenched with sweat, and I was wiping my forehead when I entered the center door and found the registration desk. "Name and service" scowled the desk attendant as she handed me a clipboard with an application form and a large brown envelope.

"Wade Dhamner, US Army" I replied, as I took the seat on the long bench against the concrete wall. I had just taken the pencil attached to a long string on the clipboard to fill out the forms when a tall soldier dressed in brown khaki's and sporting two yellow stripes on his sleeve told me to follow him.

The heels of his shoes snapped against the concrete floor. They were polished and reflected like mirrors off the newly waxed surface.

We turned and walked down a long, dark hall that smelled of cough medicine and rubbing alcohol. I could see doctors and nurses in curtained cubicles on each side checking patients dressed in boxer shorts and t-shirts as we proceeded down the hall.

"Take a seat and wait. Someone will be with you soon," he instructed us, as he turned and made his way back to the registration area.

I was turning the first page of the application when a medical assistant dressed in bloused white canvas pants, black military boots and army green sweat shirt, yanked the clipboard away. He towered over me and told me to step behind the curtain to my right.

Through the curtain he yelled "strip and put your clothes in the large brown envelope."

"Leave it on the bench. You will return here. Put on the pair of shorts and the white socks on the bench and step out to the yellow line!"

Once changed, I stepped onto the yellow line. He instructed me to follow the yellow line on the floor to all of the numbered stations starting with A-1. At station A-1, a big-boned lady told me to sit on the round, metal stool, open my mouth, and say 'ah'.

She pushed a flat wooden probe deep into my mouth and throat. It made me gag and cough as she flashed a small pen light from side to side and along the roof of my mouth.

I almost fell off the stool as she spun me first to my left, and then right, as she crowded me into the folds of her huge chest, and pushed the light deep into my ears, while circling and holding her eyes close to my head.

I could smell the sweat of her massive body as she stepped directly in front of me, and told me to follow the light with my eyes, without turning my head. She made a few marks on my clipboard sheet, and told me to follow the line to the next station.

An intern was just finishing with someone as I arrived at the B-1 marker. Another uniformed soldier told me to take a seat on a high metal table, as an officer stepped into the cubicle and took my pulse and listened to my heart.

"My name is Captain Lance. You will report back to me after your x-rays and other stops. We're running out of time and may not finish with some of you today. Take the line to the next station and come back here as soon as you can."

At C-1, I received my chest, feet and back x-ray. I was told to stay put as the technician disappeared behind a heavy glass door. She returned in about four minutes and placed the x-rays in my brown envelope, and told me to move to the next station.

At D-1, a doctor was seated on a stool and waved me into the cubical. He pulled down my shorts and pressed his fingers hard against my pelvic bone in a cavity above my testicle. He told me to cough left and right. My lower groin and testicles were still burning when he pulled his fingers away saying "you're OK" while scribbling some notes on my clipboard and checking a few boxes.

He pointed to the hall and sent me back to the line. I pulled my shorts up as I walked down the hall, and joined a line of 20 other recruits waiting at station E-1.

The large nurse who had examined my mouth and ears stepped into the hall and said "No talking! This is the final part of the physical exam. After this, some of you will be sent back to Captain Lance for more instructions, and some of you will go through the black door at the end of the hall and wait. Remember, absolutely no talking. You are the property of the US Government now, and will follow orders without question" she punctuated, as she turned and disappeared down the hall into a cubicle.

Silence.

No one spoke or joked.

I was afraid to look at the others, as we waited for about ten minutes before a large attendant dressed in 'whites' and combat boots, appeared and told us to put our toes on the yellow line, strip, and lay our shorts and shirt on the floor directly in front of us.

As I laid my clothes on the floor, I noticed that each of us had a roll of toilet paper and trash can beside us. The attendant told us with a sharp pitched voice to do nothing until he had finished his instructions.

Stepping back, he pressed the clipboard tight against his massive chest, and ordered us to bend over and forward as far as we could, while reaching back to spread our butt cheeks. The coolness of the air on my exposed butt, and the voices behind us, made me nervous and afraid of what might happen next.

I could hear footsteps and voices moving down the line in my direction. I could hear muffled voices grunting and sighing, as medical rubber gloves snapped and thumped into the bottom of the metal trash cans.

The sounds bounced off the walls across the waxed floor and into my ears. Then, I could see the white bloused pants and black boots behind me. There was a tearing sound of rubber stretching as he spread my bottom cheeks like a filleted Chesapeake cod.

Oh, jeeeeeeeeesssssshhhhh, I thought, as the large gloved finger pried my butt cheeks apart and probed my bottom-turning first left, then deeper right. I thought I was going to faint from the burning pressure when he pulled upward, almost lifting me off the floor. Then he pressed downward with a piercing jab, making my knees buckle toward the floor. I thought I was going to vomit, when I heard the rubber snap as he pulled the glove from his fingers and threw it in the trash can.

"OK you're the last one. Clean up and report to Captain Lance," he said in a harsh voice, as his assistant started picking up the rolls of toilet paper and put them in a large box against the wall.

Walking weak-kneed and a little dazed down the line, I noticed five from the group had already been sent through the black door. Wondering where they were going, I finished dressing and followed the yellow line back to the front, when Captain Lance stepped in front of me pronouncing " Welcome to the US Army, Private."

He repeated the same greeting to the others and told us to take a seat at the metal table against the wall.

"You have all passed your physical." He said.

"Unfortunately, five of your group have been turned down and will not be accepted by the service," he said, as he handed each of us a three-ringed binder.

He dismissed everyone except me and three others. The rest were told to report to the quartermaster's desk for boarding instructions. In a commanding voice, we were told that there wasn't enough time to complete our written test and start our series of shots. We would be the guest of the US Army for the weekend. We would report back promptly at 0700 hours Monday, as he instructed his clerk to place us in hotels, and provide us with meal vouchers at a local diner. Ordered to our feet, we were given instructions and told to report on time Monday morning.

I was glad the physical exam was over. No one had prepared me for it. I was hungry and sweaty, but made my way down the street toward the Hotel Roanoke.

Jamie Awake

Jamie lay awake all night thinking about the bus ride, Wade, and what she had said to her grandmother.

She wondered what he was doing right now and if he had arrived in Roanoke on time. She wondered if he would write. What would he think of her letter and of her? Was any of it real? Was she just dreaming?

It was hard to understand the feelings she had. She couldn't sleep. She went downstairs and smoked a cigarette on the front porch while listening to the cicadas serenade in the forest. If he wrote back, what would she say to him? What would it feel like? Was this love, infatuation, silliness, and only a dream? Would this turn out like all the dreams she had had before/ She felt like such a child. She didn't know anything about a boy. Even with all the reading and romance novels, nothing prepared her for the wakefulness, this excitement.

"Jamie, what on earth girl! Why are you sitting out here in the dark? You are thinking about that boy! Heavens child, what am I going to do with you? Come to bed and get some sleep and we'll go see Sally tomorrow. She doesn't have a phone. We'll tell her about your bus trip and see what she thinks. I know it will be Ok no matter what happens."

With that Jamie promised her grandmother she would go to bed and wait and talk tomorrow. She finally fell asleep around 1:00 am after smoking four more cigarettes and drinking a half a glass of her grandmother's brandy. She woke at nine to lazily sit in the window with her head on her knees and had a good cry as she listened to Bobby Vinton on the radio singing his hit song" I'm so lonely" about a soldier who was far from home.

The Hotel

"Private Dhamner," the company clerk shouted as I bounded to my feet and snapped to attention in front of his desk.

"Take this envelope and read the instructions inside. Everything you need is in there. Report back at 0700 hours Monday for further orders."

"Dismissed!" He said as he called the next recruit and repeated the same instructions.

Pulling the paper from the envelope, I walked out of the room and across the lobby. I read that I would check into the Roanoke Hotel by six o'clock. My dinner would be at the hotel restaurant. There were green vouchers for all other meals at Riley's Diner and a $10.00 bill.

I remembered seeing the hotel from the bus on the way into town. I wondered if I would see the lady from the bus, and her granddaughter there.

The streets had been full of shoppers, cars and street vendors. The hotel was a ten story building at the corner of Commerce and Campbell Street. It was more modern looking than any building I had seen in Waynesboro or Charlottesville.

I wanted to go to a pay phone to call Martin's Store on Route 6, and see if he could get a message to my father. He could pick me up for the weekend. I spotted a pay phone on the outside of the wall when the other three recruits came up and asked me where I was staying. Before I could reply, they told me the names of their hotels and headed in different directions. It was 5:30 p.m. After walking the four blocks to the hotel, I walked into the lobby to the sound of a cascading water fountain.

I was watching the water spill from the third tiered level when a sweet southern voice said, "Mr. Dhamner, we've been expecting you. Your room is number 407. It faces west and may be a little warm, so open the windows and let it air out before you go to bed. Dinner is served from 6:30-8:30 p.m. on the second floor near the steps leading to the veranda. Thank you for staying with us" she finished with a southern smile.

Walking down a dim lit hallway decorated with framed pictures of confederate heroes and heroines, I found room 407, and unlocked the door with a stainless steel key on a string tag that had been given to me by the desk clerk.

Stepping from the red and yellow paisley rug in the hallway through the doorway, I was struck by a mixture of stale, stuffy air, and the aroma of ambrosia in a bowl by the door. A large queen sized bed with stacks of quilts and butterfly patterned blankets threw a golden glow back toward the window. Trailing my hand along the cool marble credenza, I walked around the bed and cranked out the large double pane window. Looking down, I breathed in the vehicle sounds and smells from the street below.

To my left through the bathroom door, I could see the white porcelain tub with brass claw legs. A white RH monogramed towel was draped over its side, with wash cloths rolled into a triangle on the sink top. There was an oval rug on the black tiled floor in front of the sink that matched the white porcelain tub. I ran the water until it became cold and doused my face and dried it with one of the fresh towels.

I turned on the Philco television and adjusted the rabbit ears. The black and white image was wavy, but the voice was the evening news anchor, Walter Cronkite. I left the television on as I took another look out the window at the brick building with the chiseled window frames, reflecting the sun's warmth into my room.

I sat on the bed and started looking through the three ringed binder when I thought about my grandfather. He would be watching the same evening news and talking to my grandmother about me. They would split a bowl of peaches with cookies. It was my favorite dessert. My mother would be cleaning up the supper dishes, and probably crying silently, as she wiped the tears away with her blue checkered apron that I had given to her on her birthday. My father would be heading out the door to fish. He would take my little brother, Freddie, to carry the worm can. They would catch two or three 'white chubs' as we called them because of their white fatty bottom. My mother would clean them for breakfast.

I felt home getting farther away. It was just over the mountain. I could hitch a ride and be there by midnight. I could sleep in my bed tonight and maybe wake up and this would all be a dream. My older brother, Artie, would be home next. He had finished his three years as a cook at Fort Gordon. He had a job waiting for him with my uncle Henry at Henrico Electric in Harrisburg. He would be a lineman, and planned to buy a big Buick or Pontiac, if I knew him.

My younger brothers, Eddie and Freddie, would play their guitars later in the evening with Scotty Brown and Jimmie Fortune on the back porch or down by the river. My sister would be studying for summer school to make up the failed English class, so she could be a freshman next year.

I missed home. I didn't know anybody here. I was alone for the first time in my life in a fancy hotel with a fancy name, when I heard the phone ring in the room. The lady at the front desk was checking to see if the room was okay and reminded me to come to dinner.

I turned the lights off as I walked out the door and made my way down to the lobby for dinner.

Dinner for Three

Home was never like this, I thought, as I walked down the winding stairway to the hotel lobby. Mints on the bed stand, monograms on towels, pillows with silky covers, and slippers in the bathroom were all new to me. There were free postcards on the room desk. I took one to mail home.

In the lobby, people were checking in with all sorts of suitcases, shoulder bags, and dogs in cages. This was quite a place, I thought. I felt like I was an actor in Hollywood, or some other famous place that I had never been.

"Can I help you with the postcard?" the smiling lady at the desk asked. She told me it would be included in my bill and not to worry. Then with the same radiant smile, she pointed to the stairway leading to the veranda and told me to enjoy dinner.

Strolling across the lobby, I spotted Kit from the bus. There was a younger lady with her. She was dressed in an orange paisley saffron dress. She nervously held a small purse in front of her, with a long gold strap draped across her left shoulder. She kept turning the low heels of her shoes over on their sides in unflattering discomfort. Her appearance and demeanor suggested that she was nervously trying to please her grandmother. As I walked closer, she looked at me with a face that begged to be rescued.

"Why hello young man" the grandmother said extending her white gloved hand to me as she stepped in front of her granddaughter in what appeared to be an obvious message to stay my distance.

"Thank you. I will be staying here this weekend before departing for army basic training in South Carolina," I returned, hoping Jennifer would be paying attention.

She was smiling and looking back, while gesturing for me to follow them. At the top of the stairs, I followed them to the restaurant entrance. We waited without speaking.

A very attractive lady in a long black dress and menus approached and asked if there would be three.

"No, it will just be my granddaughter and me. We have a reservation" she responded. The attendant turned to let her know it would be a few minutes, and led the grandmother and Jennifer to a table by the far window, overlooking Campbell Street. It offered a view down Commerce Street and the white stone United Methodist Church across the street.

I noticed a lot of visitors coming in with reservations. They were led to their seats and provided a menu. Most ordered ice tea or lemonade since alcoholic beverages were not served in the restaurant. Soon, the attendant returned and let me know that she would find me a seat as soon as possible.

After ten minutes, she stepped in front of me and asked me to follow her. As she turned toward the tables, I smelled wisteria blooms and a faint scent of sweet vanilla. I took a deeper breath and followed the freshness to the window, and a small table toward the back of the restaurant. Once I was seated, she placed a large menu in my hands.

As I opened it, she listed the specials for the evening, which included breast of chicken with mashed potatoes and gravy. The others were roasted cut of lamb with a plum parfait, and split-breasted dove with steamed green peas over pork, cooked with rice on the side.

I ordered a hamburger with home fries and cold slaw. She told me it was a 'good' choice. She returned to let me know my hamburger would be ready in a few minutes, and poured a glass of ice water.

I was looking at the silverware on the table when a soft hand touched my shoulder. It was Jennifer motioning for me to come over to their table. Her grandmother gave me a scowling look from across the room. Jennifer grabbed my collar and pulled me up in my chair.

"This is not a request," she said, as she pulled me from my chair and guided me to their table.

"I don't think your grandmother wants me to join the table," I said.

"Come on, she won't bite you. She's just a little particular about the friends I choose," she said, dismissing my concern.

The waitress was bringing the food to my table, when Jennifer intercepted her and carried my food to their table. On the way, she told me her grandmother's name was Mildred Spencer, but she liked to be called 'Kit'.

"She'll like you. Just be yourself and don't brag. She likes to do most of the talking. She'll tell you her life story that I've heard a hundred times, about her stay here when she was young."

"Good evening, young man. I see Jennifer has been persistent in bringing you to our table," she said in a very demurring voice, as I glanced at all the silverware and the three plates on the table. I took a seat, after pulling Jennifer's seat back and sliding it forward.

Kit was having lamb roast with plum sauce. Jennifer cancelled her order and asked the waitress to bring her a hamburger deluxe, much to her grandmother's chagrin.

"Where did you go to school and what do your parents do?" Kit quizzed, as she cut a small piece of the roast, dipped it in the plum sauce, and delicately placed it in her mouth. She hardly opened her lips, I thought, as she placed her fork on the side plate. Then, in a single motion she raised her napkin to her lips as she chewed slowly, waiting for my answer. She continued to chew softly, hardly moving her jaws, as I told her that I was the first to graduate from high school in my family. I described our farm on the Rockfish River just off highway 151 in the Rockfish Valley.

Then I stopped, realizing that I must be talking too much since she kept cutting a small portion of the roast and placing it in her mouth with a "mehah, mehah" sound and piercing glances. She was bored and totally uninterested. Heeding Jennifer's warning, I interrupted her soft chewing with "Tell me about you and your family."

This released an avalanche of endless tales about her husband's travels and adventures here and abroad. It was hard to follow what she was saying, since much of her conversation was with herself and her long dead husband. As she continued to talk, Jennifer and I were able to eat a little, and dabble in the catsup bowl with our fries, while visually talking with our eyes about how dull this all seemed.

I was amusing myself with Jennifer and the home fries, when abruptly Kit said "And your father, what does he do besides farming?"

I was startled by her question, and almost knocked my water glass over, as I chewed fast and gulped down a fry so I could answer her question.

"He works for DuPont in Richmond. He leaves on Sunday evening with his ride and returns on Friday. My brothers and I are responsible for feeding the animals while he is away. The whole family pitches in. We don't have a lot of money, but we always have plenty of food...." I tried to finish, as she interrupted, and started telling me about Jennifer's plans after she finished school.

This conversation drifted back into a long, three way conversation, when the waitress returned and asked if I wanted my hamburger in a box to take to my room. It was only then that I realized that I hadn't eaten anything, except a few fries and crackers from the table. I excused myself with my hamburger and the remainder of my home fries, and left for my room.

A haunting sting of shame that I felt at times like these, but could never explain, followed me down the stairs and up the hall to my room. I knew we talked with a southern farm accent, but she was making fun of me. I was not good enough, I thought, to talk with her granddaughter. She must think I am a real hillbilly for rambling on like that. I finished the hamburger in my room. Water from the bathroom sink helped chase down the last of the fries and bun. It also helped get the foul mustard taste out of my mouth, and Mildred out of my thoughts.

It was 9:00 p.m.

The western sky was turning dark outside. The window sheers were beginning to reflect the street lights below. It would be dark soon. I wanted to call home but we didn't have a phone. Lying on the bed, I listened to the ceiling fan string swing back and forth against the frosted globe.

The twirling shadows danced against the white plaster ceiling, as I glanced at the alarm clock on the night stand. It was 9:30 p.m. I fell asleep in my clothes.

Sally

Sally Royal Dameron was a southern lady. People described her sweet-tea voice and gentle manners, as a disguise for her formidable energy and stamina, when taking on any task that required social interaction and a forced sense of tradition.

She was anything but the empty-headed and helpless damsel so many traditional southern men expected women to be in the 1920's and 30's. During WWII, she and her sixteen-year old daughter moved to Baltimore, and worked the military munition factories making clothes, boots, and bullets for the soldiers in Europe and Japan.

She was kind and tender hearted, but she could stand her ground, and was clearly the lady of the house in all matters pertaining to her six children and 14 grandchildren. It was said that she could make the finest clothes that could grace any debutante, as well as sling shovels of horse manure with her husband, Hayward, on their 26 acre high mountain farm on Spruce Creek Mountain.

On this morning she eagerly awaited her sister, Wanda, and her granddaughter Jamie, to talk about her favorite grandson, now a soldier in the Army.

"Hello Wanda! Come in out of the heat and let me pour you both a glass of tea, fresh from the cool house. My, it's hot, but you're not here to talk about the weather or my tea. Tell me what brings you here." She finished with a gesture for them to take a seat at the side table on the front porch.

"I met Wade on the bus to Charlottesville last Friday. I usually go to the University Hospital for treatment on Monday, but rescheduled for Friday. We, or I, talked all the way to the bus station and he listened. I want to write but don't have his address....."

"My, my slow down child." Sally interrupted. He will write you if he said he would. That's who he is. Had an effect on you, didn't he? He can do that. He is no nonsense, works hard, saved his money last year, and graduated 12th in his high school class. He wants to make something of himself. He was never much for a lot of silly conversation or loitering around in town like some of these other boys. He wanted to serve his country first, like his father and grandfather, and then settle down at home. He surprised everybody, but Hayward and me, when he decided on an early enlistment.

I knew he had to get away, but he'll be back."

"Sally, you know about Jamie, and what she's been through. I'm concerned about her, but this is the first time

I have seen her take an interest in any boy, or young man. I just don't want her to get hurt, but I want her to be happy too. She will be 18 in September, and has big dreams about her singing, even though she knows her physical limits, and what the medical treatment has done to her. I, we, want to know more about Wade. She has a young girl's crush on him, and has been daydreaming ever since they met on the bus."

"Wanda, he'll write to Jamie, me and his family when he has time. I don't have his address yet, either. We do have a phone, and he has our phone number. Hayward and his father know a lot about the service, and told me not to worry or expect any contact from him for a least a week or so. He will be busy from sun up to dark. Army training will be tough, but he'll make it."

Together, they spent the rest of the morning drinking tea and eating slices of Sally's pound cake. They talked about who they knew, and the big funeral last week for Charles Summers, the county supervisor responsible for getting the Spruce and Stoney Creek road graveled and partially paved last summer. He was the father of eight children, and visited Hayward a lot on Sunday afternoons to watch the rooster fights, like most of the men on the mountain. Jamie sat through most of the talk, but her mind was still on the bus ride to Charlottesville, and thoughts of her getting her first letter.

The Accident

A speeding siren jolted me from my sleep at 5:30 AM.
I ran to the window to see a man lying on the sidewalk across the street. A car was wedged between a power pole and a pickup truck. A broken power line was spitting sparks at a man hole-cover, and making grinding sounds against the pavement. Firemen and police were scrambling everywhere. A city utility truck arrived, and the driver climbed the pole and shoved a long wooden rod in the transformer window. The street lights dimmed a couple of times, and the sparks stopped, as I heard people running in the hallway.

From my window, I could see hotel guests in all sorts of night garments, spilling into the street below, as a policeman held up his hands and motioned them back to the hotel. I spotted Jennifer in the crowd on the street.

She was holding her night robe tight against her body with her left hand, while flailing the right all about and shouting at the policeman. She was trying to tell the policeman something about the accident, but he wasn't listening and kept pushing the crowd back.

He took her arm and forced her to the curb. The man was motionless on the street. A fireman threw a yellow striped jacket over his face, and pulled it down across his body. His thin trouser legs were both bent outward, making him look like a fire fly reflected against the flickering amber street lights.

There was a lot of commotion and yelling in the street, but I could hear only muffled voices through the window.
Pressing my ear against the window, I tried to hear what Jennifer was saying, when a heavy cane tapped on the door and a panicky voice screamed, "I can't find Jennifer. She ran downstairs to see what was going on. That girl will be the death of me. Are you awake in there?" she kept yelling as I open the door to see Kit grasping the neck of her robe

and sobbing. She pulled me into the doorway and pushed me down the hall and told me to bring Jennifer back to her room.

I ran down the hall and stairway in what seemed to be a singular motion to find Jennifer hastily walking across the lobby door shouting, "I saw the whole thing. The man in the car just ran over him like a dog. He flew through the air and landed on the street. The man in the car jumped out after his car hit the pole and ran away. I know what he looks like. He just ran away," she finished, as her grandmother raced across the lobby and cradled her in her arms and took her upstairs.

An officer in the doorway said he would get a complete statement a little later. Mildred acknowledged him with a slight nod of her head, as she and Jennifer disappeared up the stairs.

In the street, a panel van arrived as two policemen loaded the body. A lineman climbed the pole and restored the power. The fire truck backed into the street, made a U-turn, and headed back to the station. Down the street, a patrolman swept up glass while another one measured curved track marks on the sidewalk, and motioned a tow truck to take the vehicles away.

It was 6:30 a.m. and the street was awash with sunshine and building shadows. A spray of light was breaking against the steeple on the United Methodist Church across the street. The pavement in front of the hotel was quickly turning gray. The sun sparkled and danced down Commerce Street on waves of shattered glass. Everyone was gone now. A quiet hush of wind slipped past the back of my neck. A few cars passed by. I thought I heard a pigeon coo when the doorman asked if I would be coming inside for coffee and raisin buns in the lobby.

As I turned from the street I heard Mildred shout through the doorway "Wade, come join me for coffee. Jennifer is resting. She has had quite a night. What a dreadful thing.

45

I must talk to you, now!" She finished sharply.

As I followed her to the lobby she turned and apologized for her rudeness saying "Thank you for finding her. I don't know what I would do if I lost her. Maybe I'm over reacting, but I'm going to call my daughter. We'll take her home for the rest of the day. Maybe I'll let Jennifer write to you. I pray you will be safe in your travels. Goodbye" she finished without inviting me into the café for coffee and raisin buns.

I never heard from them. An article appeared in the Monday paper regarding the accident. There was no mention of an eye witness. The victim was not named.

Sunday Morning

After returning to the room and washing my face, I picked up the military voucher for breakfast. The breakfast diner was two blocks away down Campbell Street. The busy commercial streets on Saturday were now as quiet as a prayer room on Sunday.

It took me only a few minutes to find the cafe. Opening the door a waitress calling me 'sugar' took my Army voucher and offered me a booth by the window. It was a real train dining car from the 1950's. The owner had purchased and restored it. The baggage compartment served as a storage area for plates, cups, and an assortment of napkins and silverware. The place was packed and smelled of fried eggs, bacon, sausage, toast, biscuits, grits, and steaming coffee. Most of the people were dressed for church; the Baptist, Methodist and Presbyterian churches were all on the same street across from the diner.

"What can I get you, honey?" the waitress asked with a broad smile, as she slid the breakfast special in front of me, and whisked away to pour coffee at the next booth. When she returned, I pointed to the Sunday Morning Egg Special.

From the back of the counter came a voice telling me that it would be coming right up. A bell rang and the plate was before me. They kept bringing me gravy and biscuits on a platter steaming hot from the oven. This was a lot more interesting than the hotel restaurant last night.

I was eating and drinking coffee, when a twelve year-old boy came in barking "Get your Telegram News! Man killed in street this morning! More in the afternoon edition!" he blurted out in short commands. I bought one, but I found nothing about the accident. Maybe there would be some more details, I thought, when the paper boy grinned and shouted, "You going to eat that biscuit? Thanks for the tip" he said, grabbing it and throwing it in his paper pouch. He was gone and eating it before I could say anything.

I couldn't eat any more, so I signed the voucher and headed back to the hotel. On the way, I passed a Chinese laundry that washed shirts and pants for a dollar, while I waited. I had been wearing my clothes for two days. I entered and stepped behind a make-shift curtain, where I undressed and gave my shirt, pants and socks to a Chinese lady, with sweaty hair sticking to her face and neck. She grabbed the clothes saying "One dollar and ready in forty-minutes. Stay seated and wait."

The curtain was thin, and I could see people exchanging money for clothes. A poker game was going on by the window. It looked like the two soldiers from the induction center were losing lots of money, and were still drunk from the night before.

They were in their twenties, so I guessed they had been drafted. They argued a lot with the two other players dressed in grimy t-shirts and military pants. Without warning, the short soldier broke a beer bottle against the wall and called one of the men a cheater. The crowd froze in place among whirling washing machines and sloshing soap suds sliding into floor drains. The big white commercial driers spun around pushing out heat, humidity and the smell of dry bleach into the already sultry room.

"Sit down or I'll cut your nuts off," shouted the dealer as he pulled a hand-carved hickory cane from behind the spruce pine applecrate he was sitting on.

"Don't mess with these people," the older soldier said. We'll get in trouble with them and more trouble with the army when they find out," as he threw his cards in the middle of the table and led his friend out to the street.

I watched from behind the curtain when the old Chinese lady reached through the curtain, stripped me of my wrap around towel, and pushed my clothes into my stomach, saying "Be much trouble if soldiers come back. Romie done called the cops. They're on the way. They take you to jail just because you know them soldiers. They'll beat you up and take your money. Here, come with me out the back and home now, quick" she said, as I pulled on my still damp clothes and scrambled to the back door to get out.

The Chinese Lady

Outside I ran past rusting trash cans, and piles of soiled clothes that had been discarded and thrown out to be picked up with the trash. The smell of bleach and vomit were everywhere on the ground. I found an old green dumpster, and leaned against it, as I buckled my belt and finished pulling on my socks and shoes.

The police car was pulling up in front. One of the policemen was yelling at the soldiers and card players as I ran down the street toward the hotel. I had no interest in what was going on.

I could hear myself swearing and shaking. I had never seen this kind of trouble before, but I knew it wouldn't be good for me if I got caught. The Chinese lady had done me a favor. Maybe it was my age; she seemed to know that I was scared.

I decided that I would spend the rest of the day in the hotel reading the endless racks of farm and hunting magazines. There were plenty of donuts and coffee in the lobby. I kept eating most of the day in case I decided to not return to the diner this evening. At 5:30 p.m. I walked to the train diner for fried chicken, mashed potatoes and cranberry sauce. Once finished I walked straight back to the hotel to avoid a repeat of the day.

I read a couple of chapters in Look Homeward Angel. I wrote a bunch of postcards to mail home, finished my letter to Jamie and mailed it. I made sure I had completed all the forms in the packet for the morning. I set the alarm for 6:00 am and fell asleep.

Jamie, Sunday morning

It was a glorious Sunday morning.

Jamie opened wide her second-story bedroom window, placed her hands firmly on the window sill, and pushed her head out like a Phoenician figurehead carved directly into the stem of a ship's bow, and let the full morning sun splash across her face.

Then lifting her arms high over her head, she arched her back and let her satin gown silhouette her young adult figure against the blue sky, and pushed her hair back to let the fresh breeze flow through her blonde waves. She was a singular image of the virgin goddess Athena, as she exercised, meditated, and prayed softly to herself.

"I know I don't want to die. I don't want to have thoughts of killing myself. I want to live, God, I want to live. Tomorrow will be my last bus ride to Charlottesville, and my last counseling session. I will give them my goals,

and focus on getting a job, writing more songs, staying as healthy as I can, and start living as much as I can, for as long as I can." She said to the invisible face in the clouds above Three Ridge Mountain.

She bathed her face, placed a few light strokes of makeup on her cheek and chin, put on her new yellow dress with a blue sash her grandmother had just finished, and bounded down the stairs for coffee and breakfast before leaving for church in Wintergreen.

At church, she made a solemn prayer to work hard on getting her classes finished and getting her diploma, eating better and helping more around the house. If possible, she would take the office job offered at Waynesboro Nursery in Beech Grove, make a recording of her latest songs, and do everything possible to get in touch with her soldier boy.

After church and lunch, she walked through the tall grass in the pasture, letting the orchard grass brush against her ankles, as she raced to her water cave. There she soaked her body in the cool waters of the cascading Spruce Creek Falls.

She could not get the thoughts of Wade out of her mind. It was like a new found energy force, and was pushing her to find out more about this new feeling she had in her heart and stomach. She now had a reason to want to live and wished to do the things that would help her be a better person, a woman.

She lay against the smooth granite bolder that her grandfather had placed at the entrance to the cave, and let it warm her back, as she read and wrote down what she had read, and now believed, were some of the greatest love lines ever written by Emily Dickinson, for her second letter to Wade:

"Hope" is the thing with feathers -
That perches in the soul -
And sings the tune without the words -
And never stops - at all..."

The Recruitment Center, Roanoke, Virginia

"Dhamner!" shouted the sergeant at the door, as I entered the induction center. "Go to Station A-1, remove your clothes, except for your shorts, and wait. Next!" he bellowed as he pointed down the hall toward the large female attendant, who had examined my throat and ears on my last visit.

I had hardly stepped in front of her before a giant tattooed hand, with an army flag imprinted in blue, grabbed my left arm just above the elbow and pumped two shots into my arm with a *bimp..bimp,* from an inoculating nozzle that looked like an electric paint spray gun.

I felt sick and pale. I thought I felt my knees buckling as the liquid pain exploded through my shoulder, when another medical attendant appeared from behind a curtain on my right, pressed the nozzle spray gun against my upper arm, and pumped two more shots.

It really hurt. I could feel tears on my face but I wasn't crying as the female stepped in front of me and stopped me dead in my tracks. She pulled down the right side of my shorts, exposing my right upper buttock, and plunged a long syringe deep into my flesh, held it for a second or two, slowly pushing the contents into the large muscle.

"All done," she said, as she pulled the needle out and handed me a large white gauze, telling me to press it hard against my hip until the bleeding stopped. A weakness spread throughout my whole body. My tongue was dry. The eggs, bacon and grits from Lance's Diner were rumbling and heaving in my stomach, as I took the gauze pad away and massaged the lump of liquid under my skin. I was light headed and about to sit down when the nurse growled, "You can't sit here. Get dressed and follow the yellow line to the testing room" she finished, as she turned behind the heavy canvas curtain and filled another syringe.

This had all happened in a minute or two. It seemed longer. My body was hot and my arms and bottom were numb from the inoculating experience. I could still feel the liquid piercing through my veins as I made my way to the testing room and looked for a seat.

There was a gray metal table in the middle of the room with six manila folders stacked in the middle. Five other recruits were standing behind their chairs, as I took my place behind the last vacant chair.

We were commanded to take a seat.

As the scraping sound of the chair's legs rocketed from the concrete floor, Captain Lance instructed us to take and open the folders with our names imprinted on the cover.

There would be no talking. We were to answer every question even if we didn't know the answer.

I wanted to raise my hand and ask for some water when the Captain snapped "Do you understand?"

Everyone responded "Yes, Sir" as we reached for the number two pencils and started answering the multiple choice questions.

It was about two o'clock when I finished the test.

Putting down my pencil, I noticed a sergeant moving toward the table. He took our test papers and placed them in a large cardboard box against the wall.

He returned with a wrapped hamburger and fries. He placed a bottled Pepsi in front of me and told me to wait until everyone finished. My head was pounding and I could feel my skin getting red and hot from the shots and heat in the room.

The others were frantically marking boxes on the test papers when the sergeant stepped to the table and called "Time."

It was three o'clock. We were told to eat while the tests were graded, and someone would return and give further instructions.

While we were eating, Captain Lance gave each of us a five inch strip of card stock paper. We were told to memorize the number and save the peel off strip for later.

My strip read RA137789947 on one side. The other side had a red, peel off strip of tape. I was the only recruit in the room with an RA number and a red, peel off strip.

I was watching the others memorize out loud...

"US..., RE.., NG..," when Captain Lance put his hand on my shoulder and said "Come with me, now!"

I picked up my newly issued canvas handbag with my belongings and followed him to an army jeep waiting outside in the parking lot.

As a corporal took my bags, he told me get in the back, started the engine and scattered gravel along the parking lot, as we sped down a one-lane road toward Roanoke Regional Airport.

Captain Lance yelled over the noise of the engine and highway, "You did extremely well on your test. You're in the Army now. Memorize that number, and be prepared to give it to the airport manager" he finished, as we headed south of town past a sign that read: Airport, 3 miles.

"Remember, Son," he repeated, "before you board the plane for Columbia, SC, you will need to memorize your serial number. You will be asked for it everywhere you go for the next three years. You'll carry your bag on the plane" he said, as he peeled off the red tape strip, and stuck it on the side, just below the handle.

As he and the corporal dropped me off at the terminal gate, he gave me a thick envelope saying, "Give this to the company clerk or duty sergeant when you arrive at the Receiving Center at Fort Jackson. Do not let it out of your sight. It contains all of your test papers, physical exam report, rank, and reporting station after basic training. You will address all officers as 'Sir' and follow all orders without question. Do you understand, Pvt. Dhamner?" he said, as he took one step backwards, saluted, and welcomed me to the US Army.

"Yes, Sir," I saluted, as they jumped back into the jeep and disappeared in a cloud of brown pollen dust down the driveway back toward Roanoke.

The Flight

This was my first flight on a DC-3. It lasted about two hours. The sun was quickly disappearing behind the Blue Ridge and Appalachian Mountains below.

From my window seat, I could see farms and houses below on square, quilted patterns of gold and green.

Highway 11 South, 220 North, and a bulldozed outline of Interstate 81, crossed and crisscrossed each other, twisting and winding along the valley floor south toward Johnson City, Tennessee, and eastward to the mountain top town of Mt. Airy, North Carolina.

Tiny cars and trucks looked like summer ants trailing home to earthen dens on the asphalt highways. A Great Southern and Ohio train lumbered along the winding Shenandoah River past Shot Tower, making its round trip from the coal mines of Kentucky through Pulaski, and down across Afton Mountain to the coal-fired towers on the eastern seaboard.

At an intersection of highway 11 south, where a Great Southern train would soon cross, I could see a Trail Ways bus stopped at one of the detours along the partially paved

Interstate 81. It could be the same one I had ridden on to Roanoke last Friday.

It seemed like a long time ago. Here I was flying south in the dimming shades of June's sunlight toward Columbia, SC, on an adventure that was so different from home and the Rockfish Valley. Behind me were farms, friends and memories of my senior school year.

The smell of early spring clover and honey suckle vines faded into evening light. I continued looking out the window to see spatters of twinkling lights below, as the pilot came on the speaker thanking us for flying Piedmont Airlines and letting us know that we would be on the ground in ten minutes.

The air was suffocating as I stepped from the plane onto the stairs leading down to the sweltering tarmac of Columbia Regional Airport. The flight and snacks had dissipated the ache and numbness of the shots and trauma of the induction center.

As I walked through the cyclone fence and gate at the terminal, a limousine driver, complete with red cap, flight jacket and gray-striped pants, held up a white cardboard sign with five last names scrawled in blue and green crayon colors. Mine was on the list. I walked over to him and gave him my name. He took my bags and told me to follow him.

I recognized the tall soldier that I had seen at the laundry in Roanoke. It would not be the last time our paths would cross over the next three years. He told me to get in the front seat and slide to the middle. He smelled of beer, and was smoking an unfiltered Lucky Strike.

Flipping the cigarette out the window with his forefinger, he told me that Bud wouldn't be coming to basic. He was in the Roanoke jail. "The cops caught him and beat the hell out of him. I thought I saw you there. What happened? Did the old Chinese lady feel sorry for you and get you out the back door and send you home?" He laughed as he flipped another cigarette butt out the window, and leaned back in the seat and took a nap on the way to the base.

After a car ride through the sultry night heat, on a dirt and gravel roads that twisted westward through the rolling hills outside Columbia, we arrived at an old WWII army barrack building with a sign that read:

WELCOME: CENTRAL RECEIVING
Central Receiving Center, Fort Jackson, SC

Our limo arrived, and we joined a motley crew of forty-eight others in civilian clothes, sweaty, tired, and sitting on a variety of suitcases, shopping bags, and handbags like mine. It was 10:15 p.m.

The dim-lit asphalt parking lot was surrounded by metal dumpsters, 36 tin trash cans full of food waste and paper debris. The air was alive with the sound of cicadas, bats and mosquitoes, and smelled of molded lawn shavings and tarpaper.

In the middle of the lot was a short-haired, bespeckled singular soldier in a white cotton t-shirt, bloused khaki pants and combat boots, holding a clipboard and pencil with his dog-tags hanging from his neck imprinted with the name: Pfc Michael Shaw: US23478952.

"Welcome to Fort Jackson. I'm Pfc. Michael Shaw, company clerk for Company C-18-5. A drill sergeant will be here soon to take you to your temporary barracks. It will be your home for the next two days until you receive your uniform and clothing issue, weapon order, blankets and rations kit for basic training. Some of you will spend time at the dispensary for glasses, dental checkups, and additional shots. You will meet the base barbers at 09:00 after your morning PT and two-mile run.

Your drill sergeant will be here soon.

As I call your name and check you off my list, go to the center of the lot, and get into military squad formation, four wide and ten deep. Stay in formation, no talking. You can smoke if you got them. No questions. Your drill sergeant will tell you what to do and answer your questions."

The group gathered with a lot of murmuring and "what the hell is this shit? What the fuck is going on, and who or what the hell is a drill sergeant?"

"ME! You ass holes!"

The sweltering humid air of the parking lot froze like an artic chill in the night.

The sweat, glistening steel face of Sergeant Harmon Faison, tightened under the brim of his Drill Sergeant's hat, as his cold black eyes pierced the night air, and surveyed the group of fresh recruits.

His freshly pressed fatigue uniform was starched and pressed like plastic against his 6'4"thin-boned gladiator frame, He had a flat stomach, muscular upper arms and chest, and hands that held a horse sash in one and gripped a holstered bayonet in the other. Above his breast pocket was an 82nd Airborne patch with crossed rifles, and on his right shoulder was an embroider black and yellow 7th *Calvary* patch.

In the dark shadow of the humid and sweltering hot parking lot, he looked like a pantheon god ready for battle and defiant of any who resisted his orders or commands to move forward and take the enemy.

"ATennnnnnnHuttttttttttt!" Barked the company clerk as he motioned to Sergeant Faison.

"Forward. March!" He shouted.

"Give me your left, your right, left, right, march Stay straight, keep pace. Left, right, left, right!

Companeeeeeeeeeeeeeeee….halt," he barked.

Some of the recruits starting snickering.

Then, no one spoke or made a motion.

We stopped in our tracks as the sergeant abruptly commanded. "Stand at attention. Who do you think you are, some bunch of barrack's lawyers? Don't move until I tell you, you can move" he said as he turned, and faced another grim-faced sergeant with five stripes.

Death silence is the only way I can describe the look on the sergeant's face, as he turned to face an officer, a young freckled 2nd Lieutenant Camden Moore, commander for Company C 18 5, standing at attention on a small concrete platform to his left.

"Sergeant!" the 2nd Lieutenant says. "They're all yours."

Thirty minutes passed, and I heard two bodies hit the ground in exhaustion.

I was in good physical condition, but I was feeling faint when a drill sergeant came up behind me and said firmly so everyone could hear, "bend your knees slightly and don't lock them. You'll pass out if you do, and get sent to the infirmary. You will be recycled, and wait another week before your basic training starts," he finished.

He was right.

It helped, but my knees and thighs were burning in pain.

It was eleven o'clock. Where had the time gone?

A sergeant with a six stripes patch with a diamond inside was shouting for us to line up for inspection. It was dark. Mosquitoes and sweat bees were buzzing and biting my face and neck. The steaming heat from the freshly paved blacktop parking lot was coming through the bottom of my penny loafers and white socks.

For the first time, standing here in the dark, I was beginning to realize that my life as I knew it was gone when the sergeant with the stripes yelled, "Form a line. Extend your hand to touch the shoulder of the recruit on your left, and step forward with your left foot first and head for that building at the other end of the parking lot.

We were marched into the building, given bedsheets, and told to stand by our bunks.

It was 11:30 p.m.

It would be 0130 am before anyone lay on a bunk.

We were told that reveille was 0530.

We would meet our Platoon Drill Sergeant Harmon Warren Faison at that time. He had served two tours of duty in Korea and trained with 82nd Airborne at Fort Bragg before duty at Check-point Charlie in Germany, and Artic training in Alaska. After a thirty-year career, this was his final assignment before retiring at the age of 47. This was his first state-side US Army post since 1961. He was battle hardened, and would turn me and 120 fresh recruits into battle-ready soldiers over the next eight weeks of basic training.

We would learn quickly that he took his job as our Senior Platoon and Drill Sergeant seriously. "I will build up your confidence, and turn you into fighting men. Boot camp will break down the weak, weed-out the undesirables, and send you back home," he said repeatedly during our first night. The next eight weeks would test us physically, mentally and spiritually. There was no turning back. What we learned here could possibly save our lives, or lives of others in combats. We were a strange mix of 120 farm boys and city kids. Some had joined the army like me, out of duty, while others were discontented and never missed an opportunity to let the rest of us know they had been drafted. Bivouac would be seven weeks away, and graduation from Boot Camp at the end of the eighth week. I was already looking forward to seeing home again.

First Mail

"Jamie, you have a post card from your soldier boy!" shouted Ms. Thompson, as she returned from the Wintergreen Post Office and Harris Store, with ground cracklin corn seed, a loaf of light bread, some canned spam, and three days of mail.

"Let me see," returned Jamie, as she eagerly read the hurriedly written note on the military issued postcard out loud: *Read your letter and hope you can write me back. This is the address the recruitment center gave me along with 5 postal cards. They will mail them for me to family and friends. Say hello to everybody.*
Yours truly,

Pvt. H. Wade Dhamner, RA137789947
Fort Jack Basic Training Camp
Company C-18-5, Barrack Alpha
Columbia, South Carolina APO 41

"I'm going to put the letter that I wrote last Saturday in an envelope right now, and walk it down to the mail box. Is that OK?" She said, as she danced away and up to her room, clutching the card to her chest and singing: "He wrote to me, he wrote to me, he wrote to me…"

When Jamie returned from mailing her letter, supper was on the table: fried spam, cabbage, carrots and cornbread. Ms. Thompson, Tom and Hanna watched in amazement as Jamie ate everything on her plate and asked for seconds. This was new. It was marvelous and wonderful. Ms. Thompson had never seen her so happy. This child had endured so much sadness, loss and pain. She was more determined than ever to make Jamie's life happy, and every dream come true, for as long as they had together.

Boot Camp and Home

I had barely laid my head on the pillow when a loud speaker at the end of the barrack trumpeted reveille. A voice that sounded like the sergeant from last night, rattled over and over again "You have twenty minutes to assemble and get to running two miles. Inspection will take place during your run, and those who fail will be on latrine duty. I want to bounce a quarter on those beds.

You have eighteen minutes", the voice continued, as the barrack was frantic, with awakening recruits pulling wool, military blanket covers, and tightening their corners into folds under spring mattresses.

Drill sergeants were pacing up and down between bunks tearing some bunks apart, while others bounced quarters off tightly riveted bunk covers. All this was going as clothes were pulled on or straightened from a night's sleep.

I straightened my bunk from a night's sleep. I had watched the tall soldier from last night. He had re-enlisted. I figured he knew what he was doing. It would not be the last time he kept me out of trouble and out of latrine duty.

"Two minutes!" roared the voice over the speaker, and the last of the recruits bounded out the door into the parking lot for reveille. Damn, I thought. It's him. It was the sergeant who had told me to bend my knees. He was there last night. The company clerk yelled, "Companeeeeeeeeeeeeeee C-18-5 Attennnnnnn…..huttttttt!" Sergeant Faison stepped in front of us, dressed in combat boots, bloused trousers and a white t-shirt. He raised his right hand, and motioned forward march, double time.

Along the way, nine recruits dropped out. They were quickly escorted to a jeep for examination and recycled to the infirmary. The tall soldier was beside me in the group. I ran step-for-step with him. I heard a thud behind me and almost stumbled and tripped, as a soldier grabbed my shirt from behind and went down on the pavement. I was determined to finish and not drop out. The humidity was suffocating. My lungs were gasping against the heavy air. I thought my chest was about to bust. Sweat was streaming into my eyes. My thighs were on fire. The penny-loafers were pinching my toes and a blister was developing on the side of my foot.

A trail of vomit, beer, and salty sweat followed us across the base streets and sandy fields. Everybody was cursing and swearing about the heat. Some asked the sergeant how much further, as he sang out in military cadence:

"I don't care if I get there last, just as long as we get there fast ...A soldier's life is hard and long, just keep going and you'll get strong ....If this heat is bothering you, call your mama so she can come get you... Sound off!" he yelled back at us in a heavy voice.

We all started singing the song. We jogged two miles in sweltering heat and humidity, in street clothes and shoes, before returning to the parking lot.

Breakfast was at 0615.

Barracks inspection was at 0700.

At 0730, we assembled in the parking lot for a one mile march to the quarter master's building, for our duffle bag and military issue of clothing. We surfaced on the south end of the building. Our duffle bags were stuffed with four sets of fatigues: two pairs of combat boots, two belts with brass buckles, eight pairs of socks; dress black and combat green fatigues, two dress uniforms; summer khakis and six sets of boxer shorts and t-shirts, along with a shaving kit, water canteen and mess kit.

It weighed about sixty pounds.

My blister was killing me. I could see it bleeding through my socks as they sized my feet for my combat boots. I was worried that I might not make it back to the barracks, when the military convoy trucks arrived and transported us to the barracks, where we were told to dress out in the fatigue greens and repack our duffle bags for transport to our permanent barracks.

At the permanent barracks, we were given two things: a medicine kit with bandages, and a four by four foot piece of waxed wrapping paper. Sgt. Faison instructed us to place our civilian clothes in the paper and wrap it tight. While wrapping the clothes and shoes in the paper, I bandaged my toe. We were told to put our home address on the front of the package and place in it in the large box on the way out for mailing. I mailed mine to: Mom and Dad, Route 29, Rural Box 4, Faber Post Office, Nellysford, Virginia.

Once she opened the smelly contents, Mom threw it away. She read and kept my note. We joked about the package later. However, she never really told me what she thought or said about me under her breath when the package arrived a week after I wrapped it.

Jamie's Letter

Pvt. H. Wade Dhamner, RA137789947
Fort Jackson Basic Training Camp
Company C-18-5 Barrack Alpha
Columbia, South Carolina APO 41

Got your postcard.
Don't know what boot camp is like, but Tom, our Farm Manager, said it was pretty bad and would 'weed out' the undesirable from military service. I don't think you are undesirable, whatever that means, and know you will hang in there and do well. I am doing my best, and everybody says I'm doing better, but I think they're lying to me.
Talked with my grandmother, and plan to quit the counseling sessions at the hospital as soon as I can.

May have a part-time job. I'm reading 2-3 books a week. Will send you some. By the way, I promised my grandmother I would cut back to four cigarettes a day just for you. I do hope I get to see you again.

My grandfather has a sister, Lillian, in Columbia, that I last saw when my grandfather was alive and he took me to visit her and her husband, Ned. I was 12. She's real nice and lives in a big white house with columns in front. I think I was too much for them then. Real church going people and strict too. I would like to see them. If I can go see them again, maybe I can see you while I'm there. Hope that's OK.

They started working on the Wintergreen Golf Course up on the mountain. My part-time job may be doing price tags for all the shrubs and trees the Waynesboro Nursery is planning to sell to them. Not much is happening here except it's hot and humid. I go to the river about every day to swim and cool off. We'll go when you come home next time.

Grandmother helped me bake the cookies in this box.

Hope you like my letter and read it while eating the cookies. I really miss you and I am writing a new song for you after reading Emily Dickinson, and listening to Bobby Vinton for about a 100 times. Write soon, and hope we can talk some by phone if you have time.
Love, Jamie

Letter to Jamie

I know you got my postcard. I got your letter. Never read poetry by Emily Dickinson, but I'm sure I will. It's been so hard. This is my second week. After I wrote that note to you, I fell asleep. I got 12 shots at the Recruitment Center, took a bunch of tests, and received my guaranteed enlistment papers for photography school at Fort Monmouth, New Jersey after basic training.

I should have written before now, but this is the first chance I've had. The Army is hard. We run every morning at 6 am, and have about 20 minutes for breakfast and barrack inspection before training starts. We train and go to classes all day and sometimes at night. I got all my uniforms and sent my old clothes home to mother. I'm sure she burned them. I had worn them for three days before I got into the permanent training barracks.

Write and tell me more about you. I liked your song and appreciate the letter. Send me your phone number. I get to make a call on Thursday nights between 6:30 and 7:00 p.m. I will call you. We can only receive emergency calls from family in the company day room.

Yours truly,

Pvt. H. Wade Dhamner, RA137789947
Fort Jack Basic Training Camp
Company C-18-5 Barrack Alpha
Columbia, South Carolina APO 41

Weekend Pass to Columbia

It was Thursday evening at 1800. Sergeant Faison formed us in squads of ten men each, sitting on the lawn in front of our barracks, with our newly issued M-14 rifles.

We were given detailed instructions by squad leaders on disassembling, cleaning, oiling and re-assembling our rifles for inspection Saturday morning. We repeated the same exercise fourteen times, until all 120 trainees completed the drill in less than two minutes, stood in parade formation, ten men wide and twelve deep, on the asphalt parking lot, and presented their weapon for inspection.

At 1930, Sergeant Faison sat us all down again and told us he would issue weekend passes to all that passed inspection. I had sent Jamie a postcard and told her that I might get a pass, but was surprised when the company clerk stepped out of the barracks, came quietly up behind me, and told me I had an emergency phone call from home… I could take it, he said, in the company dayroom, and had 5 minutes to talk before returning to the cleaning exercise.

"Hello!"
"It's me, Jamie. I told them I was your sister and grandmother was sick. Don't get mad, but he asked if it was an emergency, and I said yes. Did you get that pass for the weekend in Columbia?"
"Yes, but I wasn't going to go anywhere."
"Why not?"
"I don't have much money and I'm too young to drink, so I thought I would stay here on the base."

"Well, I'm catching a bus tonight to Columbia and plan to stay with my grandmother's sister on Bull Street, just down the street from the bus station.
Take that pass and come see me on Saturday. I am bringing my guitar, and will be playing and singing at the Methodist Church on Sunday morning. I really want to see you. The address is 309 South Bull. See you Saturday for lunch at the house. Bye, I …"

I heard the phone click as the company clerk came up behind me and pushed the receiver down. "What's wrong?" he asked.

"My Grandmother is sick." I said.

"OK, sorry, return to the group. You have a lot to do to get ready for the Sergeant's inspection." He said, as I returned quickly to the exercise without comment.

I could still hear Jamie's voice as I returned to clean my rifle, make sure my locker was in order and my uniform pressed, and ready for morning inspection. Lights out was at 2100. Inspection failure meant no weekend pass.

Columbia

Saturday morning after 0900 inspection, I caught the Fort Jackson base bus to Columbia. The large white Magnolia House at 309 Bull Street made a real impression. Stately and elevated on a hill, I spotted it when the bus came into the downtown area. I wasn't sure, but I thought I saw Jamie sitting under the huge columns in the front, in a yellow dress, strumming her guitar. I wanted to yell out the window, but waited.

It was sultry hot as the bus pulled into the station. Soldiers from the base were everywhere and easy to spot, with our close-shaved haircuts and over-sized Class A summer Khakis. Cabs were everywhere, giving rides to local bars and amusements in and around the town.

I spotted some of the recruits from my company, huddled together around the front of the bus station, or walking toward bars, grills and cafes that spread out from the station to the square bricked area on Bull Street. There were tall police and sheriff deputies at every corner with "billy clubs" and 38 special pistols hanging from ammo and handcuff belts.

Once off the bus, I made my way quickly down the back alley from the bus station, remembering the incident in Roanoke, and not wanting to have that experience here.

"Wade, get in" a soft voice in a yellow dress shouted from the back seat of a 1963 Fairlane Ford.

It was Jamie.

"If you don't want to get mugged or put in jail you better get in here with me and ride. I saw your bus go by and thought I saw you, so Uncle Ned and I jumped in the car to come and get you. Get in the front seat and roll the window down. This heat is awful." She said.

"Lunch will ready soon," Ned said, as I put my overnight bag on the seat and rolled down the window for

 Jamie. "Lilly is looking forward to meeting you. Jamie has done nothing but talk about you since she arrived yesterday. I wanted to drive down to the post office where I work, but there's a large group organizing a march on Washington DC, so it's best if we just stay close to home. The bus station is not a good place to be at night."

"Uncle Ned, tell him what you do" Jamie said, as she reached over the seat and hugged my neck, and took my cap off so she could feel my hair. "Damn, what did they cut your hair with, a pair of sheep shears? You got a few bare spots, but I'll fix that tonight."

"I'm the Post Master for the town, and we handle a lot of mail for the base. We usually stay open until noon on Saturday, but with the big protest rally planned downtown tonight, and soldiers in town, we closed this morning at eleven.

There she is 'ole faithful' we call it. Last time Jamie was here she was twelve. She's changed a lot since. Been a while, but get to see the family up in Wintergreen the family reunion. We're going at the end of August. Got to get out of this heat."

Lillian had sandwiches and ice tea waiting for us. I got a major tour of the palatial house, with its wide winged white columns and over twenty-eight windows. It had a large balcony overlooking greenery and a hedge of box-woods and red tips, that completely encircled the house, some over six-feet tall. The smell of junipers and honeysuckle was thick in the air, teasing my nose, as I helped Jamie out of the back seat. She had talked the entire drive, telling me about her stay there when she was 12, and the great care and attention received from Lillian, who was a retired nurse.

We stayed home in the heat of day as Jamie re-trimmed my hair, and talked on the balcony in the late afternoon until Lillian called us to dinner around five o'clock. It was great seeing Jamie again. She was like no one I had ever met; smart, intuitive and bent on helping me learn to read more books and talk about the army.

"I want to visit you if I can when you travel to your next base. I know it won't be easy, but I have some money saved, and my grandmother has given me permission, as long as I promise to smoke less and take my medicine."

After dinner, we all took a slow walk around the block before sitting on the front porch. Ned had installed a large 52 inch ceiling fan, which circulated and cooled the summer air. They knew Jamie and I wanted time together, so Ned and Lillian retired for the evening to the lower level of the house.

"Where do you think you will go after Fort Jackson?" Jamie asked.

"I will get a leave home, and then I report to Fort Monmouth, New Jersey, for 12 weeks of photography school and advanced training for my next assignment. I don't know where it will be yet."

"Come see me at home. We're having a big family reunion at the end of August. All the family and friends will be there with plenty of good food. It will be a good time with you. I want to show you around."

As she finished, she moved closer to me and tucked her head against my shoulder, and we sat, silently until she said, "Wait here. I want to get us some cool wet wash cloths. They will cool us off.'

On her return she leaned me back against the wooden lounge chair, and put the wet wash cloth on the back of my neck and squeezed it, so the cool water would run down my back. She moved toward me, looping the wet towel on my

69

neck and shoulder, as she unbuttoned my shirt and pushed it down against my belt. She kept her cool, wet hands on my chest for a while, and then gently pressed her wet blouse against me, while wrapping her arms around my neck. She kissed my forehead, nose, and ears, and held me tight.

"You two need to get to bed, Jamie," said Mrs. Marshall from upstairs. "I'm looking forward to hearing you sing and play your guitar at church tomorrow morning. I requested *Morning Has Broken;* my favorite and your grandmother's too. Wade, I have the sofa in the living room ready for you, and you can use the hall bathroom to shower in the morning before breakfast and church." She finished, as she led Jamie to the guest bedroom, and left the light on for me in the living room and hall bathroom.

"Good night Wade," Jamie waved from the balcony outside her bedroom, as I turned off the light and went to sleep on the sofa under the watchful eyes behind the open door of Mr. and Mrs. Marshall's bedroom.

I thought I was dreaming. I felt a cool wash cloth on my forehead and soft fingers on my lips, and a voice that whispered, "Suussshh, they'll hear us." It was Jamie.

"Slide over. I want to just lay with you for awhile. They will be getting up soon. They've been awake half the night, worrying that you and me would get together here on the sofa. They're tired and fast asleep, but will be getting up at 6:30. I just wanted to be near you, hug you, and talk. There will not be much time once we get to breakfast."

"Jamie I…."

"I know you're afraid they will catch us and we'll be in trouble. Don't worry, I'll go back upstairs, but first hold me," she said, as I pulled her pajama body to me and felt the wonderful softness of her body against mine. She smelled of lilacs and Avon cream lotion. It was spellbinding as I heard her say, "I want this to last forever. I know it may not, but it's all I have for right now." She kissed me, deeply melting into my face like warm cream butter.

"I want to be with you more, and hope we can spend a lot of time together when you come home in August," she whispered in my ear, as we lay quiet and listened to the sound of the living room ceiling paddle fans. The drip of the sink in the hall bathroom had a steady cadence. It was just a few minutes, but she kept saying in the dark, "I want this forever, forever, forever."

Then, with surprising quickness, she said, "I've got to go back to bed. See you at breakfast." And with a kiss on my forehead, she was gone.

Breakfast was jelly and jams, cinnamon toast, bacon and eggs. Jamie ate everything and went to the living room to practice her songs, while Mrs. Marshall invited me to help her with the dishes. Tom fed their dozen henhouse chickens, and watered the azaleas, magnolias and red buds, growing along front steps and fence on the front lawn.

Everyone greeted me at church as we took our seats on the second row. It was a beautiful church with high mural windows and painted white pews, and satin cream painted walls. Everything smelled of sweet lilacs and lavender.

Jamie held my hands as we sat together for the morning prayers and greeting of quests by the pastor. She was invited to the front and introduced for two songs during the offering. The church pianist accompanied her on a soft, keyed Baby Grand, as Jamie's gentle strums on her guitar, and a soft melodious voice enthralled the congregation with a rendering of *Morning Has Broken* and *Amazing Grace*.

The pastor complimented Jamie, and thanked her for blessing everyone with her gift of song and music. The sermon was tailor-made for Jamie. She commented in the car later, that she often felt like the 'woman at the well', who was shunned except for a loving Savior, a gentle man of kindness and love, as she squeezed my hand and asked me to put my arm around her shoulder.

Ned approved, as he winked at me in the car mirror.

After a hamburger lunch at Chester Ham House on South Main near the court house, they insisted that I let them drive me back to the base. Since Mr. Marshall made mail deliveries on base, he knew where the barracks were. They allowed Jamie to walk with me to the guest sitting area, outside the company dayroom, hold each other briefly and kiss, before I walked her back to the car for her return to the house, and bus ride home in the morning.

As I watched them drive away and started walking to my barracks, I still could feel the warmth of her kiss and her soft arms holding me as she whispered 'I like you' and told me she was looking forward to seeing me at the family reunion in August. Her voice, music and wonderful smell would get me through the toughest training of my life over the next four weeks. I knew she would tell Ms. Stevens all about this weekend once she got back to her counseling sessions next week. She would find a welcome ear and bonding friendship, which would encourage her to leave the sessions and make as much of the time she had left to live.

I knew her wonderful voice would linger in my head and heart until the loud blast of reveille at 0600 the next morning when the world of training, running, marching, range firing and bivouac returned, and I was the property of the US Army. I would see her again at the reunion.

Bivouac

Boot camp, with all its pain, forced marches, rifle range, night maneuvers, and bivouac, passed as quickly as my first night on base. It was the last Saturday in August. Everything had been the same this morning with reveille, two mile run before breakfast and barracks inspection. It was also hot and humid but we didn't care.

It was 0900.

Here we were, Company C-18-5 sitting on the asphalt assembly lot where we had spent so many mornings. Our duffle bags were laid out in perfect rows of ten. We were positioned in squads of thirty-two with four soldiers abreast; four squads deep in full dress tan khakis.

I had managed to find a seat on a sand bag, on a tuftof grass near the curve rather than on the hard black top pavement. The company commander, first sergeant and post commander would soon arrive to announce our graduation, and present us with our orders for our next post assignment. We would be dispatched by bus to Columbia, and then on to our next assignment post.

Most of us were headed home to families, loved ones, and friends. I had twenty days leave before reporting to Fort Monmouth, NJ, for advanced training and combat photography school.

I was jotting a few quick notes in my journal and addressing a postcard to Jamie and Captain Lance, when the shadow of Sergeant Faison's wide brimmed hat drifted across my notebook and the grass at my feet.

He was standing as tall and stiff as he had a week ago, when he knelt behind me at the rifle range shouting, "Damn boy! Where did you learn to shoot like that?" as I aimed my M-14 and hit the down range black's bull eye with twenty perfect hits.

"Home," I returned without shifting my body away from the hot sand, while inserting another clip, and releasing the breach for a rapid-fire sequence.

"Stand up, soldier!" he commanded, as I fired the last of the rounds; placing the entire group in the black dot on the target. He took my weapon while cocking his right eye to look down the steel-rimmed barrel.

Watching him swiveling his head back and forth in a 180 degree direction he looked like a night owl searching for prey in the dark. He twirled it in the air and caught it on the forefinger of his hand. He checked for balance, and looked at the breach again shoving it straight forward toward my chest where I caught it with my quick hands. The other drill instructors gathered behind me. I felt a strange sense of trouble and possibly a long march to the guard house.

"Something ain't right. I can smell it." He said.

He stepped directly in front of me and stared into my face. His eyes pierced mine. I could feel his hot breath and sweat on my face. He kept gesturing "uh huh, uh huh" Then abruptly turning to other drill instructors, he ordered them to move two targets down range, another hundred yards.

He also told them to clear the firing block of everyone but me, as he grabbed an M-14 from a passing recruit.

"This is the damndest thing I've ever seen," he said to himself, as he ordered me back down to the firing block to take a firing position on the sandbag.

He placed three full clips in front of me while raising his binoculars to his eyes. My throat was dry with nervous anticipation. The summer heat drained sand from my eyes. We had been at this all morning; watching and practicing grenade throws, bayonet thrusts and target practice. What could he be thinking, I thought, as I watched the large targets placed 200 yards further down range?

"Take your time. You'll have two minutes to shoot all three clips. When finished, lay down your weapon and step back away from the block and stand at ease."

I lay prone on the sand-packed ground, and placed my rifle in the grooved mound in front of me, shutting my eyes, and wiping sweat from my face with the back of my hand. In my blind eye's mind, I could see the target, as my father and grandfather had taught me many times on hunts along the Rockfish River for deer and squirrel. Moving my finger to the curved steel trigger, I could see the invisible animal's eyes and waited.

"Ready, fire", the instructor commanded, as I closed my eyes like a rural mountain mystic; mysterious and stoic to the sensory deprivation about me, and saw the ferret's, beady eyes, the deer tail flinting back and forth in my cross hairs. I aimed for the center of his eyes, carefully not to spoil the meat with a wild shot.

All three clips were empty. The bolt slammed back and stayed open. I stepped back and waited. The targets were raised with white tags in the bull's eye.

"Damn, I ain't seen anything like this in my 30 years," he said again to himself in half belief, as he lay on the ground looking through the binoculars.

Getting up from the ground, as he looked at me with a half grin, he shook his head from side and side.

He winked at me as he snapped, "Damn soldier! Stack your weapon and report to the field mess." As I walked away, the other drill instructors picked up my rifle and examined it much like Sergeant Faison had earlier. They were still talking when I entered the mess tent and every eye was on me.

The recruits were whispering and gesturing toward me, with their arms and shoulders. Something had happened. I wasn't sure what to think, when the mess hall loud speaker clicked and Sergeant Faison's voice saying "Company, you'll be proud to know that Private Dhamner has qualified as a sharp shooter and marksman with a score of 100. Four others: Helms, Parks, Ramsey and Jackson also qualified as sharp shooters. Training resumes at 1300." He finished.

And now a week later, in the hot blazing sun, he's in front of me. "What are you writing in the notebook?" he asked, kneeling on one knee in front of me.

"Just stuff," I replied, as I shoved it in the side of my handbag.

"What's up, Sarge?" I said, hoping Sergeant Faison would not call me to attention and order me to do push-up's in this heat. "You're a damned good soldier," he said, as he pulled two black and silver, engraved metals with 'Sharp Shooter' and 'Marksman', imprinted on a tag from his right vest pocket.

Pinning one on my dress Khakis he said, "I want to give these to you personally. You're a hellva shooter and soldier. I have placed a letter of commendation in your records for the next station. You'll be hearing more from your commanding officer, I'm sure" he finished, as he stepped to another soldier, and handed him a 'marksman' metal.

As the Trailway buses pulled into the parking lot, I made a mental note to remember him. He would be included in my notebook.

The Dream

It is another sleepless night. She paces the kitchen floor. She walks up to her bedroom, and puts some Bobby Vinton and Patsy Cline on the drop down record player, and takes one last sip of warm peach brandy made by her grandmother. She lets the sweet taste linger on her lips as she places the glass on the nightstand.

She kisses the locket with Wade's heart-shaped picture, and uses it to caress the scar on the side of her cheek and neck, as the dim reading lamp spreads light across the darkening room to her bookcase, with Jane Eyre, Emily Dickinson, Chaucer, Shakespeare, and other literary classics and books. She admires most the 19th century works of art her grandfather had stacked, alphabetically, for her to read. The walls are decorated with prints that her grandfather gave her of the great neo-classic art; including her favorite titled 'The Lovers' by Guilio Romano' and 'The Girl with the Pearl Earring', as well as many attempts to paint mountains and river scenes.

Her own yellow cotton dress, with the velvet blue sash, is draped over the back of her easy rocker waiting to be worn again at the August reunion. She sits on her bed, and wraps her arms around bare shoulders, tucking her knees beneath her elbows as she looks at the twelve lit candles on the shelves, dresser, and chairs positioned around the room. She lays her head sideways letting her long blonde hair, now almost to waist length, drape over her thighs, as she pulls the palms of her hands to her lips, and kisses them softly pretending, pretending it was him.

"I miss you," she whispers to the darkened ceiling and flickering candles.

She imagines his strong hands moving down her shoulders to her back. They feel warm, firm, reassuring against her body. He whispers in her ear "I love you and miss you." She says "Oh, how I love and miss you," to the lingering scent of the Old Spice she gave him during their visit in Columbia.

"Stay with me and don't leave me now, she says to the darkness" she lays back on her deep cotton pillow, pulling the lamp chain to turn the light off, while letting him slowly to her unbutton pajama top, and place his hands on her butterfly shoulder as she pulls him to her firm rounded breast, letting him caress and kiss them deeply and passionately.

"Yes, like that" she breathes as she pushes his head to her flat stomach and his tongue traces the rim of her navel and he says, "Are you sure?"

"Yes, oh yes,' she whispers as he lifts her body to meet his lips and glides into the cradle of her waiting thighs and pushes slowly, gently, lovingly against her.

They stay motionless, very quiet, neither wanting to move, until she motions for him to roll over, tightly holding and clinging to him, as she glides on top of him and lies in  his arms, letting her long hair cover his face like a blanket of love. The air in the room cools as she rolls to her side and says,

"I want more, and know you do too, but not tonight, I love you" she says, as she moves her hand to her inner thigh as she had so many nights before, and lets her body find pleasure under the softness of the warm bed sheets, as she whispers again to the darkening room, "I miss you, want you."

And the night becomes a warm, darkened blur as she holds the small heart shaped locket tight in her palm and whispers again, "Good night, good night, my sweet love."

Jamie wasn't sure if what was happening to her was a dream, or not, but she wanted to be sharing everything, every feeling with him.

Home and Home is not the same

The ride home would take nine hours. As I took my seat, I looked out the window to see other recruits scrambling to buses that would scatter them on leaves to homes all over the east coast. My head was swirling with memories--boot camp, rifle range, reveille, night firing practice, poker games in barracks after lights out, patrols, my visit with Jamie and her family and Sgt. Faison.

I removed my notebook from my handbag and thumbed through the postcards from Jamie. She had sent a couple of poems and clippings from the local newspaper. One note was "a please to visit her" before leaving for my next post assignment.

She said that she wanted to show me a very special place that her grandfather built for her just before he died. 'Jamie's Place' on the river she called it.

The bright August sun sprayed into the bus of stoic faced soldiers and civilians headed for Charlotte, Greensboro and some to Virginia. I found myself wanting to nap, but the talking and laughter was too loud. A card game was going on behind me. A soldier was strumming a guitar in the seat directly ahead. My fellow traveler had already pulled his cap over his eyes in a vain attempt to grab some sleep. I envied his attempt. Opening my hand bag, I pulled the stack of letters from Jamie, my grandmother and sister, and piled them on my lap with the others. I read and reread them. My grandmother was mending well, and was taking high blood pressure medicine.

Artie was home now and would pick me up at the bus station in his new 1956 powder blue Pontiac. Dad was on a three day work shift at DuPont. He was putting in more time on the farm. My younger brothers and sister sent notes about summer school, and picking and packing peaches. As I read letter after letter again, I realized that I had missed home. I was also thinking of everything I had packed into the last eight weeks, when a "Welcome to North Carolina" and Charlotte City Limits sign flashed past the window. The driver maneuvered the bus on to a business 29-74 highway, which quickly became a narrowed two-lane street as we crossed the Catawba River Bridge, and emptied into a four lane highway called Wilkinson Boulevard.

Charlotte was the final stop for everyone except me and a lady holding a small baby in the front seat. The bus driver told us we had ten minutes to use the bathroom and get something to drink. Greensboro was three hours way. It was hot. I bought two drinks for the trip, and returned to the bus. I moved closer to the front and took a seat across from the lady holding her baby.

We would have a full view of the road ahead. I had never been to Charlotte. It took fifteen minutes to the northern city limits, where we turned on Highway 29 toward Greensboro. The North Carolina country side was beautiful, with its piedmont ridges and endless rivers that crossed and crisscrossed highway 29 north.

The driver announced that it would be two hours and fifteen minutes to Greensboro. We would have thirty minutes for lunch. I was getting hungry, so I drank my second Pepsi.

The bus was packed.

The passengers were mostly women and children. The mother to my right tried to entertain her child by turning the miniature black and white television away from the glare of the window. I had seen these before, but in the seats at the bus stations. The reception was not very good.

It was hard to hear over the sound of the engine and the road noise. Most of the children seemed to stay entertained by turning the knobs and watching the people talking on the screen.

I couldn't remember where, but I fell asleep.

"Soldier, this is a lunch stop" snapped the bus driver as he shook my shoulder and jarred me from a deep sleep. The early morning hours of basic training were catching up with me. This was the first in a long time that I had had an afternoon nap. The bus ride was slowing time down for me. I felt relaxed and rested. Making my way to the station café, I was confronted with an array of lunch choices from hotdogs with chili to hamburgers with bar-b-cue sauce. The café was jammed with passengers, and the smell of fried onions and diesel fuel drifted throughout the confines of the room.

I looked down Elm Street where the Woolworth Drug Store advertised coke floats and banana splits for fifty-cents. It was going to take a while to get seated at the bus station counter, so I walked across the street and down five blocks on Main and took a seat at the long counter. I ordered the coke float, the banana split and a double cheeseburger.

The drug store reminded me of JC Penny's and Payne's Pharmacy, that had just been built in Waynesboro. Every aisle was numbered and signs hung from the ceiling on strings. Big blue letters described items to be found on aisles below. I could smell the forced air aroma of cotton candy. Caramel and buttered popcorn spilled from a glass enclosed popper behind the counter. Stacks and stacks of school supplies lined the shelves. School children and their mothers were picking out all sorts of notebooks, pencils and paper.

The cool air felt good. It was 95 degrees outside.

Here, it was cooler. I ate my two slow melting ice-creamed desserts. As I finished the last of the chocolate syrup in the bottom of the banana-shaped dish, I glanced at the wall clock. I needed to get back. My bus would be leaving in ten minutes.

Pushing the wrapped hamburger into my pocket, I paid the counter attendant and opened the door, as a gust of cold air pushed down on my neck, and the street hit me with a blast of hot humid air. I felt like I had stepped into an oven. The driver was punching holes in tickets and loading passengers. I crossed the two lanes of asphalt pavement and presented my ticket.

This was an express bus for Washington DC, making stops in Lynchburg, Charlottesville and Richmond before arriving near Union Station in downtown Washington DC.

I felt that this specific part of town was set for more growth and economic development; the train and bus stopped here, the court house was half a block away, and small shops and professional buildings filled every block on Main Street. Glenwood and Elm Avenue intersected here and fed traffic north to Highway 29 and north to 301 and 220 to the South Carolina beaches. Woolworth's Drug and Department Store were the focal point for new emerging social, cultural, education and art activities in the downtown area. I knew I would be back someday.

Telephone Call and Part-time Job

"Hello, Jamie. I'm in Charlotte, North Carolina on a twenty minute stop. Just wanted to call and tell you I'm on my way home. I am looking forward to seeing you while home, and let your grandmother know that if she needs me, I can help with the hay and early corn harvest. I want to stay busy and would like to help if they need me. I will visit some old friends, my uncle and aunt in Harrisonburg, and I promised some classmates that I would come by Van

Viper's Lake on a Saturday for a picnic. You are welcome to go with me, on any or all of my visits home."

"How are you? I got that part-time job with the Waynesboro Tree Nursery over on Beech Grove Road. They like my handwriting, and I will be labeling and pricing all of the fall harvest plants for shipment to stores in Virginia and other states. It is 2-3 hours a day. I can ride my bicycle up Highway 151 to the Ewing Farm, cut through the property on the old dirt road along the river, and be there in 20-30 minutes in good weather. The exercise will be good for me. If it rains, Mr. Frank Woods will come to get me in the company pick-up truck. Grandmother is going to pay me also for helping out with the canning and peach picking here."

"Jamie, I have to go, and looking forward to seeing you soon. Bye."

"Bye, I love you."

Things Are Different Now

Sliding to the window seat, I was joined by a gentleman in his late fifties that reminded me of a portrait of Mark Twain. Dressed in a white suit and black laced boots, he placed his cedar cane between his knees and pulled a brown leather satchel on his lap. He unsnapped the buckles and pulled out a pile of handwritten notes. They were divided into sections by large paper clips and rubber bands. He was the county attorney heading to Washington for a meeting on desegregation.

He asked how I liked the service, but didn't wait for my answer and continued talking. However, the noise of the engine and the driver's voice made it difficult for him to continue his one-way conversation. I tried to act interested as he spilled out more and more information about himself.

He was headed to a 'house' committee meeting, he said, on integration and desegregation in North Carolina. He represented clients who were concerned about what the new laws might mean to the future of the state. Most of his conversation was beyond me, and I tried to interrupt and change the subject, but this proved impossible.

He was on a mission.

He read and re-read his notes. As his lips moved to the words in a whispering voice, he occasionally turned to see if other passengers were paying attention to what he was saying.

Occasionally, he turned to an unsuspecting traveler across the aisle and mentioned the upcoming city school hearing on integration issues. Most of the passengers ignored him, and turned to their magazines or raised their voices, and continued their own conversations.

At one point, his conversation became heated and he waved his hands as if he were making a closing argument to a jury. An elderly lady hunched in her seat and made a resettling motion with the sides of her dress, as she made a verbal comment about her dissatisfaction under her breath, regarding her dealing with him.

Directly addressing the attorney with a pointed finger, she said, "This is an important time we're living in. Nothing is going to be the same. Life is changing here in the South. We have a President and his fancy attorney general brother to blame for what's going on here. They don't seem to understand our ways sitting up there in their big fancy offices. I have a bad feeling about all this," she finished with a jerking turn back into her seat.

The attorney reminded himself to put her thoughts into his notes and comments for his meeting in Washington DC. A quiet pause settled over the bus with her final remarks.

There was a copy of the Saturday Greensboro News Journal in the seat pocket. Browsing the headlines, I discovered that a large conference would take place in October to review the strategies and plans for the education system at all levels. An editorial cartoon showed a white sailboat in a black turbulent sea. It was listing to the left and sinking fast. The mast with a confederate flag was visible above the water. The caption read: 'Gone with the northern wind.'

Strange, I thought: This had nothing to do with me. I would discover later the impact of this bus ride. These were city people who spoke with sharp voices. Their foreheads turned red. The sides of their necks flailed out like angry hens guarding little chicks. The side of their stretched lips and tongues pierced the air in front of them, as they expressed opinion after opinion of 'those' people in the White House.

The attorney was enjoying the debate. He was quietly taking credit for this stir of emotions on the bus. They clearly liked talking and discussing local and national issues. As for me, I just wanted to get home and spend time with my family.

The voices on the bus and the noise of the road sank back into my mind, as I closed my eyes and pretended to sleep. It kept some sounds out, but I found myself drifting back to boot camp, and then forward to home.

Occasionally, I could feel the attorney nudge my shoulder. I gave no response. My training in resistance and interrogation came in handy. Sleep came quickly, until my head bumped hard against the window, as the bus pulled into Lovingston station.

Through slightly dazed eyes, I saw Artie sitting in his new blue Pontiac. From the way he cocked his head I could tell he was listening to the local baseball game on WTVR. The cocking of the head seemed to make his hearing sharper. I'm not exactly sure if there is medical proof for this, but he believed it. Tucking his head under the window visor, he shaded his eyes as he scanned the inside of the bus looking for me.

We waved as the bus stopped.

Over the steering wheel, he shot a pistol finger salute at me, nursed the last of his large fountain coke, and headed for the station. Two other passengers and I departed the bus quickly. The driver pulled my duffle bag from the under carriage and tossed it to the curb. I gave him a dollar and hoisted it to my shoulder, as Artie reached behind me and took the handbag and patted me on the head like a stranded puppy dog.

He was always doing things like that. Even as a young boy, I could count on him to punch my shoulder or slap the side of my head in a friendly gesture of brotherly love. He was doing it again. It felt good, I thought as he asked, "Do you want to stop at Aistrop's Store for a hotdog and coke? Are you hungry? What kind of food have they been feeding you on the base?" He said, as we tossed my duffle bag in trunk and slammed it tight. He patted the trunk lid with his hand as he pointed me to the right door. He slid in and pushed the seat back as far as it would go, and turned the radio on. The announcer's voice blasted from the dash, and roars from the crowd signaled another home run. We listened as we drove through town and made our way to Highway 29 south.

Home was 30 minutes away.

I liked the way he placed his arm on the window rest and drove with his wrist gliding back and forth across the top of the steering wheel like James Dean or Robert Mitchum.

"She purrs like a kitten, don't she. It's a real smooth ride. I only paid $800 for it. Bought it from Sam Thompson at Nelson Motors," he said, as we raced down highway 29 at 60 mph, to the turn off for Aistrop's Store and home. We both knew we would have to eat again when we got home, but we didn't care. We might run into someone we knew at Aistrop's Store. It was a favorite Saturday afternoon hangout for high school students, and kids looking for a good pool game or a try at the pin ball arcade.

Aistrop's store was a disappointment as no one we knew was in the store. There were a few travelers from New York buying a couple packs of Nabs and RC Colas. They were making a stop for gas before heading south to Florida for the winter. The hot dogs and drinks hit the spot. We ate and drank an RC as we shot a quarter game of pool. Then we headed home.

Artie went through the same ritual of pushing the seat back and turning on the radio, as he started the car and turned out of the parking lot to highway 29.

As we turned right and entered Route 6, the sun rays peeled through the windshield making Artie's sunburned profile appear much like the Indian image on the side of the fender and on the dash of the car.

I was about to mention this when he said. "That's why I bought it. I liked the Indian hood ornament and his face on the grill. I've always liked Indians. It's a shame how we mistreated them, right here in Virginia," he said without further comment, and started humming the Lucky Strike lyrics

"You still writing in that leather notebook grandmother gave you?" he quizzed, as he volunteered information about his wooden plane, and attempt to fly off the barn when we were kids. He reminded me that he almost made it. We both laughed a few tears of our own, as we talked about mother and how quickly she got to the hog pen.

"I still have the plane. It's in a thousand pieces in an old box in the shed. That was a really dumb thing to do, but not as dumb as some other times I bet you didn't write about. I understand that Mrs. Rutherford, your high school English teacher, gave you a D- for it. She thought you were lying."

We were almost home, when he asked me if I wanted to take care of his car for the next two weeks, while he worked on the power lines in Manassas. He didn't have a place to park it, and the crew moved fast with the trucks, as they stretched the new power lines across the mountains. He told me not to wreck it, and to keep it full of gas and oil.

As the front tires hit the gravel pavement with a shattering blast, he said "We'll have to eat again. Mother's been cooking and fussing all day".

We looked ahead and saw her standing in the front yard crying and waving her big, white handkerchief at us. My door was barely open before she grabbed, hugged and kissed me saying "You look like you haven't eaten for a year. C'mon in, and let's have some supper. You can tell me all about the Army and the stinky clothes you sent me to wash."

It was 8:30 p.m. Crickets and cicadas were sending rhythmic chants through the forest around our house as we entered and took our seats at the dinner table.

I was home for a while.

Sunday Reunion

I finally got home on August 24th after a nine hours bus ride. I would report to Fort Monmouth, Photography Training School, on September 16th and would have just 21 days at home for visiting and time with Jamie.

It was Saturday night, and my family had big plans for us to go to the Rockfish Baptist Church reunion services, and a picnic on the grounds. It would be great to see some of my classmates: Dale Ward, Phyllis Witt, Donna Carter, Judy Hughes, Phil Dodd, Wayne, Diane and Maynard Fortune, and Larry and Becky Small. My former Sunday school teachers, Hazel Phillips and Pete Small, would give me a big hug and tell me that I needed to put on some pounds.

Old man Roades still sang in the choir and made a big fuss, until I joined him for the service. He used to give my brothers and me rides home after church, so we wouldn't have to walk in the hot sun on highway 151. I liked working for him getting up hay in the summer, because he always paid on time, and gave a dollar tip when I did a good job milking cows or picking peaches. I wanted to go see Jamie, but I hoped she would understand. She would be going to her last counseling session at UVA on Monday, and working part-time on Wednesday and Thursday. I had promised my grandmother I would take her to Harrisonburg in my brother's car, to visit my aunt Jarmie. If the pastor let me use the church phone, I planned to call Jamie during the picnic on Sunday to let her know it would be a couple of days before we could meet.

I was looking forward to seeing Jamie and working the farm with her grandmother and Tom. He had already raked the hay to dry and wanted me to start loading and stacking it in the barn before it rained. Jamie planned to work at the nursery on Tuesday and Wednesday. We would have the long weekend together.

Can't Wait

"Grandmother, I can't wait! He's here!

I know he has a lot of family stuff, and I will be patient until we can meet. I know he will call me tomorrow, and let me know when he can come see me and work with Tom.
It will be fun to have him here for the reunion. I missed him so much. I just don't want to be silly and embarrass myself. This is all so new to me."

"Jamie, you two will be just fine. I'm glad we visited his grandmother. She told me that she and Hayward plan to be here and that Wade will stay with them part of the time. That should give you and him plenty of time to work and see each other during his leave. I'm so very proud of you. Down to four cigarettes a day. All of this is changing a lot of things for us. I have always thought you could do without the counseling sessions. The travel is hard on you and I need your help here more these days.

Now tell me what you want to do during the reunion—sing, play your guitar…"

"I want to spend as much time with Wade as I can. And of course, I know I will have to help with the food. I will do that… Just want time with him…"

"It should be over and most people gone by two o'clock. Then you can have all the time you need."

"Thanks Grandma. I love you more than you know"
"I know."

Jamie felt wonderful. A feeling of being complete invaded her whole body. To have a boyfriend and just be able to say it. The counseling had been good when she was younger, but nothing was really new except the probing by Ms. Stevens and the fact that she was the oldest one in the group now. She had written out her goals and planned to hand them in at the Monday session. She was willing to attend another month, but by the middle of September there would be no more counseling sessions and daylong trips to Charlottesville. She was nervous, a little afraid, but more sure of herself than she had been about her life for a long time.

Leave and leaving for Fort Monmouth

In a little over three days, I would be catching another bus in Charlottesville for Fort Monmouth to near Asbury Park, New Jersey. I hadn't seen Jamie, but read her invitation for dinner and visit to the cave. I looked forward to seeing her again.

I had promised my grandmother Sally that I would take her to Harrisburg before I left for a visit with Aunt Jarmie and Uncle Henry. She would took one of her famous family pound cake with chocolate icing for the trip, and I could plan on spending most of the day there. She would want to be back by five o'clock to get dinner ready and help with the farm animals.

I had spent many summer days on Jarmie and Henry's farm in Staunton as a child. The last time I stayed was just before my seventh grade. Now, we only visited at family reunions and birthday parties. Something happened between my mother and Aunt Jarmie. I found out later they wanted to adopt me, and mother would have none of it. She got mad and words were exchanged.

I didn't get to visit again until toward the end of my junior year in high school. I worked the hay fields for Henry. We never talked about the adoption again. They never had any children of their own and adopted two of his sister's children, and raised them on the farm.

I always wondered what it would have been like.

After breakfast with my parents, I drove to Wintergreen and filled the gas tank for the trip. This would keep my grandmother from arguing with me about gas money for the trip. She would give me two dollars and tell me to put it in my pocket for later. I knew she would be waiting in the orchard at the end of the dirt driveway for me. She had four sacks of vegetables, a gallon of sweet cider and a side of smoked ham that Granddad had double wrapped for the trip. She believed it was impolite to visit without taking something. This was a lesson that she always impressed on me.

I never forgot.

"It will come back to you in triple" she would say. She was a great conversationalist and loved to talk about our family and how her parents and grandparents settled Spruce Creek Hollow. An early land grant after the confederate war made it possible for old man Gilbert's parents to settle on 160 acres at the foot of Wintergreen Mountain. Spring waters fed the valley and helped the Marshall clan grow corn, sorghum and rye wheat. Cows and horses filled the pasture lands, and peach and apple orchards dotted the hillsides from Harris Store and Grist Mill to Hadder Ridge, at the end of Spruce Creek Road.

An early stage coach route trailed along what is now highway 151, bringing city people and tourists to the mountains and country side. Most came to escape the summer heat, and humidity in tidewater towns like Richmond and coastal towns as far away as Charleston in South Carolina. Some stayed and called the mountains home. The aroma of Burley tobacco curing in barns and tobacco houses drifted with the late evening lightening bugs in the Rockfish River Valley, to the Afton Mountains in the west, and to the Brent's Mountain peaks to the far south of the valley basin."

She wanted to tell me more as I turned on Powertown Road, and the gravel road leading to the farm. Her stories would keep, and there would be plenty on the return trip unless she decided to take a nap.

Aunt Jarmie always had a thousand things to do on the farm, and parceled out jobs and errands for any family visitor who stayed more than an hour. I always liked the way she could send people away, relieved that they had helped her with a crucial errand, or finishing a job that would have been impossible without their help.

By 1:30 p.m. we were on our way home. We stopped for ice cream at Newberry's in Waynesboro and were heading out of town when she said, "It's a shame about Jamie you know, the fire and all. That brother was rotten as they come. He even threatened your grandfather once, but he took an axe handle and chased him back across the creek. He never came back again.

The fire was awful. Jamie's mother and father both died in the blaze. Jamie jumped out the window after her brother tried to kill her. It's been a nightmare for her grandparents, never knowing if he would show up some night and burn their house down too, or worse. Your mother tried to take care of Jamie for a while, when she got out of the hospital, but her burns and problems were more than she could handle.

The grandparents originally left her in the Staunton sanatorium, but that was no place for a young child. Your mother tried again to keep her at the house, but later Jamie started the operations and had to stay at the university hospital, and come home on weekends. As she got older the weekends became months and then Christmas and holidays. Her grandfather passed away six years ago. I had not seen or heard from Jamie until she wrote me a note and told about meeting you on the bus. She is a sweet child.

The operations and medicines have taken most of the life out of her. I adore her loud laugh and energy at times. She can sing like an angel sometimes and at other times she can be as wild and loud as that Dana Harris down in Danville.

Sometimes she can be the sweetest thing, and then suddenly the old fears come over her, and she cries and goes into trances and fits of rage. Her grandmother tells me she hasn't had any blackouts for a while. She sure likes you. Talked about her soldier boyfriend in her letters.

That's you I guess!" she finished, as we drove down into the orchard. I tried to go around the car and open her door, but she met me halfway with a hug and hurried kiss as she told me to come back again before I left.

As I drove away, I watched her in the rear view mirror, waving her white handkerchief, when not drying tears from her face, and shouting that I need to write home as often as possible, and say "hello" to Jamie.

Dinner

Ms. Thompson had everything ready for the reunion. She knew others would have their favorites, but desserts were always her specialty. The dinner table was covered with different desserts: a triple layer strawberry upside down cake, chocolate brownies loaded with black walnuts, a large jar with mixed grapes, cantaloupes, strawberries and sliced plums, a 16 inch square, three inch deep apple pie baked in a redesigned wooden apple crate. She placed a pumpkin pie in the center of the table, still in its shell with brown sugar and cinnamon spice, There was a vanilla pound cake with chocolate icing, and a blackberry bread roll on a china platter, sprinkled from end to end with powdered sugar. The main dish was a whole deep pan roasted chicken, glazed with honey and brown sugar.

Two oil lanterns lit the table with soft shadows making the food look like a Norman Rockwell Thanksgiving dinner in *Look Magazine*. For me, she made a batch of flour biscuits and sat a jar of homemade marmalade by my plate. She invited Tom, the farm manager, and his wife Hanna, to join us. She said a prayer, asking a special blessing for Johnathan, her husband, and me, since I would be leaving to go back to the Army on Saturday morning.

She then announced, "at our house, dessert is eaten first!"

During dinner, she told us she missed her husband. He always made Thursday a special dinner night for Jamie. "Life's too short, he would say, so enjoy." " Take as much as you want, but save some biscuits for Wade," she said proudly.

We talked, laughed, and ate from every dish on the table. We told stories. Dinner lasted two hours, but seemed like only minutes. It had gotten dark outside. We could hear the cicadas and crickets in the woods, and down along the pasture. Ms. Thompson made a big pot of coffee, and placed it on the front porch during dinner. Tom, Jamie and I were told to go sit on the porch and drink some coffee, while she and Hanna cleared the table and washed the dishes.

On the porch, Tom told me how Jamie's grandfather had tended the farm for over thirty years until he died. "Fine man, lived to sixty-four. He's buried on the rise just above the creek falls, where Jamie goes to swim in the summer. I guess he still likes to watch over her when she's in the river."

Tom had been hired five years ago to help with the 150 acre farm. He had grown up in Wytheville, West Virginia and had farmed all his life. After he lost his farm, Johnathan invited him to come for a visit. The visit lasted five years. He and Hanna lived in a two-bedroom, rent-free house at the end of the pasture. He tended a large garden, and raised chickens and eggs for his family, and sold some at Harris Store in the winter.

He came after the fire and death of Jamie's parents, hearing about the fire from stories circulating around the valley. Johnathan never talked about it. They became friends, worked the farm, and let their silence speak. Jamie played with their daughter sometimes. She married recently and moved to Crozet. They visited about a month ago and this was when they found out they were expecting their first child at Christmas. He talked for a while longer, sipped his coffee and left to check on the cows, before coming back to walk his wife home.

Jamie and I sat on the edge of the oil plank porch, drank the last of the hot coffee, and watched the fire flies. "When are you coming back?" she said with a pleading voice, hoping I would say soon.

I responded, "I don't know for sure. I could get a short leave at Christmas. I don't know where I will be stationed. I can't say whether I can get home or not. I know my training at Fort Monmouth is supposed to finished by Thanksgiving. I could be sent to a permanent assignment anywhere..."

"Are you ever coming to see me again?" she interrupted as she placed her coffee cup on the porch floor, turned toward me and took my hand.

"This was a special night for me. Grandmother, Tom and Hanna like you. I like you. I'm going to miss you," she said, as her grandmother came out on the porch and took a seat in the porch swing.

"Don't mind me. Did you get enough to eat, Wade?" asked Ms. Thompson. "Maybe you can come back tomorrow for more, and Jamie can show you her secret cave and swimming pool up the ridge at the back of the farm that her grandfather built for her," she said as she turned her eyes toward Jamie's smiling face.

"Sounds great. I really liked the dinner and desserts you made. Thank you again for having me over for dinner," I answered as she stopped swinging and went into the house.

Jamie looked at me through tired eyes. She seemed to fade at dinner, and perk up with the coffee on the porch. A few times, I thought she was napping at the table. The medicine made her drowsy. She looked very frail in the darkening shadows on the porch.

Ms. Thompson had turned the kitchen lights out, and the oil lanterns on the porch were burning down to a low flame.

We both knew I had to get home. Jamie was tired and needed to get some sleep. She leaned her head on my shoulder and pulled my hand into hers.

"I'm going to miss you," she said again, as she kissed my cheek and let my hand go.

As I walked down the path to the car, she yelled through the screened door, "Tomorrow, come over early for the reunion."

The Reunion

It seemed like everyone in the Rockfish Valley was showing up for the Marshall Family reunion. My parents and grandparents, who had not attended for years, showed up. Mother was busy setting up a folding table under a tree in the yard for my father and my siblings: Artie, Eddie, Freddie, and little sister Debra Sue. They were joined by our closest cousins, the Davis family, who came with their three daughters: Mickey, Ann and Betty; and their oldest son Tracey, who would be leaving the following week for the Marine Corps.

Jack and Annetta Marshall came with their eleven children from far up on Spruce Creek Road. Massey Thompson joined them with his boys: Junior, Will, William, Jake and two girls; May and Susan, who would be married this summer. Malcom Campbell was there with his family. They could eat all the food themselves if allowed first at the table. Jamie would make sure this didn't happen. Pete Small brought her son Dwayne who was home from the University, and his sister, Barbara who was recovering from a near miss car accident and broken arm, on highway 250.

M.Q. Campbell and his wife Pepper came to greet a lot of friends who frequented their store. He liked to bear hunt and killed a 400 pound male, just off Stoney Creek near the falls, in 1959. He had it mounted and displayed on the store wall for customers to see. He liked to telling the story of the hunt, and hauling the bear on his back to his truck for the trip home.

Robert Fitzgerald had just come home from the VA hospital and service, with a bad limp from a wound in his ankle. His wife Bessy was pretty and cheerful as always. She gave everybody a hug who let her wrap her long, strong arms around them, and squeeze until they said "OK, I love you too."

I watched Jamie move through the crowd on the porch, serving them home-made vanilla cookies and inviting them to the tables, which were setup in the yard with fried chicken, potato salad, fresh sliced tomatoes, apples, home-made apple sauce with cinnamon, and strawberry and blackberry pound cakes, prepared by her grandmother.

From the side porch, Ned rang an old church bell to get everybody's attention, and invited Elder Broadhead to return thanks for the meal, and offer a special blessing to those present: *"Brothers and Sisters, we are grateful for this special day. Let us pray to the Mighty and True God: Lord of Heaven and Father to all gathered here, may we offer our thanks and grateful love for your grace, and safety and good health, and prosperity in this day.*

To those who are ill or shut in at home, we ask that you prayerfully cure their infirmities and we pray for their speedy recovery.

To those here whose loved ones are unsaved, in harm's way or otherwise in need of your saving love and grace, we beg for your hand of mercy on them before the end of this day.

And to those who suffer in silence let this be a day of grace and gracious forgiveness. And lest we forget, bless those who prepared this food and nourishment and those who will partake of it, we petition your blessings and love and kindness for them all.

For it is in the Name of our Lord and Savior, we pray this day. Amen."

With this, Ned, Lillian, Mrs. Marshall and the rest of the crowd surrounded the tables in the yard, filled their plates and glasses, and took seats at an assortment of tables on the lawn to eat and enjoy the meal. I saw Jamie making her way toward me, with two plates of food, inviting me to join her on the porch swing.

She was glowing and smiling. She was so happy to have family and friends at the reunion. We talked, and she told me about some of the people I did not know. She especially wanted me to see and recognize the Hadder boys. She pointed a finger at them in the crowd, so they would know she was telling me about them. They were now friends, she smiled. She said "the oldest one had a crush on her, but he would be marrying his cousin in the fall. No worries," she said.

I knew I would miss this visit later, back at the barracks. I would especially miss my grandmother Sally and Grandfather Hayward, who were shyly perched quietly on a large stone at the outer edge of the yard, greeting and speaking to friends and relatives who passed by. They looked at Jamie and me often, as we sat together on the porch. I knew they were talking about us. I couldn't hear them, but I could read their smiling faces and sad eyes.

Jamie and I sat close. We didn't talk much, but I knew her sadness would return tomorrow, when the yard was empty and only memories of the day lingered in her mind, as she prepared for another bus trip to the Charlottesville hospital.

"Jamie, will we have a song from you today?" prodded Ned, as he handed her the guitar, and invited the crowd to join her in the hymns, *Amazing Grace* and *Morning Has Broken.*

It was the moment I had waited for. Her melodious voice would touch them with a sense of sweetness and innocence seldom experienced during the harshness of everyday farm work. In her voice was a message of hope, endurance and commitment to a higher cause. She inspired them, but few, except me knew the real deep pain in her heart and the deep need she had for relief for her mental anguish and youthful pain.

As she finished the last verses of *'Morning Has Broken'* I knew our time together was what my grandparents saw and worried about. They knew, as did Jamie, that I would have to keep my promise to make her happy while she was here, and not forget her when she was gone.

Do You Want to See My Butterfly?

"I want to show you my secret place. My grandfather called it Jamie's Falls. He finished it for me when I was ten, and recovering from the fire and first series of surgeries." She said, as we walked out the back door toward a brush pile leaning against a hedge of locust and wild cherry trees.

Ducking beneath the low hanging branches, she took my hand and pulled me through a narrow tangle of honeysuckle and fox grape vines. We rounded a large quartz rock and steep bank, leading up to a pitched rise, crowded with red and white oaks. I could hear cascading waterfalls in the distance as we went down a grassy path through a blackberry patch to a flat rock that dropped off sharply.

Reaching back for my hand again, she pulled me down the side of a cool damp rock as the waterfalls pushed a chilly spray against my shirt, neck and back. We stopped and crouched on all fours as she placed her hand on her forehead like a scout searching the horizon for danger or intruders ahead. It was obvious she had done this many times in summers past.

"I had to watch for The Hadder boys you met yesterday, when I first started coming here. They were mean and threw rocks and called me names when I was younger. My grandfather took care of them real good a couple of times." She pronounced, as she tugged gently at a twine rope draped alongside the cavernous rocks where we were kneeling and holding on to large gray streaked nelsonite boulder.

She pulled the rope again gently and looked through the opening toward the river. "Tell me if you see anything moving" she said with a mischievous smile.

At first I didn't see anything. Then the tops of the branches were swarming with bees. They darted through the limbs, toward the water and rocks, looking for intruders. They kept circling the water and rocks, as we stayed very still and silent. Jamie kept cautioning me to stay put, until the spectral cloud of bees retreated to the canopy above and into a large gray hive swarming over the river's edge.

"Those boys used to hide in the bushes along the river and sneak up on me while I was swimming or bathing in the river pool. Once, they grabbed me by my ponytail and held me under the water until I began gasping for air and begged them to let me go. My grandfather heard me and came to the top of rock with a handful of rocks and chased them away. After that, he rigged up the hornet and yellow jacket bee trap. It's still here and sure took care of them. I never saw them again but I was always careful. Always looked to make sure they weren't lurking in the grass or behind the bushes by the rocks." She finished and motioned for me to follow.

We half crawled to the rock tunnel, pushing back bushes from the opening. What met my eyes was a cascading waterfall that plunged over a granite boulder and deep into a dark, swirling pool below.

Jamie darted ahead to the top of the falls and sat on a carved oak log that had been wedged between two stones,  and a stump of a long fallen willow tree. New sprouts were shooting up from the dead decaying tree bringing new life and strength to the watery rocks. The stones and carved tree trunks had weathered many summer storms. They stood as sentries to a grandfather who loved and nurtured a young child through very harsh years.

Her life as a young child had to have been painful I thought. It was the pain of a seemingly friendless and lonely world, where one's hugs and kind words must have felt awkward to a child who was suffering and weary of people who stared at her scars. It must have been especially painful when children made fun of her, or adults searched for words to say as they made excuses to get away.

Joining her, I sat on the log and looked down at the stream through a narrow gorge that opened into a series of low mountain peaks and a green pasture valley.

"This is my sea of mountains," she said, as she waved her hand and counted the sharp peaks rising on the horizon, above the green tapestry.

"This is how I feel when the valley's fogged in. Only the mountain peaks dot the white watery clouds from this vista point. When the fog lays in the gorge and valley in early spring and sometimes in early fall. I call it my sea of mountains. My grandfather and I watched it many times. I wrote a poem about it and my grandmother loved to hear me sing it.

It was about the hard times I've seen, and the way the world treated me. I've never been on a date. No one took me to a prom. I have only one true girlfriend Marianne, who is older and moved away. The only birthdays celebrated by me were with my grandparents. And, no boy has ever looked at me and touched me the way you did on the bus to Charlottesville, in Columbia, and now here at the reunion.

No one ever came to see me in the hospital except my grandparents and your grandmother when I was very young. Sometimes I hate my life. At other times, I can laugh and be funny and think maybe it will be better. I still can't believe you wrote back. And now you're here in my beautiful secret place," she finished.

Then she quietly lowered her head between her knees and looked down toward the dark water below and listened to the cascading falls.

Then suddenly and surprisingly, she looked straight at me and softly said: "Do you want to see my butterfly?" as she stood up and faced me. She took my hand, and guided me gently down over a windowed outcropping where we planted our feet firmly on a three-step ladder.

The ladder was made of heavy oak limbs, and was wrapped securely with hemp rope from side to side where hand-grooved cuts held them together. It was cool inside the dark cave but I could feel a warm spray, pushing into the opening. It was difficult to see the walls that looked like wet rock quarry stones, but the air was the freshest I had ever smelled. We stepped from stone to stone. I could feel the moisture of the shallow stream seeping into the sides and soles of my tennis shoes.

She lit the first series of hanging lanterns along the wall. The dimness faded into softness. I could see large quartz stones along the stream bed and our shadows flickering on the rocky walls.

About twelve feet ahead, surrounded by the darkness of a rock overhang, I could see the back side of a white rushing waterfall reflecting a gray glare into the cave's mouth. My ears popped and I could hear echoes and feel the walls vibrating all around. Then the vibration of the stone walls above our head signaled the secret that lay ahead. Her grandfather had scooped out rock and debris from countless summer storms and floods, and engineered this secret passage way for Jamie. She could come here anytime and be alone. She could avoid staring eyes and talk to herself without crying.

The emotional pain of years of recovery were softened by the cool warmth of the darkened cave, carved by massive stones and surging timbers that flooded this opening when Hurricane Hazel dumped tons of water into this deep shallow pool.

The opening revealed another underground waterfall pouring into a dark, bottomless pool below. At the back of the cave was a shallow, tropical spring surrounded by smooth stones, and at the waterfall opening, we were met by a cool spray that blew into the cave.

On one side of the wall was a bench; hand-carved from a birch tree, smoothed and waxed to a brilliant brown. Once again, I could see the handiwork of a grandfather whose bittersweet sorrow for his son and daughter-in-law had found joy in this place. He let a young hurt child blossom into a beautiful young woman.

This was Jamie's hiding place, where she came to life. This was where she wrote her poems, and sometimes sang in the darkness like a caged bird waiting to fly away.

Rain

When we entered the cave it was a sunny August day, with bright sunshine and a sweaty lingering humidity in the air. Now, flashes of lightening blazed across the stone walls, and reflected along the flowing stream that trailed to the edge of the boulders to the pool below.

We had rested in each other's arms, and I noticed that Jamie's skin was getting colder, and her face was flushed red in the dimly lit cave. She was visibly frightened.

"We need to leave. The water is rising in the cave, and it will be difficult to wade out and make our way up the ledge and back home" she said, as she released her tight grip on my shoulders, and invited me to follow her to the waterfall's edge. Thunder rattled through the boulders overhead, and the current flowing to the waterfalls was a rushing white rapid.

"I got caught in here once several years ago. I lost track of time, and the water rose to my waist before I could find my way out, and up the rock wall in the dark. The opening at the top was hard to scale on the wet slippery stones", she said, as she pulled her jacket over her head and handed me mine as the water pushed faster and faster against our ankles.

We dressed quickly in the dark as she handed me her tennis shoes, and asked me to pull them on for her. As I bent over and planted my knees in the water to tie her shoes, she laid her body across my back, and wrapped her hands around my midsection as she cried, "I am so sorry. I am so sorry."

"Don't worry, we'll be okay," I returned as I took her hands, and pulled her up the same stones we had come down. The rocks were wetter now, sweating in my hands, as I held her and reached higher and higher for the outcroppings and crevices in the stone wall. It would be hard enough to climb by myself, but I realized she needed me to help her up to the opening.

She started sliding backwards down the rock face, and cowered like the girl on the bus. Her hands were limp in mine, and I grabbed her waist and pulled her hard against me and up the wall.

"Jamie, hold on. We're almost to the rock opening,"

I shouted, as the thunder grew louder and lightening flashed against the cave's entry.

"You may have to go ahead and bring help back to carry me to the house. I missed my medicine at noon and feel dizzy and may faint," she said begging me not to leave.

"I'm not leaving. We'll be alright," I said, as the danger of what lay ahead gripped me

"We may have to wait it out," I said, as I balanced her on the rocky opening while edging my feet and body against the jagged stone opening and held her tight. The up draft wind from the backside of the falls pushed the rain into the exposed opening like a massive fan. At times, it seemed as if we could be forced from our lofty perch like two frightened summer finches.

I had a half melted Milky Way in my pocket, and offered it to Jamie. At first, she pushed it away, and then gobbled it down like a fresh worm delivered by a nesting mother robin. Within seconds, a blush of red forced away the chalky white in her cheeks, and her eyes reflected a brilliant bluish green stare at me, as the lightening snapped against the outer layer of the stone cavern.

"We're going to be alright," she said as we waited and watched the lightening and rain parade across the afternoon sky.

"Some of my grandmother's blackberry pie would taste good now," she said, with a forced laugh and smile.

Suddenly, a spray of the sunlight reflected off my watch and bounced against my eyes. The rain had stopped, as quickly as it had started. The sun threw red and gold blazes against the wet tree branches above our heads, and reflected off the moist rocks at our feet. In the distance, we could hear birds and frogs emerging from their hiding places to perch and peek into the hot summer day.

"Let's go home, Jamie!" I said, as I lowered myself to the paths below and reached up for her waiting arms. She leaned forward and fell into my open hands, like a wet sack of flour, as she wrapped her arms around my neck and kissed the side of my face. She was warm again, but I knew it would be a race home before she collapsed; weak, pale and sick again.

As I forced my way up the muddy bank, clawing at the rocks and roots to keep us steady, she held tight to my shirt and belt. I lifted her step by step, up the red clay bank along the stone embankment wall, careful not to brush against the twine string rope leading to the bee's nest, until we arrived at the top of the path, and crawled through the opening in the vines and briars. The gravel and leaves from the log road paths fell into my hands, as we made the last leap onto the level path that would lead us home. Standing up, we could see the chimney of the farm house and barn in the distance through the trees, as we walked arm in arm down the rutted path.

Occasionally our feet would sink deep into the smooth marbled path and our shoes would cling to the exposed roots. We made our way down the ridge until we finally arrived at the back porch steps. At the kitchen table, Jamie poured four tablets into her hand from prescription bottles and threw them into the back of her mouth, tossing her head back, as she lifted the glass of tea to her lips. She opened her mouth, drew the glass away, and let the last drop fall to her tongue, as she curled her eyes toward me and smiled. Within minutes, she drifted off to sleep on the sofa, and I lay on the floor beside her.

It was strangely peaceful in the house, knowing that Jamie was safe. We were dry, and her grandmother would be home soon from feeding the animals in the barn.

New Jersey

As I boarded the bus in Charlottesville for the eight hour trip to New Jersey, I knew a time like this would never come again.

Passengers were talking and settling into their seats, as I slid to the right window side to get a last glimpse of my mother, grandmother, Artie and Jamie. She had given me another note, and asked that I not read it until I was on the road.

It was a promise I would keep.

For now, I just wanted to look at her and the rest of the family waving goodbye.

I wasn't sure what lay ahead, but I knew what I was leaving behind-- home and everything that I loved.

I kept watching Jamie as she hugged Ms. Thompson and my grandmother's neck. She waved her handkerchief like a surrendering soldier, as she whispered with her lips "come back to me."

The express Trailways bus moved backwards into the street and pulled away on business 29 to Union Station, Washington DC, with a final arrival at Central Station in New York City.

I turned to look back for one final glimpse of my family, but other passengers were in the way, waving and saying goodbye.

You're going to miss this someday, Jamie's voice kept whispering in my head. I hope you think of me and the times we shared often. Don't forget me... the voice trailed off in my head as the engine gears shifted and the pavement careened below the bus.

I closed my eyes and could only see Jamie. She was magical. The two days we spent together were like a lifetime. My virgin body could still feel the cool spray of the waterfall, and the warm rising mist in the cave.

I watched her again, in my mind, as she emerged from the cool water of the cave. She wrapped her arms around me and smiled. Our bodies melted like the countless wax candles, lighting the tropical pool at the back of the dark cave, as she took me from innocence to discovery.

"If you could do anything today," she said, "what would it be?" as we lowered our bodies to the sandy warmth of the water. We rested our arms on the smooth stone edges, watching the soapy water spill over glassy curves and flow away from the cave.

"Lots of things, but you tell me what you want. Tell me how you want me to make you happy today," I whispered as my voice trembled.

"Bathe me with a soft sponge. Bathe my back and touch my butterfly and massage the hurt away. This was my grandfather's favorite pleasure. I miss his words of encouragement," she said, as she turned away and let the candles' light reflect off her back.

As I reached out and pressed the sponge down the middle of her spine, making circles around the wings and gently pushing upward on the red and purple tattoo lines, I could tell that she was smiling and drifting deeper into the dark shadows against the stone wall.

"This can be our time together," she said, as she dipped her body and head beneath the warm frothing water. Then turning to me, she gathered my body in her outstretched arms and pulled me to her and whispered "love me, love me."

The sounds of the waterfall went soft in my ears as she  pressed against me, cradling me, and drew me to the warmth of the butterfly on her shoulder. She held me for a long time, wrapping her arms around my back, hard against her as we listened to the sounds and life....

The passenger beside me nudged me back into my seat and gently pushed me back to the window. I had drifted off in a daydream. "Who is Jamie, soldier?" He asked me. "A very special person," I answered and thanked him for waking me.

"Jamie," I said again, but the noise of the rain and wind outside the bus windows made it impossible for the passenger to hear me. I turned back to my notebook and jotted my thoughts into a poem for Jamie as quick as I could. I didn't want to forget her.

Union Station was ahead on the avenue through the middle of Washington DC. I would change buses here for Grand Central Station, and then south again to Fort Monmouth, New Jersey. I would get a few more postcards and send them to Jamie before the bus pulled away.

Jamie's Morning Walk

She walked through the morning dew and wet weed path down to the creek. Wade had caught the last bus in Lovingston, and would be at Fort Monmouth now.

Thoughts of Wade still lingered in her mind from their talk in the dark on the porch last night. She had never felt about anyone like this. It was a surreal experience for her. She had fought so hard to be indifferent to others over the years, especially boys who had tortured her during her young years—making fun of her facial scar and calling her names. This was different. She felt a love like none she had known, and wasn't quite sure what to do.

He was so real, so honest and wonderful with her. No one except her grandparents and closest adult friends had complimented her on her music, poetry, and her beauty.

He was so young, but so grown up at the same time. She knew he had to get away from the valley to become somebody, but she found herself wanting him here, now.

As she stepped to the edge of the ledge overlooking the pool, she heard his words, felt his hands, and the press of his body, when he held her during the storm. She lay flat on the soft stones on the creek bottom, and let the cool water run across her bare legs and wet cotton blouse that trailed and rippled in the water. She wrapped her arms around herself and pulled tight, as she looked up through the stone opening and the blue morning sky overhead.

This was a dream come true, and she knew that soon she would need to return to the house and get ready for the day. For now, she just wanted to linger, and let her thoughts drift with the clouds, and hold herself as he had, and dream as she penned another poem to him in a letter to mail later today.

She ran her hand across her face, and traced the scar to the knot, as he had, and closed her eyes as she let her fingers trail down to her tanned flattened stomach, and gently touched her lips and shoulders as he had....and silently said, "I miss you, come back to me soon."

The Road North

The nor'easter rain pierced the cooling September air and slammed huge rain drops against the windshield, as the wipers swapped back and forth through the blurry highway ahead. The crosswinds pushed hard against the side of the bus. The sound was deafening. No one talked. We were focused on the headlights streaking at us on the divided highway.

I could see road marker signs and darkened houses without lights, along the highway edge. An occasional truck driver would blast his horn and speed by on the inner lane throwing huge waves of rain across the front of the bus, as the bus driver cautiously made his way on the wet highway. At Havre de Grace, we crossed the Susquehanna River near the head of the Chesapeake Bay, and felt the full torment of the eastern storm blowing inland. Gust after gust of wind pushed the last of the summer heat from the air and forced the bus engine to struggle against the turnpike.

Writing was difficult.

Then suddenly, the rain stopped, revealing a cool autumn sun to the west and fading green pastures and maple forests along the ridges. A road sign said "New York City 113 miles." I lay back and tried to read, but sleep once again stole the day from me. A sharp bump and a large green Harlem Tunnel sign sucked us into a huge granite rock entrance and dimly lit tunnel curving downward under the Hudson River to Manhattan and Grand Central Station. The orange lights along the guard rail and speeding cars produced a noxious glow and smell of suffocation, as I waited for the bus to turn upward and out, on to the pavement leading to our next stop.

Entering the underground terminal, the bus driver told us to come to the side of the bus for our luggage, and go to the central lobby if we were making a connection. For those ending their trip in the City, he bid them farewell. After a 30 minute stop, I transferred to a local transit bus and continued on to Asbury Park, New Jersey, where a forty-five minute ride brought me to the 'Welcome to Fort Monmouth' sign.

As the bus peeled away, I felt an ominous chill in my body. It hydroplaned and sheered a wave of New Jersey street water against the Fort Monmouth sign. My black leather boots sank deep into the gutter, flowing full with trash, leaves and rain as I watched a green Fort Monmouth military bus approach in the dark that would take me to CECOM Signal Corp Headquarters, Fort Monmouth. I pulled my overcoat up against my neck, and pushed my back against the seat to find a little warmth against the night air.

The bus driver told me that everything was closed on the base, so he would drop me at the main receiving depot and they would know what to do with me. It was a three story dorm-styled building. The lights were out, and a security guard patrolling the dorm rooms held a flashlight as I made my bunk for the night. He told me that reveille was 0600, PT at 0610, and the mess hall opened at 0630. No meals were served after 0700, so I could not be late.

The day went fast, and by 1400, I was assigned to my permanent barracks, given my school schedule, and instructed to catch my bus at 0800 for Photography School.

So began my advance training in Army Field Photo Reconnaissance. On the morning of November 22nd, I would be headed to Little Silver Spring Station in Maryland, to catch a west bound train to Alameda Station in Oakland, California, to await my permanent assignment.

Photography School and Flight Training

My study schedule was intense, grades were extremely competitive, and free time would be almost non-existent. My class of 30 worked hard on field assignments, aerial reconnaissance flights, and intelligence procedures. Orders from the command post and new assignments and duties were issued daily.

Our instructor was Staff Sgt. Kessler, a combat veteran, and non-commissioned officer was demanding and a harsh critic. If we didn't perform to his expected standards, the exercise repeated until it did. We were told that our assignments were critical to military intelligence in the field of operations and sea paths around domestic and foreign ports and land masses.

We ran reconnaissance and surveillance patrols using such developmental aircraft as; modified transport C-123's, Twin prop OV-10's and low flying Bell Model 205 UH-1B

Huey Helicopter, to photograph with K-12 stationary cameras and newly advanced 35mm camera with high speed infrared film.

The weeks rushed by and I found myself in the barracks on a cold October night at 2100, when Sergeant Kessler met a group of us at the barracks door. "Dhamner, Crawford, and Beiler, you are with me in the briefing room, now! We leave in an hour! Be at PT field behind CECOM building, C48, for your transport to the flight line to the Jersey Shore. That is all."

"Yes Sir!"

By 2130, we stood in the dry night air near the old county airport just off base. We heard a distant roar and thunderous rumble of a UH-1B-Huey Helicopter. Approaching over the tower at the south end of the field, it landed in the dark. A single light flashed from beneath, and the door slid back and latched open as it swiftly dropped in front of us, rotor spinning and dust from the field piercing our eyes, sleeves of our flight jackets, and hitting our D-12 and H-200 aerial camera cases.

The helicopter pilot shouted, "Load quickly. Strap in. We have a Twin prop, open top, OV10 and a developmental, modified C-123, waiting for us to make a night aerial patrol up the Jersey Shore to Maine. You are not to talk about this! You were never away from base. We will be in night flight mode, and due to return before daybreak. We'll be twenty-seven miles out and over water. I hope everyone can swim if we go down."

We arrived at the air flight command center just 15 miles from Monmouth, and immediately ordered to our seats and flight positions. As we boarded, I thought I would have had more time before a maneuver like this one. It would be a training flight for us, but we were expected to film suspected submarine and small boat crafts reported on the Hyannis Port and the upper Maine coastal waters.

Take off was in 12 minutes, so I went through my sound check in my head gear and heard the final announcement of "prepare for take-off, seatbelts on, we will cruise at 6,000 feet. I am Captain Jim Sanders and you know our co-pilot for tonight, Master Sergeant Kessler. You have been hand-picked for the assignment. Good hunting."

With that, we rolled forward on the darkly lit runway, went into a 60 degree climb and made a sharp 90 degree back left turn in a 45 degree oblique maneuver, over the distant lights of Asbury Park and Newark, New Jersey. Our designated flight grid was 526 nautical miles north.

The seatbelt lights stayed on, and I went through a K-12 camera positon check for film, setting instructions and reloading canisters. From there, my headset was ablaze with instructions from Sergeant Kessler as flight deck commander: "Run camera now--shut off—wait—run--run again--increase speed-- reload as needed--ready camera low level pass-over—15 seconds-- low level--hold and hold on to your seats. This will be low dive to 600 feet over the marshes and back up to 8,000." I caught my breath. The G-force of the dive tightened my stomach muscles, and my head felt a little light-headed.

"Everybody okay?" Shouted the pilot over the high torc of the engines, and the stiff coastal wind pushing upward and hard against the plane's bottom structure and wings, making film blur a possibility. I drank coffee from my thermos to steady my nerves. I kept check on the time, as plane constantly made high and low altitude 45 degree oblique flight pattern loops in the night sky.

Then, it was back to base. I filmed 4-high speed, twelve inch reels, at 200 foot length, and loaded them into metal tubes for delivery and processing at the lab, on our return.

I looked over at Crawford and he was going through the same process and procedure on the right window side of the plane. We returned to the flight center and the plane threaded a route around the old asphalt pavement. The same helicopter was waiting for us and we made the return trip to Fort Monmouth to dispatch our film cartridges for processing.

We joined our classmates in the mess hall at 0600, and prepared for another day of classes in the academy building at 0730. No one noticed our absence during the night. We would go on three more night flights before I left Fort Monmouth in November.

Washington DC

A letter from Jamie, September 16th.

Dearest Wade

It has only been four days since we talked by phone, but I wanted to send you this letter. I want you to see if you can get a weekend pass, and meet me in Alexandria for a tour of Washington DC.

A good friend of mine from Wintergreen went to Washington two years ago, and has a roommate who shares an apartment in Alexandria.

She and I talked by phone. We usually talk about once a month. I told her about you and our visit this summer. She suggested that we visit her sometime.

Before Thanksgiving, her friend is going home to visit her parents. She offered us a place to stay. I know you are in training, and it may be hard for you to take time off, but I hope you will call me about it.

My grandmother has already given me permission to go by bus, offered to buy my ticket, and given me $25.00 for food and souvenirs.

I want to bring my guitar and sing some of my new poems for you. My friend would like for me to play, and sing for some of her friends while in town. What do you think? This is one I wrote to a Bobby Vinton tune, titled "It Was You."

You took my emptiness away
You gave me loving bliss, today
I have never known love like this
You stole my heart and made me live

You made me want to love and live
with so much to give
This is why I am so in love with you

Now take away every loneliness
And give me more love like this
and love me true like
a love I never knew that love could feel so good
with you

You gave me hope
And told me I could
Love again
And find myself and have everything

That is why you are my everything
My heart, My hope, My dream, My love
My everyday

With you I will be the dream
I thought had gone away
In your arms
I hope to stay in the ever after and today

Just remember that it was you
Always you
That let my dreams

My hopes
My love
Come true
And it will be your love I give
Until the day
We no longer dream.

*By the way, I called the station and found an express
bus that leaves Fort Monmouth around 11:00 a.m. and
arrives in Washington DC at 3:00 p.m. My bus would
arrive about the same time. You could catch the 4:00 p.m.
Sunday bus and be back at the base by 10:00 p.m.*
*I hope you like the poem enclosed and the list of books
I've been reading before I see you again*
Love always, Jamie

I could hardly put the letter down. I wasn't sure if I
could get a pass, but asked the company clerk as soon as
mail call was over. He informed me that the procedure
required that I fill out a pass form with detailed reasons for
the pass and the destination with an address and phone
number. I could get permission from the CO after the noon
meal on Friday. However, it required that I report into the
duty officer by 2300 hours on Sunday night for bed check.

After completing the form, I returned it to his office.
At mail call the next day, my three-day, a weekend pass
was waiting for me. I called Jamie:

"Hello, this is Jamie." The voice answered softly in the
other end.
*"It's Wade. I received approval for my weekend pass.
How are you? And by the way, happy belated birthday.
How's everyone at home?"*
*"Everyone here is fine. Grandmother says hello. She
bought me a new outfit for the trip to Washington. I knew
you would get the pass. Can't wait to see you and phone my*

friend in Alexandria to make arrangements for our stay with her."

Her voice trailed off, and I could hardly hear her on the line. *"Jamie are you okay, and up for this trip."*

"Yes, I need to see you. I have so much to talk about. I've been lonesome here. The days pass slowly here.

Next Monday will be my first full year on only four tablets a day. The doctors want to release me next year. I am driving my grandmother's car, but only short distances. Read sixteen books since you were here. I think I've earned a degree in literature and eastern philosophy.

My music is my favorite pastime. I've concentrated on folk music by Joan Baez, Donna Harris, Bob Dylan and Pete Seeger. Even threw in my own, a country-folk song...

I recorded it myself for 25 cents at a recording music booth at Broadway Music and Books, just off the university campus last week...and want to play it for you. Can't wait to see you again."

"Me too. I have to get to the mess hall before it closes, but I'll send you a postcard of the schedule and look forward to seeing you in two...."

"Bye, see you soon I...." The line went silent and the operator instructed me to put three more quarters in the slot. At mail call the next day, I received another belated letter from Jamie.

Dear Wade, Hope I don't get in trouble with you.

I need to talk to you about something I did last week. I modeled for a figure art class. They wanted to paint my back and the butterfly. They paid me $10.00 cash. I think Ms. Stevens told someone about the butterfly.

I have no shame about it. I wore a sheer champagne silk sheet over my front, and turned my back to the class-mostly women students and one young man.

They drew and painted for over an hour.

I dressed and left. It was painful, but I'm sure no one painted my tears.

It was liberating. That's why I like the photographs you've taken of me. You captured the real me.

There will be an exhibit of the best drawings next month in the university art lobby. I hope to attend to see if I am on display. By the way, one of the students from New York, Julie Harris, painted me in charcoal. She won first place and gave me the drawing. Maybe you can include it in your book someday. I like it. So does Grandmother.

With Love, Jamie

My evening call to Ms. Thompson

"Hello." I said, as Jamie's grandmother came on the line.

"Wade, it's good to hear from you. Something wrong? Jamie's not here."

"I know. I wanted to talk with you. How is Jamie doing, really?"

"Well, she would be pretty upset if she knew I was talking to you about this, but it might be the best thing for now.

The doctors want to take her off her medicine because it is damaging her kidneys and liver at a faster rate than before. She needs the medicine, but her mood is better and much improved lately, with Ms. Stevens' teaching her yoga and meditation for pain relief in her jaw and neck. She tells me she likes it, and it's working better than the medicine.

The girl is fond of you, but knows that you will be assigned somewhere faraway. That's why she wants to stay in touch.

She's writing poems all the time, and singing the best songs I've ever heard. It's how she deals with the hurt and years of pain. I know some people think I've spoiled her, but she is so smart and ahead of her times.

She reads and knows things that astonish the professors at the university. She has no interest in a degree, but is smarter than them all. She made a record last week and plays it all the time. I am sure she wants you to hear it. She bought an extra one, and sent it to a radio station in Lynchburg.

She does get tired and sometimes sleeps late. We'll just keep that between us. How are the cookies? They're Jamie's favorite. Oh, I know I'm going on and on like Jamie. She will tell you more about the record on the trip. Good night and I pray all is well with you."

Four days after I talked with Jamie and Ms. Thompson, a package arrived from Jamie, containing two dozen sugar

cookies, a vanilla pound cake, and an article by Tom Wolfe. She also included a small charcoal clipping of a drawing of two silhouetted figures bathing in a river.

She had been taught a lot by her grandparents. She had spent a lot of time sitting in literature and music classes at the university. She wanted me to know that her life, although painful physically, had been a dream come true.

Music, art, literature and common sense were her special gifts. She was insightful. She read magazine articles, and books by Tom Wolfe, Aldous Huxley, James Baldwin, Ken Kursy, Harper Lee, Charlotte Bronte, and even The Complete Works of Shakespeare, while listening to the music of Dana Harris, Bob Dylan, Bobby Vinton and Joan Baez.

She wasn't much into the 'Rock 'n' Roll' sweeping the country. She was constantly telling me that I was destined for greatness. She wanted to be a part of my life. She wanted me to understand that her time was like sand in an hour glass. She was determined that whatever happened to her, she I would not be forgotten by me.

As I munched on the cookies, I smiled and imagined what it would be like to be with her the in Alexandria and Washington, DC.

Jamie and Marianne

I watched the bus schedule flash black, then white above the information counter. It announced arrival times and departures. Jamie's bus was scheduled to arrive on time and flashed 4:15 p.m.

A walk around the smoked filled bus station as the smell of hamburgers, hotdogs, onions and sweet mustard pierced my nose. Travelers ran for late arriving buses, to catch the next one out to destinations north and south. Porters pulled large baggage carts from platform to platform, removing large Samsonite suitcases, taped and ragged boxes, and baby strollers of every description for passengers. Everyone was yelling directions above the bus dispatcher's voice as porters tied baggage labels on suitcase handles, military duffle bags and boxed equipment. Bus drivers slid and separated them into the bus baggage compartment for the next stop.

Then, I saw Jamie's bus with Charlottesville-Nashville sign above the front windshield, as the bus bounced left and right, to maneuver into the narrow parking spot. It was a high-decker Trailway Bus. I could see Jamie in the second row section waving and smiling at me. She was wearing her tight Sears' blue jeans, tucked into her doeskin winter boots, black sweater vest and my favorite baseball cap. She took it off, and tipped it toward me. Smiling and waving, she made her way down the steep center stairs with the other passengers.

She looked great as she stepped through the bus door and tossed a small handbag onto the concrete platform. She reached out for me, encircled her right arm through the insides of my winter coat and tossing her head back, and said, "Kiss me soldier!" Her slightly parted lips met mine. We held each other tight, as we moved away from the bus to wait for her other baggage. The smell of teaberry gum stayed on my lips.

"I just wanted to say that!" she laughed out loud, as we walked along the side of the bus to get her backpack and guitar. The diesel fumes mingled with the cold November air and swirled around us in the terminal.

We had so much to say as the crowd pushed and shoved us from the bus platform to the inside ticket counter and café on South Street. We were greeted by the sounds of taxi cab horns, yelling attendants, and city buses, moving in an endless circle on the street to pick up passengers and whisk them away from Union Station.

"Jamie, let's take this cab," I said, as she tightened her belt around her coat, and pushed her jeans deeper into her doe skin boots.

We jumped into the next available cab, while the driver tossed our bags and her guitar in the trunk. We headed south by the old congressional office down Pennsylvania Avenue, then swung left by the Treasury, turned left across the Seventh Street Bridge past the Washington Monument, and out of the city toward Alexandria.

I put my arm around her shoulder and held her tight. She planted her right hand on my thigh. We kissed and held each other tight as the taxi bumped, and darted in and out of traffic. We rode south along the narrow streets and broken pavement, through the avenues of Alexandria's stores and apartment buildings.

After a three-mile ride, we entered 'Old Towne' lined with identical four-story executive-style brick apartments. The driver drove slowly, trying to spot the 417 address.

"There it is!" Jamie shouted and handed the driver a $5.00 bill and told him to "keep the change."

Standing on the sidewalk, we looked up and recognized Marianne peering from behind the curtained window three levels up. She waved for us to come up, and we heard a beeping tone near her mail box. We pushed open the door and walked the three levels of stairs to be greeted with hugs by Marianne on the landing.

"Hope you both had a good trip," she said, giving Jamie a big welcoming hug and extending a handshake to me. She showed us where we could put our bags, and gave Jamie a tour of her roommate's room. They returned to the living room, and Marianne pointed at the living room sofa.

"That's for you. It's a little lumpy, but comfortable."

The apartment suite was an efficiency designed for two people. The bedroom had twin beds. The spacious living room was complete with a bathroom and small sitting parlor to the right of the stairs. Folding French doors separated the small kitchen and pantry from the bathroom and a sitting parlor. A single French door opened from the kitchen to an outdoor terrace. It was mainly used in the spring and late summer, to take advantage of cool evening breezes from the Potomac River.

"I have a lot planned tonight for you two. I have to work tomorrow, so I have a surprise for you. We're having dinner at a café I love. It's just down the street. It's called a coffee house, and it's becoming the rage in the city and here just off King Street. It is frequented by Georgetown students and faculty. There are politicians, writers, artists and business leaders who want to be seen and show up. It's very informal. Lots of tourists and city dwellers come here for the new atmosphere and talented artists who play and sing in the cafes. Dinner is simple, inexpensive, and Shaffer Beer is half-price between 7-8 p.m. They invite guest speakers and singers for an open mic session every Friday and Saturday night. This is happening all over the city. It started up north and just last week we had a young folk singer here, Bob Dylan, from New York. Jamie, I want you to take your guitar and sing some of your poems and songs for the crowd!"

"Marianne, I mainly sing for myself and Grandmother. I don't know if they'll like my songs."

"Yes they will, won't they Wade! Jamie you have a beautiful voice and your songs are good. Maybe you can do a little Patsy Cline, Bobby Darin and Buddy...."

"Wait a minute you two," Jamie interrupted, I'll take my guitar, but I want to see and hear what some of the others do first before I try to sing" she said sheepishly, as she complied with Marianne's decision.

Marianne was a clerk typist and stenographer for the Department of Commerce, and a Justice Department courier to the Executive Building. There were thousands of young people like Marianne that kept the politics of Washington going on a day-to-day basis.

She was up at 5:00 am every morning and on a bus to the city by 5:45 am and at her desk by 6:30 am. She would be leaving in the morning, just like any other day. She planned to wake Jamie and me as she left. We could catch a 9:00 am bus for downtown. Once there, we would take a tour bus to the White House, The Capital, Arlington National Cemetery, The Jefferson Memorial, and finally, the Lincoln Memorial. Marianne had secured tickets earlier in the week. It would be cold and windy. We would be able to stay on the bus for most of the trip. We would bundle up for the walks to the monuments.

Nico's Cafe was dark with small lamps on the tables, and side tables along the walls. Soft cushioned chairs were pushed into the corners. *Time* magazines and *Washington Post* newspapers littered racks by the front door. There were candles on small shelves around the walls.

Background music came from a *Magnavox Stereo* positioned on a small stage. About 10-15 people were ordering food, mostly soup, hamburgers, hotdogs, and sandwiches. The air was full of smoke. The smell of coffee, beer and fried potatoes filled the room, as cigarette smoke diffused the fluorescent and incandescent lights hanging from the ceiling, and shining from the kitchen.

At the far end of the open room was a Steinway piano and stool on a raised platform, with a single microphone. Placed in front of the microphone, and between a guitar rack and set of rock and roll drums, was a high-backed director style canvas and wood chair.

A single spotlight in the ceiling reflected off the piano top. A black and brown canvas covered box speaker, with a cord dangling to the floor was nailed, precariously to dark veneer paneling. Big band 1950's music echoed across the café from the Magnavox speakers.

"Dogs with chili are my favorite" shouted Marianne, as she took a long draw on a Black Ribbon. Most of Virginia was 'off premises' but here in The District one could drink beer as long as they showed an ID for 18 years of age. Marianne pushed two bottles across the table to Jamie and me. Hotdogs, hush puppies and potatoes chips appeared on the table in wicker baskets. Bottles of catsup, hot sauce, and mustard were place on the table.

"Is this the young lady I've heard so much about Marianne?" boomed a short, rotund and bearded middle aged man, wiping his hands on his apron in preparation to shake Jamie's hand. Jamie stretched across the table and shook hands and said "I'm not very good, but I will give it a try."

"Great, my name is Nico, and I own this place. Finish your food and I'll play a few tunes on the piano and introduce you. By the way, your dinner is on the house tonight. Enjoy and order some more if you want," he finished, as he moved to the next table with the same

 introduction to his guest, and bragged about the young talented singer who would be on stage with him tonight.

I watched Jamie slowly drink the last of her water, take a deep breath, and stand up at the table. She shouldered her guitar and kissed me for good luck as she walked to the side of the stage. She was calm, with a pleasant smile on her face. She took one last puff on her Lucky Strike, and waited with quiet confidence.

Her hands gently strummed a few familiar cords on her guitar. She licked her lips and waited. Nico was having fun playing for the crowd. He banged out a few Dixie favorites and a white key anthem. He introduced Jamie as a good friend from Spruce Creek near Wintergreen. He promised that we would hear a lot more from her in the future, as Jamie slipped into the high-backed chair and strummed a few quiet chords for the crowd. They stopped talking and the sounds of plates, cups and chatter went silent in the darkened room.

The harsh spotlight softened Jamie's face.

She pushed her yellow hair over her left shoulder, and I noticed a Rembrandt glow on the delicately outlined cheek. Her lips parted, and the beautiful Patsy Cline ballad 'Crazy' filled the room. I watched the faces in the crowd sway, as the emotion of the song and voice of the singer became one. She went on to play 'Blue on Blue', 'Your Cheatin' Heart' before snapping the crowd to their feet with 'Blueberry Hill'.

While the crowd applauded and resettled in their chairs, she promised to sing two more if Nico would join her, and play some good-night tunes once she finished.

"This one is for my two best friends in the world, Marianne and Wade. Marianne and I have known each other all our lives. She has been my friend since I was a little girl. Wade is here with me tonight, but will soon be shipping out to California and his next duty station. It's called 'Soldier Boy Come Home'. And, I just wrote another one last week and it's for all of you, but especially for him. It's titled 'It was You' and I'll sing it for you."

It was you.
You took my emptiness away
You gave me loving bliss, today
I have never known love like this
You stole my heart and made me live

You made me want to love and live
with so much to give
This is why I am so in love with you

Now take away every loneliness
And give me more love like this
and love me like I never knew
that love could feel so good with you

You gave me hope
And told me I could
Love again
And find myself and have everything

That is why you my everything
My heart, My hope, My dream, My love
My everyday

With you I will be the dream
I thought had gone away
In your arms
I hope to stay
In the ever after and today

Just remember that it was you
Always you
That let my dreams
My hopes
My love
Come true
And it will be your love I give
Until the day
We no longer dream
And I am loved again

As I sat there in the darkened room, I watched the smoke-shaded faces watching Jamie. They heard and saw what I heard and saw-- a beautiful, innocent, young woman, who sang and played beyond the hurt and sorrow that we have all felt at times. She was articulate, talented and approachable in her own loving way. We also saw a saddened and troubled face, that could force a smile to chase away old hurt and pain.

We listened to a free-spirited voice that we knew might only come our way once in a lifetime. We saw someone who could take us beyond our own pettiness, and put a smile on our faces.

As Jamie finished the last song and lowered her head, the crowd exploded with applause. They all looked at her and the make-shift stage in awe, as she walked to my table. She sat in my lap and quietly put her arms around my neck and hugged me, as she whispered in my ear "I'm so tired. Take me home."

I put her coat on, and wrapped the woolen scarf around her neck. She pulled her hat on, as I strapped her guitar on my shoulder and walked her to the street. She had a broad and tearful smile on her face. Behind us, we could hear more applause and words of encouragement to keep playing and singing. A loud and proud Nico shouted

"You're welcome back here anytime. Good night and good luck."

At the apartment, Marianne took the half sleeping Jamie to her bedroom and she slipped between the soft cotton sheets and blanket. She was asleep instantly. Marianne motioned for me to join her in the outer parlor. We pulled out the sleep sofa. She helped me put sheets and a heavy blanket on the sofa, and with a perfunctory sense of business said, "I keep the temperature at 68, even in winter. If you need another blanket, let me know. I will be up at five, and off to work. I know she will sleep until eight. She looks very pale. I know she wanted to make this trip. Enjoy your tour of Washington tomorrow.

Take her to see everything she wants. I will be home about six o'clock. We'll stay home, talk, catch up. I will make a batch of my spaghetti and southern style noodles for us. I even made her a small, chocolate, birthday cake. We'll celebrate. I have everything, so don't worry. Take good care of her and make sure she stays warm and dry", she finished, and went to bed.

I was asleep myself by 11:30 p.m. and barely heard Marianne's voice when she shook me awake the next morning at six o'clock. She told me there was coffee and donuts in the kitchen and left for work.

Marianne

Marianne had left home three years ago.

It was rumored that she had left with, and married, the young Navy Ensign who had taken her to the Senior Prom.

She was a top student, the most popular girl in school, played basketball, and performed in the band. She was outspoken and a defender of those she considered less fortunate. Jamie fit in this category, and no one teased her when Marianne was around.

The young lieutenant had left and gone his way. She worked long hours as a junior clerk for the Earl Warren court. She was smart and up to date on the scenes to see and places to be seen, in and around the Capitol.

She had been given every advantage as an only child. Her parents both worked hard and gave her everything life could provide. Her father was a part-time preacher, and the science and math teacher at the local county school. Her mother managed a small grocery store near their home. She opened the store every day at six o'clock for those driving to Charlottesville and Waynesboro for work.

The store seldom closed before 6:30 p.m.

On Saturdays, she closed at noon. She managed the store, stocked the shelves, and paid all the bills for the owner, who owned two other stores and gas stations: one in the valley along highway 151, and another on the new Route Six on the Rockfish River.

Marianne had prepared dinner since she was in the fifth grade. She enjoyed the pleasant, talkative evenings with her parents. She, of course, always made a full report of school activities, piano practice, weekly 4-H Club meetings, and special school projects. She especially delighted in letting her parents know that she had completed her homework, and displayed test papers and graded assignments returned by teachers. She was showered with accolades and money by her parents, who saw her as precocious and responsible beyond her years.

In their mind, she was the perfect child. In high school, she excelled in band, chorus, literature, math and science with a 4.0 GPA. In her junior year, she was elected class president, and school president her senior year. Her teachers saw her as their number one candidate for a college scholarship in the arts and sciences. Her parents saw their every dream and hope for their daughter as a reality.

Marianne had other plans after she graduated. She wanted to see the world, as she told Jamie, during their secret talks. She had met a young navy ensign during her junior-senior beach trip. They became instant pen pals. He was her date for the Senior Prom and the envy of the other girls in her class, as they watched the dashing navy ensign, in full military dress, twirl her about the floor of the high school gym.

As she and the ensign whispered to each other, and talked and dreamed secret plans of a life beyond her high school graduation, Marianne's parents worried. They saw their life's plan for their only child disappearing. A prom night and candles had put a love-dazed sparkle in Marianne's eyes. She looked deep into the eyes of her prince charming. He offered a mystical life of travel, diplomatic functions, and the social graces that came with being the young, attractive wife of a naval officer based in the Washington/Annapolis area.

A week before her graduation, she announced their engagement. They were married in August by her father at his church, with close friends in attendance. After a brief weekend honeymoon, he returned to his Norfolk Naval unit where he was commissioned a lieutenant. He shipped out to the south Atlantic.

On his return, Marianne joined him after six months, and they made their home in a small apartment. The marriage lasted a year. They divorced. She moved to the present Alexandria apartment, and took a job as a low level typist and clerk, at the Department of Justice. Her parents thought she would be devastated.

Instead, she thrived on the attention garnered from elected politicians, lobbyists, businessmen and educators who frequented the justice department seeking special judicial favors and appointments. After 18 months, she received a promotion and a raise sufficient to allow her to upgrade to an efficiency apartment in the three story walkup in Alexandria.

Her personality drew her to the abundant arts, music and social functions in the area. She particularly enjoyed the performing arts at the new emerging social centers. She was often invited, and joined, other equally ambitious artists, writers, attorneys, educators and social activists, who wanted to be a part of the new civil rights movement and policies of the Kennedy/Johnson administration.

She felt that she was in the epic center of a new movement that was changing the philosophies of the old South. She saw encouraging, sweeping, cultural shifts that would become the beginning of a new society.

At 22, she was a confidante to the emerging democratic power and social change which could put the President's brother in the Oval Office.

When she visited home on summer weekends and other ceremonial occasions, she never talked about her Washington life-style, or the divorce. Instead, she visited and spent time with Jamie at the river and cavern. Marianne encouraged Jamie to write, play the guitar and sing. In return, Jamie was direct and candid with Marianne. She became a voice of reason and reality for Jamie. She listened to the songs and envied Jamie's strength and honest approach to life in general.

Marianne was determined, that no matter what happened to them or between them, they would always remain best friends.

Jamie's Treatment

At nine o'clock, I woke Jamie with a hot cup of percolated coffee, and a jelly-filled donut, with a birthday candle. We laughed as she blew it out. She ate quietly in bed, while I read the morning paper, turned the radio to WVAP for some morning news, and music by *The Topps* and some old tunes by Patsy Cline.

It was just the two of us together.

"We have some time before we catch the shuttle bus for our tour of Washington at 10:30 am. I know what you want to know, and I will tell you everything I can." Jamie said, as she let me rub the Johnson and Johnson baby lotion deep into her back. It was dry from sleep, the long trip, and lack of lotion. As I massaged her back and applied the Avon moisturizing lotion, she began.

"After my brother pushed me through the window, I felt a stinging pain in my shoulder and neck. There was a lot of blood. I had tried to talk, but couldn't move my jaw. My lips sagged, and my words slurred. I could hear myself screaming, but no one seemed to hear the sounds that were only in my head. The smells of burning wood and rags pierced my nose. I rolled away from the smoldering boards and protruding nails, which made one last claw-like scar. Then all was darkness.

The fire department and volunteer rescue team arrived. I was transported to the university emergency hospital in Charlottesville. They wrapped me in cool, wet, bed sheets and sedated me for the pain. I could only sleep on my stomach for the next three weeks. It was the beginning of years of treatment and recovery.

The cut on my face and neck was bandaged for two weeks, before it was removed to see how the stitches were healing. One of the stitches pulled loose, as I turned my head during sleep. That's where the knot is. It still hurts to the touch.

I left the hospital after a month, and went to live with my aunt Lillian in Columbia briefly, and then returned to my grandparents in Wintergreen. I couldn't sleep at night. My head hurt, and I had constant nightmares where I am falling from the window again and again.

There was lots of pain as my grandfather and grandmother dressed, cleaned and removed dead skin from my upper back and shoulder, with warm and cold water and special liniment lotions. My jaw and face took longer and sometimes I couldn't chew, so I drank a lot of milk and ate softened bread. I wore a small set of braces for about a year. Although it was a long time ago, I can still remember the pain.

My head hurt some at first, but got worse as time went on. My jaw was slow to heal, and biting down sent shock waves through the side of my head. A comprehensive medical evaluation and diagnostic testing by a neurologist, showed that what was thought to be a bump, was actually a concussion and could cause long-term problems such as: loss of memory, headaches, sensitivity to noise and light, dizziness, blurred vision, ringing in the ears and fatigue. I've had them all at one time or the other over the years, but the main thing now is the headaches.

The doctors gave me all kinds of medicines. They mostly made me sick. Only the mixtures my grandfather made for me worked. He was very upset with the doctors. I think it was his frustration and anger that led to his building the dam and cave for me on the creek. It took him six hours a day for two weeks, until he damned the creek and the cave, so I could bathe and let the warm water wash the burning away.

The pills were given to him by doctors, he told me. He would cut them in half, so I could take them in a spoonful of honey and peach brandy. They eased the pain, but not the ache I felt in my heart. I'm an example of what happens to a child who takes adult pain medicine. When I was eligible for high school, my grandparents got special permission for me to spend two days a week at the university hospital ward, for treatment and tutoring in the afternoon."

She stopped talking, turned away, and hid her face in her hands. She had noticed my lips moving, trying to speak. "Tell me what you want to know." She said.

"I know you've been through a lot. Tell me what I can do? Tell me about your counseling sessions. How are you now and, and…….. are?" I whispered, as she silenced my lips with her outreached fingers.

"I am getting so much better, but a lot of damage was done when I was young. Physically, I'm healed, so to speak, but this last year, I was ready to give up. Yes, my time is short, and although I don't know when, I do know how my life will end. I have been diagnosed with depression, as a result of the headaches and a kidney disorder. It's treatable with medicines, but apparently I have inherited some other illness from my parents. My grandmother told me my mother was bipolar, and my father was an alcoholic, and may have had diabetes. I don't know for sure, but this can't all just be from the fire and accident.

As I told you in my letters, I read all the time. I have studied everything there is to know about chronic kidney diseases and the medicines that control my mood swings, but there is a lot of damage.

About a year ago, I started reading about meditation, self-healing, and a whole array of Native American Indian and Zen body approaches to my condition. I know I'm an amateur at this."

Ms. Stevens says it gives me a compass, and a way to center my life, so I will be prepared if things turn worse. She has been wonderful. It's our secret. I can't tell too many people. They will think I'm crazy or something.

I had accepted my situation, and had peace about my solitary life and future. I had seen 'the light of death' as

Ms. Stevens said, and I knew my time was short, and I could and would die. I was ready to give up.

Then I met you, and I'm here now!

I want to make the most of our time. I know it's going to hurt you. Do you understand?" she finished, as we pulled each other close.

She wanted to talk more, so I sank back in my chair and waited. I had learned that I had to say nothing, and wait until the thoughts were clear in her mind, or she would just allow me to talk more, and drive the conversation.

"I am sick, but not defeated. The doctors have done all they can do for me. I'm not going to let this beat me, and I've been okay with knowing that I don't have a long life ahead of me. I didn't want to tell you anything, and I thought we could just go on and life would be all right.

I never planned on this happening.

I never planned on liking you, loving you, or anyone.

Everybody thinks I'm tough, and I am. But, I've isolated myself the last couple of years from those who I know care about me --pretending that I could act tough, stay busy and dress the part, and I would just end and be no more.

Then, I prayed, and asked for a sign, or someone, who could make me love them more than I hated myself. Do you understand? You happened! You were on that bus on a day that I never travel to the university clinic. You become the answer to my prayer, wish, dream, or whatever you want to call it. I know it sounds a little crazy, but it's true. I like you more than you know. And I know it's selfish to want you, and ask you to be, to be my boyfriend, but I must. I must write more, sing more, and go to some of the places in my dreams before…"

"I know", I said, my voice trembling and my heart breaking as I bowed my head and whispered the words she wanted to hear.

"I have more to talk about with you, but we have 15 minutes to walk to King Street and catch our shuttle for the Washington tour. I'll wear warm clothes. I really want to see the Capitol with you."

As we walked to the corner, she acted like she had nothing more to say. Then she told me she had bought me an early Christmas present of books that her grandfather had made her read. She knew it would be good for me to read over the next few months, since I had mentioned that I may not be coming home for Christmas. I would be getting my orders soon, and it looked like I would be transferring to Fort Ord, California, in late November, and my next assignment was unclear.

She was only spending two days a week at the University Medical center, and would start working at the Stoney Creek café on Fridays and Saturdays. They also wanted her to play her guitar and sing in the evenings. She had saved money for another trip somewhere, and maybe even a car.

The green and red tour shuttle arrived and we settled quickly into a front seat with our back packs and high expectations. Our first stop was the Jefferson Memorial, with a quick photo walk to the monument and return to the shuttle. Jamie had fun pretending to read the Declaration of Independence plaque. With everyone back on the shuttle and head count completed, we drove by The Capitol, circling Union Station, and took a slow ride up Pennsylvania Avenue to the White House. The driver talked constantly, telling us where we were, and that we would have another 15 minute photo stop across from the White House. The wind was picking up, and Jamie and I decided to stay on the shuttle, as the others walked to DuPont Circle and snapped group pictures.

I put my arm around her as we sat together, as she said, "I'm going to take a chance and tell you something I really want to do, but you have to promise me you will listen, pay close attention and learn with me. I have never been with anyone. What we have together is very special, but I am under no illusion that you can take me with you, or that you even love me. I certainly like you, but it's hard to love.

I have lost so much in my life.

I want to love you, but we can't have sex. I cannot get pregnant. I am a Christian. I'm really a Zen Christian, according to Ms. Stevens since I am learning to meditate, studying kundalini yoga, and reading about a more mystical and secular philosophy than the Bible.

I am writing a lot of poetry and developing it into lyrical and folk songs. I think some of my poems are pretty good. I am also experiencing feelings and thoughts about you and being with you. I want to make love to you more than you know. I want to be in your mind and heart and make you happy. I know you can make me happy, but I don't want you to be hurt. I want to tell you and show you what I've learned from reading and studying about sex and love. Boys are different, and I know you have sexual drives, desires and thoughts that are different than mine. I have those feelings too, but together we can do things, and have real meaningful and loving experiences, that won't get me pregnant until I am married, if that should ever happen someday.

I know I'm rambling and some of this is confusing. It's confusing for me too, but don't stop me, or I may lose my nerve, and we'll never talk about this again. I want to show you what I've learned and see if you like it and want you to share some things with me." she said. When we saw people returning to the shuttle, we stopped talking, with a promise that we would talk more at the apartment.

"Do we have everybody?" the driver asked, as we pulled away and headed for Arlington National Cemetery.

"I hope we have plenty of time at Arlington National Cemetery," Jamie said, as the driver announced that we would have 30 minutes to visit the Unknown Soldier's

Tomb and walk around the grounds before returning to the shuttle.

"I have heard and read so much about it, and my great Uncle Patrick, who was killed in the Korean War, is buried there along with a lot of other heroes." It was misting and a cold breeze whipped at our collars, but Jamie was determined to make the walk to the tomb and see some of the crosses lining the green grassy hills.

"I've read so much about its history and how this was General Robert E. Lee's home before the Civil War. The Union Army refused to bury Confederate Soldiers there until well after the war was over. It's one of our most revered national monuments and every President since Lincoln has visited the site and made speeches in honor of our veterans," she finished, as the driver started to gather us back on the shuttle for our return to Alexandria.

Back at the apartment, Jamie and I made coffee, and finished off the rest of the donuts Marianne had left on the kitchen counter. With her energy returning, and a second tablet with her coffee, she invited me to the living room sofa. "I've read about things deeper, more sacred, and supposedly more fulfilling. So far I have only dreamed about them, but I know it works, at least that's what the books have said..."

"Jamie, I want to do everything with you that makes you happy and helps us understand more about each other. I'm beginning to read, and there is so much I don't know, but you can teach me, and we can learn together." I replied.

"You don't think I'm crazy do you?" She said.

"No, I don't, and we will do whatever it takes with whatever time we have, to make this the greatest time and year of your life."

"I want to sing you a verse from a song I wrote, and then try some things with you before Marianne return tonight, if it's okay. It's about a butterfly, but it's about us."

I'm just a butterfly with a busted wing
I fly high every day
My spirit soars through
The blue sky and cotton white clouds
My journey is incomplete
Until I cross the southern border
To warm in the moist air
And fresh breezes
That can heal this broken wing
And make me whole again.

If I could go anywhere
Be anybody
See anything
Do everything
I would do it with you
No sad eyes, tears, but smiles...
.... And, I'm thinkin
You back to me,
For all the world to see
That's because I'm so in love with you.

Then without a word, she laid the guitar aside, and stood up and took my hands saying, "follow me and do what I do, and I want to show and try something with you." as she pulled me down in front of her on the floor. Our knees were crossed and in front of each other on the rug, in a lotus position.

"Look at me. Really look at me. My face, my eyes, my shoulders, my breasts, my stomach, my hands, and feel me with your eyes, and touch me and caress me. I will do the same to you. Just go with me. Don't think about anything but us in this room, with the music playing, and listen to our breathing...."

As a quiet softness invaded our bodies, I watched her breathe and the movement of her body. I began to experience some discomfort and said, "Jamie, I care about you. It's just that the military can be very demanding and I am not sure of this or where I will be this week, next month, next year." She put a tender finger to my lips.

"I know, that's why I'm here now. I want. No, I need this, and you in my life. I have missed so much.

I've read over a hundred books: the classics, ancient history, biographies, and current best sellers. None of them have prepared me for this. I know that I appeared to be a free spirit but I'm not. You think I'm strong but I'm not. You must think I am weird sometimes, but I can't help my feelings for you" she continued.

"What can I do?" I asked.

"Love me, no matter what I say or do." She answered.

With that she pushed me back on the rug, closed my eyes, and gave me a long and soft kiss. I could only feel her lips as she laid her head on my chest and we napped together, as the music played in the room with only thoughts of now and each other.

At six o'clock, Marianne came home. We cooked spaghetti, made a salad, drank hot tea, ate Jamie's birthday cake, and talked about home. Marianne turned the television on to the Lawrence Welk Show for us to watch but we just listened. Jamie went to sleep in my arms on the sofa around nine. She said that she felt safe and loved against my shoulder. A few times during the night, I thought I heard her whisper, "We'll be alright, soldier boy. We're quite a pair. I don't want to lose you and what we have. I'm going to keep writing my songs and sending them to you no matter where you are. I will wait for you to come home."

Then she drifted into a very satisfied sleep, with me holding her tight, my arm around her shoulders. Sometime during the night, Marianne came in and put an extra blanket over us.

We ate Sunday morning breakfast late and talked until lunch. With a final good-bye for now, Jamie and I kissed, hugged and went down to the street to my waiting cab. I caught the 3:30 p.m. Union Station bus back to Fort Monmouth with feelings and memories of our time together, and a determined confidence to take her more and more into my life.

Little Silver, Maryland-Fort Monmouth 11-22-1963

"Pink sky in the morning, sailors take warning," bellowed from the mess cook, as we piled into the dining room at 0615 just after reveille.

We ate quickly, signed the last of the our departure forms with the company clerk, and loaded our duffle bags, handbags, and personal camera equipment, in the green military transport buses for the ride through the cool crisp New Jersey morning air south to the Little Silver rail station.

It was 1050 when we arrived.

We gathered along the brick and veneer station house, with an outdoor coffee and donut shop. I walked to the south end of the platform, and planted my Arvin transistor radio against my ear and listened to an AM/FM music station. They played the old hits: Tommy Dorsey, Pete Fountain, and Bing Crosby's Christmas songs. They also played a mix of new hits by the likes of Bobby Vinton, Ricky Nelson, Frank Sinatra, Joan Baez, and Judy Collins. The voice from the small dual speakers was clear, except for occasional sparks and spatters of electric static.

As I listened, I thumbed through my rail tickets, bus transfers and orders, to make sure I had everything I would need for the next four days as I traveled to the Oakland, Alameda Station, California. From there I would travel, by bus and train, to my permanent assignment with the Combat Development Command Center at Fort Ord, Monterey, California.

I noticed more and more passengers were moving along the platform with baggage of all kinds, wearing heavy winter coats as they pulled close together to ward off the clear, but cold winter wind pushing against us.

Then, the rails began to vibrate, as the train approached.

The cold wind whipped at the tail and lapel of my thick Class A overcoat. I kept rubbing my nose and ears to keep warm. The cold sky was crystal clear, and only the pink clouds from the morning drifted overhead, as we listened in the distance for the train. The rails tensed with a gathering motion and the wind curled harder around the concrete support of the small station, as we anticipated the Great Northern and Southern that would take us to Union Station in Washington, DC.

As the train pulled into the station and blasted steam from its belly, I noticed my radio had gone silent. I thought my battery had run down when the volume had faded. Then in an emotionally strained voice, a news reporter came on the radio, "Shots have been fired in downtown Dallas during the President's motorcade through the city. It appears that several shots have been fired from a building, and the President and Governor of Texas have been hit. We don't have a full report on the shooting, but it appears that the President has been fatally wounded, and the Secret Service has sped away. We are making our way to the Dallas hospital for more details."

Walter Cronkite's voice came on from the New York station, asking for more clarification and details, but the reporter's voice had broken away, and silence reigned over the airwaves of the transmitter for the next 3-10 minutes, as the Porters ushered us on the train, and stored baggage and belongings in overhead shelves and behind black canvas wall cabinets.

I kept the radio to my ear, but the static made it difficult to hear, as I took my seat. The conductor moved through the aisle, telling everyone to take their seats quickly so we could get underway. There were inaudible moans and murmuring in the passenger car, but no clear details of the event in Dallas.

I was stunned. I sat quietly and a thousand thoughts and concerns pierced my mind. I waited, and wanted some sense of certainty and security, as the train pulled away slowly toward Union Station.

I lost the signal on the radio, and placed it in my handbag as I heard the conductor's clippers punching the tickets and placing tags on suitcases in overhead bins.

He announced in a steady voice to all that "The President has been shot, and the situation looks very grave, according to reports on the train radio. We will give you more details, once we have checked everyone's tickets and are fully underway for Washington."

It was 12:40 eastern time when the conductors appeared at the front of the car and asked for our full attention: "Last reports are, the President is dead and the governor of Texas has been gravely wounded. The First Lady has been taken to the Dallas Hospital, and we are awaiting word from the White House and Vice President Johnson. I will keep you informed, and will have additional information for all military personnel on the train regarding your arrival at Union Station.

I have been informed that everyone will need to check the departure times and gates, once we arrive, and follow all instructions for boarding your departing trains or final arrivals in the city," he finished as he walked to the door at back of the car and walked through to the passenger car behind us.

Silence. No one talked.

I wrote in my notebook:

Clouds raced across the sky.
My heart stopped.
The air was different on this morning in Silver Spring, Maryland.
I stood with other soldiers, waiting to board the slow approaching train that would take us to Alameda Station and beyond, to a war no one had heard of;
a conflict of national crisis, a wound that would not heal,
and another generation and another time of change.
The President had been shot.
We stood at silent attention, facing Washington and the west.
It was quiet this morning by these cold tracks
heading west beyond Dallas,
to a future that would be different
and dangerous
and dark,
at least for a while.
The train arrived.
Stopped. We boarded,
We remained quiet.
Said nothing.
Looked ahead, letting our silence speak
and I faced the future, a child no more.

Union Station, Washington, DC

The ride to Union Station was under three hours but seemed longer. No details were announced on the train. "No details," kept ringing in my ears and I was having dark thoughts about the future and what this news might mean to the nation and President's family. I was sure my family had heard the news by now and could imagine my father and grandfather talking about what this might mean to them and me.

At Union Station we disembarked. Train passengers scurried and scattered quickly in all directions down the platform ramps to recover baggage, check departure times, greet loved ones. Other passengers pushed their way through the thickening crowd to find departing train platforms.

My worries and fears quickly dissipated in the rush to get to my train. I felt a vague, unexplainable sense of urgency in the station; like everyone else in the terminal, I walked without talking. The crowd was faceless. They moved effortlessly out of my way as I made my way to Gate 10, for the Chicago train.

Finally I stood in the spacious anteroom of the train car with my baggage, as a friendly-freckle faced mother with her three year old daughter, took a seat in a chair beside me. We were soon joined by a collection of passengers who listened intently to the boarding instructions. We would travel and dine together for the next four days. It would be Thanksgiving in two days.

At the far end of the room was an elderly couple; the man held a cane to balance himself, while holding a large canvas trunk for storage on the train. His wife was dressed in a heavy, black woolen coat and kept yelling at him to tell the porter to store what they had so nothing would get broken.

Between them, dressed in black cotton slacks and knee boots, waist length parka jacket, and pin striped sailor cap was an olive skinned girl who appeared to be sixteen. She kept winking at me from under the sailor cap, and stared at my uniform and metals, with an occasional lick of her tongue across her lower lip. I thought it was odd, but she was oblivious to any noise or instructions, except the music from her transistor radio. I considered it a simple reaction to music.

Beside me now, holding on to the upright pole for balance, was the attractive freckle-faced female with her winter coat and scarf tucked against her throat. She wore a Jackie Kennedy styled bonnet which graced her smooth packed hair. She exhibited a sense of comfort and travel confidence as the conductor ushered us down the narrow hallway and into our individual compartments. He would return after dinner, and show us how to lower the seat into a bed.

As the lady settled into the compartment, her young daughter pointed at me and asked her mother if they could go to dinner with the soldier. She replied yes, as she looked at me while, sliding the door closed. She said, "They would be ready to go to the dining car in about an hour if I wanted to join them." I responded with a wave of my hand and walked past and closed my door.

Finally, alone in my compartment, I sorted through my satchel bag for writing items and civilian clothes. I stored my bath soap, shampoo, toothpaste, and civilian clothes. Wearing my civilian clothes would be optional on the train, for dining or sitting in my compartment. I took them out, and placed them in the small wall closet for these occasions. However, my choice was to wear military attire at all times on the train.

I turned on the night light in the dimly lit compartment and searched through the magazines stored in the vertical rack and upright shelves beside the layered curtain window.

The train made a crunching sound. It moved back and forth with a bouncing motion as the engineer completed the final coupling of the passenger and dining cars on the track.

I could feel the forward movement and watched the terminal walls move past my window as the train pulled slowly out of the terminal through an array rail signals with blinking lights and into the cloudy gray afternoon. Soon we were speeding through the northern suburbs of DC, and into the rural pictorial countryside. There had been no new news or newspapers in Union Station. I purchased a recent copy of the *Kinsey Report* and a *Time Magazine* for the trip.

From my window, I could see fence rows and backs of wooden framed houses darting by, and evaporating into the steam and diesel smoke flaring from the locomotive engine. The sunlight was beginning to fade, and I could see street lights coming on. The train blasted its horn, and we made our way through small piedmont towns and villages. I could see a flat river basin, as the train moved like a slow trolley car around a dark gravel bed before heading up a steep incline to a high metal trestle bridge. It rattled and rumble beneath the steel wheels and seemed to cry out in the night, as we steamed deeper into the western Virginia dark winter sky.

I tried to read some of the magazine, but the dim night light and roughness of the train track made it difficult to keep my eyes on the page. I remembered that I had placed the last card from Jamie in my coat pocket. I took one of the postcards I had bought at Union Station and wrote her a note:

Jamie,

I'm on a train heading west and hopefully you will receive this sometime after I have arrived in California.

I was shocked by the news about President Kennedy. I'm sure you are nervous and worried about the future also. I miss you and enjoyed our time together.

You will need to write to me at my new address, once I arrive in California. For now, I want to enclose a poem I wrote just today. Write back and send me some of your poems and songs.

I think Vic and Marianne would like to have you back again at Nico's in Alexandria.

I don't know if I told you, but Fort Ord is near Monterey, California. They are hosting the Monterey Folk Music Festival next spring. I will send you some information. I think your Patsy Cline impersonation and folk-style poems and singing, would be a big hit back home and in Monterey.

Stay well, take your medicine, and get stronger
I plan not to forget you
Love Always, Wade

Dinner with Connie and Pam

I heard a tap on my door and a voice say, "Mr. Dhamner, are you ready to go the dining car with us?"

It was Connie and her daughter. I joined them in the hall for our four-car walk to the dining car. Pam took my hand and pulled me along, as she told me about her grandfather's cotton farm in Edisto, South Carolina, the tractor that they rode to town, and all the farm workers she knew. In her very precocious manner she named each one, to her mother's approval and lip movement. Not letting my hand go at any time she acted like an experienced train traveler, and pulled me without any fear through the four windy air channel doors between the sleeper cars until we finally arrived at the dining car.

The dining car was full when we arrived at the entry door at 5:10 p.m. It was long and slender with white clothed tables lined along both sides. Church pew benches were bolted to the car's side interior while a chain of perfectly lined chairs filled the aisle.

"There he is again," shouted the young olive-skinned girl I had seen in the ante room.

"Mama, have them sit with us," she gestured, as Connie, Pam and I, made our way along the aisle, and took our seats at their table. The place settings had 3x5 white 'Reserved' cards with a place to write our name. The silverware was wrapped in soft cloth napkins and a glass of ice water greeted us. The porter reached high over our heads and shuffled large leather-bound menus like casino cards into our waiting hands.

I chose chicken. This rendered an "Excellent choice" to me and the others, as they made their selections and returned the menus. We finished dinner quietly and went to our compartments for sleep. I was tired, but I stayed awake in my room to read and wrote more letters home and to Jamie.

The next day passed quickly after a light breakfast. I read and visited the vending machines for snacks and coffee back in my compartment. I enjoyed looking out the window and taking pictures of the changing landscape of rolling hills, bridges crossing rivers, and endless small towns that displayed signs with tributes to the late President Kennedy. At five o'clock, the porter tapped on the door and reminded me of my dinner reservations at 5:40 p.m.

As we assembled in the dinner car, I noticed that both Connie and Pam were wearing heavy knit shawls and matching blue saffron dresses, with an embroidered cotton blossom on the right lapel. Noticing my stare, Pamela told everyone that "Mama makes all of our clothes. The cotton blossom is the family's English crest symbol. Our ancestors settled in America in the 1700's and have been cotton growers ever since."

"Pam, don't tell all of our family secrets," Connie chided, as she motioned for the bread tray. She asked everyone to tell her something about themselves and why they were traveling on the train to California. As we talked, our porters removed the stainless steel covers from the lead weighted china to reveal bread, turkey and dressing. He dished up mashed potatoes and gravy, served with sides of green beans, peas and carrots. We were given ample bread with butter and jellies and jams. Desserts would come later. The water and tea glasses were constantly replenished.

Without explanation, Connie closed her hands over her plate as Pam mimicked her. The gathering around the table did the same. *"Lord, we are blessed. Thank you for this food and this time together. Be with us, our nation, and our leaders during these troubled times. Grant us mercy, in Love we pray, Amen."* As she finished, the rhythm of silver and plates joined in a symphony of celebration as we enjoyed the meal.

Connie had spent the better part of her summer with her aging mother on the Edisto River north of Charleston, South Carolina. They had been away since May. As she talked, she kept tucking a powdered handkerchief in the top of her blouse after patting her cheeks and neck. The aroma of fresh aromatic lavender drifted across the table during dinner.

She was a skilled conversationalist, and before the meal was over, she had engaged every member at the table with her sweet tea southern voice, her sharp laugh, and occasional "bless your heart," response to the most mundane or trite comment or opinion. Even an off-colored sexual innuendo from a salesman at the table received only a gentle glance, as she continued to engage everyone around the table.

"Wade, I understand you are traveling to your next station in California. You will need to stay in touch with my husband and me. We would like to have you visit us during Christmas."

I responded with a "Thank You!" as the young teenage girl sitting with her grandparents seized the opportunity to say, "You can visit us also anytime," with a loud embarrassed giggle, while pushing another mouthful of mashed potatoes between her massive lips and rolling her eyes at me.

"You better watch out for that one and don't be inviting him everywhere," Connie said in a playful scolding voice, as she reached across the table, and touched the grandmother's arm.

"She must be a real blessing to you both. Is this your first train ride across the country with a child?"

"I'm no child. I'm Teresa. I will be sixteen in December." She said with a smirk, as her grandmother assured Connie that she did not mean anything by her comment.

"Yes, this dear sweet child lost her mother and father last year in a car accident. We are taking her to San Jose to live with us. She is a junior and should finish high school next year. She can be a little trying at times, but she has been through a lot."

"Teresa, why don't you and I take Pamela to the observation car," I said.

"Can I go mama?" She begged as Teresa and I took her hand, and headed for the observation car and to find a comfortable seat before the adults arrived.

"She's a real....."

"Okay, Teresa" I interrupted, pointing at Pamela jumping from seat to seat so she could save one for her mother.

"Hey sit with me." Teresa said. "I want to give you my address. I hope you will write to me. It's a retirement community, so I won't have many friends."

She finished the address and Connie, the grandparents and a well-dressed gentleman in a navy blue suit, bright red tie and silver cuff links, encircled us on the sofa seat. As coffee was served they talked about the shocking news and what they thought it meant.

Connie leaned over and whispered in my ear "You better watch that one there. She's asking for trouble and a sex pot to boot. I wouldn't be surprised if she isn't pregnant before next summer..."

"Connie, I told her I had a girlfriend, but just ..."

She was going to make another comment, when a man in a blue pin-stripped suit, leaned over and offered her his cigarette case. "No thanks, my husband smokes. I like the smell of a good cigarette but haven't developed a taste for them myself," she responded. She waved her hands in approval as she told us how much she had missed her husband.

"He'd be sitting on the porch about now. He had probably been eating out most of the time. He went to work early this morning, building houses and setting up the plumbing codes in Tiburon. I call and talk with him by phone once a week. It's been a long time since May", she said softly and turned her head to look out the window and watch the dark velvet sky pass by.

Later in my room, I made a few notes regarding dinner, Connie's conversations, and the distant lights passing by from cities and towns, outside the observation car windows, as we continued to make our way west.

Train to Chicago

A porter poked his head in my door, and told me the dining services were available in the upper car, and a seat had been secured for me.

Sitting in my compartment, I wondered what was happening outside my windowed world, where fence rows, cattle barns, and backs of grey soot-stained framed houses whistled by in the vaporized steam and diesel dust. A huge banner, THE PRESIDENT OF THE UNITED STATES SHOT DEAD, flapped in the November chill between signal light poles. We slowly moved up a slight grade on the outskirts of town, and I saluted out the window to a flag draped at half-mast in a city park. Other white canvas banners hung from second story tenement buildings, and along iron fences near confederate and union cemeteries, as the train maneuvered carefully through a slow-down zone.

Then the engines picked up momentum, and we were once again gliding effortlessly over hills, downhill grades, and more rolling hills. Just before the afternoon sunlight started to fade, I saw prairie grass along the tracks and shadows of car lights on highways in the distance. There were dim lights in houses on high sloping hills. The outline of city buildings danced across the darkening sky, as they came to life, and car lights streaked down its arteries and avenues.

We crossed over a high trestle bridge, and a flat river basin, with coal barges and scrap metal boats floating south on the Ohio River to smelting mills. We traversed a dark gravel pit with flat rail cars waiting to be loaded, before pushing again across another metal trestle bridge. It also rattled and thundered, as we steamed into a darkening West Virginia sky, and Ohio-Kentucky night.

The dining car was full when I arrived after passing through the four air channel doors between sleeper cars.

"There he is again. Mother, it's the soldier. Have him sit with us." shouted Pam, as I made my way to the only place available at the table. A porter reached around my right shoulder and opened a large menu on the table, featuring the four dinners available for the evening. I pointed to the fried chicken, again, and he told me it was an excellent choice again.

Outside the diner windows, houses, buildings, light poles and street lights sped by in cadence to heavy, steel wheels skip tracing on the rails beneath us. Inside, the diner was alive with subdued chatter about the shooting. There was a lot of confident speculation about what it might mean to us. No one seemed to know any details, but everyone spoke fearfully in foreboding silence about the future of America.

"We'll be in Chicago early in the morning for a layover, and can learn more about the shooting," Connie said, as others nodded in approval.

She made an excellent table moderator, asking each of us around the table, to tell something about his or her families and where they were going. She started with me again, and time quickly passed at the table. She finished by telling us about her family in Summerville, South Carolina. She and her daughter had spent the entire summer and early fall with family.

Her family had grown cotton for three generations and owned most of the valley on the Etowah River. They were headed home to Northern California, where her husband, Ray, was a general contractor and plumber.

The evening dinner ended with each of us promising to gather again on the next evening to continue our conversations.

After dinner, I was still restless, and walked the entire length of the train. The air was cold, and the winter wind blew hard against the collar of my overcoat, as I made my way from car to car. I knew that pushing through the connecting air pressure doorways of the passenger cars would not be easy, but I needed the exercise.

The cold November night whipped up my legs from the rails below. Black rubber air-lock bellows walls pushed me back and forth through the connecting doors, testing my balance as the train snaked along gentle ridges, ocean waves of sand hills, and curved trails leading west into the winter night. Along the way, train workmen and porters oiled hinges, swept floors, stacked food trays, and washed windows.

On the ground along the tracks, I could see an army of workmen switching 90-foot steel rails for safe passage and checking cross-ties and graveled grades for efficiency and safety, as the Great Northern and Ohio train made its way across the American landscape on a cold and chilly night before Thanksgiving.

It took me about thirty-minutes to make it to the last car and back to my compartment. It was ten o'clock. The darkness now totally surrounded the train. The darkness outside my compartment window was penetrated occasionally by a bright reflecting and rotating light, on a passing freight train plunging through the night sky.

On the train, passengers were insulated from the sad drama in Dallas and in the Capitol. Just as we were being swept along these westward tracks, a whole population was being driven through a cascade of media events that would change them forever. The darkness in the compartment stole the night from me. I drifted into a dreamless sleep until 5:30 am, when the train surged forward with three newly connected diesel engines for the final miles into Chicago.

Breakfast in Chicago

Before heading to the breakfast, I sat alone in my compartment and watched the flat-treeless terrain gliding past the window; brown and vanilla gray through the telephoto lense of my Pentax camera. Then, making my way down the hall to the door of the dining car, my ears and eyes were greeted with the morning clatter of silverware on cloth tables, white porcelain cups steaming with fresh brewed coffee, and platters piled high with eggs, bacon, toast and butter. The room was alive with people drinking, eating and talking over morning papers that read:

"PRESIDENT KILLED IN DALLAS!"

I was half-way through breakfast when a captain and sergeant tapped me on the shoulder and invited me to the back of the dining car, where six other uniformed marines and soldiers were waiting.

The captain and the porter escorted us to the railway platform where we assembled into a 22 member uniformed garrison patrol, as the captain stepped in front of us.

"Gentlemen, you will report to the Chicago Rail Transit Station central dispatch office at 0900, for duty assignments during our six-hour layover in Chicago. All of your personal belongings and papers will remain on the train. The station police and security officers are doing a routine check of the rail lines and switching stations. We are in a Level One alert due to the current national crisis, and the local authorities have asked for our assistance. You will each be issued a military weapon and a temporary guard assignment. This is not a drill, but we do not want to alarm any civilian passengers, so go about your assignment with vigilance and calmness. You will return to the central dispatch office promptly at 1300 hours to return your weapons and continue on your travel west. All of your questions will be addressed by the Director of Security, and me, National Guard Commander for the Chicago Metro Area, when we are all assembled at 0900 hours.

At the assembly area, we were assigned to walk a perimeter patrol around the station, with a local officer or national guard military MP, to make visual inspections of rail lines and switching devices, and report any suspicious activity or persons to the local authorities.

As I walked along with Sergeant Napier with the local reserve unit, he told me that the *Chicago Tribune* had reported that major rail systems and airports were demonstrating strict security vigilance during the weekend, in the event there was more than the Dallas operatives involved. His unit had been on full alert since the first news reports, and a sense of uncertainty was prevalent throughout the nation.

He understood that this was new to me, since news was limited on the train. He was sure that calm would prevail as soon as the new President addressed the nation tonight, and we could return to our regular assignments.

We found no concerns as we patrolled the station, but noticed that passengers in the station were watching and wondering about our patrol. As we made periodic stops along the some four miles of station tracks, other patrol units could be seen doing similar inspections.

At noon, an 'all clear' signal was passed along to the patrol units, and we made our way to the dispatch office. Passengers were either on the train or making their way to the platform for boarding. Connie met me on the platform: "What's going on? The whole train station is swarming with police, security guards and your group of armed soldiers walking along the tracks. We had a station porter and security guard walk the length of the train before the order was given for passenger boarding. It was a little scary. I read the reports in the newspaper, and it seemed like the government was taking no chances during this time following the assassination. We will not hear or see the President's speech tonight, but I plan to call Ray and make sure he does. Anything I need to know?"

"No. It was just a routine patrol. A little unusual, but these are not usual times. I called home and talked with my folks. My girlfriend, Jamie, and her grandmother plan to watch the news tonight, and let me know what's going on. They are very nervous and saddened. There is a lot of speculation about the shooter. He is to be arraigned in the morning in downtown Dallas. I received a telegram from Fort Ord that they expect me to report for duty in three days. Otherwise, 'we soldier on' as my father would say."

I could not repeat what had been discussed with me regarding the station patrol, news from the Capital, or the military alert that would remain in effect, even as we left the station. According to the Captain and Sergeant Napier, there were many reports in the major newspapers across the country, that possibly Lee Harvey Oswald had not acted alone, and that some police officers and pedestrians had been injured in Dallas. It was a dark time, and the most reliable and credible news was coming from Walter Cronkite and his news staff. Security was very tight around Washington, and air surveillance and patrols were stepped up along all American coastlines, and in major metropolitan transit systems like Chicago. More would be known, once we arrived in Oakland and I went on to my duty assignment at Fort Ord.

City of San Francisco

After Chicago, we headed across the plains on 'The City of San Francisco' through the Rockies and desert flatlands, until we crossed into Nevada the Sierra Nevada-California Mountain, loomed high ahead of the train.

As the train started up the Sierras Mountains, the strain on the four forward diesels and two aft engines could be felt by all of the passengers. The vibration of the windows and scraping sound of the wheels against the rails could be heard by all as we passed over deep ravines and sandy slopes that cascaded down glacial ridges from some 10,000 feet above.

I went to the observation deck to watch the red auburn sunrise reflect off of the sides of 'City of San Francisco' locomotives twisting and turning through the high rocky canyons. Brown cactus hills turns sandy gray and gold in the morning brilliance of an eastern sunrise, as it pushed its dusty fingers up the high mountain meadows, on its journey across the plains to become a California sunset over the Pacific.

"Good morning stranger," said a voice behind me, as Connie offered me a fresh brewed coffee. "I get restless in the mornings, and like to sit on the porch sipping my coffee as I watch the hills around our Petaluma home turn green in winter and gold brown in summer. But I want you to tell me more about your family and what they think of your being seventeen, in the army, and far from home."

"Well, Connie we have a small farm and my father works for DuPont in Waynesboro and Richmond. He's on a construction crew. He leaves on Sunday evening, and returns every Friday night. Most of the farm work was done by me, my brothers and my mother. It's hard work and hot in the summer. We raise pigs, chickens, and fourteen milk cows. We sell the milk and about 20 dozen eggs a week to local stores. We cut our own firewood in winter. I hunt and fish for extra food on special occasions.

There wasn't much in our house to distinguish us from the other farming neighbors--whether black or white. We had a spring at the bottom of the hill, below the garden, where I fetched fresh water every afternoon after school. Last year my father had a well dug--it was 90 feet deep, and it always had iron rust floating in it, when hand-pumped from the well in the front yard. It settled to the bottom and rusted most of our zinc buckets.

I learned to squirrel hunt with my older brother when I was in the 5th grade. I always oiled and cleaned my 22 rifle after every hunt, and hung it on two 20 penny nails over the kitchen door. I speak broken southern English because I was seldom corrected, except by my grandmother, who liked for me to say 'House' instead of the Germanic 'haus' spoken by other relatives and neighbors. She had lived in Baltimore and Washington DC with my grandfather, during the war, and that's how they pronounced it, she'd say.

In summers, we mostly ate from the garden. We never had candy unless my mother made a plate of chocolate. We cut wood by hand with a crosscut saw, and stacked it by the south side of the house. My clothes were mostly 'hand-me-downs' or ordered from the Sears Roebuck catalog. My family doesn't have much money. I saved $450.00 from my summer work and army pay, and plan to start a savings account when I arrive at Fort Ord. My parents signed for me to join the army. I plan to send money home when I can. It's going to be hard on them. I did most everything, but there's no way to make a living there. Work is scarce, except for farming and part-time work in the next county over the mountains."

I stopped because of was tired of hearing myself talk and asked her, "What about you?"

"Pamela and I look forward to getting home. We had some illness in the family. That's over now. I probably won't go back for two years or so," she went on, as I watched her eyes sparkle in the morning sun. Her freckled, tanned face glowed in the morning reflection from the sky-view window. Her emerald eyes squinted at times, as she looked farther ahead, as if something caught her attention, then disappeared in the distant morning snow.

Then, there was silence in the car, as the engines of City of San Francisco snaked their way through steep rock canyons with swift turns to the left, and hard rights up inclines to the high Sierras.

It was 7:20 a.m. when we reached the summit and the train slowed to a crawl, as if taking a breath from exhaustion, and then paused on the tracks, with an announcement to passengers of the vistas and scenic overlooks.

Connie pointed left beyond the blue haze to the horizon, to the crimson and peach colors of Half Dome, in the distant Yosemite National Park.

"It looks like an upside-down tea cup in the morning sun. Ray and I spent our honeymoon there ten years ago. We climbed the gorge. We swam in the Mimosa River.

You need to go there someday. It's a beautiful place. Hot in the summer though," she said, as she extended an invitation for us all to go to breakfast in the dining car.

Arrival in Oakland

The trained lurched forward in the dark, leaving our passenger cars on a side track until 6:00 am. The porter woke for breakfast those of us who were departing by bus for the San Francisco Coastal train line across the Oakland Bay Bridge. Connie and Pam would be picked up at the train terminal gate by Ray, her husband, for the short drive back to Petaluma. She gave me their phone number and address to call them once I was settled at the base. They offered me Christmas at their house, since I had no family I could visit.

The coastal train from San Francisco stopped at the main gate of Fort Ord at two o'clock. I threw my heavy duffle bag over my shoulder, and walked off the train to the parking lot.

A jeep driver in the parking lot waved a cardboard sign with my name, and signaled for me to get in. I tossed my bag in the back and we stopped at the main gate where my orders were inspected. The guard handed my orders to the driver, and with a salute, backed away and raised the barricade arm for us to pass.

The jeep driver threaded us through a series of back streets and fenced warehouse buildings, until we arrived at a sign: PERMANENT PARTY RECEIVING.

He pointed to the large, two-story green clapboard World War II style building, and told me to go up the stairs and report to the Quarter Master Sergeant.

My nose stiffened at the smell of mothballs, as I entered and walked the length of the dark-gray walled barracks, with freshly waxed and buffed brown linoleum floors. At the end of the large warehouse room, just outside the door, two soldiers sat on footlockers polishing and shining their new, black, combat boots. They looked up at me and said "fresh arrival, Sarg!"

The winter air from the Monterey Bay pushed through the top openings of the high ceiling windows, and the smell of the coal furnace hung in the room like a smoke trail from the Chesapeake and Ohio locomotive, on Afton Mountain back home.

A black and white TV mounted on the wall played and replayed the cadence and caisson music from the Kennedy news that had been broadcast all week. There was a somber mood about the barracks. No one seemed to be talking. Soldiers came in, threw their packs down, lit cigarettes, and immediately found a metal folding chair and watched the parade of news and tributes presented by Walter Cronkite. While watching the news and other soldiers, I was startled by a massive figure that confronted me in front of the Quartermaster compartment door. His hands were on his hips. Without looking at me, he shoved three wool blankets, a fresh bedsheet, and a pillowcase into my chest.

Pointing at a spring-meshed metal cot three rows away, he told me to make up the bunk for the night. "You're shipping up to CEDEC at 0800. Have your duffle bag ready, bed made, and wait." With no more instruction than that, I put my duffle bag on the footlocker, made the bed, and joined the other soldiers in folding chairs, watching the news.

One by one, other soldiers in dress OG green uniforms and full combat gear, joined us at the TV, until a young company clerk with corporal stripes, ordered us to attention by our bunks, and called out names for mess hall duty. My name wasn't called, so I stayed at the TV until mess call at 1700, and then joined everyone else for the half mile march to a meal of steak, green beans, mashed potatoes, and biscuits..

The mess hall was also quiet, and a TV had been brought in to show the news. At 1745, we were ordered back to the receiving barracks for night duties, and lights out at 2100. At 1900, a sergeant in full combat dress ordered us to attention and night patrol duty. We were each assigned a specific wakeup time and barracks walk duty of thirty minutes, until reveille at 0600.

I pulled a 0400 assignment in socks, shorts and t-shirt. My responsibilities included walking the upper and bottom floors of the barrack with a flashlight and lantern, making sure the building was secured at both ends, should soldiers attempt to leave or return after lights out. I was to make sure all cigarette butts were pushed deep in the sand-filled

165

buckets below the red-night lights, at the latrine doors at the top and bottom end of the barracks.

At 0545, one of the recruits whom I had seen polishing his boots, shattered the dark silence by running the length of the barracks and banging the metal cots with a large tin bucket. Everyone was up and rapidly making their beds, shaving, or using the bathroom, before PT exercises in the parking lot at 0610 and breakfast at 0630.

After breakfast, I, along with three other new arrivals, were ordered by the Quarter Master Sergeant to wax and polish the floors in the receiving barracks, scrub the commodes, and clean the shower stalls. At noon I made the walk back to the mess hall for lunch.

I was left alone on my bunk bed to read, until I heard a young soldier enter the barrack and call my name. I was glad to see him and his jeep that would take me to my permanent barrack on CEDEC hill two miles away, high above the receiving barracks and central receiving. I made a point of not visiting the central receiving mess hall again.

First Order

I had just walked into the CEDEC barracks when I was handed a pillow, two wool OG green blankets and an envelope with mail, that had been forwarded to my new APO address at Fort Ord. The last mail I received was on November 21, at Fort Monmouth.

"Don't get too used to this place" shouted the sergeant.

"Since you are from CECOM, you'll transfer to your headquarters barracks within 24 hours. Report to the mess hall at 1900 hours. Your orders will be waiting for you from Major Lasiter, your new company CO for the unit. These orders include, assignments, flight details, lab time, and intelligence meetings and briefings.

That's all I am permitted to say at this time. Your new dispatch orders will come directly from the Major and Sergeant Toms in CEDEC unit. Understood?"

"Yes, Sir Sergeant!"

The headquarters' mess hall was jammed with officers and noncommissioned officers. The menu was chopped steak, mashed potatoes, green beans, wheat rolls, and apple pie. The line was crowded, as a mess hall sergeant barked orders to KP soldiers on duty, and a constant clatter of stainless steel pans, meal trays, silverware, and mumbled conversation blasted across the dining hall. I took a seat at a six-person table between Sergeant-Specialist Richard Edlund, and Mark Cash; both were in full combat training OG green fatigues and flight jackets, with their flight helmet strapped to their backpacks on the floor behind their chairs.

"Just arrived from CECOM?" they said, as they looked around the floor for my equipment.

"Yes."

"Eat fast. Go to the assembly room as soon as you can, and meet with the rest of the intelligence unit. We've been expecting you. From Fort Monmouth, right? Our first flight out this week is in three days, with briefing on return. Major Lasiter is tough and demanding, but always has your back. You'll get everything you need when we meet tonight. If we can answer more questions, let us know." With that, I finished eating, and followed them to the assembly room at the south end of the mess hall.

Waiting for me was Major Lasiter, and a corporal with my backpack, an envelope with insurance forms, papers to be signed, and a copy of the briefing report for the meeting.

"Gentlemen, take your seat," a company clerk announced loudly, as everyone followed orders, and took a seat in one of the straight-back chairs and pushed their backpacks to the floor and under their seats.

We were instructed to keep the manila envelope on our lap with pencils for instructions.

"Atenhuttttt!!!!!!!" Shouted the company clerk, as Major Lasiter marched in with an "At ease, gentlemen. We have a busy week ahead of us. If successful, and we meet our objectives, all of us can take a break this weekend, with minimal duty, as we head into Christmas."

The agenda followed a report of duty assignments completed, and a call to order for four reconnaissance flights over the Pacific to grid marker 4g, 5L and H2, with a return to HQ by Friday. We were instructed to read through the folder and report to unit leaders for 0400 assignments in the morning.

"Dhamner, Constanza, you are with me in the briefing room, now!" shouted the major. "You are both from CECOM, and know the drill for the recon. We leave in an hour. Be in front of CEDEC HQ for your jeep transport to the flight line at the old Monterey County Airfield, for a 2300 departure. That is all."

We stood with, "Yes Sir."

I was shocked by the rapidity of the assignment duty. I thought I would have an orientation, and a couple days to adjust to the base, but I was ready for my first recon photo flight. It would be a training flight for me, but I was expected to step in for Specialist 4th class Lawrence, who had left on medical leave this morning.

We arrived at the air command center just off base, and were immediately ordered to our seats and flight positions, aboard the modified transport C123 that was already going through a preflight checklist. Take off was in 20 minutes, so everyone went through an equipment check, sound check of our head gear, and heard the final announcement of, "prepare for take-off, seatbelts on. You will be able to move about, once we reach 10,000 feet. We will be over water the whole time, so your crew chief will take you through emergency instructions. I am Captain Sam Ull, and your co-pilot for tonight is Lt. Buz Grant. Have a good flight, and see you back on the ground at 0600 hours."

With that, we rolled forward on the runway, lifted up, and made a sharp 90 degree turn right and back left in a 45 degree oblique maneuver over the distant lights of Monterey Bay. Our designated flight grid was 604 nautical miles northwest.

Once we were at 10,000 feet, I went through a K-12 camera positon check for film, setting instructions and reload canisters. From there, my headset was ablaze with internal chatter and specific instructions from the flight deck: "Run cameras now--shut off—wait—run--run again-- increase speed-- reload as needed--ready cameras for low level pass-over—15 seconds-- low level—hold, and hold on to your seats. It may get a little bumpy....."

A stiff westerly wind pushed upward and hard against the massive plane's structure, making film blur a possibility. Otherwise, my training at Fort Monmouth had prepared me well for the filming procedure, plane maneuvers, and the challenges of my first official recon flight. Time passed quickly in the dark, and coffee was a constant companion. I kept check on the time, three turning loops back to base. I filmed six-high speed, 12 inch reels at 200-foot length, and loaded them into metal tubes for delivery and processing at the lab on our return. I strapped into my seatbelt as soon as the rough pavement vibrated beneath the plane as we landed, dispatched our film cartridges, and return to headquarters for debriefing and rest at the barracks. It was Wednesday morning. I arrived Sunday evening. I had already completed my first aerial flight assignment.

A package with a letter from Jamie was waiting for me at the Barracks mail room. *"Happy 18th Birthday" the card*

read. Call me soon! Hope you read the two books enclosed before Christmas.
We need to talk.
I'm coming to California.
Love, Jamie.

Quarantine

It was 0500 on Monday, December 9th, and the CEDEC crew was on their way to Monterey County Airfield for a routine three days out and back in reconnaissance, when Major Lasiter received a phone call to hold off and report back to command center. The recon crew would remain at the airfield hangar until further notice.

He returned to inform us that the entire base was under quarantine for two weeks, or until further notice due to a number of reported meningitis cases among basic training recruits on base. A young child had died, and all base personnel were to return to their barracks or command quarters to begin a regiment of sulfur pills and other anti-biotics. This meant all planned Christmas leaves were canceled until further notice.

I and the three others were transported back to our barracks by jeep, and given strict orders to remain there, except for meals in the mess hall and planned guard duty on base.

I was eligible for six days leave, but had no plans to use it. Instead, I planned to carry them forward to the New Year and apply them to the other days of leave, whether at home or in the area.

The side effects of the pills were cramping, some gastric distress, and a lot of farting. This made for real unpleasant conditions in the barracks, with tape-sealed windows, and heat by coal furnaces.

I was glad there were books in the barracks and Jamie had mailed me her stock of the classics, including books, by J.D. Salinger, Ray Bradbury, Ayn Rand, Jack Kerouac, Allen Ginsberg, John Steinbeck, Aldous Huxley, Herman Wouk, Edna Ferber, Ernest Hemingway, Noel Streatfeild, Betty Friedan, J.E deBecker, Harper Lee, James Michener, and Katherine Ann Porter to name a few.

The quarantine was lifted the 19th of December. Those already planning on a leave were free to go. I pulled double duty with Major Lasiter, and also volunteered twice for KP duties in the mess hall for other soldiers on leave.

I caught a bus on December 27th for a four day visit with the Hershey family north of San Francisco, in a little shoreline town called Petaluma. It was a quick visit; they had a lot of questions about my assignments at Fort Ord, my recent promotion, and my singer-song writer girlfriend back home, whom I had met on the bus to the recruitment station. If she came to California, they wanted to meet her and invite her to sing at their church.

I told Jamie all about the Hershey family and my quarantine experience at Fort Ord, on the daily phone calls the Hershey's let me make as a belated Christmas and birthday gift.

Jamie at the Window, December 1963

It was another Monday morning, and Jamie found herself opening the window drapes to a seven o'clock sun, as she had for the last nine years.

On this morning, she spread her arms wide, touched the side of the window, and stared straight at the morning sun coming up over Brents Mountain Gap. She declared to herself that things had to change.

She looked over her shoulder into the mirror and saw the butterfly tattoo on her shoulder blade reflecting back. She smiled as she reached around and touched it as Wade had, and remembered his gentle kiss on her back as he held her, and promised not to forget her.

For the first time, she accepted herself and decided she wanted more than doctor appointments, sad eyes glancing at her, and songs and poems that only she listened to. She wanted to fly and sing and live. Her life had changed, and her spirit was renewed in a way that was hard to explain, but the social worker and doctors had defined it. She had found someone to love more than she hated herself.

At least she didn't have to catch the bus to the university hospital. She could drive her grandmother's car the 30 miles down Highway 151 to Crozet, and then Highway 250 straight to the hospital. They would be waiting for her at eleven o'clock as always, but she wasn't sure she would go this morning, when her grandmother shouted, "Jamie, you don't want to be late for your appointment. I have breakfast ready for you and packed a sandwich for lunch."

"Grandmother, I don't think I can go today," she said as she slid her feet under the table for breakfast. I have a lot on my mind. Seeing Wade every 4-6 weeks is not enough for me. I miss him. Writing and telephone calls are great, but not enough."

"Oh, child, I was afraid this would happen, but I'm glad. You are so different now. You have stopped hating yourself and wishing for the end. I know it's hard. What do you think Doctor Gamble and the social workers will say?"

"I don't care. I want to go to California, and maybe wherever he goes after that, if he will have me, for as long as I last and don't get sick. I've been thinking, if I use the money I get every month from Granddad's trust, get a job and save money, maybe, just maybe, I can catch a bus and visit him. What do you think?"

"Lord, child, if it makes you happy, and you will be safe; I will help all I can."

"Thank you, Grandmother. I love you and will talk with the doctors and Wade the first chance I get."

"Now eat your breakfast and get ready. You can still make it to Charlottesville by eleven."

Jamie

"Hello, Jamie. I got your letter about coming to California. We have eight quarters worth of time in the pay phone slot for about 12 minutes. I've missed you."

"I miss you too, and want to see you sometime soon. What's the weather like in California? It's getting cold here in the mountains and will start to snow tonight."

"It's cold here too in Monterey, but no snow, and some days it gets to 70-75 degrees. What are you thinking?"

"I've saved money, and my grandmother's sister lives in Pacific Grove, California. Her husband is retired from the Navy, and teaches at a place called the 'Presidio' and Santa Cruz College. My grandmother told me about it..."

"Pacific Grove is about 20 miles from the base, and on the ocean."

"What? I thought it would be far away. Now I am really excited. I can catch a bus. I'm afraid to fly and it's expensive. Let me talk to my grandmother. So what's up? Traveling?"

"Some, and I know my schedule better now."

"I read Look Homeward Angel last week and working on Brave New World. This stuff is hard. I don't know how you do it... I read Portrait of an Artist as a Young Man; you are my 'Emma Clery'-- Stephen's beloved, the girl to whom he is fiercely attracted to. I just finished it yesterday. The guys in the barracks really keep after me to read more. I'm reading After Many a Summer Dies the Swan by Aldous Huxley. The guys in my unit say that they wish their girlfriends would read more."

"Hey, say it again. I want to hear it. I want to hear..."

"My girlfriend! I like telling the guys in the barracks about my girlfriend who reads, sings and plays a guitar.

I tell them maybe they can hear you sing someday. What is your grandmother's sister's address? Send it in your next letter. Maybe I'll go by and check it out while you are talking to your grandmother. Do you really think she would let you travel this far?"

"It would be hard for her but I think so....."

(The telephone operator came on the line to let us know we had forty seconds and I should deposit more money.)

"Jamie, I think about you a lot. I miss you, but it's a long ways. I will call next week at the same time, and we can talk more. I....."

"I love you too," she said, as the dial tone came on.

More Books

Sitting cross-legged on my OG green footlocker, I read and re-read lines from the book. It was hard for me to understand what the author was writing about sometimes, as I tried to decipher the words with my Webster's Dictionary: permeate, hermetically, hyperbolic, germane, etc., stared back at me from the acidic pages slowly turning before me.

"You're getting it," said the deep smoke-pipe voice of Richard Edlund, behind the large, pale, hand that grabbed and sweezed my shoulder, just above my PFC stripe and 6th Army combat patch.

I read on.

It was hard. Still, I could feel my sense of confidence and comprehension growing. I had already thumbed through *Red Badge of Courage* by Stephen Crane and *Catch 22* for my next reading.

My daily duties at the base Photographic Lab and Photographic Services were demanding, and the hours with field maneuvers and reconnaissance shoots made for long days and sometimes nights.

I was assigned to the Hunter Leggett Reservation's Jet-24 Props Recon Flight Unit, for practice and experimental flights, short runway take-offs, infrared tree-top fly-overs, and landings in preparation for field deployments of aircraft and camera equipment to destinations in Southeast Asia.

Once a fly-over shoot was made, my job was to remove the large bulky k-12 camera, and process the 100-foot 12 inch wide rolled film in our mobile lab unit, stationed just off the short graveled runway. Conditions in the mobile unit were cramped and hot in the southern California sun, making for short tempers among our three-man crew.

The process from start to finish took about fifty minutes. The processed, dried and re-rolled film would then go to another mobile unit, for review by their intelligence units. Everything, down to the finest details, was recorded for HQ inspection for the next flight. Our objectives were: take off and return in 16 minutes, complete the photographic and interpretation process cycle in less than 40 minutes, and take off again—for a total of 5 flights over three days. When practice was over, three of the developmental planes would be shipped out to the China Sea and other active duty locations.

In between assignments, I read.

Daryl Simms, a draftee from Chicago, and manager of the base lab, liked me and encouraged my reading. He often emerged from our smoke-filled lab with advice. He liked *Profiles in Courage,* by Senator Kennedy. It would have a different meaning he said, now that Kennedy had been shot. He was right. He gave me his first edition copy. Between complaining about his draft notice that brought him to basic at Fort Dix, the cold weather at Fort Ord, his loss of pay, and the small allotment he and his wife received as a former teacher, he gave me a copy of *The Fountainhead,* by Ayn Rand and the *Iliad* and the *Odyssey* by Homer.

It wasn't long before the other soldiers in the barrack invited me to go with them to Crusoe's late at night for pizza, and sometimes beer. Even though the drinking age in California was 21, the guys always poured me a glass to drink. After pizza, we walked along Cannery Row and the Pacific Grove shore, throwing pizza dough in the air for the seagulls. Sometimes, group of young college and high students would walk and talk with us, knowing that we were from the base.

One night, we followed a large crowd as we made our way toward Fishermen's Wharf and the Tides Restaurant. We could hear someone in the crowd say "I know they're in there... Have your camera ready and maybe you can get a shot of them."

"Who?" I asked.

"Richard Burton and Elizabeth Taylor are here filming "The Sandpiper", he said as the crowd erupted in conversation. The two stars raced down the stairs and jumped into a waiting limousine. I got a blurred picture of the top of their heads. I printed it up, sent a copy to Jamie, and gave copies to the other guys in the barracks.

Call to Jamie

"Hello, Jamie this is Wade."

"Hey soldier, what's going on out in California?"

"Not much, been busy. Flew my first night flight... Your letter said we needed to talk... By the way, I have 30 quarters lined up in the phone booth, so we can talk for about 50 minutes. There are two other phone booths, so I think we'll be okay to talk before they knock on the glass door.

"That's funny. I miss you. I can't wait to see you again. My grandmother has been in touch with her sister.

"By the way, Wade, you are talking different. No southern accent. I don't know for sure, but grandmother wrote to her sister, and asked if I could visit.

The doctors think it would be good for me, but Grandmother is concerned about me traveling that far on a bus. I have the money, but don't know if it's ok to visit yet. What's it like there? I watch TV, and hear so much about California. I even found out that Joan Baez and Bob Dylan will be singing at the Monterey Music Festival. What do you think?"

(An operator came on the phone, and asked that I pay 75 cent for three more minutes)

"Jamie, I'm back. Stay on the line, and I will pay the operator so we can talk more... I would like to see you, and I know I can get time off between assignments and travel. I wanted to come home for Christmas, but I don't have leave time built up, or money for the trip.

Some friends I met on the cross-country train have offered me a holiday visit to their home for Christmas, in Petaluma, about 120 miles north of here by bus. Wish I could see you, but..."

"I know. It's hard being here and wanting to be there..." I said. "It's so nice hearing your voice. Let me know as soon as you can about the trip and for how long. I stay pretty busy Monday through Thursday, but most weekends are free..."

(The operator came on the line again, and I put in 4 more quarters)

"Jamie, can you send me some of your songs? I'm reading a lot of books. Read about the movie 'The Sand Piper' that will be filmed here in May or June with Richard Burton and Elizabeth Taylor. The base commander encourages the soldiers here to attend as many town events as possible." I said.

"I know we are almost out of time." Jamie said. *"I love you. I miss you and I will write you another letter this week and let you know what I find out about the trip. Are you getting my mail okay?"*

"Yes, I will watch for your mail and try to find out what my assignment schedule is after Christmas, in case you get a chance to travel here. I can send you something toward your trip if that helps.

"No need, save that for when I get there…
Let's talk again in a week, and maybe I will know.
I love you. Good night…"

The phone went silent, and the operator came on the line and told me I needed to put $1.50 in the phone slot.

Another call

"Hello, Jamie. I'm on a stop, and will have to talk fast…We're doing 'tree top" level photography fly-overs, 90-200 feet, for troop training maneuvers, tank movements, and ground-to-air artillery firings, as a practice assignment for the training project we will be doing in the desert, just outside Fort Bliss near El Paso, Texas. I leave for a special duty assignment in March, and should be back to the base at Ford Ord by April 22nd. Nobody knows what it's about, but it will change a lot of our procedures and flight plans.

I sent you a letter, but wanted to call and talk about your trip to Monterey. I purchased a one way Trailways bus ticket for $62.00 from Charlottesville on Tuesday, January 14th, for an arrival in San Francisco for a transfer to Monterey, California, Friday, January 17th. So, when you get that ticket from me, you'll be all set to go. It's an express bus, and will stop eight times in major cities across the USA. Since it's winter time, they will take a southern route to Barstow, California, and then go north through the San Juaquin Valley to San Francisco. You'll see some pretty country. Maybe you won't be afraid to fly back after the bus ride. It will be fun, and you'll enjoy seeing the country and meeting people on the bus. Maybe you can write some songs about it. I hope this is OK. I am excited about you coming out, but we will have to work around my photography and flight schedule.

Our typical recon flight schedule is Monday-Thursday, and after a debriefing meetings, we are free to go off base, or travel away if we like, and have the money for it. I like Big Sur, Point Lobos, Monterey-Pacific Grove, and of course, San Francisco, which is a two hour bus ride north on Highway 101. I plan to take you there. How are you and what's going on?"

"I finished the counseling appointments, and have the okay to travel from the doctors and my grandmother," she said quickly. "What do I wear? I want to know more about my stay. How often will I see you? I have a million questions. I am reading the Feminine Mystic, and want to talk with you about..."

"Jamie, I love you and have to go now, bye, and we'll talk again soon."

"I love you, too" I heard in the receiver, as I ran for the Huey already in motion on the flight pad.

Letter to Jamie about the Monterey Jazz Music Festival

Dear Jamie, I am finishing this letter on a reconnaissance flight up the Pacific coast. I don't know where we are, but we land for refueling in 20 minutes, and I plan to mail it to you.

You are right about the Monterey Jazz Music Festival. There is a small local one in May, but the big one is in September. Everything is just starting now. I, along with four other soldiers, have volunteered to man the main gate so we can get free tickets. They had a festival last year, and want to make it an annual event.

The town festival planners are excited about Joan Baez maybe making an appearance. We understand she is *staying with friends, just south of Big Sur, and writing a new album for a US tour. There are other big stars, or those wanting to be "big stars" on the playlist. Will find out more.*

I am checking on a place for you to stay, if it doesn't work out with your grandmother's sister. Major Lasiter, my commanding officer, and his girlfriend, live in Seaside, just a couple miles from the base. She is a nurse on the base.

When I told them you were a singer and songwriter, they said they might be able to help you meet Joan Baez if you still want to.

Got to go. We are landing. I miss you terribly and just finished reading Of Mice and Men, and Jane Eyre.

Love, Wade

Call after Quarantine Alert

"Hello, Jamie,
I sent you a letter, but wanted to call as soon as I could. Remember, I told you about the quarantine on the base before Christmas for meningitis. As of February 1st, the base is closing all base housing for relatives, until they can figure out what to do about the concerns that have risen. None of us have been affected, but a young child died just two weeks ago, and the Basic Training Barracks for new recruits will transfer all future trainees to Fort Lewis in Washington State.

I am still leaving for Fort Bliss on March 1st.
A new science research lab is being built here, and everyone is taking shots again, as a precaution.
I am hoping you still want to come, but you need to talk with your grandmother about staying with her in-laws in Pacific Grove.

Let's keep the dates the same.
And there is no real health emergency here for me, or for
you, if you come out. Please reassure your grandmother
of that. Let me know if your trip is still going to happen.
I will be gone for three days, so wait until then, or send me
a telegram or letter once you know something."

"I miss you.
And, I love you, Wade.
I will talk with grandmother."

"I miss you too.
All my love, and love to the family."

California

"Hello Wade, I worked it out.
And guess what? Lilly and her husband, James, own
Crusoe's Pizza in Monterey. Have you heard of it?"
"Yes, the guys and I go there every Thursday night for
pizza and beer, poetry and music. It's great!
Tell me more..."

"She said I can stay with her, until I have to return here
for early spring planting. Grandmother insisted on that.
She and Tom will need me. I ride the planter, and put out
the tobacco. I ride the corn seeder, and make sure each
kernel is spaced and fertilized just right. I'm good with the
tractor for cultivating, and the pigs and chickens love to
hear my singing, when I put out the water and slop in the
mornings..."

"I didn't know you did all that..."

"Yes, and there's more. When she found out I was coming, Lilly asked if I was still singing and playing my guitar. She wants me to sing on Thursday, Friday and Saturday nights for them. They will pay me with pizza, beer, lodging and money. I am so excited. This was meant to be. They have a small one-bedroom garden cottage behind their house, that their daughter used while going to college until she got married and moved to Los Angeles with her husband.

James retired in 1958 from the Navy, and was stationed at San Diego, San Francisco, and Monterey. They bought a home in Pacific Grove and stayed. She's never been back to the Rockfish Valley except for her brother Pat's funeral, about five years ago, but has thoughts about the reunion this August. I plan to keep a journal of my trip for you and write grandmother every day, as I travel across the country."

The phone was quiet.

"Is something wrong?" Wade asked. "No, this just is so new and happening so fast. This place is all I have ever known and I am going to miss it. And, I am a little afraid. I don't want grandmother to get sick or anything while I'm away. I want everything to be alright. I'm doing so well. My health is good and I'm walking everyday, even in the cold and snow. Just finished reading Silas Marner for the tenth time. I love that story."

"It will be okay. You'll see."

"Wade, I'll write soon. All my love. Be safe and careful Bye."

There was a feeling of sadness in the air as she hung up. I couldn't explain it, but wondered if she was telling me everything. Was she ill again? She would tell me in a letter,

I thought. Sometimes Jamie was better at putting things on paper than explaining them on the phone. I would wait and see.

Letter About Seaside

Dear Jamie,

Seaside is a small seaside town, just south of the base on Shore Drive Highway. It's mostly motels, and a gas station. Most of the duplex apartments are rented by soldiers, with wives and children, stationed at the base. There is one Sambo's pancake house, three bars, and a pretty dumpy high rise hotel called the Carlton, where a lot of base soldiers stay with their wives or girlfriends, who visit on weekends or holidays. It's a pretty rundown place, but has a great view of the Monterey Bay and Pacific Ocean on clear days. The clear days don't happen very often in spring and summer, since the fog comes in almost every day, making it pretty cold and dreary.

In winter, the sky is mostly clear, but the winter rains start in December, and goes until March sometimes. This is where Major Lasiter, and his girlfriend Stephanie, have a condo-duplex apartment. It's pretty nice, since a major with flight pay is paid fairly well. I make $109, plus, $40.00 flight pay per month. I could not afford to live off base, but I plan to save my money for you, if we need to get something while you are here.

Jamie, see if you can bring as many of your medical records as possible. Since the hospital deals with a lot of military head trauma, Stephanie wants to set up an appointment for you. She wants to show your records to the internal medicine doctor at her hospital who specializes in kidney and liver diseases. She has arranged for a complete physical and workup for you, if you want, when you arrive.

She and the Major are great people, and I can't wait to introduce you to them. Stephanie is not only a registered nurse, but wants to be a doctor someday. The Major had mentioned this to me, and hoped he can retire in two years, and they can both make permanent plans as a married couple here in Monterey.
Wade

Tuesday, January 14th -17th Bus Trip

Jamie was up late—packing and organizing cloths for the trip. Her grandmother cried with her a little, but kept encouraging her to go and a have great trip.

"Child, you need to get to bed, or you'll sleep through the morning, and the bus will leave without you. I want you to promise to write every day…Write, phone and tell me everything," she said, as she admired Jamie's face and her figure that had matured over the last two summers. She was more confident, and sure of herself than she had ever been.

Ms. Thompson went downstairs and sat at the kitchen, table thinking about all that was happening. Johnathan would have been so happy for this time in Jamie's life. He was so devoted to her, and felt so guilty for raising a son who had caused such pain and anguish in their lives. She knew he blamed himself for being a poor father to Jessie, and maybe the cause of all of his trouble before and after his time in the service.

He wanted to be the father to Jamie that Jesse had never been. He wanted to be the grandfather she would always remember. Wanda missed him. They spent many late nights talking over coffee in the kitchen, after they had tucked Jamie in bed. She had made it her mission in life to be the mother Jamie lost, and the grandmother every granddaughter loves and cherishes.

She remembered fondly how she and Johnathan had held each other close and listened to Jamie's radio playing upstairs. She knew that Jamie had missed so much. This was an adventure of a lifetime. These two were made for each other. She didn't know where this would go, but she wanted to do everything to make her granddaughter happy, even if it meant this trip to California.

Jamie fell asleep at 11:30 p.m. and was up at six o'clock packed, ready to and making coffee and biscuits for breakfast. Ms. Thompson, Tom and Hanna joined and the talk was all about the cold weather, the bus trip, and writing home to tell them about the trip. She had packed one large suitcase, her backpack, and guitar for the trip. Ms. Thompson had bought her a notebook for letter writing, a pack of 4-cent stamps, and box of fifty envelopes. They would leave for the bus station soon.

With one final hug, Ms. Thompson watched Jamie board the bus, as she had so many times before, and waited until she settled in her seat. Jamie was smiling and Ms. Thompson held back the tears of joy she poured out in the pickup truck, before leaving for home, and the long wait until she got the first phone call and letter.

Bus Ride to San Francisco

Grandmother, the first stop was Lexington, Kentucky.
We changed buses after a 45 minute stop, and waited in the lounge. The bus drivers are so nice, and talk to us on a microphone, so we know where we are, and what might be of interest to see. This is so great. I saw a lot of mountains. I'm reading the first book from my collection of six, for the trip. Wrote two songs, and will board soon, to get a seat on the upper deck of the Vista Cruise bus, so I can see everything. I love you and will mail a postcard from Memphis. Our route is Little Rock, Arkansas, Dallas to El Paso, Tucson to Phoenix, Arizona, then San Francisco, and finally to Fort Ord, Monterey. Wade plans to join me at the San Francisco bus station to Fort Ord, California. I'll be sure to sleep and rest as much as I can, and use the wash cloths to bathe when I can in the bus stop restrooms and eat regular meals on the trip. Nothing is going to make me sick, and I plan to enjoy every

minute of the trip. God Bless and will write again, and send lots of postcards with love to you. Wade made me promise to call when I can, so we can talk on the way. This is going to be the best adventure. Love, Jamie.

Memphis, Tennessee

Crossed the Mississippi. It was beautiful and big. The sun was going down, and I took some pictures and hope they come out. Wade promised to develop and print them for me when I get to California. I get pretty tired riding on the bus, and it's hard to sleep with everybody talking and laughing, but it's fun. They have lots of magazines on the bus, and everybody shares, and sometimes people buy newspapers and pass them around. I've been reading about what's going on in Washington DC, with the big march and the civil rights protest. Here on the bus, everybody gets along, and, like me, wants to get to California. Hope everybody's okay there, and will call if I get more time when we stop in Little Rock, Arkansas. God bless you all, and I love you, Grandmother, more than you know.
Jamie

Little Rock, Arkansas

Saw the hills and mountains that they call the Ozarks. Very pretty, green, but not as tall as our mountains. Once we got into Oklahoma, someone said we need to see if we spot some "Okees". Not sure what they look like, but I didn't see any. The country is pretty dry and dreary. The sky is gray and overcast most of the time. The bus driver said that they have a lot of coal-fired textile mills, and that's why the sky is gray. The land is rolling hills, and sometimes gets pretty flat. Not much to take pictures of, but I snap city and town signs as we go by. I wrote another song today after reading an article about closing a school in Alabama or

Mississippi. Not a lot of good news in the paper, so I went back to my books. I'm reading a really hard one that Wade told me he finished --The Fountainhead. I really want to see California. Wade promised that we would walk across the Golden Gate Bridge in San Francisco, if it's not too windy or cold. He told me that Mark Twain said "The coldest winter day he spent was in San Francisco in July." I don't believe that, but we'll see.

God Bless, and will drop this in the mail when we stop.

Texas

Texas went from green trees and grassy fields to desert and cactus bushes. Could see some mountains in the distance, but don't think they will make very good pictures. The sunsets are beautiful. You hardly see a cloud all day, and then they show up bright and brilliant as the sun goes down. I hope Wade put color film in this camera, but I'm not sure.

The Dallas Skyline was pretty, but I got tired and took a nap until we stopped at the bus station. The bus driver said we would have almost two hours. Some people will get off here, and others will come on to fill the seats for the trip to California. We've had about eight different drivers so far, but we stay on the same bus. I like it. I wrote three poems today, but not sure if they are any good. I wasn't too motivated. At this stop I am going to call Wade at the café number he gave me, so we can talk a little bit.

Not sick, and not tired like I was yesterday. I've been drinking a lot of coffee from my thermos, and cookies are holding out pretty good. I smoke a cigarette once in a while, but don't seem to need them as much as I used to. They have a water fountain in the back of the bus near the restroom, and I get a Dixie cup full every time I go the bathroom. It's hard to walk down the aisle and use the restroom, because the bus shakes me back and forth.

Yesterday, I lost my balance and fell into a lady's seat, before I got back to my seat. You and I will have to go on one of these trips someday. The bus driver said Tucson is two hours ahead, and then we head northward for Phoenix. It's still all desert and cactus bushes, but pretty in its own way.
Love, Jamie

Arizona

I like Tucson. Green and pretty and feels like summertime, but no sticky, hot humidity or mosquitos. They do have flies and fruit trees and tomatoes everywhere. Big eighteen wheelers, pass us loaded to the top with juicy red tomatoes. I saw watermelons, cantaloupes, carrots and loads and loads of Texas Pete peppers on a big truck.
Imagine, summertime in February.
Is it snowing there yet? It must be 80-90 degrees here in the daytime, but the bus is air-conditioned, so I can't tell until I step off at the bus stations. They have these big fans all over the bus stations, and I wet my wash cloth real good to stay cool. I put my shorts on, but it got cold on the bus, so I put the long ones back on. Still reading and writing as much as I can. This is really a big country, and it changes every day. I love it. Thank you for letting me go to California. All my love, Jamie.

Las Vegas

We are 50 miles east of Phoenix, Arizona, and the bus driver just told us about the rest of the route to San Francisco. After Phoenix, we head north, and ride across the Hoover Dam to Las Vegas, and stop there for fifty minutes. I can play the slot machines. I have 20 nickels, and I hope

I win. From there we go to Reno, and stop again at Lake Tahoe for an hour. I want to see the Lake. This is still the best trip. I still can't believe I'm doing this. Then, onto San Francisco. I hope you like the picture postcards. Will send more, with all my love, Jamie.

Lake Tahoe

"Greetings from Lake Tahoe" is what the card says. It looks just the like the picture. I didn't win any money, but I like the music. Elvis pictures were everywhere, and all the women had big blond hairdos and smoke Pall Malls. I'm tired, but I would do this all over again. Just called Wade, and he's made a lot of plans for us in San Francisco before we go to Monterey and Fort Ord. I'm taking a nap, so I'll be rested when we finally arrive in San Francisco this afternoon. I bought a magazine about California to read on the bus. I changed my watch three times. I miss you so much, and will try to write every day, while I am here. Love, hugs and kisses, Jamie.

California Arrival

We just came into California, at a town I think the bus driver called State Line and Squaw Valley. He said we would be on route 50 through Donner's Pass, where a lot of 49'ners died in the snow, over the Sierra Mountains, and down into Sacramento, the capital. Then it's about three hours to San Francisco. We'll see the Golden Gate Bridge, and cross the San Francisco Bay, before arriving at the Folsom Street bus station. It's beautiful and green everywhere here. This is the rainy season for California, but they are having a drought, and not much rain. I see what they call aqueducts filled with water from the snow melt, in the high Sierras. Finished four books so far, and still writing poetry every day. I dream a lot when I go to sleep. The noise on the bus doesn't seem to bother me like it did at the start. There are no little children on the bus. We do have a lady with a baby. He is a really good baby, and hardly ever cries.

I did get to talk with Wade, and he is riding a bus to the San Francisco station, so we can ride to Monterey together. He told me the bus usually stays on the Interstate 101, but the bus driver will be able to make the slight detour to the sea coast highway, and take us straight to the Monterey bus station near Fort Ord. I am so happy. This is a dream come true. I played my guitar for the baby today, and everybody on the bus liked it. I will call and write again when I get there.

Jamie.

Jamie's bus would arrive at 4:30 p.m. Wade had arrived from Fort Ord on the 3:00 p.m. bus. Jamie's bus was scheduled to leave at 8:45 p.m. with a 2:10 a.m. arrival at Monterey Bus Station. Wade didn't know if he could change the ticket but he would talk with the bus dispatcher.

The Scrapbook

My Dearest Wade,

I may get to California before this letter, but I wanted to write it, so you would know more about me. This is my third day on the bus, and I've learned a lot, and I'm having a great time. Met a singer-songwriter headed to Little Rock Arkansas, who cut a record in Nashville. His name was Crash Craddick. I can't wait to see you.

I've been reading an old Bible and scrapbook Grandmother gave me for the trip. Here's what I learned: My older brother was born in 1939, and I was born in October 19, 1944. My parents' names were Mary Catherine and Jesse Lee Marshall. They were first cousins when they married. The family was against it, but Mary Catherine was pregnant..

My father drank, beat my mother, and after returning from the war, he was abusive to my older brother. He beat him and blamed him for everything that went wrong in his life. He worked the farm, but could not keep a steady job, because of his temper and drinking.
According to my grandmother's notes in the scrapbook and the Bible, he was never the same after he returned home.
I was conceived on one of his furloughs home during the war. My mother was very kind, loving and pretty. She dropped out of school in the seventh grade. She was talented, played the guitar, and wrote sad songs. I have some of them. She must have had a pretty voice and sang solos in church. Her favorite song was, "Morning Has Broken."

There are lots of pictures in the old Bible, showing my father with bottles of whiskey, playing cards and gambling, and hugging my mother. In one picture, she has a black eye and a broken nose. My grandmother wrote that he called her a 'whore' all the time, and said she was not a good wife. I don't believe it. She loved me.

On the night of the fire, he was drunk and beat my mother after having sex with her, and hit my brother with a metal pipe when he went into the bedroom where he heard mother screaming. He wanted to protect her. My father hid the pipe under the bed when he chased Jesse out.

Jesse went back later when my father went to sleep and saw my mother's face and head was covered with blood. Jesse was convinced she was dead, and our father had killed her. He took the pipe and hit my father in the head shouting "damn you, damn you" and poured gasoline and kerosene all over him and the bed, and struck a match and threw it on the bed, and it burst into flames and soon engulfed the room. He tried to get back to my mother, but could not. I was told later that they both perished in the flames.

I walked into the hall. Jesse was yelling and talking to himself "I killed the son of a bitch. He killed mama. I hope he burns in hell. I hate him. And damn her for staying with him, and letting him beat me all the time. I'm going to hell!"

The fire was scorching hot, and I fell on the floor when Jesse came down the hall. The whole room and front of the house was engulfed in flames. I could smell the gasoline fumes and rags burning. I was coughing, and couldn't get my breath, when he came down the hall yelling for me to go back. I was very scared, and he grabbed me, broke the window outside of my bedroom, and hit me on my back and legs with the pipe as he pushed me through the broken window in the hall. I have no memory of anything else until

I woke up in the hospital three days later. I was told that Jesse ran away, and was never seen again.

According to a yellowing newspaper clipping, pushed into the deep fold of the scrapbook, he was shot by Sheriff Baker and his deputies in an old barn on Brent's Mountain, when he threatened them with a shotgun. I don't know if this is true or not. This is the first details I have ever known about the events of the night.

I feel so ashamed. So much was kept from me after the fire. I stayed in the hospital, and eventually returned to my grandparents' home. I wanted you to know. I have also sent a letter to Grandmother asking for more information. She and Grandfather loved me so. I know they did everything to protect me.

I love you and look forward to seeing you soon.

January, 1964

From *Journeying the Sixties* by William Cook Haigwood

It was January, 1964, and America was on the brink of a cultural upheaval. In less than a month, the Beatles would land at JFK for the first time, providing an outlet for the hormonal enthusiasms of teenage girls everywhere. The previous spring, Betty Friedan had published, *The Feminine Mystique,* giving voice to the languor of middle-class housewives, and kick-starting a second-wave of feminism already in the process. In much of the country, the Pill was still only available to married women, but it had nonetheless become a symbol of a new, freewheeling sexuality. And in the offices of Time Magazine, at least one writer was none too happy about it. The United States was undergoing an ethical revolution, the magazine argued in an un-bylined 5000-word cover essay, which had left young people morally at sea.

The article depicted a nation awash in sex: in its pop music and on the Broadway stage, in the literature of writers like Norman Mailer and Henry Miller, and in the look-but-don't-touch boudoir of the Playboy Club, which had opened four years earlier.

"Greeks who have grown up with the memory of Aphrodite can only gape at the American goddess, silken and seminude, in a million advertisements," the magazine declared.

But of greatest concern was the "revolution of social mores," the article described, which meant that sexual morality, once fixed and overbearing, was now "private and relative" – a matter of individual interpretation. Sex was no longer a source of consternation, but a cause for celebration; its presence is not what makes a person morally suspect, but rather its absence.

Letter from Lilly

Dear Wanda,

I hope all the family is well. The weather here has been unusually mild for winter. We've had some rain, but not cold like it usually is.

James and I met Jamie's young soldier yesterday, and I promised him I would write you about a possible visit for Jamie out here in January or February.

We would be delighted to see her. I wish you could make the trip too. We don't travel much anymore, with James teaching and both of us running our pizza business. It keeps us busy.

Wade told us all about his family and how he and Jamie met on the bus. James took an immediate liking to him, and if you know James, this is rare. He was really tough on our daughters' dates when they were teenagers, and even chased one off for staying too long one Saturday night.

James and I work on Thursday and Friday nights at our pizza parlor in Monterey, just two miles from the house. We have plenty of room without the kids. It gets kind of lonely sometimes. They come home maybe every two or three months, and sometimes longer.

James built a single bedroom garden cottage in the back yard, for the girls some years ago, and it stays empty most of the time. It's decorated really nice, and sometimes I store our extra clothes in the closet. She would be welcome to the bedroom in the house, or if she prefers, the cottage is there for her to use.

If she's still singing and playing her guitar, I could let her play and sing at Crusoe's some nights. James has helped a couple of our poets and singers launch their careers. No body real big, but they have all participated in our little Monterey Music Festival every year. It's been growing and has attracted celebrities from all over the west coast. This could be an opportunity for Jamie if she's interested.

As for the young soldier, he reminds me a lot of James when we first met. James even told me that he could be "officer" material if he wanted to be; mature, sharp dresser and reads a lot. I understand that Jamie has been a big influence on him. He didn't tell us much more about his family, but I remember the Dhamners and Damerons from growing up. Are they the same family? Some were from Schuyler, Waynesboro and Nellysford.

When you get this letter, call me.
I love you and miss you terribly.

Lilly

San Francisco Arrival

I looked up into the bus and watched Jamie slowly move toward the front. She was excited. I knew she probably had talked to everyone on the express bus across the country; over four nights and five days of riding, sleeping, eating small meals and snacks. She had a tired look, but excited smile on her face, when she finally jumped down the bus steps into my arms.

She kept squeezing my neck and talking about the trip.
"I have six new poems that I think will make good songs; two are about you, and the rest are about home. I am feeling so much better these days. I've gained 10 pounds since I saw you last, and now weigh 114 she said into my ear.

"What am I doing talking my head off again? You must think I'm an idiot. I smell like nicotine, coffee and sweat. My guitar got banged up a little when I dropped it on the bus. I slept a lot, and I am so excited to be here with you..."

"Jamie, I love you. You're here and you're okay." I said, holding her while we waited for her suitcase and backpack.

"What are we doing? Don't we have to get back on this bus and leave?"

"No! I made a change. We will catch a bus Sunday afternoon to Fort Ord. Stephanie and Major Lasiter will take you to your aunt Lilly's at Pacific Grove. How does that sound?"

"I love it," She said, as she hugged my arm and put her guitar over her shoulder.

"In the morning, we're taking a sight-seeing trip, and catching another bus through and around San Francisco, and across the Golden Gate Bridge, to a town called Petaluma, where Connie and Ray Hershey live. She's the lady I met on the train traveling out here. They have a four year-old daughter that you will love. I spent time with them during Christmas, and they have become my second family. They really want to meet you and hear you sing."

"I remember you telling me about them. Is this really happening? I'm in San Francisco! You are here and we're together. I can't wait to see the town and meet them tomorrow…So, where are we staying tonight?"

"I've taken care of it. There's Howard Johnson Motel just four blocks from the bus station, and we can get you cleaned up, and rested for your trip tomorrow. They have a restaurant, and we can have dinner together and catch up on your trip and home. We'll catch the bus back here, for our trip to Monterey on Sunday afternoon."

"I love you, soldier boy, but can we get something to eat first? I'm starved."

I hailed a cab to the hotel, where I picked up the keys; and put all of her luggage and guitar in the room. I met her back in the lobby, so we could get something to eat. When I returned, she was already at one of the tables in the restaurant, with two hamburgers, fries, a side salad, and drinks for us, and waving at me to come on in.

"It's so good to just sit and know I don't have to catch another bus right away. I missed you," she said, as she gave me a kiss that tasted of catsup and relish.

"I started eating before you got here. I told you I was starving," she said, as we looked at each other, and she told about her trip, her poems, the new songs she had written, and the scary feelings she had about being in California, and meeting the Hersheys.

"I never met many people outside of the Rockfish Valley. This is our first time together, just the two of us.
I don't want to disappoint you, or act stupid or anything around your friends."

"Jamie, we'll take it a step at a time, together. Everyone is going to love you, as I do. Tell me about home."

"Grandmother cried a lot when I left. I want to call her

tonight, if it's okay. I sent her a post every day. Did you get my letter that I sent while traveling?"

"Yes, I got it yesterday, and Jamie, I am so sorry. It must be hard for you to think about all that has happened, and all that was kept from you. It was for the best, and everyone meant well."

"I know, but..."

"No buts, your grandmother would say. How's the food?" I said, trying to keep her spirits upbeat, as she ate and twined her feet around mine under the table. She was nervous. I was nervous too, but I missed her so, and was glad she was here. We would get through this time, just as we had this summer and fall, back home.

"I haven't asked you about anything. I'm sorry. You've been really busy with all your work and assignments on the base and everything."

"Yes, but this is what I have been living for, to see you and show you around and let you meet some people I've come to know, who will appreciate you, and your talents and wonderful spirit."

"I'm ready for that bath and some clean clothes. Can we go? I want to call grandmother too. Okay?" she said, as we left and headed for the room.

Inside the door, she stopped, put her arms around me and asked me to just hold her for a little while. We didn't talk. She just wanted the world to stop for a while, and be held close and kissed. It was an emotional moment for her. I knew she was crying, afraid and unsure of just what to do. This was another experience she had dreamed about, and she wanted it to last for a while. I wanted it to last for her as well.

"Are you okay?"

"I am now! Thank you for being what I need. I'm pretty tired and feel like taking a nap..."

"Oh no you don't," I said, as I guided her away from the bed where she was prepared to dive in and take a nap. "Let me get you out of those clothes and into the shower."

"I like this, and I want to let the water run until I feel clean. You stay here." she said, as she pushed me back with her index finger, backed into the bathroom, and closed the door. I heard the shower running, and her singing a song about the best year of her life... "and it was you who....." she just went on and on, and I found myself laughing and looking forward to talking with her.

I was sitting on one of the double beds when she came out of the bathroom laughing, while wrapping a bathrobe towel tightly around her.. She reached for one of the cookies I had bought in the restaurant.

"Hey, I forgot something," she said, and she put the bag of cookies on the bed, put her arms around my neck, and kissed me with a softness and passion that I wasn't expecting. The kiss was deep, and she pulled me hard against her, saying, "Thank you for loving me more than I deserve. I feel so tired, but I am also so happy to be here with you tonight, rather than riding on a bus again."

"I know."

She smelled so good. We looked at each other and smiled. She placed her hands on my chest and arms, letting them glide to my thighs, as she turned and let me put my hands on her back, letting me softly massage her shoulders and arms with no resistance. I wanted this to go on and on, but I knew she was worried that her grandmother would be expecting a phone call, so I kissed her shoulder and whispered. "It's 6:45 p.m. here and 9:45 back home. I saw a phone booth in the lobby. I have plenty of quarters for us to call your..."

"I love you soldier boy! Let me get dressed, and we'll go call her together," she said, as she jumped back into the bathroom and put on some fresh clothes, and we walked hand in hand to the phone booth.

"Grandmother, I'm here with Wade in San Francisco. I made it. It was a trip of a lifetime, but I miss you so."

"Me too child. I want you to have the best time, and write me all about it, and I can get the rest when you get back. Is Wade there?"

"Yes, Grandma. We're squeezed into this phone booth together."

"I'll take good care of her," I said. "Here she is again."

"We're going to ride across the Golden Gate Bridge tomorrow, and meet some friends of Wade's. They want to hear some of my songs, so I will sing for their church service Sunday morning. I'm famous, and hope they like my music."

"They will. You stay safe and know that we all love you here, and pray for you every day. Give Wade a big hug for me, and call me again when you arrive at Lilly's house. I told her I would pay for your calls, so don't worry about the cost. And, by the way, your sow delivered a litter of 14 piglets, and I will be mailing you a check for $100.00. I love you."

"I love you Grandmother, and thanks for making me so happy." She said, as she placed the phone on the receiver.

"Can we go back to the room, set the alarm, and lay together in the dark and talk and kiss until we go to sleep. I could eat you up. I have missed you so much!"

It was eight o'clock. We playfully, but nervously, went to the bathroom, looked at each other as we brushed our teeth and then promised each other that we would not go too far with our feelings. She made me turn away while she put on a fresh extra-large t-shirt. We turned the room light off and walked slowly hand-in-hand toward the two double beds. We stopped close to her bed. where she pulled me to her and let me caress and kiss her, while she moved her lips to my neck and whispered, "I love you."

I could smell and feel the warm air in the room. I wanted to kiss her and massage her soft back and hips, and run my hands up and down her smooth sides in the dark. She invited me to stay beside her on her bed, as I watched her tired eyes close into a sound sleep.

I woke up and looked at the clock on the nightstand in the moonlit room. It was 1:30 am.

I covered her with the light blanket and moved to my bed. As I watched her breathe, and saw her neck line so smooth, and her lips smiling. I wanted to hold her close, but fell asleep until she slipped into my bed, and nudged me awake at 6:30 am.

"I really liked last night. It's so good to be here with you. I feel so rested and refreshed. I really want you, and I trust you. I know we both want more, but for now, let's wait, and go get that continental breakfast, catch that bus, and see this town" we chimed in together," as we dressed quickly and left the room.

We checked out of the hotel, and walked to the bus station. It was a local bay area bus that made stops and pickups at several locations in-route throughout the city of San Francisco and Lombard Street, just before The Presidio and the Golden Gate Bridge. I pointed out Coit Tower to Jamie, which was built as a memorial to the famous 1906 earthquake and fire, which pretty much destroyed the city and killed a lot of people. Jamie recognized Alcatraz Island, in the distance from post cards she had seen.

We made a stop at Vista Point, on the north end of the bridge, and circled the parking lot to pick up other passengers headed to Mills Valley, Tiberon, Novato, with a final destination at Petaluma Station. Jamie was aglow with a child-like excitement. She wanted to see, feel and touch everything, so she would remember and not forget this great adventure.

Ray and Connie Hershey

Ray Hershey was raised in the Balboa district of San Francisco. He joined the navy at seventeen and learned welding and plumbing as a trade. Together, he and Connie took me into their home on weekends, as if they had known me all my life. I enjoyed their daughter, who called me 'Wadie', since she had trouble pronouncing my name.

He was the most unlikely mentor I would ever meet. He and his wife introduced me to a world of new and lasting friendships in the San Francisco Bay area. A heavy smoker, Navy veteran, and self-proclaimed working-class stiff, he lived a simple, unassuming life. On weekends, and when he needed a 'ditch digger' for his plumbing jobs, he put me to work with his crew, and paid me a dollar per hour for every five feet we dug so he could connect pipe to sewer lines or county water mains for customers.

When he wasn't working or fishing on weekends, we all went to Drakes Bay on the ocean, to picnic and collect Abalone shells. His straight forward philosophy of life is best described in his own words: "Photograph people" he advised. "They will tell you their stories if you listen. You will read books, travel to foreign countries, and hear about fortunes gained and lost. Some people will tell you that you are the smartest person they've ever met. Strange, isn't it? I just mend pipes all day, work my job, and go home in the evening to my wife and family. I'm a happy man. Most of them are not. So, listen, get smart, and live a happy life."

He, Connie and Pam were looking forward to meeting Jamie.

Petaluma

The bus stopped under the overhang at the Petaluma Bus Station, and I spotted Ray's green Nash Rambler parked across the street in front of the A&W Root Beer stand.

"Jamie, we've heard all about you." Connie said. "You must be tired, but you saw a lot of pretty country on that bus traveling here. Get in, and we'll get you to the house and have some lunch. Glad you brought your guitar for some music and singing. Pam has been practicing her 'Old MacDonald', so she can sing it with you."

Lunch was in the backyard, and Jamie felt at home with all the chickens, goats, and rabbits that paraded about as we ate. Pam threw table scraps to the animals. In the afternoon, they took us on a ride around town, and to Sonoma, the County Seat, for ice cream and a view of all the grape vineyards along the scenic Lake View Highway to Napa. We returned along the Petaluma River and the boat harbor basin.

It was late when we returned, and Connie made hot chicken soup with rice and potato cakes. Before bedtime, Jamie played some of her new songs and 'Morning has Broken' as a preview for Connie and her choir the next morning.

Jamie shared Pam's bed for the night, and Ray and I bunked in the barn. We drank one of his home-made beers, and talked about his time in the navy, my army experience at Fort Ord, and the next time I could come visit and work for him. In the morning, everyone was greeted with pancakes, eggs, and coffee, before heading to church and our return to the local bus station and return to San Francisco.

Connie let Jamie call her grandmother again and say hello, so she wouldn't worry about her. It was a short visit, but Connie and Jamie became best friends and she told her to "come back anytime." Ray seemed sad when we left, and made sure I gave him a possible time to return. Pam cried a little, hugged us both, and gave Jamie a drawing of a pretty girl with shiny reddish blonde hair, playing a guitar and singing 'Old MacDonald Had a Farm'.

Once on the bus to San Francisco, Jamie said, "They're really nice. Hope we get to see them again sometime. It was great for Connie to make sandwiches for us. Hold on to me for a little while. I need to take a nap so we can talk all the way to Monterey, after we catch the Bus in San Francisco."

In San Francisco, we caught the 3:10 p.m. bus to Monterey, where Major Lasiter and Stephanie would pick us up. There was no talking on the bus as Jamie fell asleep saying Pam talked and sang all night long. We would talk later, she promised.

Jamie to Monterey

Jamie and I arrived in Monterey at six o'clock. I spotted the major and Stephanie waiting for us in the depot, as they walked out to meet our arriving bus.

"Jamie, I want to introduce you to Stephanie and Major Lasiter, my commanding officer. They want to see you as much I do."

"Welcome to California. You must be tired, but glad to be here," Stephanie said, as she hugged Jamie. They connected immediately.

"This is Ron. He lets me say that when it's just us and no soldiers around. He won't mind. Wade is one of his best recon officers," she said as she winked at me, and I looked away nervously.

"Wade told us we would like you, and we do," said Major Lasiter, as he motioned to me to get Jamie's bags on the carousel. "I like her, and don't worry about the 'Ron' thing. We'll go back to soldiering next Monday. This is the weekend, and I know you want some time together before we take you to Lilly and Thomas' house, first thing in the morning. So let's get something to eat, and plan for the two of you to spend time tonight with us, at the apartment. We'll work out the sleeping arrangements. Stephanie will see to it."

Jamie was tired and excited to be in California. Stephanie and Major Lasiter were so inviting, and let us sit and talk on the back deck once dinner was over.

"Tell me about the army base, and how you and the major work together," she asked.

"We stay busy with reconnaissance and ground support photography. Fort Ord is a major combat training center for warfare and recruit training. There is no big conflict going on right now, but things are brewing, and we work closely with the base photographing and filming training exercises, and live-fire missions. The major is a career officer, and has seen duty in three countries before arriving here in 1961. He met Stephanie about a year ago, and they have been dating and living together for the last six months. I know they have talked about marriage, but the military is difficult on marriage, and separations can be stressful and difficult…and…"

"Hey, it's late and I know you must be tired. You two ready for bed?" Major Lasiter quietly interrupted, holding bed sheets and pillows so we could make our bed on the sofa.

Jamie called Lilly as Stephanie, Major Lasiter and I put the sheets on the large sectional sofa in the living room. She and Ron retired to their bedroom as Jamie and I brushed our teeth and dressed for sleep. We sat and talked together until midnight, but Jamie was fading away, and I was tired as well. We slept soundly together on the sofa, until 7:00 am, when the smell of hot coffee, scrambled eggs and toast, served up by the major, woke everyone up. We ate and listened to Jamie talk about her cross-country trip. By 8:30 am, we were all in the car, headed to Lilly and Thomas' house, as promised, for cinnamon rolls, coffee, and a morning walk on the beach.

Lilly and James Garrett

Lilly Marshall met a young navy ensign, who was home on leave visiting his family. She was always called the adventurous one in the family. She was first to marry, first to move away and first to graduate from college.

James Garrett was handsome, dashing, and had plans for a career in the navy, after graduation from Annapolis. He caught Lilly's eye, and she, his attention. It was love at first sight. They married the following year at Annapolis,

 and left for San Diego and his duty assignment as a 2nd officer, transporting soldiers and sailors to Pearl Harbor. They rented a small beach side cottage, and a love for the sea became their common interest. Lilly was a good wife and raised their three children, while working part-time at a local coffee shop café.

On December 7, 1941, Pearl Harbor was bombed by the Japanese, and second officer James P. Garrett was assigned to Naval Forces, operating out of San Francisco to Pearl Harbor, Midway Island and the South Pacific. During this time, Lilly made a home for their first child, James Jr., and anxiously awaited James's return home when the war was over. Their second child, Sandra, was born on Christmas Eve, 1943, and Faye was born during a Thanksgiving holiday weekend in 1944.

When Japan surrendered, James was a Lt. Commander on the Missouri, and was photographed with General Douglas MacArthur and other dignitaries. He liked showing off the photograph at family gatherings and reunions with old shipmates. He assumed shore patrol duties on the California coast, and they built a three bedroom bungalow on a high beach cliff in Pacific Grove, near Monterey Bay.

After 15 years of service, and the children in middle and high school, he and Lilly discussed their future plans, and he retired in 1958. He took a part-time teaching job at the Presidio Language School in Monterey, and a second part-time instructor's position teaching marine biology, at the new college at Santa Cruz.

Lilly continued to work part-time at various coffee shops while raising the children. In 1960, they discovered she had a real flair for pizza making, raising herbal flowers and plants in her cottage garden, and a knack for making friends with local artists, musicians, and poets. She joined a group of 'mystical gardeners' in the neighborhood, who raised their own alternative medicines and exotic curative vine plants. They cultivated native cannabis seeds in clay pots, and moved them around the neighborhood for occasional herbal parties. These were hosted by Melba, a member of the Feathers of the Rainbow Tribe; her ancestors supposedly had inhabited the Mission Valley Lands at one time.

Their children had always loved 'pizza Thursday' growing up, and constantly told her she needed to start a pizza parlor. Once the children were all older, she and James, on a 'wing and prayer' as they described the venture, followed her passion and opened Crusoe's Pizza Parlor in the Cannery Row section of Monterey.

The concept was simple, and the service was even simpler. James taught class on Monday, Tuesday and Wednesday. He place flyers around the campus and town, for a "free" pitcher of draft Shafer Beer for any party of six, who bought two ,large, 16 inch cheese pizzas. There was always plenty of extra cheese and sour dough knots placed on the tables. They added impromptu poetry readings, and a wooden raised platform for local singers and writers. They believed people came to eat, talk, have fun, and listen. They put up a microphone for the poetry readings, but no amplifiers for guitar players or singers. The business flourished, and soon expanded to a loft, where Lilly added a coffee and donut shop.

James concentrated on teaching at Santa Cruz, and helped Lilly with the pizza parlor on Thursday and Friday nights. He became an ardent follower of Rachel Carson and her books, studies and activist protest rallies on campuses and libraries, about the human destruction of the seas and oceans.

On Thursday, December 12, 1963, Wade made his first trip to Crusoe's with a group of soldiers from the headquarters' barracks at Fort Ord, for two large pizzas and his first mug of draft beer, and a startling introduction to Lilly.

Everyone liked the poetry readers and folk singers who entertained the crowd. Lilly placed an old top hat on the floor, and patrons could throw money in for the poets and singers to split at the end of the evening. Most of the singers gave her the some of the money, in exchange for takeout pizza.

However, on Wade's next visit to Crusoe's, a teacher from Monterey Peninsula College brought a poet who he introduced as Allen. He used poetry with a lot of four lettered words, and animated descriptions of sexual acts. Lilly quickly turned off the microphone and asked him "to leave and not come back. And take your G#!!##d poetry with you."

Lilly was embarrassed and upset as she yelled "who did he think he was, Jesus Christ!" as the customers cheered her on and raised their beer mugs to her. The poet made The San Francisco Chronicle news the next day, and at San Francisco State College, where he read the same poem on the college commons. The San Francisco Chronicle' news columnist, Herb Caen, called Allen Ginsberg 'the king' of the new beat generation.

February

"I like the way you look at me and make me feel like a woman. Especially when all I wear is my t-shirt, cut-off jeans and no bra. I've never had anybody really look at me, or want me," she said, as she turned to look out the cottage window.

"I want to photograph you against the setting sun," I said as she reached high again over her head, spreading her slightly tan arms with palms upward and outward in the bay window.

"I think you like that pose. Where have you seen it?"

"Never seen it, but I have read about it in *The Complete Works of William Shakespeare,* given to me at Christmas a year ago."

"My grandfather loved to read Shakespeare out loud to Grandmother and me. He called it the sonnets of intelligent people".

I remember reading a passage that went something like:

"I am Venus rising. I am Aphrodite's… Wade, I am so in love. I hope you don't mind me saying it out loud with you. This pose makes me want to cradle the sky and sunshine in my arms and hold them tight." as she tried to recite as much as she could remember from the passage. And then, turning half-way toward me, she let the setting sun spray through her long hair, as she looked heavenward and closed her eyes.

"I like this," she said. "I want to see what I look like, once you develop the photographs. This makes me feel like I'm looking out of a cathedral window, and that I am safe. I have never felt as beautiful as when I'm with you.

"Let's walk down to the cliffs and watch the sun fade into the clouds," she said, reaching for her cotton sweater and wind breaker.

"Jamie, it's getting cold. We can only stay a little while and, then, it's back here, okay!"

"Yes, it's okay! I want this to last. I want to feel and remember everything. I want to sing, and write about it," she said, as she playfully pulled me through the front door, across the garden path by Lilly's front window, and across the narrow two-lane road in front of the bungalow.

We sat quickly went to sit in a lava rock cove to get out of the cold, sharp, wind from the ocean. We watched the setting sun and listened to the sea lions on the cliffs in the distant surf.

She bent toward me, pressed her hands down hard on my sides, and kissed me with her eyes closed and lips partially opened. My brain melted like a scented candle, and she notice my arousal with an unforgiving smile.

"I love this" she said as she hugged and caressed my sides under the heavy coat that I had draped over both of us. Without saying anything, she pulled me closer, kissed me and slipped her tongue between my lips. Neither of us wanted to go back to the cottage. We kissed and pulled each other tight, as we listened to the sea gulls overhead, and the waves pounding the surf below. We lost track of time, as the cold wind pushed through our jackets, and against our faces.

"We'll have my aunt Lilly mad at us," she said, sarcastically, if you're the reason I catch a cold out here. We can go back and get some hot coffee, talk, and hold each other as long as we want," she said, as I rubbed her red nose and cheeks in agreement.

"Yes, I see Lilly peeking out the window," I said.

And, she's holding a mug of coffee up for us. Let's go get some."

Back in Lilly's living room, alone, and a fresh cup of coffee warming her hands, Jamie said, "It's hard to believe that you're now eighteen, and I'm 18, but I will be a year older in October. You know me. I talk and read a lot, and I dream about you and me. I hope you don't mind that I'm a tease with you," she said, as I watched her face redden in embarrassment and she looked straight at me.

"Come on, we need to talk about this. I have read so much about making love, the new birth control pills they have just invented, and for the first time, a new women's movement is starting right here in California. We are in the middle of a coming revolution. I know it's hard for you to talk about it. But, I want to tell you what I know, and hope maybe, you'll learn more about it."

I could see Lilly in the kitchen, looking out the front window at the golden clouds, silently drinking her coffee as she closed her eyes and pushed a listening ear to the door, as Jamie continued.

"I have dreams all the time about you and me. Do you dream about us? I know you do. I can tell. I know how we feel about each other. It's difficult to know what to do. Stephanie thinks I need to start taking the pill as insurance; she also thinks it might help my headaches. Will you get mad if I start taking them? I will try not to tease you so much, but I know you like it. I do too. I want to sing you my dream, again, like I did at Nico's, because when we do it, this is what I want it to be like."

"Jamie, I would like that, and hope I can live up your expectations, but..."

"I know, so let me take care of everything, and do all the reading and talking about this for both of us. When I have my first time. I want it to be with you. Here in California, or back home in the cave. It will be our secret. No one will ever know. Promise?"

"Yes."

"And I promise too," I thought I heard Lilly whisper in a low voice through the kitchen door, as Jamie and I sat and held each other, and watched the sun through the side patio window sink into the western clouds.

Letter Home

Grandmother,

It has been a couple of days and we've been really busy here, but I wanted to write and tell you about our trip to San Francisco and the Golden Gate Bridge, and our next trip to Los Angeles and Hollywood.

It gets pretty cold and dreary here in Monterey. It also rains a lot. When I'm not working at Crusoe's, at my medical appointments, or visiting the library, I stay in the cottage and write.

The other night after work, Wade showed me a map of San Francisco and Los Angeles, and said he wanted to take me to both places. Lilly and Thomas agreed, and offered the Volkswagen for the trip, but we decided to take a bus instead. Since we first met on a bus, it's romantic, and doesn't cost a lot. I'm working a lot at Crusoe's and saving my money. Wade always pays for everything, but sometimes lets me buy a meal.

We caught an early morning bus at Fort Ord to San Francisco, on Friday. In San Francisco, we took a city bus that travels all over for $1.00. We could get off and get back on the next bus at any one of 12 stops, in and around the city. I saw the Golden Gate Bridge, and walked a little bit, but it was so cold, we went back and waited for the next bus, which took us to the Embarcadero at the harbor. I've got lots of pictures. We ate fish and shrimp at The Three Brothers' Café, where we watched the fishing boats come in, and unload all kinds of fish for the restaurants.

Wade is checking off all the places I wanted to see.

We caught the bus again, and stopped at the zoo. I fed the guerrillas and the seals. We caught the bus again, and got off at Coit Tower, where we visited the museum of history about the 1906 San Francisco earthquake and fire, that destroyed 80 percent of the city, and killed 3,000 people. It was a very sad time.

From there, we walked to Lombard Street, the crookedest street in the world, before jumping on a cable car with a bunch of other tourists, and went downtown to Market Street. The only reason I know this, is that Wade was telling me, and I wrote down most it for this letter to you.

San Francisco is a beautiful city, but is very cloudy. We couldn't see much, but stayed warm inside the bus and cable car. It was four o'clock by the time we made the last stop, and we walked to the bed and breakfast near our bus station. We talked, and had the best time with all the people we met in the dining room for coffee, wine, cheese, muffins and bagels. I had never had a San Francisco sourdough bagel, but they are delicious with jam and butter. I didn't bring my guitar, and the owner loaned me hers, and they let me sing some old Virginia favorites, and joined me in a few other songs.

Wade is really good with me, and we slept in twin beds and talked most of the night. I am so in love, but I promise, just a lot of kissing and hugging. We joined everyone again at nine in the morning for more coffee, toast, muffins, bagels and juice. It was wonderful. I'm getting to see and do so many things with Wade here in California, but I really miss home.

We caught the eleven o'clock bus back to Monterey, and visited with Lilly and Thomas at the cottage, until Wade had to return to Fort Ord for an early Monday morning briefing, and flight out and over the Pacific Ocean.

He can't tell me anything about what he does. I want to know, but he made me promise I would not ask. I know it's important work, and Grandmother, sometimes, I worry for him. When we are together, all he wants to do is forget about it and spend time with me. I am so happy. Thank you, and I plan to call and write you soon, and to tell you about our next bus trip to Los Angeles and Hollywood.
All my love, Jamie

Talking at The Cottage

"When do you leave for Fort Bliss?" She asked in the dark, afraid to hear that it would be soon.

"We fly there around March 1st and return sometime around the middle of April. It will be a very different duty assignment, and could go longer. Major Lasiter is going to brief us Monday. Our flight crew and I have setup the remote equipment in the planes for the trip. We are ready to take off anytime."

He hesitated and said, "You will have returned home by the time I leave for Fort Bliss, but I want us to plan your next trip here."

"Do you really want me, want me to come back?"

"Yes, I'm working on taking a leave in June, to go back to Virginia, and then return with you for the Monterey Jazz Music Festival here in July or August. We'll need to get your record made for sure, and have it ready to play. We'll need to save our money and make plans with our families. What do you think?"

"I really want that. Grandmother will be thrilled. Can we call her tonight and talk about it?"

"I hope so, but let me check to see if I will be back in time; otherwise, you will just need to talk with her Okay?"

Jamie was so excited. This is what she had hoped for. She was homesick, but afraid to admit it, and wanted to see her family again. She had made her mind up to fly back, and not take the long bus ride again. She worried she would get sick during the flight, but she had a new confidence that was growing every day, with no more doubting and fearing the worst could happen. Living in the moment in California is what she had learned from reading and being with Lilly and Stephanie. They knew so much about wellness, health, and medicine, and had become like sisters and friends to Jamie. It was a wonderful time. Her strength was good, but she was a realist, and knew her body was a ticking time clock, and things could change at any moment.

Letter About Hollywood

Grandmother, Wade and I just returned from Los Angeles, Hollywood, and the Santa Monica Pier, where the famed Route 66 ends. I hope you like this giant-sized post card Wade bought for me to write you.

It was fabulous.

We left Friday morning on a bus down the Pacific Coast Highway, all the way to Los Angeles. Beautiful, but a lot of high cliffs over the ocean. I was really worried, but the bus driver assured us we were safe, as long as we didn't lean too far out the windows. It has beautiful, blue skies and weather in the 70's. Wade took hundreds of pictures of me.

I placed my hands in the movie stars imprints on Vine Street. I walked up to the HOLLYWOOD sign, and rode a trolley car all over the city, before we had dinner on Rodeo Drive, where everybody watches for movie stars.

We stayed at the Hilton Inn, back near the beach, so we could catch our early morning bus back to Monterey. Grandmother I can't wait to see you. I will call about the time of my arrival at Shenandoah Valley Regional Airport this week. Give my love to all and will see you soon. Jamie.

In ten days, Jamie would fly home, and I would leave for Fort Bliss. Before she left, I took her on a drive down to Carmel, Mission Ranch, and Big Sur. We spent time walking and talking about her trip to Virginia and her trip back to California. It became one of those unforgettable memories that Jamie would dream about during lonely nights in her room at home.

Jamie's First Flight

Jamie waved to Wade from her window seat, as the plane slowly backed away from the gate and taxied down the San Francisco Airport runway for the flight home, by way of Chicago, on February 28th. The major allowed me time to take her to the San Francisco airport by bus, and wait with her until her flight left.

She liked Stephanie and Major Lasiter. She knew they had become attached to her. Her genuine personality was infectious, and everyone she met became an immediate friend. She made them promise to keep her health private. Stephanie was a real friend, and secured on-base visits for her to make sure she stayed healthy, and she could fill her prescriptions, if needed.

She was vibrant, and seemed to be getting better. It could be short-lived if she had caught a severe cold or winter fever. We were fortunate in both cases, as she was glowing and upbeat during her stay.

Her grandmother and Hanna were waiting for her, and listened to her talk non-stop the entire two-hour drive home. She had left a shy, frightened girl, and returned a confident woman. They knew nothing would ever be the same for them or her. The joy in her heart, and the smile on her face, was indescribable. All the years of pain and worry seemed to dissipate in the emotion and excitement of the reunion.

Major Lasiter's Briefing

It was 0830, when I arrived at the Fort Ord, CEDEC briefing room, and Major Lasiter stood and addressed those in attendance.

"The media is buzzing with the impending Viet Nam conflict. It is a sad, but important! We are here for the coming insurgency along our coast lines. We will continue our night low level flights over the Pacific from San Diego to Fairbanks. However, orders from CECOM and CEDEC, may call for a new course of aerial photographic reconnaissance and surveillance in the coming months.

"We are at war with our own discontented citizens, and with the Hollywood political and conspiracy theorists who are influencing our military and civilian partners. We will continue to partnership with the air force pilots and coast guardsmen, flying modified C123's at night, and doing early dawn low level UH-1B Huey Helicopter maneuvers. We will continue to quickly return film and sound recording to the military authorities for review and interpretation.

"If there are questions, be brief. Otherwise, to your duties and assignments for the day. Be safe and silent as is our command."

With no questions, we were dispatched to our flight deck and returned by 1130. I tackled my military assignments with fierce determination, knowing that our CEDEC unit would transfer to Fort Bliss in less than six days. I relished my downtime; I did my reading between flights, readiness maneuvers, and filming tank exercises and training at Camp Roberts. I also practiced my flash cards for word recognition, and looked up definitions in my Webster's Dictionary. While assigned at Hunter Leggett and Camp Roberts, I finished eight books, and wrote two letters to Jamie.

My flight to Fort Bliss was March 4th. I wrote to Jamie: *We landed at Fort Bliss five days ago, and I've been busy day and night. I miss you terribly, and hope all is well at home. Before my flight on March 5th to begin my assignment at Fort Bliss, I read eight books. You would be proud of me. They were hard, and the Webster's Dictionary was my constant companion. It was not as warm and pleasant as you though!*

We train day and night in day-time temperatures in the 90's and night-time temperatures in the 40's. Everyone pulls guard duty at the firing sites. Conditions are very harsh, and sometimes dangerous. Meals are delivered by field transport trucks. The bathrooms and showers are WWII style, with no heat and no hot water.

I volunteer for night guard duty and down-range reconnaissance assignments--short work duties with long wait-time. This give me time to read the books you sent like, On the Road, Of Mice and Men, Call of the Wild, and more. My metal footlocker has become my off-duty reading spot, during dinner and evening lights out. When I go on jeep patrol duty with my Desert Arsenal Patrol partner, Specialist 4th Class Dennis Hopper, from Boulder, Colorado, I always have a paperback book in my backpack.

To him and others assigned to our desert unit, 'I'm a phenomenon. I wasn't sure if this was a compliment or not, but a dark veil has peeled from my eyes, and reading has become less challenging, and life more interesting. New, paperback, 1st edition novels appeared on my locker, with notes of "future reading assignment" taped or posted inside by my fellow soldiers. One came from my desert unit Commander, Captain Simmer Mosley, Combat Development Command with a "Good Luck Soldier."

I do miss you, and will write again soon. Let me know how it's going back home, and what progress you are making on your records, songs, writings, and books.

Love always, Wade

Fort Bliss 1964

The big hovering C-130's settled on the runway at El Paso Airport like a fat duck on a farm pond. They moved slowly to hanger 4J where a convoy of military trucks waited to be loaded. They would transport an array of ground to air weapons, helicopter tow drones, stainless-steel cases of motion, aerial and still photography equipment, mobile field photography laboratory units. A second convoy unit would transport the arriving 128 member combat command unit from Hunter Leggett Military Reservation, and the sixteen CEDEC army military technical specialists.

By night fall, they would be encamped 75 miles into the Argon Desert Range, north of Fort Bliss, for what was to be a 45-day experimental assignment. They would be testing ground-to-air low level artillery against modified OV10 jet prop planes on short runway take-offs and touch and landing exercises. The goal was to develop and test an array of intelligence experiments aimed at new kinds of tactical light unit fighting, ground surveillance, and night-to-dawn aerial reconnaissance of tropical and delta terrain.

The tropical and delta exercises were considered top secret, and the entire assignment disguised as a routine training convoy for live fire exercises. The US Army Corp of Engineers bulldozed and built a series of water channels, with low hanging trees. It was designed in a circular and figure-eight design, and covered about fourteen acres, just beyond our encampment at the base of the Argon Mountain Range.

Ron Critzer, Rick Beiler, Rod Brood, Dick Edlund and I were assigned to one of three photo-lab mobile units, which were mounted on a long eighteen-wheeler half-track truck base. It was equipped with water cooler units to keep the inside temperature at 75-76 degrees, for film processing and printing of 12x12 Agfa topographical photographs, for air transport back to CDEC Headquarters for analysis.

 Each unit wore colored bands on their caps and helmets, signifying their level of security and intelligence assignment for the duration of the project. Our unit was white for signal communication, and ground-to-air reconnaissance support. Guard duty was mandatory for everyone, and consisted of dark-to-dawn security checks of armaments, gunnery equipment, and the firing range. Everyone pulled three two-day shifts during the assignment, with full battle ready backpack, 45 pistol, and Carbine or M-14 Rifles. Radio contact was maintained at all times with the headquarters unit at Bliss.

No leave or weekend passes would be granted until twenty-one days into the assignment, and these were for travel to El Paso or Albuquerque, New Mexico. Most of us stayed in the desert, since transport was only by military jeep, and limited in time away from base.

During this time, I stayed in touch with Jamie, folks at home and the Hershey family in Petaluma, by field-pay-phones or letters. We worked from early daylight until late into most evenings. Night flights were held to a minimum, because of heavy daylight training exercises with the troops, and tank units operating in the desert. Sleep in the mobile bunk houses or tents were our main escape from the harsh cold at night, and high temperatures and windy conditions during the day.

Jamie gave me updates about her return home, visits to the cave, early spring planting, family, and the farm tree-pruning and grafting of young apple trees. She had reduced her counseling sessions to once a month with Ms. Stevens, and increased her reading list, and books for me to read. She was writing new songs, and recorded a song she would bring to California for the Monterey Jazz Music Festival.

The doctors at the university hospital liked the physical and medical work-up, done by Stephanie and the liver and kidney specialist, at Womack Hospital on Fort Ord. They saw some stabilizing of her physical condition. The main improvement was in her positive attitude, and efforts to do all she could to prevent any future damage, including no smoking, no alcohol, and an increase in her supplement regiment of vitamins.

Jamie's letters came to me on a regular basis. It was exciting to read her letters, and try to keep up with her on articles and paperback books she sent. I knew I was her literary pen-pal because the subject of most of our letters was, "what did you think of the plot in this book or that book."

Her new record: "It Was You," was getting regular play on WTVR radio in Lynchburg, and WVHS in Staunton, Waynesboro and Charlottesville. A religious organization in Richmond, Virginia, contacted her for a live performance on their new Sunday morning TV show. They invited her back for two more performances and offered to produce her record under their label for one year.

I shared her record with the Fort Ord radio station, and it caught the attention of the base commander and his USO communications director, who wanted to meet her on her return for some possible USO appearances in Monterey and surrounding cities.

I loved every letter, and her enthusiasm about her return to Monterey, hopefully in Mid-April or May.

Cooper

I lost track of my good army buddy 'Cooper' from basic training and Fort Monmouth, until I received a letter from his mother, while on assignment at Fort Bliss in 1964.

After Fort Monmouth, he was sent to Fort Benning for training, and then, shipped out to a new assignment as photographer to Camp Holiday, based south of Pleiku. His  mother sent me a picture of him dressed in fatigues, with his Specialist 4th Class stripes, smiling and holding an M-16, much like the photo I took of him holding his 4x5 Speed Graphic Camera at Fort Monmouth in 1963. With the picture, she enclosed a letter. I knew it was hard to write. There were ink smears along the bottom where she wrote:

Coopers gone.
He said it was hot on patrol.
He said he was headed out
and would write when he got back
and prayed he would be safe.
It was a nice funeral. They gave me a flag.
They said some nice things about him. The army paid for
the funeral and put a brass marker on the grave.
I knew he would want you to know.

With Love, Cooper's mother, Elsie Crawford

At the bottom of the letter, she taped his obituary.
The first line read: Specialist 4th Class,
Cooper William Crawford, US Army,
July 16, 1945-April 2, 1964.

Top Gun and Viper Scope

After forty-five days in the desert, I was glad to be assigned duty at the base photography center at Fort Bliss.

On Friday, April 17, I was due to transfer back to Fort Ord, when Major Lasiter asked me if I would take two additional assignments at Fort Bliss before leaving. The first was to photograph the Sac Unit (Strategic Air Command) flight crews and officers flying in and out on 24- hour around-the-clock surveillance maneuvers from Holloman.

"I told them that you were our best. I hope you don't mind. I know it's a delay in getting back to Ord, but it's a great assignment. It is strictly a PR assignment, and Fort Ord and the CECOM at Fort Monmouth are looking for some great still shots, as well as dramatic action shots for a PR campaign to be launched in October," he said.

This was where I met Base Communication Director, Lt. Josie Rodrigues, a striking, six-foot, auburn haired commander, who spent most of her off-duty time on Sundays at her family's home in El Paso. She was also dating an ace F-4 jet fighter pilot, stationed at Holloman Air Force Base.

A devout Catholic, her father was very protective of her. The family was also suspicious of the military and didn't like soldiers. They made an exception for the young Arizona native Lt. John Cainly, whom she had taken an interest in over the last six months.

A University of Texas at El Paso graduate, she spoke five languages, including Spanish, and was seen as one of the rising stars in the Army Officer Corp stationed at Fort Bliss. At 26, she had been engaged to be married at one time, and saw herself as gourmet cook and marketing sales representative of fine California table wines. It was my understanding that both her family and Lt. Cainly like hot, spicy foods.

She, and a 6th class airman assigned to her, became my jeep transport to Holloman and for the introduction to the flight crews for the photography shooting assignments.

The second assignment came as a surprise, when Major Lasiter called me to discuss my personnel file. "Dhamner, I've been reading your personnel files, and talked with your Drill Sergeant Faison at Fort Jackson. He had some pretty nice things to say about you. When I told him about our desert combat development assignment, and the light rifle team combat development project with the new M-14e1 Rifle, he recommended I talk with you, and include you in the firing range drill. He told me about the incident with you at Fort Jackson, and thought you would be a good candidate to try out the new weapon for the army. What do you think?"

"I'm flattered Major, and will do what I can to help, but haven't fired an M-14 since basic training." I said.

"It will only be a day, and I'm curious about how you might do. I think your personal insight would be helpful."

"Thanks Major, when do I report?'

"This afternoon, 1500 hours, and again for a night fire drill at 1900 hours. They know you are coming. You'll report to Sergeant Faison, who is arriving at 1400 hours to meet you, with the new M-14e1 scope mounted rifle."

It was like old times at Fort Jackson. Sergeant Faison still had his waxed mustache, wore mirrored, aviation sunglasses, and talked in his usual no nonsense manner.
"Dhamner, you're the best damn shooter I've ever met. This is quite an assignment for you. You remember Sgt. Cash here" as he turned to the second platoon and drill sergeant that I had also met at Fort Jackson.

"Damn Dhamner we called you at Jackson. We're at Benning now, and your major has given us an opportunity to fire the new modified M-14e1, which may be the new sniper version for the army, if we can show it's marksmanship at 500-720 yards. Has not been done yet, but we are hoping you can use the same methods you used at Fort Jackson, and show us how you did it. We're pretty good at 400-500 yards, but shit, whose counting? We want to take a long shot at 650-720 yards, with a fresh lemon."

"What? A lemon, Sarg?"

"Hell yah. Can you do it?"

"I mean, can you do it and show us how you did it?"

"Don't know, but let's try and see. I'll talk and let you know my thoughts, if that helps. Who's spotting, and who's shooting a second rifle?"

"What? How did you know we had a second rifle? We didn't tell anyone."

"I've made this shot a thousand times in my mind's eye, but I figured one of you would try to out shoot me, and see if I'm really any good." We laughed as the transport jeep picked us up and took us to a location with trees, near a swampy area on the edge of the newly-dug pond at the range.

Once there, Sergeant Faison recorded the conditions: wind, humidity, temperature, sun's position, time and ground level, and surroundings for the shooting exercise. Head targets, and a few illuminated lemons on one-foot rebar stakes, were placed at 200, 300, 400 and 600-yards distances. Some targets were also placed on the pond's bank, in trees, along ridge lines above the campsites, and on distant sand hill embankments. One 600-yard target had a thin dragline, and a soldier behind the embankment was instructed to pull it slowly, a foot after each shot, for a motion firing, to see if a motion target could be hit with accuracy.

Just like at Fort Jackson, we lay on the ground, on a small hilly mound, with sand sacks positioned in front of us for the rifles. We each had a modified Springfield Armory Winchester-Harrington Rifle, with 20 magazines with 7.62x54mmr modified rounds, aperture rear sight with a barley-corn front sight, and what Sergeant Faison called a new Viper PST Generation One mounted scope.

We completed both of the firing exercises at 1500 hours, and later that night. I carefully writing down my thoughts, on aiming and firing the rifle. Out of 400 rounds fired by both Sergeant Faison and me, we had a 98 percent hit result. Sergeant Cash, our spotter, wrote everything down in a folder for the report to Major Lasiter and the Fort Benning Combat Development Command, which was sponsored the exercise for the army.

"It's late, but do you have any beer at that campsite back at the base?" asked Sergeant Faison. The jeep driver and soldier who pulled the dragline targets took us back to the base. We signed-off on a verbal agreement to stay in touch, and meet together the next morning 0800 to complete full report to Major Lasiter.

I wrote Jamie, and told her about the additional assignment with Lt. Rodrigues. I gave her my full description of the flight with Lt. Cainly in his F-4 jet and aerial reconnaissance at 20,000 feet, and the G-force on the rapid descent and return to the Holloman.

Lt. Rodrigues paid for a copy of Jamie's 'It Was You' record. It received a lot of play on the base radio station, and a local El Paso station for six weeks.

Later, on my return to Fort Ord, I received an engagement announcement and wedding date, after Lt. Cainly's planned return from deployment in the Philippines and the China Sea. Jamie's comment was "love and military uniforms were a perfect match made in Heaven."

Chad, A Hero's Story

Language Specialist 4th Class Chad Wong had just returned to the US from a brief assignment at the US Army's military arsenal base in the Philippines, via another 10-day assignment in Stuttgart, Germany. He would be assigned to CDEC for training with me on aerial and ground photography reconnaissance before shipping out to a base on the China Sea.

So began our friendship and short term assignment. We were together on all training assignments. He kept his French and Vietnamese language active, by occasionally conversing on occasions with our two Vietnamese officers interpreting the exercises and assignments for Major Lasiter.

His parents had come to America in 1943. They settled in Alexandria, Virginia, just off King Street. Chad's father opened the Happy Day Café and Laundry, with a small, two-bedroom apartment above.

It had steam heat, running water, and a large bathtub in a 5x6 hallway bathroom. Chad's father was proud to be an American. He wrote to his aging parents in Korea, telling them about the café and his new apartment. He liked to send them black-and-white Polaroid pictures of his patrons. He mailed them pictures every Saturday morning at the post office across from his café.

His café did a good business. Travelers and tourists heading into Washington DC, were enticed by his window sign: "99 cent special breakfast" of two eggs, toast and grits. Customers could drink unlimited coffee up until ten o'clock for an additional five cents. Attorneys, naval officers, congressional staff and their executive assistants frequently tipped him an extra dime after breakfast, to stay and read *The Washington Post* newspaper he put on the counter for free.

Customers liked his wife's white, porcelain coffee cups. Each cup had a hand-painted cherry or dogwood blossom in red, white and blue. They were displayed by the cash register, and customers purchased them for souvenirs.

This was a great life, thought Chad, an 11th grader at Alexandria High School, as he walked his twelve year old Sister Taneka up the four tree-lined blocks to her school. He would then walk, and sometimes run, the six blocks to his school. He liked the smell of the freshly-painted picket fences in front of the brownstone apartments that lined most of the streets.

He touched and tapped each picket with his fingers, as he turned away from Potomac River Street, and headed for his school on the Chesapeake Highway. As he walked, he glanced through the pink mimosa trees lining the street, and imagined the Capitol in the distance, as it magically appeared glided through the tops of the trees. Its tall rotunda pierced the morning sky a symbol, he thought, of America's pride and perseverance. After finishing high school, he wanted to go into the US Army to serve his country, and return home to help his father, mother and sister in the café and laundry.

On June 22, 1963, he boarded a bus in the front of the café, for the four-hour ride to the recruiting station in Lynchburg, Virginia, and then on to Fort Jackson, South Carolina for his basic training. In August, he would go home for twenty-one days, before leaving for a language training assignment at the Presidio in Monterey, California. There he would complete two months of intense Vietnamese and French language training, before flying to Thailand for a temporary assignment.

In February, 1964, he returned to the US, and was assigned to Major Lasiter and the CEDEC unit. The first time I met Chad was on the C-130 flight to Fort Bliss. He sat quietly, directly in front of me, and only stared down at his field pack and a book in French, titled, *Pride and*

Prejudice. He never looked at me. He just kept his head down.

Occasionally, without turning his head, his eyes glanced toward the two uniformed Vietnamese officers sitting in officer's rows ahead of us. He listened to them.

"My name's Chad. They're talking about you're your CEDEC unit and this assignment." he said. "They know a lot about us, but more about you. They're saying you're the senior photographer, and will be having a permanent base assignment here, when the desert patrol is finished."

"That can't be right. I am due back at Ord at the end of April."

"That's what they're saying, is all I know" he whispered in my direction, through the drone of jet-pro engines."

He was involved in all reconnaissance briefings and discussions about the modification of armaments and battalion ground maneuvers that I was photographing in the desert. At night, he would take out his harmonica and serenade us in the tents and bunk house, with his version of *Dixie in Texas Country Western Swag,* he called it. It reminded me of low coastal tunes and Virginia blues, and I told him so. He liked that.

His personality and charm had a calming effect on the tensions among the ground troops practicing what they thought was for a combat zone assignment. It was clear and obvious with Kennedy's death, and the new President sending more advisors and ground troops to the Southeast Asia area, creating growing civil unrest and draft protests, that something ominous was afoot. They were young like me, and trained to follow orders.

But, I had to ask myself, why were South Vietnamese officers here? What was Chad's specific assignment, and why was I carrying out assignments with clear instructions to photograph everything on the ground and in the air, that could reveal detailed troop movements, live-fire air, and down-range damage results? And what were the night time helicopter drone towing flights and artillery fire we were photographing and analyzing? The major only asked me to get the job done, and equip the modified OV-10 and C-123 with photographic equipment they needed so that, "we could get the hell out of here and back to Ord" he said with an irritated voice.

In May, Chad shipped out to a place called, Khe Sanh, and later to the Vietnam's delta and hill top country. I remained at Fort Bliss for my assignments, and then back to Ord. The CEDEC unit was never de-briefed on the assignment in the desert. It was as if it never happened.

Two weeks into my return to Fort Ord, I received a postcard from Chad---*the weather is awful here—hot, muggy most of the time, like Fort Jackson in August, just more bugs. Thanks for sending the photograph of us on the Huey, and the group shot of everyone, before boarding the C-130 at Bliss. I sent it to my father at the café. I'm sure he tacked it up on the wall near my other postcards and pictures. I will transfer to the highlands next week, as an interpreter and photographer for some US Rangers and advisors. Maybe I'll meet our old officer friends. Look forward to returning home in 10 months. Maybe I'll look you up, and we can catch up. Maybe we can work together again. Chad*

The details are unclear, but Chad was killed while on patrol in the Highlands in June, 1964. His name is on a cross in Arlington National Cemetery. His mother and father placed fresh flowers on his gravesite every Sunday, until they passed way within four hours of each other.

His sister Taneka, who lives with her grandmother and attends Alexandria High School. She rides the bus to Arlington the second Sunday of every month, in memory of her parents and Chad. There she places a small U.S. flag below his name.

Remote

"Everything's going remote!" pronounced Major Lasiter!" announced Major Lasiter, as he opened our weekly briefing.

"We will be looking at our photography and reconnaissance surveillance operations and procedures for some modifications. Some of you, with special skills and assignments from CECOM, will continue your flights until we hear from Command. Many of you who just joined us will be reassigned to posts which need more ground control support and laboratory processing of films.

"Over the next several months, we will be experimenting at Hunter's Point with military technicians, who will travel with us, and observe the way we can transfer hands-on skills to the pilots and flight crews.

"We know CEDEC will be in the forefront of most of the development here, and at temporary assignment bases in the southwest for the next couple of months. The reason is more of a cargo and equipment weight issues, than personnel. Command has made this very clear. If any of you want to have a further discussion with me for reassignment, please do so. We serve a very important function, and our superiors have made this very clear.

"Some of you may have ideas that can improve the process, and I have been told these are welcomed. We will continue to work out of Hunter's Point and Ord, but critical assignments will be made to insure the confidence and security of our domestic shores. That is all!" He finished.

With a nod of his head, he gestured for me and Sergeant Keen to join him in an adjoining room, where he laid out the upcoming travel assignments for training, which included a duty assignment for us back to Fort Bliss, Texas.

He said that, "a trip to Fort Belvoir, Virginia might be in the work for us in June. Be advised that we will take the point on any technical modifications, and make recommendations for a speedy transition by this June."

"This is a real change" Keen said, as we left the major office and walked to the mess hall for lunch.

"We have been on the grid assignment since my arrival here in 61. I've been seeing a lot of news about Senator Fulbright's concerns about the US Army build up, proposed by President Johnson. Apparently, we are participating in more critical assignments, which may have something to do with our increased advisor roles in the Philippines and Okinawa. I can see you and I both on permanent reassignment within a year. In the meantime, let's keep working as hard as we can to make this project a success for the major."

I nodded in agreement, and we continued our duty assignments as we had for the last several months.

Jamie in Monterey

On Saturday afternoon May 2nd, Lilly, Thomas, Stephanie and I, watched the DC-7 land at Monterey Airport, with Jamie on board. We spotted her in a window

seat waving and smiling as the plane taxied to the airport's fenced security area. She was waving as she came out of the plane's doorway and made her way down the stairway to the asphalt pavement, quickly walking into the baggage area with her guitar strapped on her back.

"I'm back soldier boy," she said, in her high-pitched southern voice. There were hugs and kisses with everyone, as we made our way to the carrousel for her luggage.

"Look at that long blonde hair," Lilly said. "That's what you get in the south, when you work on a farm and plant tobacco in the spring."

"Thank you, Lilly, I needed that. What's for lunch?" She said, as we made our way out of the airport and piled into Stephanie's Volkswagen van for the trip to Crusoe's for lunch, and then on to the cottage. We sat in the back seat and held each other close, as the van erupted in conversations about the south, the beautiful weather in California, her grandmother, the farm, everything, but no comments or questions about her health. She was back, and the next couple of weeks would be filled with activities and events.

At Crusoe's, she was greeted by the staff, who paraded her into the café bar where Lilly served us a large pizza, salads and a pitcher of beer. It was just what Jamie needed. There was laughter, and an unending commotion of loud chatter that vibrated in the café and pizza bar. She was glowing and happy, and among friends who loved her and wanted her return to be festive and joyous.

Lilly announced that since this was a Cinco de Mayo weekend, and the Monterey Jazz Festival was in town, Crusoe's would close Sunday, but would host a special Monday-Tuesday, weekend' celebration with music and poetry by local poets and singer-song writers. She invited everybody in the room for pizza and free beer celebration.

The major and other members of the CECOM unit joined us at 3:00 o'clock to welcome Jamie back, as patrons began to fill the café. Jamie was right in the middle of the activities, joking, singing songs, and playing her guitar at the microphone. The afternoon passed quickly, and a very tired Jamie, who was still on Eastern Time, asked Lilly if she could leave at seven o'clock to go to the cottage and rest.

The major and I spent time catching up on the plans for the unit, and his request that I join him for a flight to Fort Belvoir and Washington, DC for a briefing the following week.

"Things are speeding up at a much faster pace than anticipated. We will work around the clock and Jamie's USO schedule, but you and I will be at Belvoir for two days during the middle of May. Glad she's back. Stephanie and I will be around all weekend if you two need anything. But for now, I need to return to the base. I look forward to seeing you bright and early Wednesday morning. Enjoy your time together," he finished, and made an exit to his waiting military jeep.

"I want to take a walk on the beach once we get to the cottage, and spend time with you," Jamie said with a wink and smile.

"Lilly will close and Stephanie has already agreed to take us to the cottage. I'll meet you out front after I say good-bye to everyone. I love you, soldier boy and I'm going to love you tonight."

Still holding my hand, she pulled me into her embrace and I lowered my head to meet her lips. It was a kiss that was so passionate that she knew her knees would buckle if she didn't pull away and walk outside in the cool air on the beach.

"I love it here," she said, as we strolled arm in arm. She pressed her head against my chest and talked about Virginia. "Grandmother is so happy for us, but I promised her I would return for the reunion in August. Tell me about you. I saw you and the major talking. Is something going on?"

"Yes, he and I will be flying back to Ft. Belvoir the middle of the month, but I will still be available for you and the USO schedule in May and June. After that, things may be different. I am so glad you're back. I have missed you so much. Let's walk back and talk at the cottage. It's eleven o'clock for you, and it would be a good idea to get you some rest. And even though tomorrow is Sunday, I need to go in for a couple hours and work on my report for the major, so I can spend time with you tomorrow and Monday. I have a helicopter flight briefing on Tuesday morning and Wednesday, but will be ready to travel with you on Friday of this coming week."

"I did a lot of thinking about us while I was home," she said. "Coming back here was like coming home. You are here, as well as Stephanie, Lilly, Thomas and our friends at Crusoe's. Back home, it was kind of the same as before. Just didn't have you there. Grandmother does her best, and Ms. Stevens and Marianne stay in touch, but this feels like home. It feels like this is where I belong. Does this make sense to you?" She asked, as we crossed the road to Lilly's house.

"I know. I feel the same. It was busy while you were gone, but I thought about you all the time. I want to have everything you want here, but I do think my time in California will change," I said.

"I know, and I want everything with you here too," she said, as she led me to the sofa where she pressed her fingers against the back of my neck. She returned my kiss with a feverish enthusiasm, meeting my tongue with a boldness that surprised me. She let my hands nervously seek and find the curves of her breasts, before pushing her blouse off her shoulders, down to the arched curve of her back. She gasped when she felt the clasp of her bra give way, and realized that she was naked from the waist up.

The warmth of our mouths drew muted sounds of pleasure. We were sinking into a dreamy sensation, with our eyes closed, wanting each to touch our most intimate places. I didn't know how to tell her how I felt. Instead I let her pull me tightly against her breasts as her right hand moved up to the top of my shirt, unbuttoning it one by one, until she was able to push it back off of my shoulders and down each arm, until it fell it to the floor.

We returned each other's' caresses and kisses. I reached up and pulled the lamp chain; we were surrounded by darkness and the sounds of our breathing. We were skin to skin from the waist up, our bodies poised hard against each other, as our eyes met in the dark. We lay quietly listening to our hearts beating, enjoying the feel of each other.

"Wade," she said, "I want to wait, but it so hard. I love you so much," she whispered as we lay half naked on the sofa. We didn't know what to say, as we held each other tight and laughingly looked at our tops tossed together on the darkened floor. I held her close, stroking her shoulders, arms and sides gently.

"I'm so happy, and tired," she said, as we looked into each other's eyes. "Thank you for helping me make this a perfect day. I know you... I ...." she said, pausing.

"I want it too, but let's wait," she said, as she moved my hand down the length of her warm body and let it hand rest on her soft, excited stomach.

"I've been reading a lot about how others handle these feelings we have. Soon, we'll do more," she said. "Let's be patient with ourselves. This is all I can handle for now. I love you and want you, but you and I both know, we must stop for now," as she gently kissed his lips and lay her head on his chest.

The next morning Jamie lay in bed where I had taken her after she fell into a deep sleep. She looked over to see me still sleeping on the sofa. It was 7:00 o'clock. I opened my eyes and we looked at each other across the cottage living room. Our thoughts were mutual, even though unspoken. We were in love. She invited me to her with a smile and playful wink.

"I could get used to this," she said, "but I know you have to get back to the base."

"I'm sorry I kept you up so late," I said.

"I'm not," she said, as I reached for my clothes and bent over to give her a kiss.

"Will I see you again later this afternoon?" she asked.

"Count on it" I replied.

Marriage and Engagement Proposal

Major Lasiter invited me to his office, after a seacoast and Pacific training flight with one of our new pilots. After going through the training and procedures for activating the aerial cameras, and recovering the film after the landing, I reported to Major Lasiter for debriefing as usual. He was in a somber, but cheerful mood, and we quickly reviewed my paperwork as he said, "Specialist, I need to talk to you about an important matter, and I want you to consider what I say as friendly advice for careful consideration."

This was different, as I wasn't quite sure what was coming. It was a surprise to me as he began: "You and Jamie are very special to Stephanie and me, and we've discussed something we want to talk with both of you about over dinner this week at our place. As you know, Stephanie has been monitoring Jamie's medical condition. They are also very close and talk about many things. In confidence, Stephanie has shared some of their talks and has a very interesting proposal to make to you both.

"It could help you both focus on your feelings for each other, you on your job, and on concerns for Jamie and her medical expenses that will increase over the next several months. I know this is strange, and I don't want to make you uncomfortable, but Stephanie asked me to talk with you first, and then you can talk with Jamie before we meet." He paused, took a deep breath, and slowly released it as he looked straight at me.

"We think you two should get married!" he exclaimed, almost not believing he had said it himself. Surprised by his statement, I pushed back in my chair as he noticed the puzzled look on my face.

"I know you're young, and there's a lot of uncertainty, but there are some real benefits to you both. I know you love each other, and this is a surprising conversation, but you would receive an additional pay allotment, and Jamie would be eligible for all the benefits of a spouse," he paused.

"I know this, because Stephanie and I have talked about this ourselves, and a wedding is in our near future. I am talking to you as a trusted friend, and as a soldier for whom I have the utmost respect."

"Major, with all due respect, this is a lot to think about. I love her, and we have talked a lot about her illness and our feelings for each other, but we take it a day at a time. I want what is best for her. I'll talk with Jamie about it tonight. You can imagine how nervous I am about this. I'm only 18, and this is a lot of responsibility."

"I know. Believe me, I know, but this is a unique situation, and this is an arrangement I think you may need. At the same time, we don't want to surprise her, as I think I have surprised you. I'll leave it to you, and will await your call."

Rather than expecting a salute, he shook my hand and walked me to the door, putting a friendly hand on my shoulder.

I left his office as I had many times before. This was different. Marriage...Wedding...Spouse...went through my mind as I smiled and hung on his words as I entered the barrack to change. I called Jamie to let her know I would be coming by the cottage tonight after her performance at Crusoe's, so we could talk about something really important. She pressed me for more, but I told her that it wasn't about my duty assignment, but about us.

She said she could wait.

Jamie Wondered

Jamie put down the cottage phone, and her mind raced in a thousand directions. What could be so important that Wade would call me and want to talk? She couldn't get it out of her mind as she walked out into the garden to gather some fresh aloe vera and Echinacea for herbal tea.

Lilly stopped her, saying, "I heard the phone. Anything wrong?"

"No, Wade called and wants to talk about something really important tonight after work. Is it okay for him to come by? I'm worried. He wouldn't tell me anything on the phone."

"Don't fret, it will be all right. Why don't we go down to the beach and wade in the surf. It will clear your head. I also have something to show you. Take the aloe vera. I'll put it on your back."

Jamie stood in the cold Pacific surf, the water lashing at her ankles, as she raised her outstretched arms to the sky, revealing a finely sculptured silhouette of her body, beneath the soft, wet, cotton, knee-length dress. She stood in the surf, her feet firmly planted in the soft sand as the breaking waves teased her legs, driving her into a deeper state of awareness as the pill Lilly had given her began to take its effect.

The change in supplements and the mystical ingredients of Lilly's garden were having wondrous effects on her. She could hear the rush of the ocean as she touched herself, and explored the feel of her body. She listened to rhythmic musical chords that drifted through her head, waiting anxiously to be played on her guitar.

She wanted to know more about what Wade had on his mind. Lilly beckoned her to come and sit with her and pulled a dry towel over her shoulders. She kissed her cheek as they lay in the sun and let time drift away across the sky.

"Lilly, can I get addicted if I smoke too much, or get used to the pills? The aloe vera plant is so soothing and healing. I've never felt so good, and had such a sense of peace. Grandmother would freak out. Wade might get upset. This is so great," she said.

"No, James and I have occasionally smoked this after work to calm us down. Mabel has assured me it is not addictive, and everybody's in the neighborhood is trying it. We meditate. It's like an out-of-body experience. It opens our minds to new fantasies and thoughts."

"Me too. I read about it. It opens our pubescent gate, and sometimes my head throbs with an ecstatic rhythm. Sometimes, when I'm with Wade, I'm on fire, but we stop before we go too far. I can't believe I'm talking like this with you," she said. She drifted into a quiet napped on the beach until Lilly shook her awake. They headed back to the house for a snack before leaving for work.

Jamie had only taken a half of one of the pills given to her by Lilly, on the promise it would relieve some of her work stress and anxious internal feelings. It was a first. She was reading more about eastern faith, mostly a blend of Zen Buddhism. The mescaline pill, aloe vera potion and cannabis leaves and seeds, opened her mind to fantasies and feelings that were producing new poems that pushed her beyond the pain of her adolescence. They sealed the old wounds in her soul, and opened her mind and body to a new, thunderous beat she read about in On the Road , and in the beat poetry of Allen Ginsburg.

When she and Wade were together kissing and touching, she felt no carnal need, but a feeling of deep closeness. She deeply loved him and wanted everything he wanted, but held strong to her promise to God that she would not have sexual intercourse with any man until there was a spiritual union of their soul, mind, spirit and body. She was both puzzled and fascinated by the newness of her inner nature, and consequential religious intermingling that was so different to her strict Baptist faith. What she knew was that she would die before the end of the year. The doctors knew she was on borrowed time. What she had finalized in her mind and soul was how to live, until the last days came. She believed that life would go on for her if she found a way to make her poetry, songs and voice live. Maybe, she thought, she and Wade had found the secret; living, knowing death is a certainty, but life can go on, whether in joy or pain. She chose joy and the wonderful mystical peace that was hard for her to understand sometimes. She believed it, and had a strong growing faith in herself and a wondrous eternity that would be hers in the new chapter of her life.

Her prayers were being answered, and the pitying of herself was far away. A new dawning was waiting for her and Wade.

The Engagement

"What? I love you, but never thought we would actually talk about it."

"Jamie, it's a good idea, and they want to talk with us over dinner."

"Do you love me that much, that you would ask me to marry you?"

"Yes, I want you," I said, "And everything a marriage could give us both, for as long as it may last. I want to wait like you, but this would make me so happy, to make you happy. Yes, I'm nervous and scared like you, but ready to take care of you and love you, if you will have me."

"Christ!" Jamie said. "I've got to really think about this. Just this morning I was just trying to get through the day, with everything going on with us--your assignments, my health, the USO travel--and now an engagement and a wedding.

"What do you think grandmother will say? She may not give permission. I don't know about this," she said, as she drew me close and kissed me. She closed her eyes, turned off the lamp and settled her head on my shoulder in the dark silence.

"Maybe I want this," she said. "Yes, maybe I want to do this. I don't know if it will work out, but I am so crazy in love with you. Nothing can hurt me as long as I have you. I feel so safe and secure with you. It's the details of planning and going home for the wedding that I am not sure about."

"Okay, me too, but let's call your grandmother in the morning. It's too late there now. We can call Stephanie tonight and confirm dinner, and find out more about the military benefits from her."

"Okay, but just hold me tight for a while. I need to tell you something too, before we call."

Jamie appeared to be napping in my arms, but then started talking about not taking any of her medicines. She and Stephanie had worked up a regiment of vitamin supplements, weekly vitamin A and D shots and a vegetarian diet. She and Lilly had been using aloe vera natural lotions from the garden, for her back. Both were working. She asked me not to get mad, and told me she had smoked cannabis leaves and seeds, every Thursday for the last three weeks, with Lilly. It was wrong, but it helped more than any pain killer she had ever taken.

She was so full of surprises, but I felt I could not scold her and told her not to tell anyone else, as I reached for the phone and dialed Stephanie's number.

Dinner with Stephanie and Major Lasiter

Jamie and I drove to the apartment in Sea Side as planned. Lilly and Thomas were so good about letting us use the Volkswagen that they had bought for their daughter, when she lived in the cottage.

Before we could ring the doorbell, Stephanie opened the door and reached out to us with a hug. The major and I shook hands. For the occasion Stephanie had planned the major's favorite meal for the occasion: California baked spaghetti, a mixed salad, and Napa valley wine.

Jamie was the first to speak. "Wade and I have done nothing but talk about this since we called the other night. We called my grandmother in Virginia, and she was nervous for us, but also excited. This is all so weird, but wonderful. Oh, oh let me stop. You know me by now, and when I get excited I talk."

"It's okay," the major said. "Let's eat and talk. Stephanie will explain what we talked about, and we can all discuss this together."

"All right!" said Stephanie. "Go ahead and eat and I will tell you what I've learned. Jamie's medical tests are all back, and I may not tell you anything you don't already know. What is new, is what we may be able to do to improve your condition, and set in motion a better plan of treatment. I can't make any promises, but Captain Lofton, our chief internal doctor, has lots of expertise in this area, and gave me the information we need to talk about." She paused to wait for questions, and continued.

"First, since you both are eighteen, and already have parental consent, marriage is what you two have to decide. The medical benefits begin as soon as Wade submits the marriage certificate and paperwork for military spousal support. The main thing is that you, Jamie, can receive the same medical care as Wade, to treat your kidney, liver and headaches. We are calling them disorders and not illnesses, because under this definition we can begin treatment.

"Captain Lofton said we can't promise a cure, but stabilizing and improving your current health will be the main goal for treatment. Womack is the best facility in the area, and has some of the best doctors and specialists available."

She stopped, as Major Lasiter asked, "By the way, how's the spaghetti?"

"Great, and just to knowing you care means a lot to us."

"Yes", Jamie said. "I've been prodded and poked more than you can imagine since I was young, but no one just talked to me, or told me what was going on. I just took medicine and did what I was told. My grandfather and grandmother did the best they could and I…know my future. What I care about is staying as healthy as I can, and being with this man I love. You are so wonderful. I have never been so happy, and yes, this spaghetti is really good," she said, as we all laughed and kept talking.

"Major, I met with my company commander and company clerk today about the process and paperwork, and learned that we can apply for a civil marriage certificate in Monterey County that can be used for spousal benefits, and off post housing if we want it. A formal announcement and wedding is up to us, but not necessary.

"However, with my duty assignments, Stephanie's appointments, Jamie's work at Crusoe's, and her pending recording with Broadman Music back in Virginia, I will continue to live on post. She will stay in the garden cottage at Lilly and Thomas' house," as Stephanie asked Jamie what she was feeling.

"I feel like this is still a dream coming true. I'm better at writing and singing my feelings than talking sometimes. Wade and I have agreed to write a letter together to his parents and to my grandmother explaining everything. We want to plan a simple, outdoor, engagement party, here in Monterey near the beach, and a wedding Feast and musical festival on my grandparents' farm in Virginia. I am sure Grandmother will insist on this. She will want to invite all of her valley friends and relatives. Wade is from a big family and this will be a little bit of a shock for them too. They would feel left out if we married here. We're working on our schedule and saving money for the trip late in June. I hope you understand, and that this makes sense to you," she said, with a pause, offering to sing some of her latest songs of love for us.

Jamie and I planned an engagement party on the beach in front of Lilly and Thomas' house, where we had talked as we held each other so many times. Lilly posted an invitation on the wall at Crusoe's for their friends and my friends from the base. The major joked about being my best man, and Stephanie agreed to Jamie's request to fly to Virginia to be her maid of honor.

Together, Jamie and I visited the base PX and purchased matching engagement rings. We agreed to wear blue jeans, with a long-sleeve white shirt for me, and a long sleeve paisley blouse for Jamie. We promised her grandmother, my grandparents, and my parents' photographs from the engagement party. It would be an event on the beach with lots of music, dancing, pizza and beer.

The future could wait for now. We were in love, and loved by the people around us. For now, at this time and place in our lives, nothing could hurt us.

For a little while, the news of the day, military and work assignments, and time drifted away like the note in the bottle that we tossed into the surf.

You Are Invited

To an Engagement Party
At our house and on the beach

On Saturday, May 16th at two o'clock.

Bring your favorite desserts to share.
We are serving twenty extra-large cheese pizzas
and a forty gallon keg of our best beer.
Jamie is marrying her soldier boy, Wade, back in Virginia
on the 4th of July.

This is an engagement gift from all of us at Crusoe's.
No house gifts or presents,
but we will take up a collection of money for their trip back
to Virginia, so bring something in an envelope with your
name and address on it so they can write and thank you.

Beach House Music and Books in Monterey
has made fifty 45 rpm records
at my request of
"It Was You" and "Blue Mountain Highway Home"
as a signed gift for those attending and making a donation.

They leave for Virginia on June 29 and return on July 7th
to begin Jamie's USO tour in California.

Call or come by Crusoe's and let us know you'll be there.

Lilly and Thomas, Owners and Friends

Engagement Party on the Beach, May 16, 1964

Lilly and Thomas placed a 40-gallon keg of draft beer and paper cups on the beach for the party. Jamie and I carried the 20 super-deluxe cheese pizzas to the beach and placed them near the fire pit, where the major had gathered drift wood for a celebration fire.

It wasn't long before guests and friends started arriving, pouring themselves a beer and taking slices of pizza. I turned the transistor radio up as loud as it would go to listen to music from WTOB-Salinas.

Within twenty minutes, about thirty people were dancing, playing in the cold low-tide surf, or sitting by the fire pit,

Thomas placed a large sack of pine cones for guests to pitch into the flames as they spoke 'wishes or prayers' for our future wedding and life together.

I sat on a large volcanic rock with Jamie, as Stephanie tossed the first pine cone, "For all who love you and know you, we wish everything this good earth and heaven can give you. We love you, and you have come to mean so much... I, I, I..."

"Stephanie and I," the major said as she began to cry, "will also be there for you as you have been there for all of us through your steadfast commitment, spirit and songs."
One by one others offered additional accolades as they tossed cones, as the fire making it flame a brilliant white and red.

And then it was Jamie's turn, as the tide brought water closer to the fire and a low Pacific fog pushed its way into the cove. "This is not a sad occasion. I want us all to sing together and realize how blessed we are. This is a great country and I love it. I love all of you, and especially this soldier boy. So dance with me, and sing a song with me.
I'm just learning to play an old Pete Seeger tune, and will be singing it on our USO tour starting next week:

"This, ... and hold that 'this' as long as you can, *"*
she shouted, and sang,
"This is my country, Land that I love..."

The beach became a twilight scene of dancing figures, moving and serenading, as the fading orange ball appeared to drifted into the ocean.

Letter To Grandmother

Dear Grandmother,

I hope you are sitting down.

You will probably get this letter after Wade and I call, but we wanted to write you and tell you about our engagement and wedding plans.

We are just as surprised as you. We hadn't planned on this, but some pretty exciting things are happening, so we wanted to write. First, my health is really good, and the nurses and doctors here have been taking good care of me.

Lilly and Thomas have been wonderful with work, my singing, and letting me have time off to spend with Wade. I have been practicing and recording my songs, and making plans for our USO tour this summer. The US Army Post Commander at Fort Ord offered me the invitation, and Wade will be on special weekend assignments with other members of the band to take us to the locations.

Stephanie, my friend and nurse, and her fiance Major Lasiter, and Wade's commanding officer have been great friends to us. We have enjoyed dinner and talks at their house in Sea Side, near Fort Ord. It was they, who first talked to us about the idea of marriage, and the benefits for me as a military wife. I am responding well to the new medicine and treatment, but I am aware that there is no cure but my health is doing much better. I quit smoking cigarettes and only drink beer now.

Wade stays busy with his assignment, but we have most weekends together.

Now, the really big news. We got engaged, and will have an engagement party at Lilly's beach front house, on May 16th. We want to fly back to Virginia on June 29th, and plan for what we want to call a "Wedding Feast and Musical Festival" at our farm. You have always said grandpa would have loved something like this. So, hope it's okay. Wade and I have been saving our money, and I plan to send you some money to help out with the wedding.

I will have hospital privileges and my medicine, what little I take, is free. I will stay at Lilly's Cottage, and Wade will live on base, except for Friday-Sunday when we work together and travel for the US Army USO tour, in California.

Grandmother, I'm writing, playing and singing some of my best songs. I have two records now, and get paid for the USO tour. Lilly pays me $1.00 an hour, plus tips and all the pizza I can eat. I've gained a little weight, but everyone comments about my suntan, good health and that they love my songs... Wade's a Corporal/Specialist 4th Class, and still flies reconnaissance flights, but mostly is helping train pilots and crewmen to operate the photography equipment for special patrols and assignments.

He sends his love and is looking forward to coming home with me and seeing some of his friends and family in June and July before we return.

With all our love, and kisses, Jamie and Wade.

Letter to My Parents and Grandparents

Dear Mom and Dad, Granddad and Grandmother

You will probably get this letter after I call Granddad and Grandmother, but we wanted to write you and tell you about our engagement and wedding plans.

I hadn't planned on this, but we, Jamie Marshall and I, are engaged and will be back in Virginia in June for our wedding and musical festival at the Thompson Farm.

I'm a Specialist 4th Class, and still fly reconnaissance flights, but mostly help train pilots and crewmen to operate the photography equipment for special patrols and assignment here at Fort Ord.

I'm looking forward to coming home with my wife to be, and seeing some of our friends and family in June and July before we return.

Your son and future daughter-in-law, Wade and Jamie

You are invited

To a Wedding Feast at my house
On July 4ᵗʰ at eleven o'clock

Bring your favorite baked vegetable.
I am serving two-whole bar-be-cued and roasted pigs and
all the desserts you can eat with fresh tea or water.
(BYOB if you like, but no one can overdo it.)

Jamie got engaged to her soldier boy, Wade, on a
Monterey, California beach on Saturday, May 16ᵗʰ.

This is their wedding feast and reception gift from us.

No house gifts or presents,
but I will take up a collection of money for their trip back
to California, so bring something in an envelope with your
name and address on it so they can write and thank you.

Broadman Records and Books in Waynesboro
has cut 100 records at Jamie's request of
"It Was You" and "Blue Mountain Highway Home"
as a signed gift for those attending and making a donation.

They leave for California on July 7ᵗʰ.
Call or come by and let me know you'll be here.
Wanda Thompson, Grandmother of the Bride

Wedding Feast and 4th of July Musical Festival 1964

It was good to see people at our wedding who had become the tapestry of our lives.

Ms. Thompson, Tom and Hanna, quickly called everyone together at the front porch with the following announcement:

"Thank you all for coming. We are here today for a special celebration, to join my granddaughter Jamie Catherine Marshall in marriage to Wade Hamilton Dhamner. This is a special time, but it is also a time for food, fun and music at Jamie's orders. So gather close to the porch, and Pastor Woodson from the Rockfish Baptist Church in Nellysford, will lead us in prayer and marry this young, loveable couple. Pastor Woodson."

"It's a blessing to be here today, and I, Jamie and Wade do not want to be the ones to stand between you, food and a great time together, here at Ms. Thompson's farm.

"I have known Wade since he was nine, and I baptized him in the Rockfish River when he was eleven. Jamie is a special visitor to the Wintergreen Christian Church with her grandmother. Pastor Jack Hughes, the pastor there, will have a few words to say in just a few minutes.

" Jamie and Wade, I understand you want to recite your vows for those gathered here, before Pastor Hughes and I formally perform the ceremony."

"Yes, thank you Pastor Woodson. It's so good to see you again." I said, as I took Jamie's hands and we turned to face the gathering of friends and family.

"Jamie, you go first."

"Ok everybody, here goes. I have been so blessed this past year by this wonderful man, and your thoughts and prayers have meant the world to both of us.

"My grandfather, Johnathan, always told me that I was a beautiful butterfly, with a slightly busted wing.

He…", she stopped as the crowd laughed out loud, and even some spoke kind words about him. "He meant so much to me and would have really enjoyed this day if he were here. I'm sure he's watching and smiling, so, Wade, I love you and promise my love and faithfulness to you only. You have made this more than a perfect dream for me, and God is smiling on our lives. I will be everything you love about me, and sometimes, I know I will be difficult, but we promised each other to love and stay together, no matter what this life gives us. And with these words I pledge my heart and life to you," she finished.

"Jamie, you are the love of my life, and there is no other. God has been kind to us. He blessed you with a cheerful voice, a loving heart, and a soul and spirit that lifts me up and keeps me going each and every day. We are among friends who know us and love us and want every happiness for us together. I love you, and there is none other than you. I pledge my life to you," I finished nervously, as we turned to face Pastor Woodson.

"Wade and Jamie, these are cherished words of love, devotion, and faith. I am so glad you have made us a part of your marriage ceremony today.

"It is written," he said, "in Ephesians 5: 25-32 from Saint Paul: *Brothers and sisters: Live in love, as Christ loved us, and handed himself over for us. Husbands, love your wives, even as Christ loved the Church, and handed himself over for her to sanctify her, cleansing her by the bath of water with the word, that he might present to himself the Church in splendor, without spot or wrinkle or any such thing, that she might be holy and without blemish. So also, husbands should love their wives as their own bodies. He who loves his wife loves himself. For no one hates his own flesh, but rather nourishes and cherishes it, even as Christ does the Church, because we are members of his Body. For this reason, a man shall leave*

*his father and his mother, and be joined to his wife, and
the two shall become one flesh. This is a great mystery, but
I speak in reference to Christ and the Church. The word of
the Lord."*

With the reading complete, Pastor Hughes stepped
forward and sang the Lord's Prayer, with Jamie on guitar,
as the assembled crowd drew closer and joined them on
the final verse and amen.

"Thank you Pastor Hughes and Jamie," said Pastor
Woodson. "I don't think I have heard the Lord's Prayer
rendered as lovely as you two have done this afternoon.
God bless this prayer. And Jamie and Wade, you may put
the rings on your fingers and face your friends and family
here, as I pronounce you 'Husband and Wife'."

With the ceremony concluded, Ms. Thompson walked
to the steps on the porch, and with tears in her eyes invited
the families to assemble for a photograph, as Pastor
Hughes prepared to say the blessing for the food.

The front yard was a swarm of people Ms. Thompson
had invited. They ate and tossed envelopes into a basket on
the front porch. Everyone was in a festive mood as Ms.
Thompson and Hanna kept the tea flowing. Tom and I
served up barbeque for guests, and Jamie moved her new
drop-down record player to the front porch, and plugged in
the dual speakers so everyone could hear her record and
dance.

Jamie and I sat on the porch while I identified most of
the guests for Jamie as we sorted through the envelopes to
see who had come: were, BC Small and some of his family
were there. He always gave me summer work, and trusted
me to be part of the farm work crew. I was sure we would
talk a lot. Whit Huffer lived just down the road, and he
gave me countless rides home from the Yanceyville Saw
Mill after football practice; Mable Napier always helped
me deliver my Grit Newspapers along Route 151 with her

jeep; Oakley Quick recruited me as a member of the Keep Virginia Green that fought grass and forest fires in the valley; Pete Small, my Sunday school teacher held me while Pastor Woodson baptized me in the Rockfish River at eleven years of age; Rudolph Small took me hunting, where we killed my first black bear; Son Small drove the 18 wheeler every peach and apple season to the cold storage plant in Arrington where I loaded them; Snip Davis who the best eight layer strawberry cake every Christmas; Pete and Morfred Campbell ran a family grocery store in Nellysford; Thelma Magan, was the head cook at Rockfish Elementary School; old man Martin and his wife Mary, worked at the store; Marianne came from Alexandria; Big Ray Harris and his wife Christine, my grandmother's sister were there; my swimming buddies from Stoney Creek: Betty, Ann, Tracey, Donald, and Mickey Davis, Gary Small, Dale Ward, Phil Dodd, Judy Hughes, Freddie Phillips and his daughter Lynna, JP, Phyllis and her older brother 'HT' Witt, Zane Meeks, Maynard, Wayne, Diane, the twins and their little brother Jimmy Fortune; Lucy Ewing, our librarian, H.T. Witt, who graduated before me and went to Florida last summer as an artist for a florist studio in Miami; Junior Thompson, friend of the family and member of the County Sheriff Department; Artie and Dean Irving, who liked to pitch baseball in the big field just old Route 151; Tuck and Flaxie Hughes and their sons, Grady and Gene from Spruce Creek Mountain. Also in attendance were Ms. Stevens, who sat watching and thinking quietly; Joann Newberry who tried to teach me to tap dance in the sixth grade; Pop Painter, a war hero and worker at Small's Packing Shed; Margaret Garth, my seventh grade teacher; Mr. Rhodes from Rhodes Farms and choir director at Rockfish Baptist Church; Dolly Garth, who owned the first 53' Mercury convertible in Nellysford; and Faye Dodd, our high school drum majorette.

Just as at the family reunion, my parents and grandparents, along with my brothers and sister, gathered around a table with the Davis family, under a large sycamore tree at the far side of the yard. Jamie went to their table and talked for a long time with my mother and Sue about singing some songs. I helped Johnathan and my father clean the fire pit as I watched Jamie laugh and talk with my family and friends about living in California.

The sun was directly overhead and blazing down on the group, forcing some to head for the river for a swim or wade among the rocks with their food. The food was disappearing fast and people were beginning to drift toward their cars for the trip home. Only close friends and school mates lingered and talked with Ms. Thompson, Jamie and me.

By two o'clock, the yard was empty as we put paper plates in bags and boxes to burn later after the sun went down. Jamie and I counted over 75 envelopes, and put them in the empty box where her give-a-way records had been. Jamie smiled, knowing that her songs would be enjoyed by those who attended.

After the Wedding Feast

After the last of the guests left, we cleaned the tables and placed the dishes in apple crates for washing at the creek. Ms. Thompson said, "Jamie, why don't you and Wade go down to the cave to cool off, and some time alone. We'll clean up everything here. Stay as long as you like. Tom, Hanna and I will plan dinner for you around six o'clock so don't rush. Spend time together, talk and dream. We'll be here."

With this suggestion, Jamie and I put on our bathing suits, took four large towels and headed for the cave hand-in-hand with thoughts of love making.

At the cave, Jamie pulled me down to her in the cool water and said, "This is where I always wanted to do it first with you. Let's take our time," she said as she lay back on

the cool stones and sand, letting the clear water flow through her soft wavy, blonde hair. She looked like a goddess as the shallow stream flowed around her creamy, white neck and shoulders.

She closed her eyes to the hot afternoon sun peeking through the opening in the ledge, while whispering for me to touch and kiss her. She cupped the back of my head with both hands and pulled me to her for a deep kiss, as we held each other, and time drifted into the darkening cavern.

"Let's take it slow and easy. This is our first time," she whispered and closed her eyes. I closed mine, and felt her velvet smooth tongue slide between my lips in a passionate kiss as we pressed against each other.

"I want to do everything with you," she said, as she took off her bathing suit and lets it floats to creek's edge with mine. "I want to taste, smell and feel you wet on my lips like a fresh summer flower from my Grandmother's garden," she said as she breathed and exhaled a deep sigh while relaxing in the cool water.

Then she pulled me to her and I lay wet and naked against her. She spoke softly in my ear saying "I need to feel you. I want you," and pulled me into the soft wetness of her thighs.

"Wait, I'm not ready yet! And I'm afraid it may hurt."

"I know what to do," I answered as she put her soft hands gently on my shoulders and let me move down to taste and feel her soft body with my tongue as she eased her head back against the flat stone in the shallow water and closed her eyes.

"Yes like that," she said, as I moved to her belly and ran my tongue around her navel. She pushed me again to go lower as I kissed her again and again and pressed my tongue against her.

"I feel so good and wonderful," she repeated as she softens in my arms; exhausted from holding me so tightly. Then, she released me and I moved up her body, and our lips met as she spread her legs to mine as I pushed into the softness of her thighs.

Jamie gasps at the hard feel of me in her hands. Then guiding me inside, opening her legs wider, enticing me to push slowly, and deeply, as I felt her inner smoothness and satin softness.

"Stay right there, and push hard. I need to feel your hardness in me," as I stayed still. I felt her body tightening again against me while arching her hips up to me, with an, "I'm okay, I want this. It feels so full" as she squeezed me tighter, pressing her heels hard behind my knees and inviting me to begin the driving rhythm, we both craved and had waited for, so long, forcing us higher and higher until I felt her quickening breath hot in my ear.

"I love you so, keep going, don't stop!" she groaned, as she pulled me to her and I felt myself starting to come and slowed my movement. Aware of this, she kept her arms around me and held me tight saying, "It's okay, we're okay, and I feel so good with you," as she cradled her arms once again around me while caressing my back with deep penetrating strokes, and I surged forward deep into her; stopped, and relaxed, letting the full weight of my body engulf her.

We lay still in each other arms, holding each other while breathing to the sounds of the cascading water.

"Stay close, don't move yet, she said, I want to feel you, on me and, I want to kiss you forever," as she opened her eyes and looked up at me.

"Let's stay like this. I want to close my eyes and see and feel us together, again. I want to feel you holding me, keeping me safe. I want to love again and again," as I noticed, she had drifted into a dreamy sleep.

I pulled her up and carried her to a flat rock where we could sit at the edge of the creek. I held her close and wrapped the large dry towels around us, letting the warmth of my body, warm hers, as she lay her head back against my chest.

"I feel wonderful," she said again through closed eyes. Let's help each other dry off and put on our bathing suits, and go home. I love you soldier boy for loving me."

Jamie was happy with a wonderful glow and giddy, embarrassed look on her face, as we walked, hand-in-hand, back to the house. We hardly spoke, only walked with our arms around each other. Ms. Thompson was on the porch with an expectant smile and welcoming gesture inviting us to dinner in the kitchen.

First Night

Ms. Thompson welcomed us back to the house with a tight, warm hug before we joined her at the dinner table.

"If only Johnathan could see this. I know he's looking down and smiling at you two. I am so happy for you. I prepared some of the leftovers from today, and a big piece of five-layer strawberry cake for you, Wade. I hope you don't mind, but I did some special things to your room, and hope the two of you enjoy your honeymoon night here." She began to cry, and Jamie reached over and hugged her, as she looked at me to say something.

"I plan to help Tom with the hay and apple trees tomorrow, after I get back from my folks in the morning. My dad wants to talk about our farm, and I need to do my four-mile run to stay in shape. I promised him I would be there by seven o'clock, so I'll need to leave on my run around six and will be back by nine.

"I'm sure my mother will make a big breakfast for me, so I'll have my father drive me back. He will help with the hay and apples as well. I told them that Jamie and I would come by on our way out of town to say good-bye. Hope that's okay. They're not much for socializing. It will be a quick visit."

"When will you two be back?" Ms. Thompson asked.

"I don't know for sure Grandmother, but we would like to come home for the reunion. I'm doing well with my health, and may have some radio and TV appearances here in August."

"Major Lasiter is working on my orders, and there is a chance I may be re-assigned to Fort Belvoir, or maybe to the Army Pictorial Center in New York City, by this August or September. So, we both may be here. I'll let you know as soon as I can," I said.

"Wade, you hadn't told me that! When will you know for sure?" Jamie inquired, with a surprised smile on her face.

"Maybe on our return. I have to call the major tomorrow and will know more. It shouldn't interfere with the USO tour. I am so happy for you about that."

"That would be so good. I could visit Grandmother more, and you could come home on weekends. I can't wait to hear more," she finished excitedly, as she looked at the clock and told her grandmother she would help with the dishes before going to bed. I offered to help, but they told me to take a walk outside, and come back in 30 minutes or so.

I knew Jamie wanted to talk with her grandmother about us, the wedding, our time at the cave today, and tonight, so I welcomed the chance to walk to the barn, check the animals, and talk with Tom about the next day.

When I returned, Jamie and her grandmother were sitting on the front porch singing old gospel songs Johnathan loved. I joined in, and we sang and hummed along until Ms. Thompson stood up and said, "Good night. See you in the morning for a cup of coffee."

I took Jamie's hands and kissed both palms, as her grandmother said, "I love you. I love you both," and disappeared to her room.

"I have milk, cream, and sweet buttered biscuits for us tonight. Their magical ingredients will take us on a magical journey so that tonight will be one of the best memories we'll ever have. And I'm a little tender down there," Jamie whispered in my ear, as she moved close to me. I think we over did it at the cave, but I want to do it again with you tonight.

"While you were gone, Grandmother and I talked about everything, and I hope you don't mind, but we called Lilly in California. We talked about the wedding feast today, and our time at the cave. You know, girls talk. She wanted to know how you were. I told her pretty wonderful, and it was the best.

"Lilly told me, without hesitating, to use the aloe vera if I was a little sore and have you lubricate me with Rosebud Salve tonight.

"So let's just stay here on the porch, and talk until Grandmother's asleep. Then we can go up. I have so much to show you, and tell about in my room," she said, excitedly.

"We can take as much time as you need, and if tonight is not good, we'll wait."

"We'll see. I want to know about your orders. What can you tell me?"

"The Major told me, before we left, that he was getting a promotion and reassignment to the east coast. I'm not supposed to say anything, but he wants my team to go with him. There are three of us. We will serve as his support, as the military works on a potential buildup of troops, and reconnaissance and surveillance equipment. I may get a promotion in the assignment as well.

"He has a lot of confidence in my surveillance data reports, and my analysis of the desert troop maneuvers. I had never done any actual film interpretation, but he thinks I have a knack for it and this assignment could play a crucial role with his officers. You may not understand this, but I know you care about what I'm saying. It's important that we keep this between us until I know for sure on our return. I'm thinking late August or September, but I want to make sure your health is good and it's best for you."

"I love you, soldier boy, and my lips are sealed except for...this," she said, as kissed me with a tenderness and passion that consumed me.

The Room

Ms. Thompson had lit eighteen scented candles for Jamie and me. On a side chair there was a card with our names and a note. Jamie put three records on the drop down player, and we undressed for bed, slid under the covers, and took the note out to read.

Hope" is the thing with feathers -
That perches in the soul -
And sings the tune without the words -
And never stops - at all...

I found this in the book of Emily Dickinson's poetry that your Grandfather loved so much.
I hope you will always share this love with each other. With love, Grandmother.

Jamie and I sat on the bed, and she put the last of the creamy milk between us, as we shared one final buttered biscuit. As she placed the note back on the nightstand, I said, "I love your room. It's you. Tell me about it. I want to know more about you."

"I have always loved this room. It's where my grandmother and grandfather brought me when I returned from the hospital. It's been the place where I dreamed. I've lived here for ten years. It's my world, and they helped me make it through all those years. They are the parents I never had, and the grandparents I always wanted.

"When I first came here, I was scared and missed my parents and brother. I didn't really know them. They always seemed so old to me and worked the farm all the time. My father used to make fun of them and called them names. I wasn't sure what my life was going to be like here. I must have put them through hell. I cussed at them and even hit my grandmother, when she tried to make me wear a dress to church and short pants in the summer. I was a pretty bad little kid, and continued that way until about a year before I met you. I hated the world and everybody in

 it. Can you understand that? I was nobody. I was all alone and life hurt. I hurt, and I wanted to hurt other people. Sometimes, it still comes back.

"Look at the drawings I did on the wall over there, over my dresser and mirror. Grandmother saved every one and put them up for me. I drew stick people with angry faces and later tried to draw pictures of the mountains and river, but they never came out right. The one piece of art I really like is over the head of this bed. I will tell you about it. Look up at it. My grandfather got it for me when he bought that big set of Encyclopedias and the World Atlas, over there on the bookcase. It's a large folded, poster of a painting, by a man named Giulio Romano', who had a penchant for erotic subject matter.

"It is supposed to show the encounter between Zeus and Alcmene. The alarmed dog at the maidservant's feet, points to a breach of marital fidelity. That's pretty heavy stuff. I memorized it for a test in the seventh grade, and it really impressed the teacher. My own take on it, is that it's two young lovers, and a very loving grandmother protector. She is hiding in the closet with a loving dog named, Sampson, who is my grandfather incarnated back on earth...Hey don't laugh at me.

"Anyway, the female is learning and reading a lot about sex, flirtation and love-making, and she's putting her hand on her lover as she raises the sheet to see what he's got under there..." as I began laughing so hard, that she shushed me so her grandmother wouldn't hear.

"Now, let me finish. You wanted to know more about me. I spent a lot of time in this room last year looking at that painting and fantasizing about you-know-who. My grandfather had no idea what I would become when he put it up there. That's a secret I've kept. Grandmother has always been my protector. I tell her everything and always have. She was who I told about meeting you on the bus after the counselor pissed me off, and I came home crying that day. Bet you didn't know that, did you?"

"Now look at that painting." She slid her hand under the cover and held me and kissed me hard, and let me go when I started laughing.

"Ok if you want some tonight you better pay attention soldier boy!" She teasingly glared at me with a smile.

"Did you see the charcoal nude painting over there of me modeling my butterfly for an art class? It's by an artist named Linda Harris who was a student at the university. The other one is the famous painting, *Girl with a Pearl Earring,* by the Dutch painter Johannes Vermeer. It ought to mean something to you, since your great ancestor who came to America in 1754, was also named Johannes. It is an oil painting of a girl wearing a headscarf and a pearl earring. It is shrouded in mystery, like me, and she is thought to have been a lover of Vermeer's. Others are intrigued by the fact that a poor peasant girl is wearing a very expensive pearl earring, leading some to interpret that she may have been a prostitute who worked in one of the many taverns or boarding houses close to where Vermeer lived and painted.

"My grandfather used to call me 'Pearl' when we were at the cave and told me I was beautiful like the girl with the pearl earring. She looked alone in the world, but her real beauty and essence was captured by a famous artist for the entire world to see.

"That's me: The Girl with the Heart Shaped Amber Earring and Diamond Shaped Tattoo." She said, and started to reach for the lamp chain, saying, "So, what do you think of my little tour around the room? Got something else on your mind?"

"Wait Jamie, this is important. You know so much. You have learned so much, and you have a gift for writing songs and poetry like no one I know. What am I going to do....when...?" I paused.

"You're going to love me like crazy while I'm here!"

She kissed me, and then pushed the last of the biscuit crumbs into my mouth, and pulls the lamp chain to darken the room. We made soft, tender and easy love to the Bobby Vinton songs on the record player.

Running Home

It had been a wonderful day, and an even more wondrous lovemaking night with Jamie.

It was six o'clock, and the bed squeaked I got as I got out of bed. I washed my face in the night basin and dressed for the four-mile run to my parents' house south of Nellysford, on Berryhill Road.

At the wedding, my father had asked me if I could come to the farm early so we could talk. I sensed something was not right. The mornings were always best for us, and sometimes my grandfather joined us to milk the goats and feed the chickens while we finished the cows.

As I walked down the stairs, I waved at Ms. Thompson making early morning coffee in the kitchen and told her that my dad and I would be back before nine to help Tom with the hay and orchard spraying. "I left a note for Jamie," I said, as I jumped off the porch into the yard, and set out across the pasture to Spruce Creek Road.

The morning was fresh, and there was just enough moisture in the air to cool my skin as I ran down the steep, gravel road to the pavement at Harris Store. I set a seven-minute mile pace to run the four miles to my parents' farm.

As I ran, I reminisced about this familiar pathway to Nellysford, and how many times I had ridden my bicycle on cold winter evenings, delivering *Grit* newspapers to customers from Nellysford to Beech Grove, and then back to Nellysford before nightfall. I had to deliver 90 papers before getting home for chores and homework.

On I pushed past FP Phillip's Packing Shed, stopping on the Stoney Creek Bridge to look at the falls cascade some two hundred feet down the mountain until it emptied into the creek bed and made its way to the Rockfish River. The village of Nellysford was just waking up as I ran past Small's store. I waved at some orchard workers fueling a tractor to head into the orchard for peaches. They would later haul them to the shed on Highway 151 for packing and shipping.

Ole man Dodd was in his front yard walking his dog and throwing a stick for him to fetch. He turned and looked at me and waved the stick as if inviting me to stop. "Wade, come see me!" he shouted. "Wish I could, but I need to get home. Take care, and see you another time."

At the steep entrance to the Rockfish Valley Baptist Church, I pushed myself up the gravel road and made my way to the cemetery in back. As I walked among the tombstones, I touched and remembered relatives buried beneath the thick, lush grass offset by family stone markers. I thought I saw Mr. Roades at his wife's marker, but on closer inspection realized it was Pastor Woodson kneeling and praying in the cemetery, as he was known to do in the cool of the morning.

The he looked up, waved at me, and then returned to the marker of an infant and prayed for the parents. He waved me on saying, "Be well and God be with you." I headed back to the road to resume my morning run. At Small's packing shed, I ran up to the loading dock and said, "Hello" to Rudolph Small and his brother. They were loading a truck and invited me to join them with a shout of, "Same pay as we always paid you five dollars a truckload."

I shouted back to them, "I'll work another time. I needed finish my run and will see you again soon."

It would be a long uphill run before I turned off on Berryhill Lane for the last half-mile to our farm. I knew my father would be waiting. He had just finished with the last of the milking and returned the cows to the pasture. He looked tired and invited me to sit on the barn railing.

"You know the price is going out of apples, and it's hard to get help in the summer for harvest. Without you here and my back injury, it's more than I think I can handle. So, I've decided to sell the farm land, or lease it out to other farmers. Your grandparents are still working their place as best they can, but I think this will be the last year for me. I remember you and the kids playing the old Victrola in the chicken house. I remember the day your brother tried to fly off the roof of the barn and almost killed himself. I remember fishing and teaching you to hunt. I remember all you kids swimming in the river, until they opened Van Riper's Lake, and then you went there all the time. I remember everything, and I especially remember driving you to the bus station a year ago when you went into the Army.

"It's sad times here in the mountains. Twenty-six more of our boys left, like you, for the service. There are bad times ahead for this country. I felt it in '43 when I left and joined the army. I served in Italy and Germany. It's the same thing all over. Many will die, and many will return, but none will ever be the same.

"That's why I'm selling the farm and moving back to Waynesboro. It's the place I know; this is the place I have always loved. You were here, but you're leaving, and you won't come back. If you do, nothing here will be the way you remembered it. Your grandparents have told me they plan to move into Nellysford. It's just too far for them now to go for groceries and medical care. Your mother has made up her mind that this is not the life she wants. I don't know what we'll do, with my retirement and social security, but we'll survive somehow. We always have.

"Your mother and I got your letter and were surprised, but happy for you. Real nice party yesterday. She's a very special girl. You two have some hard days ahead of you, but we will pray for you both.

"I guess I need to get you back to help Tom with the last of the early apple spraying. I can bale hay, but I can't load the bales anymore, so you will have to do it all. Your mother wants to go and talk with Wanda and Jamie while we're working, so I guess we better move along and get her and the breakfast she made for you.

"I saved some of the money from the sale of twenty-four hams and shoulders for you, and I hope it will help a little as you make your way back to California. Promise us you will stay in touch and not forget us here. I know it will be hard to travel, but I hope to see you two again for that reunion in late August, if possible. I see your mother on the porch waiting, so I guess we better go."

We didn't talk much on the drive to Ms. Thompson's, but I knew my father and mother always meant the best for me. They always did. I think I surprised them with the wedding, but they were supportive as always, and it meant a lot to me. My father didn't move as well as I remembered, but he worked hard and always hoped for the best. Tom had sprayed the lower trees in the meadow before we arrived.

Once we finished the last of the apple tree on the steep mountain rise, we applied ourselves to baling the hayfield. It was wetter and heavier than we liked, but rain was on the way, again, we decided to put the hay in the barn and let it dry there. By three o'clock we were finished, and we enjoyed a nice picnic lunch on the porch before my mother and father departed for home. Jamie and I headed for the cave to bathe and cool off, before packing for our trip to California via Charlottesville the next day.

She kept saying "This can't be the last time. I want more," as I bathed her with the cool water. She moved to the feel of my touch on her back and pulled me tightly to her smooth, velvet body for one last time. We had to leave, but we knew we would remember this faraway loving, place, with fondness while we were in California.

Fort Ord Post Commander Briefing

Major Lasiter entered the post commander's office with a salute, and took his seat at the conference table with the two other division commanders already present.

"Gentlemen," General Gerard, Post Commander for Fort Ord said, as he stood to address the group. "I have invited you here to review our roll-out plan for Fort Ord, should President Johnson sign the Gulf of Tonkin Resolution. These are orders direct from Army Command, and need our utmost attention.

"The desert exercises you and your troops participated in have been reviewed and accepted for forward action within the calendar year. I don't think I need to mention the secrecy in this matter, but if the buildup is imminent, our units will be in the thick of it by 1965-1966.

"In September Major Lasiter is receiving a promotion to Lt. Colonel. I believe this is a well-deserved promotion. Furthermore, I consider you all my closest advisors, and that is a term we need to get used to in the coming year. If there is a conflict, we will be 'advisor units' doing ground force training by native troops. I am sure there will be engagements that put our officers and troops in harm's way. They can react if fired upon, but otherwise, we will be ready and advise the country soldiers to fight any insurgency that comes their way. The details will unfold in the months ahead, as Army Command releases orders to post commanders for readiness and implementation.

"Major Lasiter will be our eyes and ears in Washington, and Communication Command Headquarters at Fort Belvoir. We will ready our troops and new recruits as orders proceed and overt action is required.

"We will meet on a weekly basis as orders are posted to me. Otherwise, training and maneuvers will continue as planned, on a routine and normal basis. Our CEDEC Unit with Major Lasiter will be the first to go through the reorientation and training assignments. I believe he has hand-picked some of his best officers and enlisted men for assignments already. We look forward to hearing more as we go into late summer and fall. That is all. Thank you gentlemen, and God be with us."

With the smallest divisional unit of two lieutenants, one master sergeant, and eleven top flight army sergeant/specialists, Major Lasiter knew three things for certain: his unit, though small, would be important to the total operation; he would be promoted to lieutenant Colonel in the near future; and his next two years of service would be different from any assignment he had had so far.

A number of thoughts went through his mind as he returned to his office. With me and the other enlisted men and specialists on leave, and due to return in late July, he would talk with Stephanie tonight over dinner. This was sure to affect her and their plans to marry in the near future. Jamie and I would be back soon. He looked forward to reviewing training and maneuvers with me and the other trusted leaders in his unit, who he knew would be responsible for implementing the command orders and his work with the Fulbright committee.

He would commit to a future of a possible military buildup, domestic insurgency, and the general unrest and protest movement that was sure to start with a draft increase. He would keep his thoughts and concerns about the new assignment, to himself and follow orders, no matter how dangerous or conflicting in nature.

Conflict and Domestic Unrest

I read reports in the newspapers as media columnists, and political analysts, coast to coast, speculated about ships in the vicinity of the Tonkin delta and Pleiku.

Major Lasiter now attended the now weekly meetings at the Post Commander's office. A new readiness was in the making, should President Johnson gain the Congressional support he needed to move ahead with the Tonkin Resolution.

The news reported not only the military speculation on Vietnam, but also the domestic uprising and protest movements which started with the founding of the National Convention of Students for a Democratic Society in 1962. The UC Berkley Free Speech Movement began with a handful of disgruntled veterans at Port Huron. It progressed to a full-blown movement that voted down the university's stand on student activism in 1964. With the fears and paranoias of a military buildup and student unrest, the nation's colleges and universities became breeding grounds for students who felt politicians and military lobbyists were driving society to its demise and self-destruction.

Our CEDEC weekly briefings took on a new and fearful direction. Colonel Lasiter had moved into his new role as advisor to Senator Fulbright and confidante to the post commander on matters of the impending and sure fire military action, that would put us all in the forefront of a dark and uncertain future.

During this time, Jamie and I read everything we could and tried to understand more about what the San Francisco Chronicle called the 'mind numbing life' as described in Roszak's The Making of A Counterculture.

Jamie read, and encouraged me to read: Sex and the Single Girl, which she believed would force a new community of radicalism in women like none before. She believed it would create a national movement of angry and disenfranchised women that would be equal to the men's movements and protests festering in the bay area.

The Amex Theater, Fort Ord, California

The crowd could not stop their applause.

We knew the USO event had to be a success on base with the Post Commander and his staff in attendance, or it would not be successful at the other six locations, already scheduled.

Jamie had won them over with her guitar playing and singing of hit songs, while the Fort Ord band got soldiers on the dance floor to dance with partners who attended and supported them. She told her story and invited soldiers from the audience to come to the stage and tell theirs. It was an unforgettable evening for her and the audience. The Amex Theater had not seen the likes of a female singer who could command the stage and touch hearts like Jamie.

At her invitation, soldiers talked about home, duty and honor. They talked about friends, families, wives, and husbands waiting for them. They talked about the news and what it could mean for them, but mostly their thoughts were about now: the music, the words of encouragement, and the soft voice that sang about a butterfly, and other songs of patriotism and encouragement for those far from home.

In addition to Jamie's singing and playing schedule on Wednesday and Thursday at Crusoe's, she performed at several other locations. She especially liked singing at the Monterey Broadman Records and Books, where her music enjoyed good sales. Her income and appearance receipts exceeded anything she had ever imagined. She donated twenty percent of her proceeds to support the USO. She was indeed having the best year of her life and thanked her audiences at every opportunity.

I continued to work my military schedule Monday through Thursday. The post commander and Colonel Lasiter supported me in my three-day weekends off to travel with Jamie and the band. It was an intense, exciting time for us all. Jamie was always our cheerleader, and because of her, we kept going with little sleep and lots of food that appeared magically at every stop.

After the Fort Ord appearance, I loaded Jamie's guitar and the sound equipment into a 1962 Fairlane Ford from the motor pool. She was visibly tired, but still willing to return words of appreciation and encouragement to passing soldiers and friends who had attended the event.

"I have to sit in the car and rest before we leave," she said. "This is more than I ever thought possible. They really liked my music. They felt something. I love you for all your support. The General was so gracious and I think Colonel Lasiter and Stephanie danced and applauded every song. I watched you all night. I love you." she smiled, as she put her arm around me and kissed me.

"Get me to the cottage, so we can rest up for tomorrow. I am so happy." She laid her head on my shoulder and hummed to a Frank Sinatra song on the car radio on the drive home.

After Jamie's performance at Saint Augustine Catholic Church in San Francisco, she and I decided to stay at the Sheraton on Fisherman's Wharf to treat ourselves to a day off before returning to Fort Ord and Pacific Grove.

At the hotel, we undressed and showered together. I washed her back and gently massaged the butterfly tattoo. She lifted her arms high, slid her hands up the wall of the shower. "I am so open for you," as she leaned back against me. We stayed wrapped in each other's arms as she tenderly said, "I'm afraid sometimes that I will lose you, if I don't hold you tight. I want to make love to you every day. I want to sing my songs and plan together. And, I feel wonderful and excited. Hold me close, so I know you will never go away." Her lips came to mine, and we kissed and caressed as the shower drained the last of the day's delights from our bodies.

We stepped from the warm, steamy shower, toweled each other's bodies and pulled on our over-sized cotton t-shirts. We slipped between the sheets and enjoyed final good night kiss before drifting off to sleep.

Love Me Like Crazy

We were settling into a precise, but rushed schedule and making every opportunity to be with each other until her planned trip to Virginia for the reunion. She had a number of radio appearances planned with Marianne in Charlottesville, Waynesboro and Lynchburg. The tentative plan was for her to leave on August 28th, after a follow-up medical appointment with Stephanie at the base hospital.

On the night of August 27th, I woke up 1:30 a.m. and started nervously pacing around the cottage living room. Jamie walked in and asked, "Why are you up at this hour?"

"Jamie, I have a recurring dream. I wake up in the middle of the night and reach for you." I spoke in a low, guilt-ridden tone. The words came from the very depths of my soul as I poured out my heart with a flood of tears. "I'm sorry. I want you here all the time. It's an emptiness that I can't fill. It's a pain I have, and sometimes I want to die for you. Forgive me, but so help me, I mean it. I want to be strong, and I love you so. I want to believe this will go on. I, I," my voice stumbled in the dark as we made our way back to bed.

Jamie sled back to her side of the bed and grabbed her stomach. She struggled to get her breath. It was apparent that it had been my strength that had kept her going. She knew it might come to this. Ms. Stevens told her this might happen. She turned away, and planted her face deep in her pillow and smothering her voice into fabric, "God, Lord Jesus, how can we talk about this? I don't want this. I don't want to be this important to this wonderful, sweet man," she stopped, in a cold sweat that chilled her bones, as she shouted, "Wait!"

She turned over to face me and gathered me in her arms. "We've got to talk about this and not avoid it anymore. I love you, and I'm hurting too, but I don't feel it, as much as you. You'll still be here when I'm gone, so let's talk. Damn it, I love you and hurt for you, but I've got to tell you something. I want to talk it out, and then, I want you to come at me more passionately than ever before."

"What's going on Jamie?"

"Everything!" she screamed at me. "We are so in love. I want to tell you what I believe is going to happen. I've read everything you can imagine about this, and as long as you love me and remember me, I will never really die.

"So, Wade Dhamner, let me tell you what I know, and believe for sure. I've read the ancient philosophers and about the Hindu Avatars, the most famous being Buddha, Krishna and Rama. I've read everything about Jesus Christ himself. They don't know what we know. This time we have together will last forever. I will go on living for you in my songs and poems. Every time you read one of my poems, or someone sings one of my songs, I'll be here. Understand?

"And yes, I will reach out for you too, in the night, and in the day time, and will keep reaching out for you. So you better be there! You are an amazing man, and I'm going to watch you every minute of every day from now and into eternity.

"We've been reading the classics together, and through that you've become more than my literary soulmate. I've gone higher in my understanding of poetry, music, and love than I ever imagined. So, let's finish this journey to infinity, and go wherever it takes us."

It was a new awareness for both of us. She was on fire, and I wanted to hear more. She went on to tell me what she really believed about God, and the gods and goddesses of myth and fantasy. "Hold me, love me crazy, and tell me everything you want, because I'm going to do it. Got it?"

"Got it!" I said, as we reached for each other in the dark. "We are so married now!" she exclaimed. "I want to do everything, every day, if possible," as she pulled me tight and returned my every thrust, with one of her own as she kissed my lips, along my neck and wrapped herself around me.

We slept in each other's arms until the alarm clock woke us at seven o'clock.

Exciting but Conflicting Times

Jamie's successes in California had set off an avalanche of events. She took every opportunity to express her appreciation for her supporters contributions to her success. She was sure to have a spot on the playlist at the upcoming Monterey Jazz Festival in September.

With Jamie's USO Pacific Coast tour finishing, we made plans for another trip to Virginia on August 28th. We would go to her family reunion and make guest appearances in surrounding towns for her records, "It Was You", and "Blue Mountain Highway Home." She was already booked at the very popular Van Riper's Lake Resort in Nelson County for a Labor Day performance.

The post commander wanted to continue the USO tour over Christmas, with three appearances in and around the Monterey base. The colonel and the post commander provided print ads, transportation, use of the Fort Ord Spring Band, and Stephanie offered medical support.

The colonel and Stephanie announced their engagement and wedding plans in late August. Lilly and Thomas were having growing success with Crusoe's, and were attracting others to play and sing with Jamie on the Thursday "Pizza and Beer" nights. Broadman Records became the exclusive sales point for Jamie's music. Jamie and her grandmother scheduled phone calls every Thursday afternoon and talked for an hour.

I enjoyed my back stage support, and the time we shared on our special 'Sundays' in Monterey. We walked along the beach, read and discussed books, enjoyed cinnamon buns at the local coffee shops, and made love on leisurely afternoons at the cottage.

In a magical way, it seemed as if there was a heavenly glow over this time. We could forget the inevitable of outcome of Jamie's condition. She was stronger, and the medical care administered by Stephanie and base doctor, was having a positive effect.

I knew about the Thursday afternoon 'gatherings' in the garden. I didn't want to let Jamie know I knew about the private parties at the cottage with Lilly and her 'herbal' gardening friends in the Pacific Grove neighborhood. Lilly understood, said they worked, and kept the contents hidden from curious neighbors in an assorted plant containers and flower boxes.

The 'magical garden' as Jamie described it, appeared to have a positive effect on her creative and inspirational writing and singing. I chose to not make this part of our conversations and silently gave it my approval.

The base was becoming a fast-paced nerve of recruitment activity, and my assignments were becoming more and more focused on the domestic counter-culture and protests that were most likely to erupt on several California campuses. The draft and deferments became a focal point for student unrest and protests in the summer of 1964. It was during this time that I made my first cross-country flight to Fort Belvoir to review and finalize my plans for my transfer in October.

The briefings by the colonel and troop activity on bases around the country, as reported by the media, led everyone to think that even though there was a military buildup, the real conflict would be fought by very young soldiers on foreign soil. Protestors would be influenced by a domestic counter culture, as reported in the media, who were committed to mobilizing a seemingly apathetic community on the one hand, and a very large group of college students on the other.

It was a very difficult and conflicting time for me. While I was a soldier serving in the US Army with critical military responsibilities, my conversations and life with Jamie led me to listen carefully, and sympathize with the greater issues of the day. I knew these issues would have an important effect on my future as a soldier, as well as my life with Jamie.

Phone Call From Grandmother

"Hello, Jamie. It's so good to hear your voice. We miss you desperately and hope to see you in August."

"I'll be there, Grandmother. We are having the best time and traveling. Wade and I are so happy and the USO tour is what I really want to do. What's happening at home? You sound sad."

"No child, we're okay. Just miss you and love to hear your voice. All the neighbors tell me about hearing your songs on the radio. The Waynesboro newspaper wrote an article about your upcoming appearance at Van Riper's Lake Resort on Labor Day weekend. We will all be there. How's your health, Jamie?"

"I'm doing better, but still have the headaches. No one stares at me anymore, except to applaud. Stephanie, my nurse, has been so good to me. Lilly and I have become the best of friends, and I think I have talked her into coming back with me in August for a visit with you."

"I know Jamie. She called and told me the other day. She, like me, has never been on an airplane. I think I would get sick. I am so happy for you. Everyone sends their love. How's Wade? I talked to his mother the other day. Sally is

having a checkup for high blood pressure and Wade's father is selling the farm. I am so sorry about that, but with all the building and construction here at the Wintergreen Resort, the prices and taxes are going up. It's hard to make a living on a farm. We had a good year. I will have the pigs ready for our barbeque when you are here."

"Grandmother," Jamie pleaded, "you would tell me if something was wrong, wouldn't you?"

"Yes. Tom took a fall, and I have had to get Wade's father to help with the apple harvest. He's so good with the workers and does the best he can with all he has to do with his own place. He talks about missing Wade all the time, but knows that the Army is best for him now. I love you Jamie. Be sure to hug Wade for me and we'll see you soon."

"Good-bye, Grandmother. I love you."

As Jamie placed the phone on the receiver, she felt something was wrong at home. Was grandmother sick? Something wrong on the farm? She knew she wasn't going to hear bad news. This is the way it had always been. She would be patient until she went home and would learn more then.

人

Labor Day at Van Riper's Lake Resort

Lilly, Thomas, and I watched and waved, as Jamie's plane took off from the Monterey Airport on Friday, August 28th. I took a later flight on a military transport to Fort Belvoir for my briefing, and then on to New York City and the Army Pictorial Center in Queens. At APC, I met with the CECOM team and together we planned intelligence and pictorial strategy as part of the colonel's assignment for the Fulbright commission.

On Monday, I boarded a train in Central Station for Charlottesville, where Jamie was waiting for me. From the train station in Charlottesville, we drove straight to the university for her medical appointment. The headaches were bothering her more, but she tried not to complain. The supplements and weekly steroid shots seemed to take care of her lingering jaw and shoulder pain.

We took our time driving down highway 29, detouring through Schuyler to visit the childhood home Earl Hammer, Jr., before stopping at Aistrops Café for one of their famous hotdogs.

Jamie was in a positive mood and talked excitedly about the Monterey Jazz Festival and our life together. The evening meal with Ms. Thompson was just like old times. Jamie joked, as we enjoyed a pot of green beans, boiled potatoes and salted country ham. Ms. Thompson informed us that she and Hanna had been going to the cave to soak in the cool water. She commented that she felt close to Johnathan, and even wrote a few poems of her own for Jamie to read and maybe turn into songs. Tom and Hanna joined us for cake and coffee on the porch as the sun was setting over Three Ridge Mountain.

As darkness settled on the porch, Jamie nudged me and we excused ourselves to her room. We held each other more than usual and made love once again to the flickering candlelight and our favorite Bobby Vinton songs and Jamie's recording of *It Was You*.

On Wednesday and Thursday, we stayed close to home so Jamie could rest and practice for the weekend festival. She had brought new sheet music, and had even written a few new songs. She took great delight in working on one of her grandmother's poems and hoped to include it in her performance. It would make her grandmother cry a little, but she would like it.

We arrived early for the Van Riper's Lake festival for a sound check before taking a walk around the lake. We stopped at the headwaters of the lake where a fisherman was reeling in a largemouth bass.

Cars began to arrive at five o'clock, and occupants quickly took their seats on the grassy knoll above the dam. This area gave people a good view of the make-shift bandstand built for the occasion. The sun was still reflecting hot off the lake, but quickly dropped behind Pinnacle Mountain. A cool breeze flowed across the beach sand, as spectators bought drinks, hotdogs and hamburgers. The wooden stands filled quickly as families, friends and guests returned to their seats for the concert.

The crowd stopped talking in expectation as Jamie lifted her guitar. She did not disappoint them. She sang old favorites and sing-alongs including a blues version of her song *Blue Mountain Highway Home* and *It Was You*. The crowd listened in awe and wonder as she told them her story and reflected on her memories of being a young hurt child who was loved by her grandparents. She told of her dreams and hopes. She told them about meeting a soldier on a bus who made her promise—a promise that would help her chase her dream to sing in California.

She told them, for now, she was home with the people she knew and loved who had come to hear her. She could feel them with every note, every chord, and every word that poured from her heart.

Here, she was the queen, and no one was her rival. She earned their respect and heartfelt adoration by letting them know her as she invited them come closer to stage for her closing song.

As she closed with her very favorite Pete Seeger song, she sang out: "This...This...This..." and hold it as long as you can and don't let it fade away... "is my country, land that I love..." to a crowd of young and old, who only now had heard her voice, but would never forget this night and her songs.

Jamie knew and understood that when she was gone, her gifts of love, songs, poems, letters, books, and the very essence of her life as a hurting soul who had been healed, would be remembered in the hearts of those who knew her.

She deeply believed that the many of the sparkling moments of her life, including the melody of the brooks and streams near her beloved Spruce Creek home would live in the memories if those who knew and loved her.

As she placed her warm hand on my shoulder during the slow drive down Rockfish Lane to Highway 151, she leaned back against the seat. She turned to me saying, "Promise me again you'll bring me home when I get sick. I want to be home when I get worse."

I looked straight ahead, as I fought back the sad feelings and I took her hand and kissed it saying, "I will. Don't worry, I will, I promise, I promise."

Flight to California

It was like a dream. There was a faint smell of wisteria and freshly mowed grass in the air, as we left the house for the airport on Tuesday morning. Ms. Thompson was quiet until she said, "It's strange that we sometimes only get together as family and friends during homecomings wedding, and funerals."

At the airport, we all smiled, laughed, and hugged as never before, while waiting for the Charlottesville regional plane that would take us to Washington DC, for our flight back to California.

My mother repeated to me what she had a year ago, "Get on that blue mountain highway, come home. And bring Jamie with you."

Ms. Thompson wouldn't let Jamie go, pulled her close, and whispered in her ear, "I love you, I love you."

My father put his hand on my shoulder, and shyly said, "We'll be here for you son, when you come back. Take care of that girl, and hold her whenever you can."

Hanna and Tom tried to conceal their sadness. "It is hard, Hanna said, to let you go, and wait for your return. Come home please."

My grandmother kept wiping tears away as she hugged and kissed us, "I'll be here when you come home."

We didn't want this to be a sad parting, but we all knew that this was the last time -- the last time -- that Jamie would be so happy, so thrilled and so full of life.

I wasn't sure why, but it felt like we were in a play, a midsummer night's dream, and this was the final curtain call. The curtain was coming down slowly, and even stopped in a quiet moment of selfish animation. The very air around us paused and took its own silent breath, swirled in place and settled to the stage floor. We looked at each other.

Our eyes were clear. We were all smiling. Our lips were moving but there were no words. There was a quiet calm, as I watched what appeared to be a choir of angels, their glowing hair blowing in the gentle breeze and sparkling with crescents. Their silken dresses swayed rhythmically to a gentle, mystical guitar in the shadows and a soft sweet voice sang, as all eyes pivoted toward Jamie's soft angelic face "I love you. I love you all."

Then the melody faded, and I felt her hand on my shoulder and her fingers on my lips as her voice said, "It's time for us to leave, so we can come back home again."

Monterey Jazz Festival, September 18, 1964

Jamie had a determined assurance in her step, as we paraded into the old fairgrounds for the second day of the music festival.

The Friday afternoon kickoff with *The Weavers,* still lingered in my head. The smooth voice and musical melodies of Miles Davis drifted from the stage, as he practiced and gave some final instructions to his band for the afternoon event.

Jamie turned her head side to side, as we walked behind an old make-shift shed that housed speakers and other sound equipment. She had been told Pete Seeger's fans liked to hang out here and join together for a few jam sessions before going on stage. We found him, and a very young talkative and unpretentious Janis Joplin, who passed us with a wink and smile on her way to the coffee tent.

"Let's follow her," Jamie said to me, as we turned quickly and found ourselves in a smoky, canvas tent full of band members and local folk singers. In the middle of the crowded tent was, as someone said, "Joan Baez, harmonizing with Pete Seeger."

They waved us in and invited Jamie to take out her guitar and join in for a couple of sessions. She was ecstatic. This is what she came for. It was just like she dreamed it would be. She lifted herself up on to the side of the timbered picnic table and joined in with the group singing, *We Shall Overcome, East Virginia* and *All My Trials.* Jamie had only played these songs a few times before, but she joined in and sang melody or harmony.

Someone raised their hand and pointed at Jamie, "I want to hear her." So she sang out her favorite, in a high pitched voice:

"It was you who taught me love
It was you who put the sun back in my sky

*It was you who made my every dream come true
And it was you..."*

They all joined in as one with her, as I sat on the end of the table and watched the swaying heads of ten or more players and singers, pick up on the song, and play to the last line:

*"And I will never forget you for giving me
The best year of my life."*

Newcomers kept drifting into the tent, pressing against each other to find a standing space, and joining in on songs with different folk-jazz singers. As applause rang out, the room then got deafly quiet and a singular voice of a folk singer hit the metallic strings of her guitar and led the group in a final of chorus of *Amazing Grace.*

Outside the tent, Jamie, excitedly said, "Saw them, heard them, and sang with them! Who's ever going to believe it? I've got to call Grandmother later and tell her. How did I do? What do you think?"

"I think you were incredible, and it was a real bold move to hand Joan Baez a copy of your record and say, "I hope you like it. I love everything you write and sing. I can't wait to hear more. Thank you for letting me sing with you."

"I don't think I can top that!" Jamie said, as we walked back across the straw grass field to the stage area, where a young, straight-haired young man was humming and playing, as he climbed the stairs to sing his song about living in the Rocky Mountains outside Denver.

A late evening fog was settling over the Monterey Bay, pushing a chilly wind into the wooden stadium and stage area of the fairgrounds. Jamie pulled her heavy jacket tight around her. We ate hotdogs and onion rings, and drank hot coffee from one of the concession stands. She couldn't stop talking about singing with 'the group' earlier. Others sitting nearby leaned toward her to breathe in every southern word she spoke. I saw some of them looking at the scar and wondering. A lady said, "I like your earring and body art." She had never heard it called art. I could only watch her and think to myself that she was a masterpiece of fine-tuned art.

Epilogue

After the July wedding feast and August family reunion, Jamie and I returned to Monterey. We had Sunday and Monday together with her family and mine, before we caught our flight back to California.

Once back, it was a fast-paced whirlwind of activities for both of us. Jamie had signed on to do eight appearances for the USO. Most of them were in Monterey, where she continued to sing and work at Crusoe's, on Cannery Row and occasionally Angelo's Restaurant on the Wharf.

One night she was fortunate enough to meet Richard Burton and Elizabeth Taylor, who were in Monterey for the filming of the movie, *The Sandpiper*. It was more than a thrill for her, as they exchanged autographs.

Jamie kept her Monday morning appointment with Stephanie to monitor her kidney functions and to review options for a new experimental treatment called dialysis. The headaches were getting worse, as she tired from the USO travel and work at Crusoe's. She was reluctant to start any long-term treatment, and instead, stayed on the supplement regimen and low dose medicine to filter and hopefully cleanse her kidneys. She was stronger from the walking and biking to Crusoe's.

My schedule had changed. Instead of coastline and ground reconnaissance, the colonel and I, plus a small team of civilians and military advisors, worked on a detailed report for the Colonel Lasiter. He would present his recommendations in early October to Senator Fulbright, who chaired the Foreign Relations Committee.

One night, after the group had finished, the colonel invited me to his office for a beer and a private conversation.

"These are troubling times Specialist Wade, but I have deep trust and confidence in your ability to consider an assignment I want you to take. It is almost a certainty that we are going to see a shift in our CEDEC operations. With the meningitis threat here, reassignment of basic training units to Fort Lewis, and aerial photography equipment going more and more to pilot control, we at CEDEC and CECOM, will see reassignments. There will be to more signal corps support and intelligence gathering, in the event congress approves the Gulf of Tonkin resolution--the sure fire measure that will mobilize us all for a military conflict."

He paused, became very sullen, and sank deep into his chair like a man who had said too much too soon.

"I am going to need your help and reassignment to Fort Belvoir, and possibly back to Fort Monmouth or the US Army Pictorial Center in New York City. These two locations will be the focus and return areas for foreign and domestic film surveillance and intelligence on military conflicts, counter- insurgency, and domestic unrest over the next year or so.

"I know it may not be the forefront assignment you want in a hot zone, but our photographic aerial and ground data gathering will become just as important, if not more important, to a war effort, should it come. You will be promoted to Sergeant/Specialist E-5," he finished with a deep drag on his cigarette and a long swallow of beer.

I sat silent. I knew he needed my help, but my thoughts drifted to Jamie, and what this could mean. He was guessing my thoughts and said, "You and I have some very important women to consider. Stephanie's commitment is to me. I am very aware of your situation with Jamie, and you can count on me to assist in any way I can. She has had an impact on us and the troops who have attend the USO. Stephanie sees her as a dear friend. I do too. So soldier on, and we'll work on this together. Understood?"

"Yes Sir!" He reached across his desk and shook my hand.

After this meeting, my schedule settled into a routine of less direct reconnaissance, and more laboratory assignments and film reviews at CEDEC headquarters. Colonel Lasiter left for a temporary assignment at Fort Belvoir. Stephanie kept up her work and Monday appointments with Jamie.

Jamie kept a full schedule of singing and playing with the USO and at Crusoe's. Sunday was the one day we could count on being together, to enjoy the beach, or to just relax at the cottage. We listened to the Four Topps on the drop-down record player, and watched the Dick Clark' American Bandstand on the black-and-white television that Lilly had recently installed in the cottage.

Jamie had also seen her dreams come true by singing *"It Was You"* at the Monterey Jazz Music Festival, to a crowd of four thousand cheering and chanting attendees. She had mingled with the likes of bandleader Miles Davis, the newly emerging civil rights advocate Joan Baez, a very shy Bob Dylan, an almost unknown Janis Joplin, the Weavers, and a parade of others who sang and became well known as the times changed, and a new dawning of Aquarius was appearing over the horizon.

It was a very happy time for us all. I wanted it to last forever.

But, it didn't.

On Thursday night around nine o'clock, September 18th Stephanie called from the hospital. "Wade, I'm here with Jamie and Ron. You need to get here as soon as you can. It's Jamie. We admitted her this afternoon with a high fever. She is dehydrated, and we are monitoring her. They think she has had a minor stroke or temporal seizure, but…"

"I'm on my way," I said as I hung up the phone and a very worried Sgt. Dick Edlund drove me to the hospital.

Stephanie met me at the lobby door and ushered me quickly to the ICU.

"It's not good. She has been keeping a lot from us. She was in good spirits at our last appointment, but I knew she was getting weaker and she had a slight jaundice appearance around her eyes. She was as happy as I have ever seen her. This is what she wanted, and you gave it to her, Wade. She hid this from us all. Go now and be with her." She took my hand and guided me into the darkened room where Jamie lay on the bed in her yellow cotton dress. With loving arms she reached out for me.

"I love you. You've kept every promise you made to me, but I think it may be time for me to go home."

She looked so beautiful, so at peace, so very happy. This was 'the time' she had talked about so often, as she had tried to gently and lovingly prepare me. I had prayed it would never come. I only wanted to kneel by her bed, encircle her in my arms, place my head on her chest, and listen to her heart beating in my ear and in my heart.

The hospital released Jamie on September 23rd, with the understanding that she would go home and rest. Just as she wanted, we boarded a Trailways bus the next day and took a window seat. She wanted to be able to wave good-bye to the Fort Ord Drum and Brass Band, officers, enlisted men, USO friends, Colonel Lasiter and Stephanie, Thomas and Lilly and the Crusoe staff, and other friends.

As the bus moved forward, and the last of the crowd drifted to their vehicles, I covered Jamie with a light blanket and let her settle back into the seat for a nap on the way to the San Francisco airport. Every once in a while, she took my arm, pulled it close, and kissed my shoulder, saying "I'm so in love with you, soldier boy. Get me home safe." I tried to read to her from *Of Time and The River* by Thomas Wolfe, when I could, but my mind was on her and our future back in Virginia.

When we went to board the plane, the flight attendants were wonderful and took Jamie in a wheelchair. They helped us settle into the First Class seats Thomas, Lilly, the colonel and Stephanie, had purchased for us.

Ms. Thompson, Hanna, Tom, Marianne, Ms. Stevens, and my parents and grandparents met us at the Shenandoah Valley Regional Airport. We drove home caravan style; no one wanted to let Jamie out of their sight on the 'blue mountain highway home' as Highway 151, had fondly been named by the family in her honor.

I initially took five days of leave to maximize my time with Jamie. I took her to see the animals and carried her to the creek for baths and quiet naps. We would return to the house to lay in bed together and listen to music that she asked me to play.

The colonel and his staff let me drive into Fort Belvoir two days a week, take my paperwork home, and spend time with Jamie. It was a special time for her, her grandmother, my parents, and my grandparents. Marianne and Ms. Stevens were steady visitors and Jamie always brightened up during their visits. She picked up her guitar, played and sang when she could. At other times she sat by her window and watched the sunsets. I was almost constantly with her. We shared a lot of soup and butter biscuits at night before we went to bed.

She had the family attorney from Lovingston come and complete the paperwork and contracts for her records, songs. We agree that all of her music residuals would be earmarked for the university hospital and local schools.

She also spent time with me, talking about her eulogy. This was really hard on me, but she insisted that my life should go on.

"Dammit, Dhamner!" she said to me one day, while sitting by the window. "This has been pretty good. I have had everything, and you gave it to me. I have no fear of my future, and I'm not afraid for yours either. We're going to do this together. You have kept every promise you made.

"But, this is another one I want. I want you to be the last voice I hear, as I fly away and leave this earth." We laughed so hard we nearly cried.

Ms. Thompson came into Jamie's room, and with a trembling voice, jokingly said "It almost makes me want to go with you." It was a light moment we all needed. We burst out laughing and crying again, as we quietly ate blueberry pie with a glass of milk.

On Friday October 16th, Stephanie, Marianne, Ms. Stevens, Ms. Thompson, Tom and Hanna, my mother and grandmother, and I gathered for a weekend vigil with Jamie. Stephanie was now working at the Ft. Belvoir hospital and came on weekends to monitor Jamie for the family. She realized more than I did, that Jamie was failing fast.

I had stayed with her when I was home, holding her close and reading her poems, and sometimes strummed her guitar and hummed her songs, so she could hear my voice and know I was close by. On Saturday morning, she drifted into a deep coma. I took a bath at the creek, and returned to her side as quickly as I could to hold her close and read to her. Everyone gathered in the house and took turns holding her hands. It was all I could do to stay awake and hold her sometimes, but I needed to keep my last promise.

Sometime during the night, she squeezed my hand, got up and opened the window wide and lit every candle in the room. A warm, moist breeze from the cave blew into the room, as she sat by the window and let a choir of exotic silk moths with large, purplish eyespots on their wings circle her face, and alight on her golden hair.

She returned to bed, kissed my lips and forehead and sang softly, "I will love you forever, forever, I love you forever. You are the world to me and you made my every dream come true."

I was in a dream like sleep but kept reading her poems, until Stephanie put her hand gently on my shoulder and said, with tears in her eyes, "She's gone, Wade."

"Wade, she knows you kept your promises," I thought I heard Colonel Lasiter's say, "It's time to let her go. We are all here for you now," he said.

I couldn't let her go. I wasn't sure if I was asleep, or in a dream state. My body felt heavy, as I opened my eyes to a room of people.

"Yes, Wade, you kept every promise. She listened and I'm sure she heard your every word," Ms. Thompson said.

I felt my mother's fingers threading through my hair, as she and my father said, "We loved her and lost her too. Come home with us for now, for some sleep and food."

"We all lost her. We loved her so, and will miss her wonderful smile. You have done all you could to make her happy. She's at peace now. Let us take over and help now," Marianne said, as she joined hands with Ms. Stevens and the others gathered around the bed.

As I walked out and down the stairs with my father, I thought I heard Ms. Thompson say, "She looks so beautiful, but I could swear I closed and locked that window last night and put all of the candles out. My heart is breaking. I loved her so, but I know she has a smile on her face and there are no tears now in her heart now."

I awoke in my old bed at my parent's house around two o'clock, to the smell of eggs, grits, ham, biscuits and coffee. My mother had piled my plate with food, and my father was already sitting at the table reading the *Farm News*.

By my plate were Jamie's amber earring, her mother's wedding ring, and a small penciled drawing of a butterfly.

"You were holding those tightly in your hand when you went to sleep this morning. She must have given them to you with love, sometime during the night." His mother said, as she wrapped her arms around my shoulders and let me sob into her apron.

Jamie died in the early hours of Sunday morning, on October 19th, her birthday.

As she made me promise, I made all of the arrangements. There would be no funeral and no internment. Her ashes were to go in the secret sterling silver box she kept hidden in the top chestnut dresser drawer in her room.

Ms. Thompson and I called all the people on Jamie's list to let them know. They were gracious and loving on the phone, and thanked us for making this the best year of Jamie's life.

On a beautiful, sunshine Saturday afternoon, six days later, my parents and grandparents, Ms. Thompson, Tom and Hanna, Marianne, Ms. Stevens, Lillian and Ned, Lilly and Thomas, Pastor Woodson, and a gathering of some eighty friends and neighbors, followed me, as I carried Jamie's ashes to a high green meadow above Spruce Creek and placed the silver box, as instructed, by her grave marker, next to her grandfather's, in the Marshall Family Cemetery.

Once everyone was settled on the wooden chairs that surrounded the marker, I read the eulogy that Jamie and I had written, just ten days before she died, as a young singer from Nellysford strummed softly on her guitar.

Jamie's Eulogy

I left here sixteen months ago on the Blue Mountain Highway, as my mother likes to call it. On a bus, I met a Blue Ridge Mountain poet and singer-song writer, who said she had come to earth, I believe, looking for a sign, and to write, sing and teach us all how to live.

I want to thank each of you for being here today. Jamie would have enjoyed seeing your faces again, and I'm sure she would have liked to have sung your favorite song. If you don't mind, I want to read this just the way she helped me write it for this occasion.

It's a mystery, that sometimes we meet people early in our lives and late in theirs.

Jamie told me to say her name today, Jamie Catherine Marshall, so we would not forget her. She wanted us to listen to the cascading waterfall in the distance, and remember her music, her laughter, her smile, and sometimes her tears. And she asked that we not be sad, as we look back, but smile and kiss and hug each other, as we move forward into our futures with our hopes and dreams.

Touch each other and hold hands and feel the daylight and the warmth of the sun, as it refreshes our souls and spirits.

Keep all the promises you make to one another. Write everything down that you believe, and believe in. And read, read every book you can. Because sometimes, life gives us a second chance, many second chances. Treat them all as sacred and seize them, and hold on to them as if maybe they are the last breath of life you will ever breathe.

So, take the life you have been given, and live it fully, forsaking nothing and accepting everything that is good, wonderful and kind. And when life hurts, hurt together, never alone, never in sadness, and glory in the day when you will be whole again.

And, always listen to the Blue Mountain Highway: its music, its mystery, and its rhythm. It will help you solve the mysteries of life.

So, I will say it again, this is not goodbye. We will meet many times along the Blue Mountain Highway Home. So watch, and always be aware of the needs of others. Be mindful of those who read, and read the great books of life by writers who give us windows of knowledge, and feelings for a compassionate world against the dark tomorrows.

I want you to look into the faces of all the people you meet along life's highways. Help them find the wisdom they are seeking and the understanding they need, so they can decide where their road of life can take them. And lastly, help them to accept the life they have been given and invite them to live it, to its fullest.

As we all remained still and bowed our heads in a silent prayer, a young singer sang a verse of 'It Was You' and 'Blue Mountain Highway Home' on a beautiful sunny afternoon, as the soothing, peaceful cascades of Spruce Creek Falls could be heard in the ravine below.

Jamie's poems and songs

Angel with a Busted Wing, June, 1963
When I know Love, June, 1963
Blue Mountain Highway Home, 1964
Singing Until Jesus Comes to Get Me, October, 1963
It was you, April, 1964
Still Beautiful in Your Eyes, February, 1964
Faint Heart, March, 1964
How Many, June, 1964

Acknowledgement

I wish to acknowledge my proof reader and editors:
Linda P. Angel, Author and former elementary school
teacher, Vicki Lynn Smith, Author, Singer, Song-writer
Earl Smith, Talented Musician, Sound & Recording expert,
Singer, Song-writer, Sharon Duncan Hughes, Former high
school classmate, Retired teacher/educator, Kathryn Keck,
My neighbor and editorial mentor, Tina Brown, Friend and
Smith Mountain Lake adventurer and curiosity seeker,
Linda Seldomridge, Monterey, California, Former Chaplin
Ralph Spear, US Army UH-1B Huey Chopper Unit,
stationed with CEDEC at Fort Ord, California ,Melanie
Dellinger, Author and creative writer, Jay Williams,
Former Art Gallery Curator, Mentor, and Friend

*I want to especially thank the 2017 National Novel
Writing Month for inspiring and challenging me to
write and publish: Blue Mountain Highway Home*

*National Novel Writing Month is an annual, Internet-
based creative writing project that takes place during the month of
November. Participants attempt to write a 50,000 word manuscript
between November 1 and November 30. Well-known authors write
"pep-talks" to keep them motivated throughout the process. The
website provides participants with tips for writer's block,
information on where local participants are meeting, and an online
community of support. NaNoWriMo focuses on the length of a work
and encouraging writers to finish their first draft so that it can later
be edited at the author's discretion. The project started in July 1999
with 21 participants. By 2017, over 200,000 people took part and
wrote a total of over 2.8 billion words.*

Book Reading List by Jamie

Pride and Prejudice, by Jane Austen 1813
A Sports and Pastime, by James Salter 1960
The Feminine Mystique, by Betty Friedan 1963
Leaves of Grass, by Walt Whitman
Portrait of an Artist as a Young Man, by James Joyce
Brave New World, by Aldous Husley 1963
The Mouse Trap and Others, by Agatha Christie, 1937
Grapes of Wrath, by John Steinbeck
Travels with Charlie, John Steinbeck, 1962
Ship of Fools, Katherine Anne Porter, 1962
Great Gatsby, by F. Scott Fitzgerald
Look Homeward Angel, Of Time and the River, Thomas Wolf
The Call Of The Wild, Jack London, 1960
Zelda, by F. Scott Fitzgerald
Catch 22, Joseph Heller, 1962
Catcher in the Rye and Short Stories, J.D. Salinger
The Bell Jar, Sylvia Plath, 1963
Animal Farm, George Orwell, 1946
Charlotte's Webb, E.B. White, 1952
Last Exit To Brooklyn, Hubert Shelby, Jr., 1960
The Sea Around Us, Rachael Carson, 1961
Return to Paradise, James A. Michener, 1961
Long Day's Journey Into Night, Eugene O'Neill, 1957
The Innocents Abroad, Samuel L. Clemmons
The Call of the Pentlands, Will Grant, 1951
A MidSummer Night's Dream, W. Shakespeare, ed.,1903
Hamlet, W. Shakespeare, Ed., A. Shower, 1911
Odyssey Of Homer, English Prose, S. Butcher, 1925
Silas Marner, St. Martin's Classic, George Elliot, ed., 1930
Chaucer's Canterbury Tales, T. Speight, ed., 1602
Cinderella and The Butterfly Ball and Tales of Peter Parley
Golden Treasures, by Hans Christian Andersen, ed., 1865
The Complete Poems of Carl Sandburg, 1960
The Complete Works of William Shakespeare, ed. 1936
Howl and Other Poems, by Allen Ginsberg 1956
One Flew Over the Cuckoo's Nest, 1962
Good Bye Columbus, Phillip Roth, 1959

About The Author

Wayne Drumheller, who is a native of the Rockfish River Valley, Nelson County, Virginia, is an awarding winning photojournalist, book editor, and published author. He became Editor and Founder of the Short Book Writers Project in 2010. He offers free workshops to interested and aspiring authors and writers groups.

Since 2010, he has helped over 125 regional writers publish their biographies, children's books, memoirs, collections of prose, poetry, photography, and full-length nonfiction and fiction books. All net proceeds from his consulting, editing, workshops, book sales, photography illustrations and cover designs go to the Short Book Writers Project.

He received his Bachelor's Degree from Sonoma State University, California and his Masters of Education from the University of North Carolina at Greensboro. He is an active member of the Burlington Writers Club, North Carolina Writers' Network, Virginia Blue Ridge Writers Club, the Rockfish River Valley Writers, Burlington Artists League Gallery, and The Ansel Adams Society.

His advanced education in photography and writing began at seventeen when he left his home near Wintergreen, Virginia to serve in the US Army. As a photographer and student of the history of photography, he learned early that he could create, reflect and even mirror the simple things in life and celebrate the goodness to be found in most people.

"Wayne has celebrated his life and family in narrative poetic prose and contemporary photography. His books richly illustrates the landscape of our youth and if you were fond of The Walton Family, you will meet another memorable family in his books headed by a mother who sang in the kitchen while baking bread and a father who plowed his field of corn and also worked, as mine did, at the DuPont Plant in Waynesboro, Virginia."

Earl Hamner, Jr., creator of The Walton's TV series, Falcon Crest, Twilight Zone and a native and dear friend of Nelson County, Virginia.

A Brief History of My Family
and The Rockfish River Valley

The Rockfish River Valley encompasses the area from Brent's Mountain and Three Ridge Mountain to Afton Mountain. It lies in the shadow of the eastern slopes of the Blue Ridge Mountain. Two hollows located near streams within the eastern slopes are named Spruce and Stoney Creek. The upper Stoney Creek has a falls.

Rockfish River Valley is named for the fact that before the dams on the James River were constructed, rockfish ran from the bays to the farthermost points west on the rivers into the upper valley; therefore the name Rockfish Valley.

The Rockfish River has a north and a south fork and flows through a major portion of the valley, from the Blue Ridge Mountain ridges on Reed's Gap to the northernmost peaks of Three Ridge Mountain, then down even further, dropping 3000 feet to meet the Tye River and the south fork of the Rockfish River. Humpback Mountain area near Rockfish Gap at Afton, Virginia feeds the north fork. The two forks merge near the southern intersection of Routes 6 and Highway 151.

I am a descendant of the first Drumhellers in America,

314

Johannes Leonard Drumheller and his wife Henrietta "Hetty" who were born in now Ingelheim, Germany. They arrived in Philadelphia, Pennsylvania on the ship "Mary and Jamie" which sailed from Amsterdam via England to Philadelphia. It landed October 26, 1754. Leonard's signature is on the ship's passenger and port list. They had three or four children at the time of arrival and settled in the Western District of Berks County, PA. Several of their children stayed in Berks County but Leonard and Hetty and four of their other children move to establish a permanent home near Fabre's Mill/Scottsville, Albemarle County on the lower Rockfish River.

This was probably sometime between 1774 and 1783. Leonard bought land near Appleberry Mountain and established a thriving milling and oak wood drum making trade.

Because they were strong abolitionists and active traders, it is thought that they interacted with the Monacan Indians who camped near creeks and small streams in the Rockfish River Valley. I have also learned that some of the first white settlers came to the Rockfish Valley area prior to 1734 and to the Nellysford-Wintergreen vicinity before 1740. They were mostly of Scotch and Scotch-Irish origin.

The first trail in the valley, 'The Thoroughfare,' was cleared in the 1740s. The present day Patrick Henry Highway--Route 151-- closely follows this passage way.

My personal ancestry search shows that I am a distant relative to some of the first settlers to purchase land in the valley from the 1750s to the early 1800s.

Among them were the Colemans and Ewings. In 1812

Mr. Coleman built his hilltop home, "Wintergreen." The Wintergreen Resort uses the name today. He also built the Ewing home, "Elk Hill," around 1825. A mill, a church, a general store and post office were once located at Wintergreen named for the Coleman home.

My grandparents, Hayward and Sally Marshall Dameron, lived on a small farm on Spruce Creek Road. He was a retired World War I Veteran. She was a descendant and relative of many of the original settlers. The farm was just a short walk to the original Wintergreen community general store located just off the roadway that leads to Spruce Creek and the nearby Wintergreen Resort.

I was born in December 1945 to Author B. Drumheller and Catherine Dameron Drumheller in a house on Berryhill Road near where the north and south fork of the Rockfish River merge. It was a 48 acre farm bought by my father in 1947 on a G.I. Loan. In 1953 he built a new house on a section of the farm fondly called the "Old Stage Coach Road." According to family legend and stories, it was an early colonial road traveled by many notable and noble settlers, traders, Native Americans, dignitaries, military leaders, sons of liberty and American Presidents making their way to the very outer edge of the Appalachian Frontier.

This was the home and place in the Rockfish River Valley that I left when I joined the US Army on June 23 1963.

Source: The Drumheller Family Records at the Albemarle Historical Museum in Charlottesville, Virginia and Heartbeats of Nelson by Paul Saunders... Source: Historian Gene Crotty and The Drumheller Family Records at the Albemarle Historical Museum in Charlottesville, Virginia.

His published photography is recognized by collectors of fine artisan photography for his creative approach and commitment to the finished print. His original photographs and limited edition prints are in private homes in Virginia, North Carolina, New York, Florida, California and Canada. They have been published in his books:

Appalachian Sunrise, Blue Mountain Highway Home, A Rockfish Valley Poet and His Camera, A Rockfish Valley Photographer and his Poetry, Fifty Over Sixty, Living Above The Waterfall, Light in the Dark, My Alamance: A Photographer's Notebook, and Writing As Art, Editing and Publishing

Wayne Drumheller, Editor and Founder
The Short Book Writers' Project
waynedrumheller.com
waynedrumheller.hd@gmail.com
Host and Founder of the Rockfish River Valley Writers
www.Balartists.com
www.burlingtonwritersclub.org
VirginiaWritersClub.org
North Carolinawritersnetwork.org

Wayne H. Drumheller

Made in the USA
Columbia, SC
23 January 2021

31454492R00176